SUNRISE SURRENDER

He dropped an arm around her, and drawing her against his body, set his gaze on the distant hills. "There, do you see the first glow?" Nicolette watched as spears of light fell across the hilltops. The warmth of his body seemed to enflame her senses.

It occurred to him that he would die if he could not have her—and that was the plain truth. He suspected she wanted him just as eagerly, for he seldom misread the look in a woman's eyes. And who would care? Had they not already been punished? All night he had thought of her, thought of everything that might happen.

"What are you thinking?"

His answer was to bring his mouth down on hers. The fierceness of his grasp startled her. She had never known such pleasurable sensations, such excitement. She was bewitched by the wild pulsing thrill. Only when his tongue stole between her parted lips to invade her mouth did a soft cry gather in her throat and the odd constricted excitement she felt turn to fear. The thought tumbled in her mind that she must stop, stop now or it would be too late . . .

PUT SOME PASSION INTO YOUR LIFE... WITH THIS STEAMY SELECTION OF
ZEBRA *LOVEGRAMS!*

SEA FIRES　　　　　　　　　　　　　　　　　　(3899, $4.50/$5.50)
by Christine Dorsey
Spirited, impetuous Miranda Chadwick arrives in the untamed New World prepared for any peril. But when the notorious pirate Gentleman Jack Blackstone kidnaps her in order to fulfill his secret plans, she can't help but surrender—to the shameless desires and raging hunger that his bronzed, lean body and demanding caresses ignite within her!

TEXAS MAGIC　　　　　　　　　　　　　　　　(3898, $4.50/$5.50)
by Wanda Owen
After being ambushed by bandits and saved by a ranchhand, headstrong Texas belle Bianca Moreno hires her gorgeous rescuer as a protective escort. But Rick Larkin does more than guard her body—he kisses away her maidenly inhibitions, and teaches her the secrets of wild, reckless love!

SEDUCTIVE CARESS　　　　　　　　　　　　　(3767, $4.50/$5.50)
by Carla Simpson
Determined to find her missing sister, brave beauty Jessamyn Forsythe disguises herself as a simple working girl and follows her only clues to Whitechapel's darkest alleys... and the disturbingly handsome Inspector Devlin Burke. Burke, on the trail of a killer, becomes intrigued with the ebon-haired lass and discovers the secrets of her silken lips and the hidden promise of her sweet flesh.

SILVER SURRENDER　　　　　　　　　　　　　(3769, $4.50/$5.50)
by Vivian Vaughan
When Mexican beauty Aurelia Mazón saves a handsome stranger from death, she finds herself on the run from the Federales with the most dangerous man she's ever met. And when Texas Ranger Carson Jarrett steals her heart with his intimate kisses and seductive caresses, she yields to an all-consuming passion from which she hopes to never escape!

ENDLESS SEDUCTION　　　　　　　　　　　　(3793, $4.50/$5.50)
by Rosalyn Alsobrook
Caught in the middle of a dangerous shoot-out, lovely Leona Stegall falls unconscious and awakens to the gentle touch of a handsome doctor. When her rescuer's caresses turn passionate, Leona surrenders to his fiery embrace and savors a night of soaring ecstasy!

Available wherever paperbacks are sold, or order direct from the Publisher. Send cover price plus 50¢ per copy for mailing and handling to Penguin USA, P.O. Box 999, c/o Dept. 17109, Bergenfield, NJ 07621. Residents of New York and Tennessee must include sales tax. DO NOT SEND CASH.

PAIGE BRANTLEY
PRISONER OF MY HEART

ZEBRA BOOKS
KENSINGTON PUBLISHING CORP.

ZEBRA BOOKS are published by

Kensington Publishing Corp.
850 Third Avenue
New York, NY 10022

Copyright © 1994 by Paige Brantley

All rights reserved. No part of this book may be reproduced in any form or by any means without the prior written consent of the Publisher, excepting brief quotes used in reviews.

If you purchased this book without a cover you should be aware that this book is stolen property. It was reported as "unsold and destroyed" to the Publisher and neither the Author nor the Publisher has received any payment for this "stripped book."

Zebra and the Z logo Reg. U.S. Pat. & TM Off. Heartfire Romance and the Heartfire Romance logo are trademarks of Kensington Publishing Corp.

First Printing: August, 1994

Printed in the United States of America

One

anno Domini 1314

Nicolette de Chesneaux gave her silken skirts a scandalous flounce. "Bienvenue," she cooed, lifting her petticoats to reveal a shapely leg and the lace trim of her short linen chemise. "To you." She mimed a kiss. "And you, and you." Then with a toss of her pretty head and a whirl of silk, she pirouetted across the chamber, her voice bubbling into giggles as she sang out in a clear, musical voice:

> "Welcome to the court of France,
> where noble ladies sing and dance,
> and brave knights woo them a'outrance."

Her laughter was echoed by that of her sisters-in-law, Joan and Blanche, who frolicked about the room in various stages of undress, laughing unrestrainedly as each added a further line to the risque little ditty.

Despite their high-spirited antics and the splendor of their surroundings, their young lives were not happy ones. Their marriages, each for a different reason, had failed miserably.

In the glow of their forced gaiety a brace of candles flared and guttered, showering the splendid chamber with a mellow dancing light. Opulent eastern carpets adorned the floor and scarlet wall trappings laced with golden threads glittered like jewels, lending the room the appearance of a chapel lit for night mass.

The three princesses had conspired to be absent from the feast given in honor of King Philip's daughter, Isabella, by complaining of headaches, which they would undoubtedly suffer by morning considering the liberal amounts of wine they consumed. By prearrangement they met in Joan's suite. All three young women were enamored of acting and had squandered a fortune to hire performers for the lively soirees they hosted in the gardens of the nearby Hotel de Nesle. Away from the prying eyes of the court, impromptu plays were staged, plays in which the royal princesses often took roles.

But all that had changed with Isabella's arrival from England. Her vendetta against her brothers' wives, for her actions could be construed as nothing less, had led to their being severely reproached by the king for their free and easy ways of life. At his daughter's urging the king had expressly forbidden any further soirees in the gardens.

By forbidding their amusements, the king had made such activities all the more attractive to his rebellious daughters by marriage. Tonight they

PRISONER OF MY HEART

would have their revenge. True, it was for their eyes only, but it was delicious revenge nonetheless.

Preceded by a chorus of giggling, Nicolette de Chesneaux, daughter of the Duke of Burgundy and recent bride of the king's eldest son, Louis, screwed her pretty face into a laughable expression and assumed the stance of a bobbing waterfowl. Nicolette, the youngest of the princesses, had a flair for mimicry, and she often made funny faces behind the backs of the king and his ministers. No one was immune from her mischievous capers, and so it was not surprising that she perfectly captured the pose so often struck by the king's infamous inquisitor, Gullimae de Nogaret. He was said to have murdered a pope. Even his appearance was evil, for he was fat and soft as a spider, with wire thin legs and greedy black eyes. He was a man obsessed by hideous tortures, the most feared man in France, deadly, yet somehow absurd.

Nicolette stalked about the chamber poking her nose into everything, the intricately carved chests, the sewing baskets, even beneath the bed where Joan and Blanche sat stitched with laughter. With much ado Nicolette peered behind the tapestries, then whirled about, exclaiming, "The Baron de Conches is missing! Oh where, oh where could he be?" Her mimicry of the inquisitor's shrill staccato voice and her ludicrous delivery sent the pair on the bed into hysterics. It was known by all in the palace, save for the prudish old king, that the Baron Raoul de Conches was Isabella's lover.

"Ha, a mystery worthy of the great inquisitor,"

Nicolette declared, rubbing her hands together and bobbing her head comically. In the process her long luxuriant hair tumbled free of its restraints. A wealth of dark curls swirled about her face. "Never fear, I shall find him. I have a nose for such pursuits," she pronounced, tapping her nose and pointing to a chamber pot. A rill of laughter swept across the chamber.

Nicolette could hardly keep a straight face as she lifted her arm in a dramatic sweeping gesture. "Ah, but here is Madame de Pernelle. I shall question her." She then skulked near her audience and contorted her face into an even more fiendish expression, before slyly stating, "It may be necessary to torture her."

Her dramatic aside was Blanche's cue. She was the shortest and stoutest of the king's three daughters by marriage. Her plump childlike face was perfect for the silly Madame de Pernelle, the lady of the bedchambers. The poor woman was sweetly daft and by rounding her eyes Blanche perfectly executed madame's vague expression. "Oh dear, oh dear, what brings you to the royal bedchambers, Messire de Nogaret?"

"I am seeking the Baron de Conches, have you seen him?" Nicolette demanded, bobbing her head.

"Is he lost?" Blanche asked, distractedly.

"Of course he is lost, you silly cow, that is why I am searching for him!"

"Oh, tragedy! Poor Isabella. How ever will she warm herself in bed this night?"

Joan, who could not keep from laughing, stumbled from the bed dragging with her a pillow to which a silly hat had been pinned. Quickly she adjusted her skirts. Egged on by Nicolette's and Blanche's giggles, she kicked off her satin slippers and pursed her lips into a moue, looking for all the world like a pickled gudgeon—by all accounts a fair facsimile of the imperious Isabella. "Who dares approach Isabella, Queen of England, France, and all else in the world?" Blanche intoned in a regal voice.

"It is I, madame, your faithful servant de Nogaret."

"And I," Blanche twittered, rolling her eyes. "Oh, I've forgotten my name."

"Out of my way, you clumsy wench," Nicolette sneered, elbowing Blanche aside to address the smirking Joan. "Madame," Nicolette drawled, bobbing her head as she spoke, "I regret to inform you that the Baron de Conches is lost."

"What! You fool! I shall have your nose twisted off!"

"But madame, I am the inquisitor; that is what *I* do."

"Then twist off your own nose, you dull old fart, and hers as well," she screeched, motioning to Blanche.

"Yes, madame, I shall do it at once," Nicolette complied, comically crossing her eyes and gripping her own nose. Suddenly she asked, "But wait, a decision must be made! Whose nose shall I twist off first?"

"Idiots," Joan shouted, flogging the pair with

her silken scarf. "You must first kiss my royal foot," she commanded regally, raising her skirt and wagging her toes at them. As she did the rising hem of her skirts revealed the pillow adorned with Raoul de Conches' hunting hat pinned at a jaunty angle and a crude caricature of his face. The hat had been pilfered several days before when the princesses plucked it from a low branch during a hawking party. Joan had concealed the hat in her cloak even as the baron scoured the area for his lost chapeau. The incident had been the highlight of the princesses' day. But it was Nicolette who had dipped her finger into the ink pot that evening, when a stylus could not be found and, laughing along with her audience, scrawled two thick black brows upon the pillow, appropriately narrow, shifting eyes, a hawk-beaked nose and droopy, sensual lips—the face of Raoul de Conches.

"Huzzah!" Nicolette shouted with glee, pointing to the pillow and bobbing her head furiously. "There is the Baron de Conches, madame! He was between your legs all the time!"

This was the scene where Blanche as the daft Madame de Pernelle fell on the bed in a scandalized swoon, and Joan, realizing her lover had been exposed, threw one of Isabella's infamous fits of rage and began kicking the pillow about the room. All three were convulsed with laughter when the chamber door abruptly opened.

Before their disbelieving eyes stood the king, his daughter Isabella, and half a dozen stone-faced guards.

The king's cold gaze raked the chamber. "So, my daughters by marriage, this is how you convalesce from the mal de tête. You have much to explain."

For a long terrible moment, the three young women were speechless. They looked for the world like three little girls caught at mischief. In truth they were, for Joan, the eldest, was but nineteen.

It was Nicolette who found her voice first. "We did not hear you announce yourself, messire." A wealth of dark ringlets bobbed before her large dramatic eyes.

"How true," the king agreed. "On this occasion you had no opportunity to put on innocent faces." The tone of his voice sent a chill through Nicolette.

"It was only silly play acting, messire." Nicolette pleaded, her tongue stumbling over the words. "We meant no harm."

"No harm," he repeated, his voice rising to a bellow, "no harm, indeed! You have disgraced your husbands, shamed the kingdom and destroyed the royal succession! No harm! You are harlots, the lot of you! Do you also deny your rendezvous with the commanders of my guard, Laire de Fontenne and the brothers Pierre and Gautier d'Aulnay?"

Nicolette did not understand. Was the king referring to their actions of the moment? Or the gatherings of young people in the gardens? In retrospect, the play acting had oft times been risque. But the king had already forbidden any further celebrations, and a week or more had passed since their last fete. It was true many young nobles had been present, including the d'Aulnay brothers. But Laire de Fontenne, she could not recall the name nor the person, no, not at all. "They were harmless fetes," she insisted. "Perhaps the plays were somewhat lively, but there was no lewdness, certainly no lascivious behavior."

Joan, at last finding her voice, muttered, "Yes, that is the truth, messire." Her sister Blanche inclined her head, too cowed by the wrath of her autocratic father-in-law to add her voice to her sister's. They sat huddled together on the bed, clutching hands.

"Then you admit to the rendezvous in the gardens?"

Nicolette felt a little dizzy, and her mind was reeling. "They were innocent fetes," she protested, pushing her disheveled hair from her eyes and running her hand distractedly through her curls. "There were many young people there. It is true we were guilty of high spirits and laughter, and perhaps—"

"Adultery?" The king's voice cut across hers like a knife.

"No!" Nicolette answered. She was suddenly afraid. The king, normally cold and taciturn, seldom displayed any emotion, but at that moment rage sparked from his pale grey eyes and his voice was edged with contempt.

"There are witnesses to your shameful behavior," he said.

Nicolette felt a great weight pressing upon her breast, so that she could hardly breathe. "Then they are false witnesses, messire, for we are innocent."

The king's only response was a brutal snort. "Where are the rings your dear sister by marriage, Isabella, presented to you upon her arrival from England?" he demanded.

Nicolette, forgetting her first finger was yet stained black with ink, thrust her hand forward, displaying the ring. But Joan and Blanche made no move to do so.

"I did not choose to wear mine this evening," Joan managed. Blanche, clutching her sister's hand, muttered, "Mine did not suit my gown."

"Shall I send a servant to fetch them, or could it be they are on the hands of Pierre and Gautier d'Aulnay?"

Nicolette's blood turned to ice in her veins. Too vividly she recalled the game in the gardens, the foolish game of catchers and seekers among the maze. She bit her lip to keep from speaking, imagining that anything she might say, particularly the truth, would only make matters worse. The rings had been lost to a childish dare, nothing more.

Nicolette's warning glance was too late. Joan blurted out the truth, denying that the rings were gifts of affection. She needn't have bothered. The king shouted her down. "You are harlots, and you will suffer hell for your sins! Take them from my sight!" he commanded the guards.

Adultery, the word seared itself into Nicolette's brain like a red hot iron. She was being accused of adultery. "It is a lie," she wailed. "I am innocent! We are all innocent!"

Isabella, who stood at her father's side, remained unmoved. She had not said a word, though her eyes glowed with satisfaction and her expression was one of triumphant scorn.

Nicolette's gaze seized upon her gloating smile. She was certain her envious sister by marriage was behind the accusations. "We have committed no sins!" she screamed. "If it is an adulteress you seek, ask your pious daughter who comes to her bed chamber each night! Shall I say his name?" Nicolette knew she had gone too far, but she could not stop the words. Even the noisy advance of the guards could not silence her.

Through her streaming tears, their faces appeared like pale discs, a blur of color and motion above a grappling mass of sweaty hands that roughly seized her and dragged her from the chamber. She fought against them, kicking, biting. One of them struck her, a hard, sharp blow. Nicolette screamed, or perhaps it was Joan or Blanche she heard? Iron hands propelled her forward. She was jostled, half carried, down the long darkened passageways, shrieking out her innocence. Doors jolted open at their approach and the stomp, stomp of the guards' boots rang out upon the stones. On and on they went, down worn stone staircases and passages that grew progressively dank and narrow until she was shoved into a cell blacker than the night and the door slammed shut behind her.

For a long while Nicolette stood there in the foul-smelling blackness, aware only of her own misery and the hushed whimpering sobs that escaped her lips. To whom could she appeal? Certainly not her husband of barely a year. He had despised her from the moment he first laid eyes on her. Nicolette would never forget his words. "What a scrawny, dark mare you have brought for me, Father. She is not to my liking." He had said it aloud, before everyone present. Worse still had been their wedding night. Afterwards Louis had arranged to be absent from her bed. Since that fateful night a state of war had existed between them.

As Nicolette's eyes became accustomed to the blackness, she examined the confines of her tiny cell. The only furnishings were a crude wooden pallet strewn with straw and an evil-smelling bucket.

After a time, Nicolette slumped down on the straw pallet and buried her face in her hands. Of all her chaotic emotions, rage was the uppermost, a sudden violent fit of anger directed at her foppish husband, Louis, and his scheming sister Isabella. Had Louis conspired with her to rid himself of a wife who did not please him, one who knew too well his inadequacies? Was it Isabella's revenge for the play they had staged in the garden? Or was it no more than the envy and jealousy she had always shown toward her brothers' wives?

Slowly, as Nicolette's fury subsided, a horrible dread descended on her. *For the wages of sin is death.* The phrase careened through her mind like a maddened beast. By law a husband could put his wife to death for adultery. She had seen others wrongly accused. They had received no justice, no mercy save that of the Almighty. Those who had not succumbed to de Nogaret's hideous tortures had been beheaded or burned at the stake.

No, Nicolette thought, the king would not dare to pass a judgment of death upon Joan, Blanche, and herself. They were high born, not peasant women. He would not dare risk offending all of Burgundy. Though the more she thought of it, she realized that her brother and her uncles could little afford to be offended, not in their present circumstances.

How treacherous fate was. None of it had been their fault. Her cousins, Joan and Blanche, had also suffered loveless marriages to the king's two younger sons. Their husbands would not offer one word of support. They would do as they were told, just as they always had. No one would dare to defy the king, or even attempt to defend them against Isabella's lies. They would be condemned, burned as adulteresses or locked away and left to die of cold and misery.

At length Nicolette lay down upon the spiky straw and sobbed herself to sleep. A human cry rang down the corridor, startling her to full consciousness. She leapt up and held her breath. It came again, a horrid scream of panic and torture. She had not thought of the d'Aulnay brothers until that moment. Again and again the piercing screams rang out, until she could not bear it. She crouched against the stones of the wall, and clasped her hands over her ears. Louder and louder she sobbed, attempting to drown out the awful howling screams with her own wretchedness.

Far above the filth and gloom of the palace dungeons, Isabella angrily thrust aside her lover's caressing hand. "Have you no sense of propriety?" she snarled. She needed time to arrange her thoughts and moved away, walking up and down the chamber. She was an ideal beauty of her age, tall, slender, and blond-headed. Had it not been for a certain masculine coarseness about her features, her beauty might have rivaled that of the fabled Helen of Troy.

Raoul de Conches did not stir from the chaise, but his heavy-lidded eyes followed her. A faint smile snaked across his lips. "You spoke to me less harshly last evening in your bedchamber."

Isabella abruptly halted before one of the tall lancet windows that lined her suite's west wall, and directed a withering glance at her lover. "Why has he not been found?"

"Do not trouble your thoughts over Laire de Fontenne," Raoul de Conches soothed, smiling once more. He was a large man, powerfully built, though not particularly tall. In height he and Isabella were of a like size, though in coloring they differed greatly. Isabella was as fair as her dispassionate father, where as de Conches was swarthy as a Spanish brunette. His dark hair lay in deep waves and his beard was so dense that even freshly shaved his chin was tinted by a blue haze.

Isabella postured, folding her arms across her breasts. She was dressed in a gown of deep emerald velvet trimmed in ermine, and the September night felt suddenly stifling. "He may have been warned."

"By whom?" Raoul de Conches remarked in an amused tone, for none but a trusted few knew of the arrests. "You are fretting needlessly," he chided, crossing to where she stood before the window and sliding his hands about her velvet waist. "I am more concerned that de Nogaret's tortures may reveal the truth."

"They shall reveal my truth," she said, raising her pale eyes to her lover's. "Messire de Nogaret will not fail me."

"Then there is nothing to fear," he chuckled softly, putting his blue chin close to her cheek.

"There is Laire de Fontenne," she reminded him in a strident voice.

Raoul de Conches raised his head, inhaling deeply. "I and my villeins have joined the search for him. He will be found. It is only a matter of time. His servants said he left early in the day. Mayhap he has gone in search of amusement, gaming or whoring? In any case he can not have gone far."

Isabella said no more. She frowned and stood staring into the blackness of the great forecourt. She would not rest easy until this last commander of her father's bodyguards was in the grasp of the inquisitor de Nogaret.

Two

Earlier that day, hours before the scandal unfolded, Laire de Fontenne left his quarters in the Palace of the Cité and went to purchase a pair of boots. Later he would pay his sister a visit. A brief visit, for that evening he intended to meet his fellow commanders, the d'Aulnay brothers. The trio, good friends, had planned an evening's entertainment to celebrate Laire's return to Paris.

As he rode out from the palace, Laire took in the beauty of the clear, pleasant September morning. In the glancing sunlight the towering spires of Notre Dame appeared touched with gold and the Island of the Cité gleamed like a jewel set upon the sparkling river. Beneath an azure sky, the Petit Pont reverberated with a confusion of sounds. The smaller of the two bridges spanning the Seine was invariably mobbed with people as were the shops constructed along its course. With its pointed towers and jagged rooftops, the pont was like a great wayward boulevard of the city that had flung itself across the river. Upon the pont's course, the cries of wine sellers, pie merchants, and beggars calling for alms intermingled with the hammering of goldsmiths, the constant trample of feet, and the creaking of cart wheels.

Only the day before, Laire had returned from the peaceful monotony of the king's favorite chateau at Pontoise where he served as commandant. The king's love of the hunt was his single remaining pleasure in life. At times it seemed he cared for nothing else. Since the king spent much of his time in pursuing game in the wilderness surrounding the chateau, a force of guards were kept in residence.

The command was an easy duty and Laire led a quiet, if somewhat boring life. In the beginning he had missed the excitement of the court. But now Laire found his months of solitude had left him unprepared for the bustle of Paris, and already he was becoming disgusted with the crowds.

North and south, coming and going, the roadway was jammed with all manner of people and conveyances. Overcrowding and delays were a fact of life in Paris, but in the three months Laire de Fontenne had been absent, the traffic on the city's two bridges seemed to have increased tenfold.

Being trapped in its midst could only be compared to experiencing the height of battle. Indeed the streets and bridges of Paris had much in common with warfare, as muleteers and carters jostled for the rightaway amid throngs of people, livestock, and barking dogs. Laire's mount, a tall bay, was equally frustrated by the crush of traffic and moved forward slowly, ears plastered to its head. The stallion, dubbed Ronce, was prickly as his namesake, the bramble, and invariably struck back when pressed beyond his dignity. The bay was particularly quarrelsome with other horses and was notorious for retaliating at any offense, real or imagined, with a swift nip, kick, or a mighty well-aimed thump of his muscular hindquarters.

Perhaps Laire would have kept a snugger rein on his mount had he not been so absorbed in his own thoughts. In any case he could not have seen the carpet roll from the cart. The street before him was too jammed with tumbrils, oxen, horsemen, and pedestrians. Neither did he hear the string of oaths uttered by the marchand de tapis as he hauled at the reins of his mules and swayed to a halt, blocking traffic in both directions.

Directly behind the carpet merchant, another carter driving a load of dye stuffs saw too late the obstacle in the roadway and rolled to a halt atop the now sullied and partially unrolled carpet.

The marchand de tapis, a fat man with a red nose, leapt from the cart, howling with fury. Before and behind the embattled merchants the catastrophe continued to unfold as carts swayed and jolted to a halt, fists flailed the air, oxen bellowed, and horses sidestepped and snorted.

Laire's first hint of the disaster occurred when the three horsemen before him, Lombard bankers judging from their flamboyant dress, suddenly began bobbing up and down and sawing at the reins of their stamping palfreys. One of the unfortunate beasts sidestepped, blundering into Ronce. Before

Laire could prevent it, the bay bared its teeth and sank them into the offending palfrey's rump.

The terrified horse shot forward, knocking pedestrians aside and pitching the banker into a goldsmith's booth amid screams and curses. The Lombard's two associates dismounted with great difficulty and ran to pull their friend from the clutches of the irate goldsmith.

Laire reined in the ill-tempered stallion. He was inordinately fond of the horse, despite the fact that the beast had made more than a few enemies for him over the years. After a moment, Laire stood in his stirrups to survey the disastrous chain of events.

It was worse than he imagined. Farther along the bridge, amid the snarl of carts, several fist fights had erupted. Above the furious dint of tongues, shouts rang out and from both ends of the bridge, guards elbowed and shoved their way toward the altercations.

With a shrug, Laire settled back into the saddle. "Do you see what you have done?" he said to the horse's twitching ears. "We will be here for the rest of the day." Indeed, the better part of an hour passed before traffic began to move along the bridge's course.

At the bootmaker's shop, Laire was fitted, and chose a length of fine cordovan leather. He left the customary small advance and advised the bootmaker that he would call for the boots later in the week. The sext bells were tolling as he took leave of the bootmaker's shop. The morning had passed quickly, but all that was about to change.

Laire dreaded the visit to his sister Agnes. She was forever attempting to mend the quarrel between him and their brother, Thierry. Laire had never been able to decide if her actions were prompted by her devout religious beliefs or simply because it amused her to meddle in the affairs of others.

Yet another mystery was the gift Agnes had sent to his quarters during his absence, a pair of fine riding gloves of extraordinary workmanship. But the most remarkable thing about the gloves was that Agnes, who had been known since childhood for her tight grasp on money, indeed whatever fell into her hands, had sent them. She wanted something from him, of that he was certain.

The house stood among half a dozen other equally grand homes on a square opposite the church of St. Jullian. Wealthy lawyers, doctors, and tax collectors had built their homes there around walled forecourts and small, pleasant gardens. The abundant trees and shrubbery lent the square a peaceful, almost pastoral quality.

At the iron gates, Laire was admitted by the wrinkled old porter. The man looked as glum as the last time Laire had seen him. He never spoke and moved in a curious weaving gait which perfectly suited the side-stepping stallion.

Laire crossed the courtyard at a leisurely walk, preparing himself for the visit. At least he did not have to ask Agnes for another loan; tucked away at

Pontoise, he had no opportunity to spend his money. He was met at the door by a youthful serving maid, one he had not seen before. She smiled at him several times as she directed him to a small solar.

He waited, strolling aimlessly about the chamber. The room apparently adjoined the one where his brother-in-law conducted his affairs, for he could plainly hear him and another man, one dissatisfied with the tax he was charged to pay, engaged in a heated discussion. Agnes had married wisely; Jerome de Marginay, a cousin to the king's treasurer, was understandably employed as a tax collector.

Laire heard the slamming of a door. He had been correct in his assumption. Presently his brother-in-law, having finished with the angry merchant, appeared at a small door set mid-way along the room's length. Jerome was a short, pudgy man of middle years, whose face was as pink as if it had been scrubbed with a brush. After extending his greetings, Jerome said, "It is good of you to visit us at last, brother-in-law."

"I have thought of you and Agnes often these past months," Laire responded in a convincing tone. "Unfortunately my duties permit me little liberty."

"Oh, I understand completely. I seldom escape my duties."

"Is Agnes well?"

"Oh yes, very well," Jerome nodded. "She is looking forward to seeing you."

"She is not here?" Laire asked, almost hopefully.

"She is at church. As you know, she is very devoted to the Virgin. She should be returning soon."

As if on cue the large door to the passageway moved on its hinges and Agnes entered. She was a stout woman, solidly built, with large expressive eyes and a generous mouth. As always her most formidable feature remained intangible. That was her uncanny ability to induce people, from the vilest peasant to the most influential courtier, to do her bidding.

Laire smiled and said, "How good it is to see you, sister." Upon their mother's death, Agnes, then fourteen, had taken charge, quite literally. Everyone, including their father, who had completely dominated their poor mother, dutifully did Agnes's bidding. As a boy of eight, Laire had been overjoyed to be sent to his mother's brother, Marshal de Orfevres, for military training. Anything was preferable to Agnes's reproaches and sermons.

His sister came toward him without so much as a smile and offered him her cheek. "Have you only just arrived?" The question and the tone of voice put Laire on the defensive at once.

"I was delayed in the crowds," he offered. "The bridge is really intolerable."

She gave her brother a skeptical look, then addressed her husband. "You are keeping your petitioners waiting, Jerome." It was a command, really.

Her husband's pink face flushed a shade deeper and he replied in a flustered voice, "Yes, my dear. Forgive me, brother-in-law, but I must return to my tax rolls. We will talk again over dinner," he promised, retreating into his office. Through the open door, Laire caught a glimpse of several scriveners seated at a table stacked high with parchments. The draft of air from the room smelled of dust and ink, like a monk's robes.

"Come," Agnes said, attaching herself to her brother's arm. "We will sit for a time in the garden. We have much to discuss."

As they made their way through the house, Laire thanked his sister for her gift of the riding gloves. But she passed it off as if it was a mere trifle, which was unlike her. She rarely allowed anyone to forget even the smallest favor. Once they were within the confines of the garden, Agnes said in a blunt voice, "I hear you have been behaving disgracefully."

Laire was about to deny it, when Agnes shut his mouth with a scathing lecture. "The scandal has spread even to my ears," she said, her gaze boring into him. "Lewdness is offending to the sight of God, as is drunkenness. It will only bring you to ruin," she continued. "It is serious enough that you care so little for your eternal soul, but can you not see that such conduct will ultimately disgrace our family and wreck all our fortunes!"

Agnes lived for gossip; she used it as a tool, a very profitable one. Her contacts at King Philip's court kept her fully informed. But Laire was at a total loss to understand her.

"Do not look at me like a lost lamb," Agnes reproached her fair-haired brother. "You know perfectly well my meaning."

As fond as she was of her brother, Agnes did not delude herself concerning his character. He was a handsome youth, broad shouldered and narrow of hip. His merry, sparkling eyes were blue, almost violet, and in his smile there was a certain reckless charm which young ladies found irresistible.

"No, I do not. I have been at Pontoise these three months past, sober and chaste, regrettably."

She appeared so surprised by his admission that she forgot to frown. "Three months, you say?"

"Yes, which is the reason I have not visited you before today, nor thanked you for your gift." He considered mentioning to her that if she paid as much attention to her own family as she did to court gossip, she'd have known. He decided against it.

"You are not lying to me?"

"I saw the futility of that years ago," he muttered beneath his breath, bringing his eyes back to meet his sister's searching gaze.

"What?"

"No, of course not, Agnes."

"Then perhaps you are not involved."

"Involved in what? You are speaking in riddles."

"I have heard rumors, dangerous rumors. It is whispered that the royal princesses have taken lovers—the d'Aulnay brothers. Your name was mentioned as well."

"That is ridiculous."

"Are you certain?"

"Yes." His palms felt sweaty. Agnes invariably had that effect on him. He averted his eyes, setting his gaze on the small artificial pond to the left of the bronze sundial. Lily pads crowded its surface and a dragon fly hovered in mid air. "Only a fool would play at that game," he remarked.

"Nature often causes men to do foolish things."

"Not so foolish as that. You said yourself it was a rumor."

She reached out and took her brother's hand. "Swear to me you are not involved, Laire."

"I am not." Their eyes met. Laire shifted uncomfortably. "Why should I lie to you?" he said at last.

"Because you have always been a liar—you do it for the fun of it. No, do not deny it. Have you forgotten the time you filled madame ma tante's sewing basket with frogs? Or the day you pretended to drown yourself in the stream before Père Gregory's horrified eyes?"

"He was a tyrant," Laire mumbled. The memory brought a ghost of a smile to his lips. He had gone to great lengths to avoid learning Latin.

"And then there was the occasion when you tricked your brother into making a fool of himself before—"

"That was all years ago," he interrupted. "I was a child. I did it to be amusing."

"Messire our father did not find it amusing."

"No," he agreed, recalling he had been soundly thrashed.

Agnes narrowed her eyes. "Why should I believe you now?"

"Because I am telling the truth."

"Then swear before God, here and now, that you are not involved in this scandal."

Laire, sensing there was no other way to silence her, wearily complied. "Before God, I swear to you, I am not involved."

"Had you any knowledge of these indiscretions?"

"No! In Christ's name, Agnes!" He was about to say more, but she held up her hand. "Enough," she said. "I believe you, Laire. But you must promise me to avoid the d'Aulnays. Do you?"

"Of course."

"Now," Agnes said, smiling broadly, "we will speak of more pleasant matters." Agnes's promise of a pleasant conversation lasted only as long as it took her to broach the subject of the long-standing quarrel between Laire and his elder brother, Thierry. By the time dinner was served, Laire's ears were ringing.

Since Agnes and Jerome de Marginay had no children, the three of them sat at the huge table. Presumably Agnes's ladies, one was an impoverished distant cousin of the family, and the several scriveners employed by Jerome took their meals in the kitchens when guests were present.

It was warm in the hall, uncomfortably so, and servants milled about, dragging their sleeves across the table as they served. They were constantly sidestepping one another. There seemed to be too many of them. Jerome ate with the same sort of dogged determination he applied to his tax rolls and said not a dozen words during the course of the meal.

Agnes, on the other hand, scarcely had time to fill her mouth between subjects. She had opinions on every matter. One subject she was particularly keen on was the public burnings of the Templars earlier in the summer. The spectacle had caused much unrest among the common people. They feared retribution from God. For even as the flames blistered the old grand master's flesh, he had called down a curse on the king and his progeny.

The entire affair was a shameful one. Simply put, the king, in desperate need of revenue, had accused the religious sect of devil worship and plundered their wealth. And though the king's inquisitor had found the Templars guilty, it seemed far more likely that their vast caches of gold and jewels, rather than their heresy, had brought about their fall from grace. Agnes talked endlessly on the subject, though it was the curse that truly excited her curiosity.

It was evening before Laire at last escaped her hospitality. With the advent of dusk, traffic had thinned to a trickle of carts and a few pedestrians. As Laire rode through the darkening streets, the aroma of food hung in the still air and here and there a light appeared in the homes of the more affluent.

At the Grand Pont, the larger of the two bridges that joined the isle to the left and right banks of the river, the guard collecting the toll was in a hurry to return to a noisy dice game which was being played by torchlight in the dusty street. The

PRISONER OF MY HEART 31

sounds of the game, laughter, and cursing followed Laire onto the bridge. The larger part of the Grand Pont was of wooden construction and newly erected. The span ran parallel to the original bridge which had been washed out several years before by a violent winter flood. The span often shuddered under heavy traffic. Laire mistrusted it.

On the right bank, his destination was an area of shabby taverns off the Rue Vielle Joillerie. Music throbbed and rowdy crowds pressed past. Laire found a stable for his horse and went to meet his friends. His tête-á-tête with his sister had disturbed him and set him to thinking. He was not in his usual good spirits. The music, loud, unmelodic, and from many sources, jarred on his nerves and the crowds irritated him.

At The Laughing Cat, he had an ale as he waited, then another. He drifted past the dice games, halting occasionally to watch. In the course of an hour he turned down several tempting offers from prostitutes and had a third ale. Still there was no sign of Gautier and Pierre d'Aulnay. Laire thought it odd, for the three of them had met in Gautier's quarters only the day before to make their plans.

Laire knew only too well that a soldier's time was seldom his own. They had been detained at the palace by some unexpected duty, he rationalized. Still it disturbed him. He drained his ale, unable to dispel the uneasiness that had dogged him all evening.

Three

Young Albert Drouhet paused at the door of The Laughing Cat, taking his breath in ragged gasps. He had come a long distance, running most of the way. The fact that Albert had eluded the guards and managed to slip from the palace was in itself a testament to his resourcefulness. He hung there at the door frame swallowing great gulps of air.

Smoke chuffed from the huge oil lamps which lit the interior. An oily haze hung just above the heads of the shoulder-to-shoulder crowd and the smoky air reeked of sweat and stale ale.

His gaze swept searchingly over the crowd. Squinting his eyes, he looked again, hoping against hope that Laire de Fontenne was still waiting for his comrades. At last he caught sight of his master and pushed into the crowd. Only a moment before in the torch-lit street, Albert had nearly crossed paths with the men who had come to his master's quarters that evening with questions and threats.

The men were ten steps behind him. Albert cursed beneath his breath and lunged forward, making a path through the moving mass of humanity.

PRISONER OF MY HEART

Laire pressed his way slowly, elbow and shoulder with the crowd, toward the tavern's rear door. His intentions were to cross the back lot and collect his horse from the stable of a neighboring tavern.

A fat tavern maid momentarily halted his progress. She had no sooner squeezed past, when he was hailed by a familiar voice. He turned to see his squire, Albert, weaving his way through the crowd. The lanky boy with the shock of unruly reddish hair cut through the mob like a swimmer. As soon as he drew abreast of Laire, the words burst from his mouth, frantic and all but unintelligible. "They came to arrest you tonight, sire! Do not return to the palace! They are searching for you—I saw them, just now! Here, before the tavern! We must hurry!"

In the fraction of an instant it took to comprehend his squire's words and the devastating implications behind them, Laire sensed it was already too late. At a glance, the image of Raoul de Conches and eight or more of his villeins imprinted itself upon his retina. They stood together at the doorway, solid as a wall, their eyes searching the crowd. They had not spied him, not yet.

Albert's eyes widened in terror. "You must go quickly, sire. Perhaps I can distract—"

Laire caught his youthful squire by the arm. "No, it is too late." He took a coin from inside his tunic and pressed it to Albert's palm, then speaking rapidly, but in a voice devoid of emotion, instructed, "My horse is stabled behind The Red Kitchen, fetch it. Go to Marshal de Orfevres. Rouse him from bed if you must, tell him what has happened. Quickly, before they see you," he said, propelling the boy toward the rear door.

De Conches rallied his villeins with a quick motion of his hand. They surged forward as a body. Laire stood his ground. From the edge of his vision he caught a last glimpse of Albert, his pale blue tunic, silver in the smoky light, as he slipped through the crowd like a darting fish.

Confronted by Raoul de Conches, Laire was cautious with his words. He responded as any innocent man might, and his stunned expression was genuine. Laire surrendered his sword and went without argument. What else could he do? To resist against so many would have been suicide, and there was still a chance that it was all a mistake.

Outside in the noisy darkness of the street, he was given the horse of a villein. "A pity I've only a mare from Artois to offer you," De Conches mocked, suggesting, "I'm certain she is not nearly so lovely as what you are accustomed to riding."

A smattering of crude laughter rang out as a burly villein wrestled Laire's wrists behind his back and lashed them together. The vassal who had been forced to give up his mount to the prisoner trotted before the riders, lighting the way with a torch. One by one the shadowy streets with their sounds and scents gave way to the pointed gate towers of the Grand Pont. Boxed in by the baron and his vassals, Laire rode in silence. De Conches, however, never shut his boasting mouth. He seemed to take a perverse pleasure in recounting the charges against Laire. As they entered the palace gates, de

Conches concluded, "Take your last look at the world, Fontenne, for you are a dead man."

At the far end of the courtyard, three huge guards with doltish faces and meaty forearms appeared from the blackness of a door arch. They did not wait for Laire to dismount, but seized him and pulled him from the saddle. He scuffled with them briefly, receiving a blow to the side of his head that momentarily paralyzed him and sent the lights of the firmament dancing before his eyes.

He was dragged along a hall, then down several flights of worn and tilting stone steps. Here and there a sputtering torch lit the rank-smelling underbelly of the palace. Somewhere amid the labyrinth of passageways, Laire was shoved into a cell, stripped of his clothing, and shackled to the wall.

Before an hour had passed, the flaring light of a torch cut across the blackness of his cell. The blazing brightness dazzled Laire's eyes, rendering him half-blind. He blinked, squinting into the smoky light. Slowly a trio of hazy figures took shape and he made out the weasel-sharp features of the king's inquisitor and two of the burly guards who had dragged him from the horse.

Gullimae de Nogaret stepped from between the two brutish looking men. "It seems fate has placed you in a most unenviable position, messire," the inquisitor said with an unpleasant smile. Before him, de Nogaret saw yet another strong, young body, much as the d'Aulnay brothers had once been. Broad shouldered, athletic, well endowed. None of it would be of any further use to him.

Nogaret motioned the guard with the torch to step forward. To Laire, he revealed, "Your comrades have fully confessed to their crimes. Of course, they were at first reluctant, but in the end they were glad to tell me all I wished to know. I hope you are going to be more sensible."

"I have no knowledge of a crime," Laire said, "aside from your wrongful arrest and detention of the king's loyal guards." His voice sounded remarkably even, considering his state of undress and that of his nerves.

De Nogaret affected an amused posture. "Sadly, you are misinformed. It was his majesty, King Philip, who ordered the arrests."

"On what charge? Of what am I accused?" Laire demanded, feigning ignorance.

The inquisitor clucked reprovingly. "I can see that you are going to be foolish. Very well," he smiled, bobbing his head. It was a nervous tick, as was the sudden jerk of his head to the left which invariably followed.

Laire's eyes were trained on the brute standing near the door to the cell. Without a word, the heavy browed man ducked into the passage and returned with a small three legged stool and sat it beneath the inquisitor.

The other brute lifted the torch he had been holding and dropped its base into a metal wall bracket. As he turned, he took something black from his belt. It looked to be a short length of wood, a cudgel of sorts. But as he drew nearer, Laire saw it was fashioned of leather.

"Now," de Nogaret said, lowering himself onto the stool, "You will state when and where your liaisons with the lady Nicolette of Burgundy took place."

Laire's gaze flashed back to the paunchy figure seated in the center of the cell. "Since you have invented them, perhaps you should tell me!"

The brute with the cudgel moved closer, weighing the savage-looking bit of leather in his hand, flicking it. Even more menacing was the ugly change that had come over his face. In the sickly wash of torch light his heavy jaw had taken on a bestial slant and his narrow, darting eyes appeared glazed.

De Nogaret, noting the effect on the prisoner, began again. "Witnesses have confirmed your involvement. By denying it, you will only cause yourself needless pain."

Laire made no reply. His eyes were on the brute with the cudgel. He was truly frightened now. They intended to beat it out of him, and eventually, he thought, they would succeed.

"I will ask you once more," de Nogaret said, crossing his thin legs, and waiting. The corners of his eyes creased, but his lips did not move. Presently he nodded to the man with the cudgel.

The brute made a grunting sound and came and stood in front of Laire. Suddenly he raised the cudgel over his head. Laire clenched his teeth, straining at the shackles. He saw no more than a flash of motion as the hairy, hamlike forearm brought the cudgel down in a vicious arc, and halted a hair's breadth from his cheek.

De Nogaret slowly smiled. "What do you say now, my blue-eyed chevalier?"

Again the brute swung the cudgel, halting it just before it crashed into the bridge of Laire's nose. Laire broke into a cold sweat. He set his lips in a determined line and remained silent.

In the deep shadows of the cell the inquisitor's profile took on the grotesqueness of a marionette whose nose and chin all but met. Again he nodded.

With a savage flick of his wrist, the brute slammed the cudgel into Laire's face.

The pain blinded him. He thought his jaw had been shattered. He could not have spoken even if he had tried. He could not even scream.

De Nogaret looked on indifferently. "My patience with you has come to an end, Fontenne. I have no time for games. Dates and places?" he reiterated. When no response came, he gave a quick nod of his head.

The brute with the cudgel moved in, savagely hammering away at Laire's face, his knees, his legs. The rain of blows ended as abruptly as it had begun. Laire was near to fainting from the pain. What little remained of his determination to resist was quickly ebbing away.

"Are you willing to be reasonable now?"

Laire coughed, strangling on the blood that poured from his nose and mouth. When he was able, he raised his eyes to the paunchy figure seated on the stool, and gasped out a single word, "No!"

Another such assault, he reasoned, would render him unconscious, and mercifully he would feel nothing. He shut his eyes, tensing his every muscle for the blows. None came.

Instead, he heard voices, and when he painfully opened his eyes he saw de Nogaret had risen from his stool and now stood by the door. A fourth man had entered the cell. He was dressed in the king's livery. The conversation was brief and when it ended, de Nogaret turned to his torturers and instructed, "Release him from the shackles and dress him, then see to the others. We go before the council within the hour."

In a cell not too far distant, Nicolette lay on the filthy straw pallet. She had lost all sense of time. When her body could stand no more tears and self-recrimination, she had fallen asleep, only to awaken a short time later with a start of horror and realize nothing had changed. Tears stung her eyes once more. Once not so very long ago she had been happy. As a child surrounded by her sisters and brothers she had been free to laugh and play, certain that she could find comfort and sympathy for all of life's hurts in the loving arms of her nursemaid, Ozanne.

In those days the world was a magical place. She had not known grief, save for that suffered over a broken doll. No, there had been no sadness, nothing to blight their days and nights, not before the hour she and her siblings were taken to the chapel to view their father who lay before the altar, between two rows of candles.

There was no smile on his blackened lips and his large hands were cold and hard. That was the beginning of childhood's end, for during the winter her eldest brother died of lung fever, and Etudes, her only remaining brother, was sent away to be educated. But life went on, until the summer of her first flux.

It was then their mother took a second husband. He was younger than their mother, greedy and domineering. It was his wish that Nicolette's two sisters be dedicated to the church. Such would have been Nicolette's fate as well, had her stepfather not hoped to propose her as a suitable bride for the king's eldest son.

There was no doubt that she was a pretty child. It had become obvious to Nicolette at a very early age. Her father constantly bragged of her beauty, and the serving women never tired of telling her how pretty she was. People were always whispering about it. She saw it in their eyes. Even her nursemaid, dear Ozanne, told her that one day, because she was so beautiful, a noble chevalier would come and offer her his heart.

Because of the story, Nicolette had not been at all surprised when shortly after her sixteenth birthday the king sent courtiers to look at her and ask her questions. In some strange way she believed it was just as Ozanne had foretold.

Nicolette's mother suddenly took an interest in her. Even her stepfather treated her with a new respect. Nicolette was the center of attention. Dressmakers flattered and fawned over her. The king sent jewels for her to wear and a fine charette in which to enter Paris. She arrived with the first warm days of April, filled with foolish hopes and dreams, only to have them dashed by the sniveling, sarcastic youth who was soon to be her husband.

Tragedy had marked their marriage from the first hour. When the remains of their wedding feast was cast into the great forecourt to feed the poor, more than a dozen people were trampled to death. Nicolette was horrified. But her bridegroom, Louis, made a jest of it. "They are only peasants," he sneered, "they breed like rats."

No, Nicolette thought, I do not regret hating him. I regret nothing. Her fears, though, were not so easily set aside. "They will burn me," she whimpered, abandoning herself to despair.

She feared the flames, for she had witnessed the public burning of the Templars. Not by choice, but by the king's command. All the court had been present, as had half the population of the great city, whom to her profound disgust seemed to consider the spectacle a form of entertainment.

Months later the images were still vivid in her mind. She heard again in her memory the almost joyous shouts of the crowd and saw once more the old men dragged to the summits of the pyres and secured. Too well she recalled the bright breath of the torch as it touched the fringes of the faggots and pine boughs, the crackling voice of the flames and the scent of the fragrant smoke carried on the wind like some wild incense. Above all was the horror of seeing human flesh melt in the flames like wax. She had turned away sickened by the sight, the piteous sounds of their cries.

"God in your mercy, do not let me die in the flames. I am innocent," she cried, throwing herself down on the straw. Afterwards she lay there exhausted, with no more tears to shed for herself and her two cousins. She began to pray, finding some solace in the monotony of the verses. At some point, almost unaware, she fell silent and merely stared into the gloom of her cell.

A scuffling of boots beyond the door roused her. She jolted up, her heart pounding against her ribs. A key scraped in the lock, making a rusty, grating sound that tingled her spine.

Two coarse-looking men entered. Their filthy clothing reeked of urine and long dried sweat. With them was a shorter man, fat and bald with a flat expressionless face. In his hand he carried a barber's satchel. Nicolette drew back against the wall, curling herself into a ball at their approach.

Four

The day dawned with a chill grey light. Milky white vapors rising from the River Seine drifted like phantoms across the Isle de la Cite, shrouding the embankments and bridge towers, the sprawling markets, the royal palace and the grandeur of the great cathedral of Notre Dame.

At the gates of the palace, a mob gathered in the morning mists. Word of the scandal had quickly spread throughout the city. Because the affair was of a sexual nature and the accused were young and noble, the curiosity of the lower classes was insatiable.

Those waiting vigilantly by the massive iron portcullis hoped to catch a glimpse of the drama. Porters, carters, errant maid servants, laborers and merchants who had delayed opening their shops, jostled for a better view. "The judgment is certain to be harsh," an elderly merchant predicted. All had an opinion. Some argued that the princesses should die.

"They are common bawds!" a burly carter exclaimed. Others blamed the king's feckless sons. "What sort of men are they?" posed a plump maid servant. "Aye," her companion agreed. "If they can not even satisfy their wives, then how can they hope to rule a realm?"

A babble of voices from beyond the iron gates greeted Laire as he was thrust into the chill morning air and wrestled across the forecourt. His ears were still ringing from a cudgel blow delivered by one of his guards when he attempted to shout to his friends as they were dragged, a guard on either side, into the council hall. Clearly Gautier and Pierre were unable to walk, for their legs bounced and dragged along the stones uselessly.

Once inside the great hall with its lavish tapestries of blue and gold, the accused were maneuvered through the noisy crowd of nobles, lawyers, and palace servants, who had also come to gawk and gossip, and dragged to the rear of the cavernous chamber.

The d'Aulnays were dumped on the floor. Their faces resembled nothing human and only groans escaped their torn lips. Blood still flowed from their wounds and their clothing was soaked with it. To Laire they appeared more dead than alive, and he was overcome by pity and rage. He himself was standing only by sheer force of will, and because there was a wall at his back.

Pages scurried about the immense hall, some with only the pretense of being busy, others carrying stacks of parchment and ink pots. While on the raised dais, servants of the royal household positioned chairs for the king and his ministers.

Laire's gaze roved over the chamber. He noticed

three young postulants with shaved heads kneeling before the dais as if in prayer, and a number of Celestine monks among those who packed the galleries. The blandness of their tonsured heads made a pale patchwork amid the dim mass of spectators.

A sudden movement rippled through the assembled crowd, and heads turned. The insectlike buzz of conversations ebbed away and the king entered the chamber by way of a door to the right of the dais. Philip IV, tall, spare and grim-faced, strode onto the dais and took his seat beneath the canopy of velvet trappings on which the symbol of France, the fleur de lis, had been embroidered in golden thread.

The king's brothers, Monseigneur of Valois and Monseigneur of Everux, trailed after him. Both were shorter in stature than their kingly brother. Monseigneur of Valois was quite fat. He was also vain, and wore his elegant brocaded jupes longer than was the fashion in order to disguise his expanding girth.

Next came the king's three sons. Louis, the eldest, looked mortified and much agitated in his role of the cuckolded husband, Philippe with his long, blank face appeared equally displeased, and Charles, the youngest, lagged behind like a fat, reluctant child.

They were followed closely by their sister, Isabella, whose cold and unrelenting demeanor made her seem much older than her twenty-five years. The Baron de Conches with his heavy-lidded eyes and oiled hair skulked at her side like a hungry hound.

Then came de Marigny, the coadjutor of the realm; de Bouville, the king's grand chamberlain; Bishop D'Enbeau, and a host of other ministers. One by one they took their seats at the lengthy table.

Lastly, the king's marshals and the provosts entered in a solemn line. Laire did not at first see his uncle among the marshals and his heart fell. A moment later, he saw him enter with rapid strides, like a man late for an appointment. A page with a sheaf of papers in his hand hurried to keep abreast of Marshal de Orfevres.

De Nogaret, the king's inquisitor and keeper of the seals, was already entrenched at a table before and to the left of the dais. His clerks sat opposite him, writing feverishly as he leaned forward with his hands on the table, scanning the material he would present to the council. Several times he glanced anxiously toward the dais, and turned to his clerks, haranguing them and calling for alterations in the text. It was the most important moment of his career. All else paled in significance, for today the fate of kings was in his hands.

Laire de Fontenne's view of the proceedings was narrower in scope but no less profound. His gaze wandered once more to the postulants. Only then did he notice their unevenly shaved heads and the fact that their hands were bound by the ropes that cinched their waists.

Suddenly it occurred to him. They were not

young men at all, but women—the royal princesses! The revelation was as staggering as a blow to the stomach. For if the king had ordered his daughters-in-law to be humiliated in such a way, then there was no hope for Gautier, Pierre, and himself. They were already condemned. The whole of their lives could be measured in hours, and he was made sick with regret that he had not died with his sword in his hand at The Laughing Cat, and taken Raoul de Conches to hell with him.

Nicolette of Burgundy, on her knees before the dais, blanched in horror at the sight of the once handsome d'Aulnay brothers. Tears glistened on her long black lashes and it seemed to her that all the world had gone mad. She could not bear to look at them again, nor at the third prisoner.

She presumed he was Laire de Fontenne, the man with whom she was accused of committing adultery. Yet there was something about the tall, broad-shouldered young man that drew her eyes back, almost against her will. She had no recollection of ever having seen him before, though his face was so swollen, disfigured by bruises, she could not truthfully say.

His close-clipped fair hair was matted with blood as was his jupe and shirt which gaped open, exposing his chest. Even in chains there was certain youthful arrogance about the splendid shoulders and muscular chest, the way his leather hosen clung like a second skin to his hips and the faultless line of his long, athletic legs.

They had not defeated him, not broken him.

From the top of his battered head to the toes of his boots, he was everything that her hollow-chested husband with his long sneering face had never been. And she wished with all her heart that she had known this man's touch. At least then, she thought bitterly, they would have reason to punish me.

A blare of trumpets reverberated through the cavernous chamber, bringing the proceedings to order. De Nogaret stepped forward, parchment in hand, and read out the charges against the royal princesses and the king's commanders. He then gave a recital of the interrogations. The dates on which their liaisons began, the times, the places of their meetings. The names of servants were then called out, those who had aided and abetted in the crime.

From his seat on the dais, Marshal de Orfevres listened attentively to each date, each time, to each damning word that fell from de Nogaret's lips. For all his efforts the inquisitor appeared to be totally unaware that throughout the dates given, Marshal de Orfevres's nephew, Laire de Fontenne, had been on duty at Pontoise, a full day's ride from Paris. When the inquisitor paused for breath, the old Marshal seized the offensive. "You are a liar, messire!" he bellowed, rising from his seat.

De Nogaret's bulbous eyes shot up from the parchment as if he had been struck with a whip. Who had dared to call him a liar? Before the inquisitor could respond, the old Marshal addressed the king directly. "Milord," he said, "as you must surely be aware, my nephew, Laire de Fontenne, has for more than a year faithfully served as the commander of your majesty's guards at Pontoise. Indeed, he has for the past three months been without leave of duty, having only returned to Paris the day prior to his arrest." The marshal's deep, rich baritone rose to a thunderous crescendo, as he went on. "Despite this fact, Messire de Nogaret has produced testimony to the contrary, testimony contrary even to the laws of nature. For my nephew's appearance in two vastly distant places at the same time is beyond the realm of possibility, and in my estimation raises serious doubts as to the accuracy of all Messire de Nogaret's charges!"

De Nogaret howled with indignation. "I have proof!" he shrieked, "Indisputable proof!"

The king silenced him with a slight gesture of his hand, and inquired of his old friend de Orfevres, "Have you proof of your nephew's presence at Pontoise?"

De Orfevres, a contemporary of the king who had fought at his side in their youth, replied, "I do, Milord, I have here depositions signed by those soldiers of my nephew's command who served under him at Pontoise, and who have only recently returned with him to Paris."

As the marshal concluded, Monseigneur de Marigny, the coadjutor of the realm, rose slowly to his feet, explaining, "If it pleases your majesty, there are also these receipts. As commander of your guards at Pontoise, the Chevalier de Fontenne was required to sign for and to distribute the pay of those in his command." De Marigny gathered up the papers set before him and handed them to a page. "The dates are clearly stated, milord."

Silence reigned throughout the chamber as the king perused the documents. De Nogaret, momentarily at loose ends, recovered more quickly than did the king's daughter, Isabella. Her face had gone livid.

"Obviously," de Nogaret began, "my investigators failed to inform me of the accused's recent duties." The wily inquisitor regained control of his voice and quickly took another tack. "Even so," he began, "there can be no doubt as to the Chevalier de Fontenne's guilty knowledge of the affair, to his complicity, to his boldness and license.

"Might I remind all present that there is no crime more foul than for a vassal to seduce and betray the honor of his suzerain's wife. The crime is made even more heinous when the wife is a member of the royal family, where a question of legitimacy of heirs is concerned. It is for this reason I find the Chevalier de Fontenne no less guilty in this vile matter than his fellow commanders."

The old marshal leapt up again, slamming his fist on the table with such force that the papers before him scattered onto the floor. "And I shall call you liar, messire, no matter how many times you say it!"

De Nogaret's waspish voice was no match for the old marshal's roaring baritone. The king put a halt to the shouting match. The chamber again echoed with silence. De Nogaret was motioned to come forward, and the king and those nearest him fell into a hushed discussion.

Marshal de Orfevres could hear nothing of what was being said. He was seated some distance from the king and he was rather deaf, as the result of a blow to the head in battle some years before. His youthful page, however, had sharp ears and what scraps of the conversation he caught, he dutifully repeated to his master.

The conversation among the king and his ministers ended. De Nogaret returned to the table, instructing his clerks to make the appropriate changes. When he returned it was to take up the fates of the royal princesses.

Nicolette, Joan, and Blanche, who had been forced to remain on their knees before the dais, could hear quite plainly each damning word. Their exchanged glances were filled with misery and fear. Nicolette wanted to scream out her anguish, blot out the thought of her ruined life. How could this have happened to her, to Joan and Blanche? What crime had they committed? What sin was there in playful flirtations, in courtly love? Troubadours sang its praises, poets dedicated endless verses to its glory. Perhaps their rebellion had been childish, and their play acting offensive, but what other recourse had they to the ill-treatment of their husbands and the stifling life at court? She was guilty of nothing more. And if Joan and Blanche had behaved less than virtuously, she had no knowledge of it. Nay, in her heart she could not believe they had. Like her, they were victims, entrapped by Isabella's lies.

The wild shrill voice of Nicolette's husband, Louis, destroyed the last vestiges of her composure. "Let her die!" he ranted above the voices of his brothers. "She has sullied my honor. She is a bawd, she deserves no better!"

Nicolette had expected as much from her weedy husband. He was petty and cruel. His squeals of rage brought images of her wedding night flashing through her mind, and again she felt the shame and revulsion.

"A sentence of death is a serious matter," Bishop D'Enbeau cautioned. Charles, the youngest of the king's sons and husband to Blanche, agreed. He was young and frightened, hardly old enough to carry out the duties of a husband. Philippe, husband to Joan, was several years older, but of a like sentiment.

"Have you no sense of honor, brothers?" Louis squalled. "Our wives have shamed us! All of France is laughing! They are whores and deserve to burn!"

Louis's words pounded against Nicolette like hammer blows. Tears streamed down her cheeks and she began to pray silently. Because she had refused to confess, she had been denied the sacraments of the church. What did it matter, she thought, hell could be no worse than the torment into which she had been plunged. So intent was she in her prayers that she was not at once aware of Isabella's voice.

"It is noble enough to love honor, Louis," Isabella said to her elder brother. "But you must temper it with wisdom. If your wife is put to death, then you will forfeit her doweried properties and their revenues."

The king's brothers added their voices, Monseigneur of Valois most emphatically, for he had already seen the possibilities. With their wives imprisoned, the king's sons could sire no legitimate heirs. And the throne he had coveted all his life might yet be within his grasp.

De Marigny was next to voice an opinion, saying, "The loss of such sizable revenues would be a catastrophe for the treasury." He suggested locking the wayward princesses in a convent, until the matter was forgotten.

That did not suit Isabella's plans, and she prevailed upon her father. "A convent is too light a punishment."

Louis, in his haste to again condemn his wife, was taken by a fit of coughing. While he hacked and choked, de Nogaret seized the moment to suggest a prison. "Lock them away in separate fortresses, prisoners for as long as God grants them."

"That is only proper," Isabella said, pointing out, "They have sinned and should be prevented from ever passing on the blood of kings."

"No! Louis croaked, "I will have vengeance on her!"

"Be silent, Louis," the king commanded. "You must learn to control yourself. Few will have respect for a prince who can not rule his own wife.

You have been a weak and foolish husband. At least now, try to show some strength of character."

De Nogaret waited expectantly for the king's command. The bishop, having paled at the thought of putting his signature on the death warrant of his kinsmen's daughters, added his voice to those who favored imprisonment.

"So be it," the king intoned. De Nogaret scurried back to his clerks, as if he feared the king might change his mind. In a rash of feverish activity, the clerks took down the inquisitor's rapid dictation. The scratching of their quills rose on the silent air like the angry drone of bees.

Presently the inquisitor took up the parchment and, clearing his throat, began to read. "The brothers Gautier and Pierre d'Aulnay, having freely confessed to crimes against the honor and royal majesty of their suzerain lords, shall on the morrow be flayed alive, decapitated, drawn and quartered and hung upon the gibbet for all to see."

Laire de Fontenne expected no less, yet his mind shuddered at the reality behind the words. Neither Gautier nor Pierre gave any indication they had heard the terrible judgment. They appeared beyond caring. Laire had steeled himself for the same fate, and now, not hearing his name, wondered what punishment de Nogaret had reserved for him. For he would be punished, of that he was certain. He glanced to where his uncle sat among the marshals. Their eyes met, and in the look that passed between them he saw the silent resignation, as if his uncle meant to say, "I have done my best."

PRISONER OF MY HEART 55

De Nogaret continued. "The ladies Joan and Blanche of Burgundy, having brought shame and dishonor upon their husbands and the majesty of the royal household, are henceforth to be imprisoned without comfort in the fortress castle of Dourdon and there they shall remain until such time as they are called to face the judgment of God."

Nicolette heard her cousins' breathless sobs. An instant later she saw Joan slump to the floor. She turned to Joan, only to hear de Nogaret's sinister voice call out her name. Her breath caught in her throat and her heart seemed to throb violently to a standstill.

"The lady Nicolette of Burgundy and Navarre, having been proven to be an accomplice to the grievous crimes of her sisters by marriage, having brought dishonor to her husband, and to the majesty of the royal household, shall be imprisoned without comfort and the solace of the Holy Church in the fortress castle of Gaillard and there she shall remain for as long as it pleases God to grant to her."

Nicolette reached out to Joan, deciding it was useless to sob or scream in protest. They were condemned, just as surely as Gautier and Pierre. In a flash of terrifying premonition she saw the future. They will send us away to be quietly murdered, she thought. For only with their deaths would the king's sons be free to take other wives.

De Nogaret read on, "The Chevalier Laire de Fontenne, for his willful silence regarding the crimes of Gautier and Pierre d'Aulnay, for his complicity and culpable compliance, shall be exiled from court, installed as commandant of Gaillard, and it is there he shall remain as jailer to the prisoner, Lady Nicolette, for as long as it pleases God and the pleasure of the king. This is the judgment of his royal majesty Philip IV, our most gracious, most mighty and most beloved sovereign."

It was over. The king rose from his chair. Marshal de Orfevres shook his head wearily. He consoled himself with the thought that he had spared his favorite nephew a horrid death. But in exchange for what—a life long exile. The old marshal's eyes settled on de Nogaret. How puffed up he was with his own importance, his skinny legs bowing under the combined burden of his paunchy gut and his conceit. The day would come, the old marshal thought, when de Nogaret would himself be ensnared in his own web of lies and deceit. The day would come, Marshal de Orfevres vowed, and he would do all in his power to hasten it.

The hall began to empty. Agnes de Marginay rushed toward her brother, but she was halted by one of the king's guards. "No one may speak to the prisoners," he told her, blocking her determined efforts. Her husband, Jerome, caught her arm. "Be thankful, Agnes, he will live." But Agnes looked past him, and her eyes burned on Isabella. "There is the queen of whores, she is the cause of this," Agnes said from between clenched teeth. "She has shamed my family and caused my brother to be condemned to a living death. She will live to regret it, I promise you."

Laire did not see his sister and her husband amid the throng of spectators. He moved like a blind man, shoved forward by the guards, hardly daring to believe what his ears had heard. He would live. Yet he felt nothing, not relief, anger, or guilt—not yet.

Isabella lagged behind her brothers. She was regally attired in purple velvet and wore a thin gold crown on her head. Twice she paused, a contemptuous smile frozen on her lips as she watched her sisters-in-law be led away. She had prevailed on the matter of her brothers' wives, but there remained the nagging problem of Laire de Fontenne. Her father, either out of weakness or a fondness for his old friend the marshal, had spared him. The reason mattered not. So long as he lived, Laire de Fontenne posed a threat to her plans.

Raoul de Conches hung at Isabella's side, impatiently fingering his riding gloves which were tucked into his belt. He too was dressed in velvets and his black hair gleamed with scented oil. "You should be pleased. Everything has gone as you planned," he murmured to her.

Isabella regarded him with a cold stare. "I want him dead. Do you hear?"

"De Fontenne? What harm can he cause at Gaillard? He will be three days ride from Paris and under sentence of exile." The fact that the king had readily given his consent to Nicolette of Burgundy's imprisonment in Gaillard was a great success. Raoul de Conches was enormously pleased. His Norman holdings all but surrounded the fortress and its lands.

"I want him dead," was Isabella's snarling reply. She glanced over her shoulder at the inquisitor gathering up his papers, and still keeping her voice low, said, "Bring Nogaret to me, within the hour."

Later that day, after a heated meeting with de Nogaret, Isabella strolled onto the portico. The train of her gown rustled through the dry leaves that littered the stones. From her vantage point, she observed Raoul de Conches and a trusted villein, Simon Quarle by name, locked in a discussion. With them was a third man, a compactly built youth with a long humped nose who stood by silently, listening.

Isabella watched with satisfaction. Laire de Fontenne would die. At first Nogaret had been opposed to the idea, arguing that his untimely death would only further complicate matters. Nogaret had stubbornly cautioned: "His uncle, old de Orfevres, has always been a troublemaker and the king is fond of him. No, I do not like it." But Isabella had been adamant. In the end the inquisitor conceded, and now everything would go as she planned. She was rid of the d'Aulnays and soon she would be rid of de Fontenne. He was the last of the three commanders of her father's loyal bodyguards.

It annoyed her that de Fontenne had escaped the fate of the d'Aulnays. She harbored a special hatred for him. Isabella was a vindictive woman and she had never forgotten the summer at Wallingford when de Fontenne, his uncle, de Orfevres, and a number of French knights attended the tournament near London. At eighteen, de Fontenne, who had won his spurs fighting in Flanders with his uncle, had emerged victorious, the darling of the tournament.

At Wallingford, seemingly without effort, he had defeated her champion, unhorsed him and driven him to the dust. Isabella had been outraged, particularly when de Fontenne rode up to her with irony shining in his blue eyes and a calm half-smile on his lips. There had been a daring recklessness about him, a charming defiance that Isabella found at once infuriating and disquieting. On this occasion she would be the victor.

Five

Several days later in the pre-dawn darkness, Laire de Fontenne rode into the inner court of the Palace of the Cite. His face was yet swollen, his body littered with bruises from the beatings he had suffered at the hands of de Nogaret's tormentor. He was stiff and sore, but of all, his broken ribs pained him the most. The night before a physician had come to his cell to bind his chest with linen strips so that he might sit on a horse.

On Laire's right rode his squire, Albert Drouhet, and to his left a sergeant at arms appointed by the king. They were followed in close file by a troop of fourteen heavily armed men. A steady rain fell, pelting their faces and pouring from their horse's heads. They proceeded into the courtyard, riding two abreast. The hooves of their horses clattered over the cobblestones, and splashed through black pools of water. Across the courtyard, a door opened. Torch light spilled into the bleak morning and a group of dark figures appeared in silhouette, then merged as if consulting together.

Laire brought his horse to a halt before the door. Albert Drouhet drew up a moment later, leading a riderless mount. There was an exchange of documents, and a small pathetic figure was thrust forward and boosted into the saddle.

The lady Nicolette of Burgundy and Navarre rode from the courtyard dressed in the rough woolen robes of a penitent with her hands bound before her. Only a year before she had entered its gates dressed in silks and jewels. She did not look back.

Behind the drenched, plodding entourage, the massive iron portcullis slammed to the stones, echoing on the damp air like a thunder clap. The great bells of Notre Dame sounded lauds as they passed the gate towers of the Grand Pont. Below, blurred by rain, the Seine slid past, black as basalt.

It was the king's wish that the women be taken through the city without attracting undue notice. Joan and Blanche had been delivered to their jailers an hour before. From her cell Nicolette had shouted to them, but there had been no reply.

Laire and his troop rode out the hours in silence. By mid-day they passed through the last of the small villages that ringed the great city. The rain slackened to a drizzle and along the country paths, a heavy mist filled the hollows and clung, drifting amid the black barked trees.

He had not once looked at his prisoner. In truth he could not say whom he despised more, the lady Nicolette or himself. No matter how he tried he could not rid himself of the sight of Gautier and Pierre's broken, brutalized bodies. As irrational as the thought was, he felt somehow responsible. They had died and he had lived. He had lost his friends, he had lost his freedom, he had lost everything, and the sluttish daughters of Burgundy were to blame for all of it.

No human sound broke the silence, only the squeak of saddle leather, the clanking of weapons and the slog of their horse's hooves in the mud of the road. From the back of her palfrey, Nicolette observed her jailer as he rode beside the barrel-chested sergeant at arms.

Two days before in the council hall, she had thought him brave and honorable. Now she realized she had deceived herself. He was no less cruel, no more a man than her husband; worse, perhaps, for had he not bought his life with hers? The thought tormented her. The king, she suspected, never intended for her to reach Gaillard, and she wondered how Laire de Fontenne would kill her, where and when.

The hours passed miserably for Nicolette. She was soaked to her bones. Her wrists were bound so tightly that she could no longer feel her fingers, and the jolting gait of her palfrey jarred her bladder with every stride. Soon, she thought, she must relieve herself and she dreaded asking her jailer's permission.

Late in the afternoon the rain ended and they halted to rest their mounts. The dense woods surrounding them were bathed in a grey watery light and rain still dripped from the trees. In the west a reddish glow low to the horizon tinted the clearing sky with streaks of scarlet and purple.

Nicolette watched as the soldiers around her dismounted. No one came to help her dismount, no one gave a thought to her discomfort. Some stood with their backs to her, others did not trouble themselves.

She turned her head, setting her gaze on the veiled and shadowy surroundings. The woods were deep and dark. How easy it would be to hide herself in them, she thought, just as she had done as a child, much to Ozanne's annoyance. If she could but manage to reach the woods, she would be free. She did not think beyond that—where she might go, to whom she might appeal—only of a means to reach the woods. She was about to speak out, when she saw her jailer dismount and walk toward her.

Her first instinct was to refuse his help, but with her hands bound it was difficult to climb from the saddle. Laire lifted her from the horse, at once aware of her warm female scent and the soft, supple body beneath his hands. Her effect on him was immediate and impossible to ignore. "Have you need to relieve yourself?" he asked, forgetting for a moment that she was the cause of all his misery. She was shivering, soaking wet, and the patches of bristling hair beneath the cowled hood lent her the appearance of a little drenched bird.

He could not help but feel a measure of pity for her. "I can offer you only the privacy of a bush."

She nodded her consent. She did not look at him, fearing he might somehow read her thoughts. Mud oozed over her slippers as she picked her way through the mire of the road.

He took her arm when they reached the trees, but halted only several strides from the road. In sidelong glances Nicolette eyed the hollow beyond. "Might I have a more private place?" she pleaded. She still refused to look at him, but she heard his sharply exhaled breath and knew that she had won.

He took her a short distance further. The brush was denser there and he kicked down the weeds to make a place for her. The weeds trampled beneath his boots filled the clammy air with a wild, pungent scent. Nicolette held out her hands to him and, looking from beneath her long dark lashes, asked, "If you would free my wrists?" He could hardly refuse, for how else could she see to her own needs?

Laire had not noticed the condition of her hands and now felt shamed by the sight of her swollen fingers. He had not ordered her to be treated with such cruelty. The deep, ugly indentions left by the leather strap prompted him to inquire, "Who was it bound your wrists like this?"

"One of the tormentors."

Laire took her hands in his, attempting to rub the blood back into them. "Why did you not speak out?"

"To whom? To Nogaret?" she mocked, taking back her hands, unwilling to accept his grudging kindness. She looked away, suddenly disturbed by the clear blue eyes, the strong, warm hands. He was confusing her. She could almost believe he meant her no harm, but she was not so foolish as that. She stepped into the small clearing he had made and waited, kneading her aching fingers. She hesitated, expecting him to turn away. When he did not, she raised her eyes, and asked, "Will you turn your back?"

He smiled at her, a funny little half-smile, and asked, "Can I trust you not to run away?"

She did not answer, but lowered her eyes demurely. She felt about to burst, and the instant he turned away, she gathered up the robe and squatted. A feeling of blessed relief washed over her and she felt instantly warmer. Covertly she watched him position himself, took note of his spraddle-legged stance and the drilling sound against the sodden ground. She rose stealthily to her feet, and with one final glance at his broad back, bolted away.

The crack of a limb whirled him round. He caught only a glimpse of her fleeing figure. He stumbled forward, stuffing himself back into his hosen, and charged after her. Brambles and roots dragged at his boots, checking his speed. Twice more he caught sight of her through the tangle of vines and windfalls. The dull brown of the robe seemed to merge with the undergrowth and dreary light, and just as quickly he lost sight of her once more. Everything was sodden, the brush, the mat of leaves on the forest floor; soft and spongy so that every sound was muffled.

Deeper into the hollow the ground fell away quickly in a steep descent that ended in a shallow creek, where the water pooled and trickled across the rocks. Halfway down the hill, Laire halted, silently cursing himself for his stupidity. He stood there heaving, taking his breath in great greedy gasps, unable to decide which pained him more, his broken ribs, his aching jaw or his pride. There was neither sign nor sound of her. She had slipped through his hands like a wisp of smoke.

It galled him to think he would have to call to the strutting sergeant for assistance. He rejected the thought. He would find her. She could not run far, he reasoned. She weighed no more than a sack of grain. Surely she was as winded as he? The days of little sleep and less food would have taken their toll on her as well.

He was considering all this when he heard the sound of rocks clattering, as if something or someone had swiftly crossed the creek. The sound sent him careening recklessly down the rock-strewn hillside. But at the creek there was nothing to see, and the only sound was the gurgling of the water as it rippled over the rocks. He leaned forward, resting his hands on his thighs to catch his breath. But it set his swollen jaw to throbbing and he raised his head again to scan the hillside.

Nicolette crouched in the thicket, scratched and trembling. Her heart pounded in her throat, and her lungs burned as if they were afire. She could not see him. She dare not turn her head. But she could hear him moving about, hear each labored breath. She too was breathless and fought back the urge to gulp great gasps of air, fearing she would cough and betray her presence. Unbearable moments passed. She heard the pebbles crunch beneath his boots.

A rock clattered as he stepped on it. He was moving away from her. A little grey bird alit on a branch above her head, then fluttered elsewhere. Rain dripped from the branches, and farther along the creek bed, she heard her jailer curse softly.

Another sound, much closer, reached her ears. A soft irregular rustling, as if someone had crumpled a handful of silken cloth. Suddenly something queerly cold touched her outstretched hand. She recoiled violently. She saw the snake, slim and dark, as it darted across her hand.

The yelp of terror that escaped her lips was involuntary, as was the uncontrollable impulse to dash madly through the woods regardless of the direction. She bolted up in panic, clawing her way up the steep bank.

She heard him crashing after her. She looked wildly over her shoulder. He was nearly on top of her. She dodged sideways, but he seized her by the shoulder and brought her down. The impact of his body stunned her for a moment. Recovering herself, she thrashed from side to side, kicking out viciously with her legs and pounding her fists against him. But she was no match for him, he was too large and too strong. With alarming swiftness he pinned her arms above her head and straddled her. "Ough," she gasped. He was crushing her. "Let me go!" she squalled, threatening, "I will scream that you are raping me!"

Her threat elicited only a vaporous laugh. Though he did shift his weight from her somewhat, he did not release her wrists. "Why? Why should

I rape you, when I have had your consent all along?"

"That is a lie!"

"Of course it is a lie. One even Nogaret could not make credible. That is why my body parts are not hanging from the gibbet beside Gautier's and Pierre's. As for you being a slut, well, that is another matter."

"No! I am innocent!"

"Are you? Gautier had a mistress. A royal. He as much as admitted it. Which of you was it?"

"Not me! I do not know! Please, you are hurting me!" His voice was deep and fierce and for an instant she thought he was going to kill her. She was terrified and shrank back, turning her cheek to the ground. Tears stung her eyelids and she felt shamed, exposed in every sense, for beneath the robe she wore nothing and now she was painfully aware of the material tangled about her waist, the cool, clammy air prickling her bare legs.

"Please," she cried, attempting to free her hands, to wriggle from beneath him.

Slowly, he raised himself to his knees and released his grip on her wrists. "We will talk again," he promised, rising to his feet.

With lightning swiftness, Nicolette thrust down the rumpled woolen robe and scrambled to her knees. She had covered herself, but too late. There was no mistaking the look in his eyes and she stared back at him, hardly daring to breathe, or even blink.

The startling glimpse of pale slender leg split

by a mass of dark feathery curls struck him with the impact of a hammer blow between eyes. It was a moment before he recovered sufficiently to pull her to her feet. "Hold out your hands," he commanded, suddenly angry with her, with himself. He took the leather thong from inside his jupe and lashed her wrists together, though not as savagely as before, and dragged her toward the hill.

As they stepped from beneath the trees, Laire noticed the frown of concern on Albert's face. He caught the reins of the mare and turned her, leading her forward past the knots of slyly smiling soldiers. The sergeant settled his sword belt on his hips and strutted down the line of horses, remarking, "I was about to come after you. I was beginning to think you had lost your way." Laire sent him a black look and boosted the girl onto the mare. Only then did he notice the leaves and mud on her back.

Nicolette was also aware of their smirking stares. Her face burned with indignation, but she straightened her spine, and faced them off defiantly. She was innocent, despite what they thought, despite what her jailer suggested, and she vowed that she would not allow him, or anyone, to terrorize her again. He was no better than Nogaret, no better than her coward of a husband.

Row upon row of neatly tended vines lined the approach to the Abbey of Bon Enfants, and the pleasant, fermenty scent of ripening grapes filled the cool, clearing dusk. Laire reined in his bay stallion before the Abbey's gatehouse. The Angelus bells began to toll.

A lay brother admitted them, a comical-looking fellow with unruly hair and a lame leg, who stumped down from his post to open the gates. "The Father Abbot is conducting the Angelus," he explained, craning his neck to view the prisoner. He did not mention that a courier of the king had brought word of their coming, though clearly the abbot was expecting them, for the lay brother added, "Our abbot offers you his greetings and extends the hospitality of the order's guest house." The lay brother continued to stare unrestrainedly at the cowled figure astride the brown mare. His intense interest had been fired by the courier's recounting of the scandal and, despite the abbot's admonitions concerning the evils of gossip, there had been much loose talk in the abbey's kitchens. So that now he could hardly tear his gaze away to call for the grooms.

One by one the troop divested themselves of their cross bows, swords, and bucklers. At Bon Enfants, as in all holy places, the weapons of war were forbidden. From the back of her mare, Nicolette saw her jailer unbuckle his belt, remove his sword and dagger and pass it to his groom to be placed beside the other weapons in the gatehouse strongroom. It gave her little peace of mind.

Perhaps he could not slit her throat, she thought, but there was nothing to prevent him from strangling her or smothering the breath from her as she lay sleeping. A young groom grasped the reins of her horse and, at a glance, she saw her jailer approaching. The touch of his hands sent a chill racing up her spine.

The lay brother led them toward a stone and timber structure. He hopped across the darkened forecourt in an odd, stiff-legged gait, a large ring of keys jangling at his waist. The abbey was like a little world unto itself. At its center was the church with its tall spires and pointed arches. Clustered around the holy structure were numerous buildings: dormitories, the refectory, the cloisters, as well as many handsome stone and timber barns, storehouses, and workrooms. The lay brother seemed eager to point out the gardens and small orchard, though little could be discerned in the gathering dusk. He mentioned with pride that the abbey had its own slaughterhouse and tannery and that leather goods made at the abbey were sold in the Paris markets. He seemed compelled to talk, even though it was obvious no one listened or even cared.

Several times Nicolette balked at the strict grasp of her jailer as he propelled her forward by the arm. As a pampered daughter of the nobility, she was totally unprepared for the austerity of the guest chambers. She viewed the interior with a look of disbelief. Even her servants had enjoyed more luxuriant surroundings than the unadorned stone walls and pallets of straw that lined the walls of the open chamber.

She was relieved when the lay brother pointed

out a narrow wooden staircase at one end of the room which led to the floor above. "Follow me," he directed, and, limping like a wounded crow, took to the stairs, escorting Nicolette, her jailer, and his squire to the floor above.

There, a long dreary passageway ran the length of the structure. It smelled musty and unused. A long line of heavy iron hinged doors lined either wall. It was to one of these chambers halfway down the passage that she and her jailer were escorted. The squire, carrying a leather satchel for his master, followed them inside. Much to Nicolette's dismay, the chambers were small and as spartan as the main floor.

"These rooms," the lay brother explained, "are reserved for the honored guests." Nicolette looked about the room. Were it not for the tall carved chest that all but encompassed one wall, it appeared no more comfortable than her cell in the dungeon of the palace. There were no luxuries. Four straw pallets with feather mattresses lined one wall. A single bench stood beside the door, and beside it a small table which held a dented pewter water ewer.

When the lay brother and the boy had gone, Nicolette slumped onto the pallet nearest the door. She was miserable and afraid, and watched with apprehension as her jailer dropped the leather satchel onto the pallet beneath the high narrow window. He then recrossed the room, halting before the table, and lifted the water ewer. It was empty.

Laire was about to call for his squire to go and fetch some water when a brethren in a black scapular appeared at the door. "You are Laire de Fontenne?" he inquired.

"Yes," Laire responded, replacing the water ewer on the table. It seemed he would not escape the abbot's hospitality after all.

The solemn-faced monk addressed him once more, though his gaze was set not on Laire, but on the slight figure in the rough woven robe. She sat, unmoving, with her pale hands in her lap and her features lost to the depth of the hood. "The Father Abbot awaits you in the sacristy," he advised. "If you will follow me."

"A moment, brother," Laire said, moving past the curious monk to shout down the passage for his squire. There was the sound of running footfalls and an instant later a lanky boy with flushed cheeks and an adenoidal, open-mouthed expression topped the stairs. "Stay with the prisoner," Laire instructed. "I won't be long."

Albert Drouhet nodded and, sliding past the figures in the doorway, took a seat on the bench.

The monk seemed reluctant to move, and only when Laire set off down the passage without him did he manage to curb his curiosity and recall his mission.

In the sacristy a single cresset burned, its wick floating on mutton tallow, and giving off a rank odor. The abbot was an elderly man, thick-set and jovial, with ruddy cheeks and a bulbous nose. After the usual pleasantries, the abbot expressed his regret at being unable to welcome Laire and his companions to sup at his table that evening. "It is due entirely to the state of the prisoner's soul," he explained. "I am forbidden by church law to offer an unrepentant sinner the abbey's food. However," he continued, "food and wine will be brought to the guest house, and you may, in your charity, choose to share this with the prisoner. I leave that decision to you." He smiled once more. His chalice sat nearby, prepared for the next mass, and he aimlessly rearranged the altar cruets as he spoke. Occasionally he glanced at the young man with intent blue eyes. His face was marked by bruises which had begun to fade around the edges. The skin was broken in several places on the young man's jaw, and the abbot surmised it was still too painful for him to shave, for he had several days' growth of beard. In appearance he looked more a criminal than an officer of the king. The abbot continued, almost as if he were speaking to himself, "It is my belief that justice should be meted out in equal parts with mercy, do you not agree?"

"I do, Father. I will see that she is fed."

The abbot made a pleased expression. "And now," he said, "I must not keep you any longer. There is a guest who wishes to speak with you. You will find him in the chapel." With a slight gesture of his hand he directed Laire to the first of two doors. The other, Laire imagined, led onto the altar.

Laire entered the chapel through the choir stalls. He did not at first see his brother, Thierry, kneeling at the altar rail. It was quite dark in the chapel, despite the flickering light of a brace of altar candles. Laire supposed it would be no brighter at mid-day, for only two narrow slitlike windows high above the altar broke the monotony of the thick stone walls.

The familiar figure, large and bulky, turned before Laire had a chance to speak, and said, "You look surprised to see me, brother."

Laire was astonished. "How have you found me?"

Thierry smiled in the candlelight. "Agnes," he replied simply. Even in the gloom, Thierry de Fontenne could see the marks of violence on his younger brother's face. "Come and pray with me," he said.

"For what shall we pray, Thierry? That messire our father will forgive you for seizing Vezeley? It was his wish that I should have it. He made it known more than once. He spoke of it on his deathbed."

"Never did I lay claim to it," Thierry defended.

"You refused to grant me title."

"I would have done so, in time. You had no interest in Vezeley until messire our uncle, that scoundrel de Orfevres, whetted your concern. You have always favored madame our mother's people. You are more an Orfevres than a Fontenne!"

"Vezeley was mine," Laire replied hotly. "I had every right to claim it."

"Particularly when messire our uncle promised you Gien and the village of Breneol which adjoins it. Oh yes, it was all to his advantage. For if you held Vezeley and Gien, he would be certain of success when he pressed his case against Baron Gardiner, my father-in-law."

"Gardiner is a snake, he deals openly with the English."

"And I suppose you will tell me that our devoted uncle does not?"

"Only to serve the interests of the king."

"Well, it seems the king has repaid you both handsomely."

"You came to gloat, didn't you, Thierry?"

"To gloat! I am your brother."

"So you never tire of reminding me."

"In Christ's name, Laire. Why must our every conversation fall into an argument?"

"Do not look to me for fault. You are the one who first hired a lawyer."

"What did you expect I would do? Gardiner's estates will come to me eventually through Odeline. Did you think I would stand by, wringing my hands, while you and our dear uncle, de Orfevres, carved up his lands like a roasted stag?"

"That was never my intention, nor was it Auguste's. He wanted only the forest lands of Lagrume which were his by right and deed."

"By right and deed! Ha!" Thierry blustered. "Why then did the court not rule with favor on his petition?"

"Because your wife's father holds them in terror of their lives, and you well know it!" Laire accused, slamming his palm against the altar rail. "Why am

I arguing with you, here before God—or at all! I should know better!"

"I did not come to argue with you!"

"Yes, why else would you have come?"

"To give you title to Vezeley."

"Now! Now that it can not matter! How generous of you Thierry—with you as administrator, of course!"

"You will receive its revenues! You might at least be grateful for that!"

"So Agnes has prevailed upon you? Or could it be your conscience, at last?"

"Agnes had no part in my decision," Thierry denied. "Nor has my conscience, which is clearer than yours, I dare say!"

"Then it is because you and your father-in-law have hatched a better scheme to claim Lagrume woods!"

"Do you refuse to accept it?"

"I did not say that!"

"Then come with me before the abbot, and we will have done with it. Laire, we are brothers. It is not right that we should be in contention. We are no longer children, we are grown men, and I am concerned for our souls."

For your own, Laire thought angrily, though he did not give voice to his opinion. A wise decision, for just then a black clad brother entered the chapel with a purposely heavy tread, and clearing his throat, to give further notice of his presence, said, "Seigneurs, if you have finished with your devotions, the father abbot will receive you in his solar."

While the abbot looked on with a benevolent smile, Laire carefully read the document. Thierry sat opposite him, drumming his fingers on the slab-topped table. In his own good time Laire took up the quill, dipped its shaved tip into the ink pot, and scrawled his signature beneath his brother's. Vezeley was his, in name at least.

Later in the cloister as they parted company, Thierry asked, "Will you hear mass with me at prime?"

His brother's condescending good humor was beginning to rankle Laire. There was too much between them to be forgotten or forgiven so easily, and he remarked testily, "So you might convey to Agnes that all is right between us, and God?"

"Would I be wrong to do so?" Thierry smiled.

Laire grimaced, thinking all his smug brother lacked was a halo. He felt a child again, and somehow annoyed with himself. "Do what ever you like," he grumbled.

"Will you come?" his brother called after him.

"Yes, I will be there."

Thierry wished him good night. Laire did not answer.

At the guest house, Laire found the sergeant and his troop noisily devouring the meal provided by the abbot. Several cressets filled with oil provided a sickly light. The sergeant rose, his mouth filled with bread and cheese. "The brother who brought this food told me that you were praying in the chapel. You should have left more coins in the alm's box.

There wasn't enough black bread and cheese to feed a mouse, and the wine is half cow's drink."

His opinion was seconded by the men surrounding the trestle table. There were no benches. Some leaned on their elbows, others against the wall. The floor all around was marked with muddy boot prints.

Laire paused. He was furious. First his brother and now the fool of a sergeant. He turned toward them, pulling his face into a roguish smile. "Now you have spoilt my meal," he remarked. A ripple of laughter passed round the table. It was not at all what the sergeant had expected. He swallowed the cud of bread and cheese, and watched as the young chevalier accepted a bowl from one of the men and sampled the wine.

Laire was much more skillful at handling soldiers than he was his siblings. By the time he had gulped down half a bowl of wine, grimaced at the taste and joked with them, even the pugnacious sergeant was in a mellower mood.

"Tomorrow," Laire promised, "we are to be the guests of the abbot of Saint Severin. I am told he is generous to a fault. Perhaps we should pray it is so, for our stomach's sake." Laire left them in hearty agreement and made his way up the darkened staircase and down the passage.

Albert's head lolled against the wall. He looked up as Laire entered, lurched to his feet and stood blinking in the candlelight.

Laire spun him round, riffling his hair, and good naturedly teased him for walking about with his eyes closed. He then glanced toward his prisoner, who was now lying on the pallet beneath the window. At some point, his satchel had traded places with her and had found its way to the bed nearest the door. "It was her choice," Albert mumbled, still stupid with sleep. "I did not think you would care," he added with a note of uncertainty.

Nicolette lay with her back to them. She did not turn or give any sign she had heard. The boy had been clay in her hands, so eager to please her, but now her jailer had returned and so had her fears.

"The food is there," Albert indicated the table. "I could find only a single candle," he reported, "a puny thing. In that huge chest, only one candle, nothing else. Are the Dominicans really so poor?"

Laire sampled a chunk of black bread. "So they would like us all to believe. Did you not eat?"

"I thought I should wait for you." In private Albert addressed his master with the familiar toi, as a family member might, rather than the formal vous.

"Did you free her hands?"

"Yes."

"Did you offer her food and drink?"

Albert inclined his head. "She said she was not hungry."

"It has been my experience that women seldom mean what they say, nor say what they mean," Laire confided with a wink and, crossing the chamber, called back, "Fill your stomach, but beware the wine, it is foul."

Nicolette lay curled upon the narrow cot, her face

obscured by the hood, save for the tip of her nose. He stood above her for a moment, then gently touched her shoulder. "Milady, there is food and wine. You should eat something, a bit of bread, a little wine. We have far to ride on an empty stomach."

His voice was deep and smooth, kind as a priest's, kind as her father's had been. She wanted so desperately to trust him, but she dare not. "Leave me be," she spat, her voice no more than a harsh whisper. "I do not want your miserable food."

Laire's second effort met with even less success. He turned away and walked back to where Albert sat on the bench stuffing a chunk of black bread into his wine bowl. The boy sogged the bread several times, then skillfully scooped it into his mouth. "It is passable for dipping bread," he said, quickly setting aside his bowl and pouring one for his master.

When Albert had washed down the last chunk of bread, he asked, "Shall I go search for another candle?"

"No. Did you fetch some water?" As soon as he said the words, Laire recalled the boy would have had no opportunity to do so, not without leaving the prisoner. He was about to acknowledge his oversight, when Albert informed him, "A lay brother came with a pail of water and filled the ewer." Albert stood up, dusting the crumbs from his jupe. "Where should I sleep?" he asked, adding, "I left my blanket below, on the pallet by the stairs."

"That would be best," Laire said, lowering his voice. "I saw but a single staircase, and you would hear someone pass by."

Albert gave a quick nod; he did not trust the sergeant either.

After Albert had gone, Laire asked Nicolette if she would like a moment of privacy before he doused the candle.

She raised her head and slowly sat up. "Yes," she said, her voice small and brittle as she perched stiffly on the edge of the cot, waiting for him to step into the passageway.

Laire heard her pull the pot across the boards. From the floor below he heard muffled sounds, someone moving about, Albert, perhaps, or one of the soldiers. At the opposite end of the passageway, moonlight filtered in through the shutters of a large window. It would be a clear day on the morrow. Presently he heard the pot scrape across the floor again, and when he glanced over his shoulder, she was lying on the cot with her back to him. Once inside he closed the door, heard the latch click. There was no means to lock it. He snuffed the candle with his thumb and forefinger, and lay back on his cot. He did not fall asleep immediately, but lay there plagued by restlessness. Try as he might he was unable to dispel the image of her lithe body, the glimpse of slender leg and that part of her that had sent his blood to racing and left him feeling as clenched as a fist.

Six

Laire did not know what woke him, but he came instantly awake, straining to focus his eyes in the swirling blackness. There was no sound, nothing, aside from the disagreeable sensation of something moving in the darkness. At first he thought it was his prisoner risen from her pallet, out of restlessness or the need to make use of the chamber pot. But glancing across the small room, he could make out a humped form, blacker than the black of the night, lying on the pallet below the window. She was there, seemingly asleep.

What he saw next sent the blood rushing to his head with a sort of giddy horror. For in the smoky shaft of light falling from the window he perceived something taking form in the darkness, a head, shoulders. A knife blade glinted in the ashen light and the shape sprang toward the lady's pallet.

Laire lunged across the chamber in a desperate attempt to intercept the shadowy intruder. He was uncertain then, or later, as to the exact sequence of what followed. For in the space of seconds, he heard a wild scuffling, and a shrill scream. The shadow's upraised arm seemed to hesitate, then flung the girl aside. Her body thudded to the floor. The black thing wheeled about just as Laire collided into it.

There was no doubt the shade was flesh and blood; it stunk of sweat and horses. The momentum of the collision sent both men sprawling across the floor. They grappled, gaining their feet and staggered against the tall carved chest. Laire felt his fist sink into flesh. The shade groaned, throwing itself to one side. In the utter blackness, the face was a blurred form with only darkened hollows for eye sockets, a mouth. With an animal-like fury it slashed out at Laire.

The blade went wide, flashing sparks as it glanced from the chest's ornate iron hinges. Again the knife sliced the air, hack, hack. Laire felt something hard strike his hand. His hand went numb. He struck out savagely with his foot. The impact slammed the intruder against the wall. A loud grunt tore from the featureless lips.

Laire heard something clatter across the floor. The knife? But before he could lay hands on the intruder, the shadowy figure rampaged into him, driving an elbow into his broken ribs.

All before Laire's eyes dissolved in a flash of blinding white light and he collapsed in an agony of pain. When the sharp edge of it had dulled, he dragged himself from the floor. He was still dazed, gasping for breath, and only vaguely aware of the lady Nicolette's screams, the intruder's fleeing footfalls. He staggered to his feet, noticed the door of the chamber ajar, and plunged into the passageway in pursuit.

By the time Laire cleared the door, the girl's screams had brought a dozen men stampeding up the stairs. Albert was with them, Laire heard him call out. He swayed to a standstill. Clearly the intruder had not fled down the stairs.

"A murderer," Laire croaked; he had not yet recovered his wind. His ribs felt broken anew. "He is here among us!" The shrill sound of his voice made him shudder. "Search the chambers!" he commanded. He did not wait for them but dashed down the passageway like a mad man, flinging wide one door after another. The men swarmed after him, crashing into the darkened chambers and shouting back and forth.

"Here!" Laire called. "In here!" He staggered across the room and leaned out the open window, whose shutters had been shoved wide. Directly below was the roof of the stable. At the far end its gently sloping roof abutted the curtain wall. The wall rose above it, but not beyond a man's ability to leap up, catch its top and pull himself over.

Laire felt something wet, slippery, beneath his hand on the embrasure. He realized it was blood. He raised his hand, flexing it, and for the first time felt the stinging ache. His hand was slashed, how badly he could not tell in the dark. Several men crowded in around him, then dashed away to search the courtyards. It was useless, but he let them go.

In the passageway the dancing yellow arc of an

oil lantern dazzled Laire's eyes. The lay brother and the monk who had earlier in the evening escorted Laire to the abbot stood in the hazy light. "I am told there has been murder done tonight," the monk said in a stunned voice. "Surely you do not believe the abbot has sanctioned such lawlessness?"

Murder? Laire brushed past them, striding down the passage, breaking into a run. His ribs ached, shooting him through with pain and his legs felt as if they were pulled by strings. The lady Nicolette dead? She was alive enough when he charged from the room, he had heard her screaming. The sergeant and several men ganged before the chamber door.

"What has happened?" the sergeant demanded.

Laire shoved him aside. The men at the door parted and Laire entered the room. The sergeant followed him inside with a determined face.

"Take my hand, milady," Albert pleaded. Nicolette glared at him in refusal. She had scrabbled away from the combatants in the darkness, and now crouched in a corner with her back to the wall. She would not budge. Someone had lit the candle; it guttered in the draft from the open door.

Laire's gaze returned to the sergeant. It was impossible to read his expression, whether he was relieved or disappointed to find her alive. "Someone tried to kill her?" the sergeant queried.

Laire gave him a hard look. "It appears so."

"Who?"

"Why were no guards posted?" Laire demanded.

"I saw no need of them, this is a holy place."
"Do it now, sergeant."
"It makes no sense to . . ."
"Now," Laire said, a growl of temper in his voice.

The sergeant bristled. It seemed he was going to say something, then changed his mind and stalked toward the door.

Laire watched after him. To Albert, standing at his elbow, he said, "Go and see that he does. Close the door." The boy melted into the shadows, pulling the door to after him.

The room was empty now. They faced one another. "Are you all right?" he asked. She was white and shaken. The hood of the robe had fallen back and her stubbled head shone grotesquely. He held out his hands to help her. She ignored him and defiantly stood up by herself.

As she rose from the darkness into the light of the candle Laire saw her throat was smeared with blood and there was a dark stain on the shoulder of the robe that spread with every pulse beat. "You are hurt," he said.

Her eyes looked enormous, all the larger for the whiteness of her skin, and her lips trembled when she spoke. "Did you think I would not be hurt?" she accused, thinking he was a part of it, mistrusting even her own memory of the incident. In her mind she saw again the blurred, dim shape rushing toward her, the furious confusion and the sickening blow to her shoulder. She swayed a little, hanging dangerously on the brink of consciousness, no longer certain of anything.

Laire took hold of her arm. "Let me help you."

"I do not need your help," she hissed, throwing off his hand with a violent motion. She clasped her aching shoulder and, startled by the warm stickiness, just as quickly withdrew her hand. Only at the sight of so much blood did she feel the full impact of what had happened. Her lips moved soundlessly, her eyes widened and set in a fixed stare.

Laire just had time to catch her by the shoulders. As he guided her to the bench, she came to sufficiently enough to protest. He told her to be quiet and left her on the bench as he rifled through the leather satchel. With his razor he cut a strip from the hem of her robe.

"Open your cowl," As he spoke, he dipped the woolen cloth in the ewer and painfully wrung the water from it. The gash on his hand stung with a fury, dying the water dark with his blood.

"Send a woman to me," she said weakly.

He looked at her as if she were a stupid child. "We are in a monastery."

She raised her chin, stubbornly. "Then I will wait."

"You are witless." He cursed, fumbling with the rough cloth. She would have fought his hands with more determination had her head not been spinning like a top. The room grew smaller, distant. She felt as if she were floating. "No!" she squalled, sensing his intent. She grappled with his hands, squirming against the wall, trying to slide away from him. He grasped a handful of cloth, she wriggled free with a lunge. The robe gave way, baring her breasts. They were small, pink nippled and round as apples. She gasped, clawing at the robe, and raised it to cover herself. While she fumbled to save her modesty, he caught her by the shoulder and soundly sat her straight.

"Damn you, sit still. You are fortunate it wasn't your throat."

Nicolette pressed her lips together and fixed her gaze on the little window. She sat stiff as a marble statue, letting him touch her and despising him with all her heart.

Once the blood was washed away, Laire saw that the wound was neither deep nor long. It was crescent shaped where the blade had veered away, and appeared almost unintentional.

"Your man is clumsy," she said with a cold fury.

"What man? Albert?"

"The man you sent to kill me tonight."

"If I wanted you dead, I would do it myself."

"The king has ordered my death, or perhaps it was Louis?"

"I had no part in it."

"Liar," she rasped, swiveling her head toward him.

"Hold still." He ran his finger over the gash. There was nothing more he could do. There was no way to bandage it, and perhaps the air would heal it quicker. The instant he moved away, Nicolette quickly drew the robe over her shoulders, flinching when the rough material rubbed across the wound.

Laire rinsed the strip of cloth and bound his hand, looping the cloth and tugging on one end with his teeth to secure the knot. He glanced after her as she padded across the floor barefoot. One of her slippers lay beside the cot, the other he did not see.

He thought of the knife and, taking up the candle, went to look for it. He was certain he had heard it hit the floor, but now he could not find it. He picked up the slipper and dropped it beside the cot were she lay.

She had whipped the deep hood over her head and curled up on her side. The sharp sound of the shoe striking the floor caused her to jolt forward with alarm.

"What have you done with the knife?" His voice brimmed with anger. When she did not answer, he jerked the hood from her head. She raised her face and sent him a look of pure loathing. He crouched down beside her, setting the candle on the floor. "What have you done with the knife?" he asked once more, glowering at her.

Her lips tightened in mute refusal. He grabbed her face, gripping her cheeks in a vicelike grip. "Where did you hide it?"

Tears welled up in Nicolette's eyes, but she remained obstinately silent. He squeezed her cheeks, grossly distorting her lips, and threatened to thrash the truth from her. He did not. Instead he dragged her from the cot and, taking her by the scruff of the neck, roughly searched the robe. She twisted and kicked, but she was barefoot and her determined attack on his shins only made him madder.

He shook her, rattling her teeth together. "Where is it?" His breath hit her face like a hot wind. She countered by pounding her fists against him and trying to bring her knee up between his legs. He caught her by the thigh and whirled her about, bending her over and running his bandaged hand hard between her legs. He knew full well she could conceal nothing beneath the robe. The sole purpose of the maneuver was to unnerve her. It was wildly successful.

"In the straw!" she sobbed, defeated. "I hid it in the straw!" She had been prepared for a beating, but not for that. Laire dragged her to the cot. He flipped the mattress aside, one handed, and groped through the straw. His fingers touched something hard and cold. He felt for the knife's hilt and, closing his fingers over it, pulled it free. He was still furious with her and threw her down on the straw. "Evil little slut! Did you intend to leave it in my back?" he growled, retrieving the candle.

Nicolette hid her herself beneath the hood. Miserable and beaten she tugged her mattress onto the cot and crawled on top of it. The inside of her thighs smarted from his assault and she lay there choking back her tears. She heard him walk away, and saw the light retreat after him.

Laire stowed the knife in his leather jaque. After he had set the candle aside he tried the door, deciding it must have been the click of the latch that woke him. He shut the door and pulled the bench before it. The act left him feeling mildly foolish. It was unlikely the intruder would return, but he left the bench in place all the same. He lay down and snuffed the candle. He did not sleep again, too many thoughts crowded his mind.

Perhaps there was some truth in what the lady Nicolette said? Clearly someone had tried to kill her, and who else but the king or his rash, malicious son Louis would have reason to want her dead? But why had the assassin hesitated? Had he seen Laire rise up from his cot? It was possible. Laire lay there staring into the blackness at the ceiling, trying to recall what he had seen. He had been close enough to the assassin to smell his stinking breath and yet he remained featureless. The man's size, his strength, all those Laire could gauge, but he could not put a face to him.

Once while he lay there in the dark, he thought he heard her softly crying. He felt like a beast and regretted handling her so crudely. It seemed he could no longer think clearly where she was concerned. From the moment he had first laid eyes on her, he had been aware of her childlike beauty. There was something almost exotic about the shape of her eyes, the velvet black of her long lashes and the cream and rose of her skin. Little by little, without a word or a smile, she had seduced him. For he could think of no other word to describe his feelings, the tenseness, the irritation, the excitement. And he wondered if she affected other men in the same way.

* * *

He slept little that night. It was still black as pitch when he lit the candle and, with the bloody water in the ewer, attempted to shave. With the razor gripped in his bandaged hand, he awkwardly removed his beard, and from the feel of it several layers of skin as well.

Laire made his way through the frost-scented morning and entered the church. At the altar the liturgical prayers were being recited. Candles glowed in the darkness and the air of the chapel was redolent with the scents of beeswax and incense. A young priest with a wavering voice led the Latin prayer.

Laire and his brother spoke in undertones. "Are you accusing me?" Thierry asked pointedly, when told of the incident.

"Not on this occasion," Laire replied. "You had nothing to gain. Had the abbot other guests?"

"Several churchmen and a merchant, why? Surely you don't think the church is—"

"What sort of merchant?"

"Spices, he talked of nothing else. It was a boring meal. Are you bound for Saint Severin?" Thierry coughed softly, then advised, "The abbot is a good deal more generous, and the food is better."

"Was he alone?" Laire persisted.

From the altar the priest intoned, "Requiem aeternam dona eis, Domine."

"He had servants, I suppose."

Laire's gaze roved over the chapel. Aside from

his brother and him, the worshipers were all monks. "Why is the merchant not at mass?"

"He is gone, I expect. I heard him clattering past my chamber hours ago."

"You saw him leave?" Laire questioned, keeping his voice down.

"I heard him speak of an early departure last night. God's teeth, Laire, the man was old and the size of a Michaelmass hog. He could barely fit through a door arch. Did you not just say to me that this intruder leapt through a window?"

The mass continued. "Et ne nos inducas in tentationem . . ." The smoking incense tickled the inside of Laire's nose and he sneezed.

Thierry turned to his brother, whispering, "Your lady prisoner, was she harmed?"

"Only slightly, I got the worst of it," he indicated, displaying his hand wrapped in the bloody bandage.

"Ite, missa est." The mass ended. Feet shuffled on the cold flagstones, the monks filed past. Laire and his brother followed the brethren from the nave.

Outside the chapel the sky was streaked with light. Thierry walked with his brother into the cool morning. "There is still hope," he said. "Agnes believes you will be pardoned from this wretched duty at Gaillard. Know that I will do all in my power to aid her."

Laire understood perfectly. Either way Thierry had won Lagrume wood. He shrugged, remarking, "Only a miracle could bring that to pass."

"Do not be too certain. If there is an annulment, the lady prisoner would be handed over to a convent and you would be free. Agnes says there is already talk of it."

A group of monks passed by, entering the chapel, and Thierry broke into a discussion of Vezeley. Laire noticed Albert waiting for him beside the chapter house. He was standing beneath a large chestnut tree. He had picked up a fallen nut and was diligently removing the husk. When Laire swiveled his attention back to his brother, he was still rattling on about Vezeley. Laire didn't bother to listen, imagining his brother would do as he pleased in any case.

"I see your squire is waiting for you," Thierry said at last, noticing the boy. "I will bid you farewell."

Laire clasped his brother's hand. "Thierry." Abruptly they embraced. Thierry reached out once more and clasped his arm as they parted company. "God keep you, brother."

"And you," Laire answered.

Albert fell in with Laire as he strode toward the stables. "The sergeant is chewing on his moustache," he advised.

Laire smiled. "Let him wait. Perhaps he has pulled off his nose by now."

Albert grinned. A group of lay brothers carrying scythes and rakes passed to their right. Albert's gaze followed them. When they were beyond hearing, he said, "A spice merchant spent the night in the abbot's house."

"So I've been told."

Albert tossed the nut aside. "I learned from a groom that the merchant brought three servants with him, but when he left, he had only two."

Laire raised an eyebrow. Albert, obviously pleased with himself, continued, "The groom said, when he asked them what happened to the third man, they told him that they caught the fellow stealing and ran him off during the night. I asked the groom if he remembered the man, but he said no. Only that he was young like the other two. What do you think?"

Laire shrugged. He fumbled inside his leather jacket for the knife. The makeshift bandage on his hand made him clumsy. "Whoever it was dropped this in my chamber."

Albert took the knife, turning it over in his hands as he walked. "It is handsome."

"Yes," Laire agreed. "Pay careful attention to the silver work on the hilt."

Albert ran his fingers over the silver tracery.

"I'll wager it was made to match a sword," Laire said, for he had seen similar sets at tournaments.

Albert nodded, returning the weapon. "I will not forget the design."

Before the stable all was in readiness. Horses snorted and stamped restlessly in the smoky ramps of sunlight. A mutter of conversation filled the still air, and men shuffled about. Laire gave the sergeant a curt nod as he made his way among the stomping horses. All around him men began to mount up, except for the heavy-set youth standing guard over the lady prisoner. Laire sent him to join the others. Before he took Nicolette by the waist to lift her into the saddle, he dropped his head close to hers and whispered, "I seem to recall I have been cruel to you. Forgive me."

Atop her mare Nicolette twisted in her saddle, her gaze following him. He glanced back. For an instant their eyes met. As he turned away a hint of a smile touched his lips. Albert rode up leading his stallion. Laire caught hold of the mare's lead rein and passed it to him, then took the bay's reins, found the iron stirrup and mounted, thinking what an overwhelming and singularly strange emotion temptation was.

Miles to the south in King Philip's Palace of the Cite, Isabella's serving women carefully packed away the last of their mistress's twenty-eight state gowns. The return journey to England promised to be challenging, for the channel waters, late in the season, were often rough. Each gown was scented down with pomanders containing aromatic spices to protect it from vermin. A snow white gown of finest sendal silk, trimmed in ermine, embroidered with golden unicorns, and set with sixty rubies, required the energies of five serving women to solicitously wrap it in a cocoon of filmy silken cloth. Madame de Pernelle bustled about, overseeing the immense project. There were innumerable sets of slippers, some gilded, others jeweled to match a gown. There were coifs, underpinnings of

Flanders linen, of silk and lace, fur-lined cloaks and gloves, as well as a king's ransom of jewels. Madame de Pernelle crossed herself devoutly each time she gazed at them, for it was rumored many had been wrested from the treasure rooms of the Templars.

In an adjoining chamber, Isabella sat before the hearth wrapped in a bilaut of silk and sable. As she spoke, she picked over a plate of glazed fruit, rolling them over, inspecting one, then another, finally choosing the plumpest. "I need you here in Paris, close by Gaillard and your Norman holdings," she said to Raoul de Conches.

The scent of the baron's cologne filled the air, the sweet mingling odors of cypress and hyacinth. The cologne was imported from Italy, as were the baron's elegant, tall boots of purple dyed calf. He was disturbed not to be returning to England with Isabella. Yet nothing in his demeanor betrayed his thoughts. "Know that I am pleased by your confidence in me," he said, toying with the silver pomander that was tied by a silken ribbon to the arm of the chair in which he sat. "And also know that my heart sorrows at the thought of our separation." Slowly he rose from the exquisitely carved and cushioned fauteuil and went and stood before the hearth. Little tongues of flame licked over the remains of several blackened logs.

Raoul de Conches was not a fool. He knew full well that a crown did not make Isabella any less a courtesan. In England there was Roger de Mortimore, a powerful English magnate and her husband Edward's sworn enemy. He was consoled by the fact that he, and even de Mortimore, was but one of a dozen lovers, none of whom were stupid enough not to know it. Moreover, his loyalty to Isabella might well give him all of Normandy. And that would pleasure him far more, far longer than any of her charms.

He turned to her and smiled, thinking in ten years hence she would be fat, slovenly. Greedy sow that she was. "I shall mourn the loss of our nights of pleasure," he said in a fond voice.

Isabella met his gaze, her lips pursed about a plump, sugared plum. "I, too, dear Raoul," she murmured, devouring the fruit and licking the sticky sweetness from her fingers. Her tongue flicked across her lips, not unlike a snake. "It is necessary," she began, halting at the appearance of Madame de Pernelle. "What is it?" she asked crossly.

The eternally flustered Madame de Pernelle sighed, "Messire de Nogaret."

In a darting glance, Isabella saw de Nogaret step through the door arch. She dismissed the woman with an impatient twitch of her white hand.

"I have come from council," the inquisitor announced, sidestepping Madame de Pernelle as she hurried from the chamber. "De Marigny and Bishop D'Enbeau have suggested that the Holy Father might agree to annul the marriages of the king's sons. The process may take years," he assured, only to add, a moment later, "However, de Orfevres was there. He and Marshal l'Aiguillon came to petition the king to transfer Nicolette of Burgundy to Dourdon."

Isabella dropped the plum she had just selected. "Dourdon," she repeated, as if she had tasted something bitter.

De Nogaret bobbed his head, nervously. "It is all for his nephew's benefit, of course. As was his theory of how the Flemish or the English might spirit the lady away and hold her for ransom. I may still be able to placate the king, but when he hears of de Orfevre's nephew's death, he will be convinced that the danger is real. I warned you this would happen."

Isabella's pale eyes flashed to her paramour. "You must stop them, then. They must not kill de Fontenne."

De Conches regarded her with a stunned stare. He had been against it from the first. "It is too late," he said. "It is done."

"Do not tell me it is too late," Isabella threatened. "You said Simon Quarle was like your right hand."

"As a liege lord, yes. He is loyal unto death, but I doubt he has the ability to read my thoughts." His sarcasm did not go unnoticed.

Isabella's face grew sharp as a blade. "A messenger on a swift horse might be more effective," she remarked coldly, commanding him. "See to it at once."

The muscles of Raoul de Conches's jaw tightened beneath the blue sheen of beard. He sent Isabella a surly look, lurched to his feet and walked swiftly from the chamber.

To de Nogaret, she said, "Persuade messire my father that placing the lady of Navarre with her accomplices at Dourdon would be unwise."

"Yes, yes," the inquisitor muttered, already considering which arguments he would use.

Seven

Laire de Fontenne's hand was stiff beneath the blood-caked rag that served as a bandage. They rode north from the abbey, passing more fields of vines. Here the grapes were being picked. For the most part the laborers were sun-bronzed peasant women and children. They must have set to their task in the grey light of dawn, for already they were delivering basket after basket of fruit to lay brothers who emptied the produce into ox-drawn carts. One cart was already filled, its cargo rising like a purple mountain above the cart's slabbed sides.

By late morning the sun was warm on their shoulders and the sky blue as lapis. Little clouds like tufts of wool sailed past overhead and in the weed-choked meadows white and yellow butterflies danced above the nodding wildflowers.

At mid-day they halted by a stream. Through the trees they could see a scattering of huts on the opposite bank. A few women and children moved about the hovels. The sound of children's voices and the scent of woodsmoke carried on the breeze.

Once the horses had been led to water, the loaves of bread from the abbey were divided. The abbey's charity ended with the bread, they had offered no wine. Albert and several soldiers took their empty wineskins upstream of the huts and, wading into the sun-sparked shallows, filled the skins with water.

Seated beneath the trees with her jailer, Nicolette condescended to accept a chunk of bread. She forced herself to eat slowly, savoring each morsel, though when she had finished her stomach was still knotted with hunger. Laire carved another slice from the loaf and offered it to her. But she turned her head away, too proud to accept it. As she sat waiting, she ran her fingers through the grass, glad for her momentary freedom, finding pebbles, a pretty yellow leaf, a little grasshopper. Later when Albert returned with the skin filled with water, she did not refuse a drink. Her throat was dry as dust.

Throughout the crystalline afternoon they rode north. In the distance the hills were still clothed in green, but in the trees above them, the rustling leaves were speckled with clear yellows and golden browns. One of the soldiers sighted a fox bounding through a weedy meadow, its bright cinnamon tail floating after it. "Hoy," he shouted, directing everyone's gaze with an outstretched arm. "Look! Look at Reynard run!"

Slowly the countryside rose in little hillocks marked by deep ravines. For a time the soldiers around her exchanged anecdotes about foxes and taller tales of hunting. Presently they fell silent once again.

Flocks of birds passed overhead, wheeling and veering away in a great dark swarm. Nicolette raised her eyes in envy. If only she could fly away, she thought despairingly. A sudden leaf shower caused the mare to toss up her head and snort. But it was not the swirl of fluttering leaves that had jolted the mare from her plodding gait, rather a group of riders halted on the road ahead. Nicolette viewed them with alarm, fearing each moment to be her last. Had Louis sent them?

Laire reined in his horse. The sergeant signaled to his men. Horses moved forward. Nicolette's mare pranced nervously sideways, fighting the lead rein as the soldiers jostled their horses into a defensive position.

Laire rode on a short distance, halted and, shortening his rein, held the sidling bay in check. A distant rider raised his arm, signaling that he wished to parley. Laire nudged the bay forward, breaking into a canter. Ahead, a single rider separated from the others and rode toward him. They met mid-way, drawing up short, their horses bumping shoulders and rumps as they circled.

"Be you bound for Saint Severin?" the helmeted rider shouted.

Laire kept a tight rein on the bay. "Yes, who inquires?"

"I am Jean Gouin, steward to the lord Cacchot. The abbey of St. Severin was today attacked by bandits and many brethren were killed. The abbot regrets he can not welcome you and your entourage. I have given the good abbot my word that I would forewarn you and in lieu of his hospitality offer that of my lord Cacchot. His chateau is but two leagues distant."

As they rode toward the chateau, the steward, Gouin, related what had occurred at the abbey. "No one is safe from these bandits," he said. "They terrorize our roads, prey upon merchants, not even the holy men of mother church are spared. So have many of our farmsteads been put to the sword, the peasants slaughtered and their huts burned. The villagers believe we can no longer protect them. They are losing faith with us."

"Who is responsible?" Laire asked.

"You have only to look north to the king's enemies," the sergeant advised, bringing his horse even with theirs.

"The Flemish, perhaps," Gouin shrugged, "but there is no proof of it. Some believe it is malcontents among our own peasants. Life for them is hard. If the crops are poor, they go hungry, or beg at the chateau gates." Gouin had more to say on the subject. He was himself the son of the chateau's blacksmith, and had been taken as a squire by the old lord. "His son is lord now," Gouin told Laire. "He is a brave man, but he has no sense where horses are concerned."

"He has bad luck with horses," one of the bolder of Gouin's men laughed.

"Bad judgment," Gouin retorted with a chuckle. "Nothing will do for him but a beast of a horse. The last nearly killed him," he confided. In two leagues' time Laire learned a good deal about the corner of Normandy to which he'd been exiled.

Gouin seemed trustworthy enough. Laire did think it curious that he had made no mention of the scandal, nor the royal prisoner. Though, certainly, the abbot would have had more on his mind than gossip. Glancing back at the small robed figure astride the mare, Laire decided he, too, would have thought her merely a novitiate, the younger son of a noble who had been pledged to the church. With her face concealed beneath the floppy hood, and draped in the enormous folds of the robe, she appeared formless, without gender.

The sun was still high when they caught their first glimpse of the chateau, a curtain wall and three pale towers standing amid the wild countryside. Despite the chateau's dauntingly impressive walls, it had a peaceable, prosperous look about it.

At the gatehouse, Gouin, the steward, stood in his stirrups and shouted for entry. He shouted twice more before a young man leaned from a window, and grunted, "Who goes there?"

"It is I, Gouin, you fool! Open the gates!"

The guard looked down with a dazed expression, like one roused from a sound sleep. "I did not see you," the youthful guard called as he ran to give them entry. The stout gates were tall but narrow, barely wide enough to enter two abreast.

Inside the walls the smoky air was perfumed with baking bread and frying. Dogs barked and milled about the horses' legs, and servants and soldiers put aside their work and came toward the riders, calling out in greeting, asking questions.

The chateau, though small, was stoutly fortified, three towers projecting from the circuit of its walls. It was built for strength. Even the living quarters were square and plain, save for the large highly arched window openings on the second floor. On the far side of the court were the barracks and stable. Numerous other wooden outbuildings leaned against the walls of the courtyard. Beneath an open-sided shed, cows were being milked, and pigs rooted in the weeds near the base of the curtain wall.

A gawking and curious knot of women came from the door of the living quarters, raising their hands to block the late day sun and gabbling among themselves. The group parted and a plump young woman dressed in blue came out to greet them.

The sturdy Gouin dismounted. Dogs bumped against his legs as he reached to remove his helmet. His curly dark hair was damp from sweat, plastered to his head in ringlets. He said, "Milady, the abbey of Saint Severin was attacked this day. There was little damage, though sadly lives were lost. It was the abbot's wish I deliver these travelers to your hospitality."

The lady Cacchot was plain but pleasant faced with thick, chestnut brown hair braided and coiled over her ears. She appeared visibly shaken by the steward's news and crossed herself devoutly. "Abbot Gregorie?" she asked, breathless.

"He is unharmed, madame, though mad with outrage."

Her features darkened with anger. "As we all should be." To Laire, she said, "Welcome, good sire. It seems the English and their Flemish allies have sent a plague of criminals to infest our roads. We Normans are a devout, hospitable people."

Laire dismounted and stepped forward. He was bareheaded and the dying sun sparked his light brown hair with gold and red. "I have no doubt you are, madame. For only an angel could have so fair a face." He took her proffered hand in his and bowing slightly, introduced himself.

Atop her mare Nicolette heard his words and saw his handsome smile. She turned her head, tempted to cough sharply into her hand, were they not bound together. How conceited he was, how self-possessed, with his broad shoulders and smooth deep voice. And she wondered if the lady of the chateau would have smiled so fondly at him if she had been subjected to his anger.

"I am Adela, wife to lord Cacchot. You and your entourage are most welcome within our walls." She smiled, somewhat self-consciously. "We are so seldom blessed with guests. We must seem very provincial to one from Paris."

"On the contrary, madame, I find you charming."

Nicolette clenched her teeth. He was outrageous, a flatterer, worse than the king's fat brother, monseigneur Charles. Just then the horse beside her passed wind. How fitting, she thought. If she had not been so miserably angry, she would have laughed. She watched them go into the living quarters, the plump lady, Laire de Fontenne, and Gouin the steward. A voice, close by, cut across her thoughts. It was Albert, de Fontenne's squire, waiting to help her dismount.

As the trio walked toward the hall, the lady Adela explained that her husband would have come to greet them himself were it not for his injuries. "He was laid low three days past in a skirmish with bandits." A sudden gust of breeze molded her skirts to her legs and sent leaves scattering before them. She brushed a wisp of stray hair from her eyes as she related to Laire the many lawless acts that had occurred in recent months. Her voice broke with emotion when she spoke of the abbey of Saint Severin.

The lord Cacchot was propped upon a couch in the hall. He was little older than his wife, twenty, perhaps, a robust tow-headed youth with pink skin and pale blue eyes. He was not tall, for the bare legs protruding from the velvet robe were stocky and short boned.

Like most of the lesser nobility, Cacchot lived a rather isolated life and the coming of travelers to his gate meant a chance to hear news from afar, the trade fair cities and possibly even the king's court in Paris.

After being informed of the incident at Saint Severin's by his steward Gouin, Francois Cacchot warmly greeted his guest. He was as open and friendly as his plump wife and spoke to Laire with the familiarity of an old acquaintance.

"I've no great wounds," he confessed. "My damned horse fell on me. I've not even a broken bone to brag over, but I ache like a rotten tooth from head to toe," he jested, and noting his guest's battered face, ventured, "You look to have met a similar fate yourself, good sire."

"My injuries are more deliberate," Laire assured him with a leading smile. "But first tell me of these bandits, have they a leader?" Two household varlets brought folding stools for the men.

Adele remained standing. No sooner than the lad had set up the stools, she sent him to fetch the seigneur's squire and the novitiate whom she assumed they were escorting. She then bustled away, shooing the gawking serving girls back to their tasks, before returning with the wine. She served it herself, guarding her guest almost jealously, such was her eagerness to be the first to hear the news of the world beyond her gates.

The youthful Cacchot was not at a loss for theories. "To my mind they have no leader, but are freebooters, deserters from the English and Flemish armies, or those turned out for lack of means to pay them."

His steward agreed. "In the past they rode in small bands and struck from ambush, but today at the abbey, a brother told me he counted more than twenty horsemen. Their numbers are growing, as is their boldness."

Cacchot shook his head, as if to indicate matters

could not get much worse. He said, "Our neighbor to the north insists they are rebellious peasants. But how could a peasant arm himself? And who would teach him to fight with a knight's weapons?"

"If they were peasants seeking vengeance against a cruel master," Gouin remarked dryly, "Simon Quarle would have been the first to die."

"At least the most deserving," Adela concurred, taking a sip of wine from her husband's cup and handing it back to him.

"My wife considers our neighbor a churl," Cacchot chuckled. He had a curious little laugh, more of a giggle.

Gouin smiled and finished his wine. He rose, set his empty cup on the oaken sideboard that sat against the wall and, after making his adieus, took leave of the hall.

After the steward had gone, Cacchot and his wife began to ask Laire about Paris and the court of King Philip. He had no trouble keeping them entertained with amusing tales from court, and news of the latest styles and new and innovative goods from Italy and beyond.

He purposely waited until he saw Albert and the lady prisoner cross the far end of the hall, escorted by the serving boy, to speak of the scandal. Since it was inevitable that Cacchot and his wife would hear of it, if not from the loud-mouthed sergeant, then surely from one of his soldiers by way of a kitchen maid, with his third cup of wine in hand, Laire told them the story.

Adultery was common enough in every village,

but when it involved the royal family people became avidly curious. Francois Cacchot and his wife were no exceptions. They listened with rapt attention, as wide-eyed and credulous as children.

When Laire had finished his narrative, Adela sighed, "How tragic for the lady. Oh, I have heard many tales of the wickedness of the Paris court. I do not believe a young girl could long avoid being touched by its immoralities."

"You must forgive my wife," Cacchot said with a gleam in his eye. "She has never traveled farther than Rouen. She gathers her information from tales told by peddlers."

Adela sent her husband a sharp look. She had little else to say, and shortly afterwards recalled a task left undone and excused herself.

A drab little serving girl appeared from the kitchen and refilled their cups. Cacchot sipped at his wine. "I'm glad Gaillard has come under your hand. The lord for these two years past has been Briard Lachaume. He has let the chateau fall to ruin. The bandits ride over his lands as if it was their own, and what little justice survives in the village of Andelys, well, that has been left in the hands of our neighbor Quarle." Cacchot was well-informed and seemed eager to help.

"Between us we shall put a stop to these bandits," he exclaimed, seemingly pleased by the prospect.

Eight

Away from the hall, Albert stood at the door of the guest chamber. He did not know what to say to the very determined lady Cacchot, and so he repeated, "But no one is allowed to speak to the prisoner, madame."

"I have your seigneur's permission," Adela countered most convincingly.

Albert glanced helplessly up and down the passageway. He was torn by indecision. What was he to do? He could hardly leave the lady prisoner unguarded and go search out his master. Neither did he wish to offend the wife of his master's host. Finally he frowned and stepped aside.

Nicolette heard the rise and fall of voices beyond the door. They did not concern her. She lay on a bed, her mind battling the boredom that had settled over her. At the sound of the door she glanced up, startled to see the young mistress of the chateau enter the chamber. She was young, no older than herself. Nicolette wondered why she had come and what thoughts she had as she stood there looking at her. Nicolette sat up abruptly.

"I am Adela," the young woman said, coming

forward and awkwardly holding out her hand. "Is there some way I might comfort you?"

Nicolette looked into her eyes. She seemed kind and caring. More than anything in the world Nicolette needed someone with whom to talk, to share her feelings, her fears. With tears in her eyes and her lower lip quivering, Nicolette clasped her hand in greeting.

Adela squeezed her fingers. "How awful it must be for you," she said, taking a seat beside her on the bed. "The seigneur who is accompanying you told me of your misfortune, how you were wrongly accused and of the indignities you have suffered."

Nicolette did not know what to say. She was disarmed by the sympathetic young woman beside her, and even more so by the reported words of her jailer. Perhaps de Fontenne was less an ogre than she had first thought.

"He told me of your shameful treatment," Adela said. "He told me also that you were stripped of your clothing and left with only this robe to cover yourself."

A painful lump rose in Nicolette's throat. "My hair," she sobbed, "all my long, beautiful hair."

Adela was inordinately proud of her own thick chestnut locks, and could well imagine the poor girl's anguish. Her woman's heart went out to her. She embraced the sobbing girl.

"They can not prevent your hair from growing once again," Adela soothed. "In time it will be long and lovely as before." And as if for proof, she related, "One of my serving girls lost her hair to a fever, but in a year's time it grew incredibly. She was even able to braid it again."

Beneath Adela's fingers the penitent's robe was rough as a cow's tongue. She felt suddenly angry, offended by the cruelty of such an act. "How could they treat you so wickedly?" she murmured. "This winter you would surely die of chill-blain."

Once Nicolette found her voice, she told Adela of her husband's hatred of her, and of his sister Isabella's spiteful lies.

Albert stood outside the door, occasionally listening. After only a short time, two serving girls approached, their arms filled with clothing. They seemed to be waiting for their mistress, and quickly struck up a conversation with Albert.

One was pretty, fair and blue-eyed, a buxom girl whose voice was sweet as music. Albert heard not another word from inside the chamber. He was too busy impressing the serving girls with tales of Paris and its many wonders.

To Nicolette, Adela said, "I know you are accustomed to finer gowns than I have ever seen, but if you would accept it, I will bring you a gown of mine. It fit me well enough before I bore two children. Alas, now it is too snug. It is of Flander's weave, serviceable and warm. I have linen garments to spare, a chemise and petticoats, and there is a wimple and a coif as well. It would please me beyond measure to offer them to you."

Adela's simple act of kindness deeply touched Nicolette, and she thought, with a catch in her throat, of her own wicked pride. At times, she, too, had been thoughtless and cruel. In Philip's court there had been no kindness, they had all been too wealthy, too selfish, caring for no one, for nothing but their own selfish indulgences. "How will I ever repay you?" Nicolette tearfully asked.

"There is no need. In my heart I know, and that is reward enough." Adela smiled, patting her shoulder. "Now," she said, rising and going quickly to the door, "I will call for my serving girls."

Albert could hardly refuse to allow them entry, and watched helplessly as the girls swept past him into the room. What had begun with allowing one woman to enter quickly escalated into a flock of women coming and going, carrying towels and water warmed in the kitchen for bathing.

Albert paced restlessly back and forth before the door. He heard them chattering and giggling, and he wondered what his master would say when he learned of it.

Since Francois Cacchot could do little else, he monopolized his guest, discussing everything from the disgruntled merchants of Andelys and their opposition to the king's unreasonable maltote tax, to the rumors of the English allying themselves with traitorous northern barons and the Flemish.

While they drank wine and discussed the matters of the world, the aroma of food grew stronger, and across the hall, the servants placed pewter plates and goblets on the lengthy oaken table. They had just completed the task when a surly-faced serving woman appeared with an armload of cloth for covering the table. Such niceties were only brought out for guests.

The other servants had not been informed. Grumblings rose above the clatter of plates, and when the woman turned away, a little serving girl, with tufts of reddish-brown hair escaping from her braids, stuck out her tongue at the woman's back.

The sour-faced woman, with some inkling of her foolishness, spun round and nearly collided with what appeared to be a walking platter of bread, for only a pair of skinny legs in baggy hosen were visible below the mountain of loaves. The small lad staggered about in her wake, then continued on without dropping a loaf. And from the direction of the kitchens a woman's carping voice heralded noisy debate over the seasoning of a sauce.

Laire was enjoying himself. The wine which was stout and blood-red was quite good. Cacchot was an interesting conversationalist, and the atmosphere, the scent of food, the comfortable domesticity, was all together pleasant.

Cacchot, Laire learned, was a man devoted to apples. He talked for some time about his orchards, and the grafting techniques he had learned from a monk at the abbey of St. Severin. "Later," Cacchot promised, "you must sample my apple wine. It is extraordinary. My cleric, Georges, shares my devotion to the apple. You will meet him at supper. He and I have developed a brewing process. Ah, but words do not do it justice."

As Cacchot had foretold, the cleric's appearance coincided perfectly with the preparations to serve the food. He was a slight man, small in stature, with a long bony nose and an ingenious smile. After being introduced, the cleric took his place among the young lord's other retainers. Adela arrived in time to supervise her husband's journey to the table, as he hobbled between two sturdy serving boys.

The meal began with pastries filled with forcemeat of chicken and scallions, followed by a brewet of meats, simmered and drenched with the thin cinnamon sauce of the debate. Larger cuts of roasted pork were brought to the table on wooden planks, and bowls filled with melanges of dried peas, beans, and cabbage. Later there were fritters dipped in honey and apples stewed in almond milk, all washed down with quantities of spiced wine and cider.

Adela sat between her husband and their guest, the cleric, Georges, nearby. The youthful Cacchot was clearly proud of his estate, and the good food he served up to guests. He mentioned that normally there was a lad who played the lute at meal time. "I'm told it is good for the humors," Cacchot added, remarking, "Damn boy mashed his fingers in the apple press, now he can't even keep himself amused."

Laughter sounded round the table, several ladies snickering behind their hands. The cleric grimaced, whether from disapproval or the discovering of a bone in his pastry, it was difficult to tell.

As the meal continued, Adela leaned close to Laire

and said, "I have sent food, a sample of what we have here, to your lady prisoner and your squire."

Laire thanked her most genuinely and complimented her hospitality.

She smiled in gracious acceptance, confessing, "I have given your lady prisoner a gown." Before he could muster a word, she hurriedly said, "I know I have not asked your permission, but I am telling you now, so that you will not be surprised."

Laire laughed softly. Quantities of wine invariably had that effect on him. "You are the surprise," he murmured. "I envy your husband more each moment."

"Will you allow her to wear the gown?"

"Did you believe, even for a moment, that I would refuse?"

A servant came between them with a tray of fritters. The rosy-cheeked Adela selected one. "I do not think you would refuse a lady anything," she replied with a merry smile.

The meal ended, but the food had not yet been taken away. Only Cacchot, Adela, Laire, and the cleric, Georges, lingered at the lengthy oaken table. A nursemaid had brought the couple's two small children from the kitchens. The little girl climbed upon Adela's lap and rubbed her round face fondly against her mother. The little boy, who was as towheaded as his sister, climbed upon the bench and contented himself by fishing for stewed apples in the bowl of almond milk.

While the nursemaid stood by wearing an indulgent smile, Cacchot and the cleric entertained Laire with tales of their wine-making prowess. In due time an elderly manservant appeared with an ewer of the fabled apple wine and set it before them.

The cleric was remarking on the brew's magical bouquet when a stable boy raced into the hall and up to Cacchot. "Sire," the boy exclaimed breathlessly, "the seigneur Simon Quarle is at the gates."

Adela turned to her husband and made a face. As she did, their tow-headed son slapped his hands into the bowl, showering everyone with almond milk. Cacchot laughed, Adela did not. She seized her son by the ear, and pulled him away from the stewed apples. He howled with anger.

Cacchot was still laughing as he brushed the milk from his jupe and nodded to the servant waiting obediently at his elbow to pour the wine. "How many riders accompany him?" he asked the stable boy.

"Two, sire," the scrawny boy replied.

"Tell Martin to admit them. Direct them here." The boy gave a bob of his head and sprinted away. Cacchot turned to Laire. "I do not particularly trust Quarle," he said, raising his voice to be heard above the squalling child. "But as I told you, he has been my only ally against these bandits. I am curious to know what you think of him. You and he shall be cheek and jowl, so to speak. His lands border Gaillard and the village of Andelys."

From what Cacchot had imparted to him earlier in the afternoon, Laire expected a drunken brawler. He was not disappointed. Simon Quarle swaggered into the hall with his sword jangling at his hip and two villeins trailing at his heels like dogs.

Cacchot greeted Quarle heartily, waved him to be seated, and afterwards introduced Laire as the newly appointed seigneur of Gaillard. The prisoner was mentioned, and the scandal, though not Laire's involvement in it.

Quarle was of that indeterminable age somewhere between twenty-five and thirty, a deep-chested man, and a formidable sight in mail and leathers. The scandal seemed to amuse him; he opened his broad mouth and laughed. Laire noticed several teeth were missing from his lower jaw and a long scar seamed the right side of his face. He looked, Laire thought, like Attila the Hun, or at least how Laire imagined him to look.

His laugh was loud, as ugly as his snagged teeth. "So Gaillard has been handed to you? I hope your prisoner is comely," he said with a lecherous wink. "You'll find little else to comfort you there." He looked to Cacchot. "Have you warned him about his murderous peasants?"

"There is no proof of that. Are you hungry? Eat your fill. You have arrived just in time to sample my apple wine."

"Wine is made from grapes!" Quarle scoffed, reaching out a calloused hand and ripping off a hank of pork ribs. "These bandits, as you call them, murder and steal. Isn't that proof enough they are peasants . . . de Fontenne, did you say?"

"Yes," Laire responded, watching as Quarle and his two villeins helped themselves to pastries, pork and all else within their reach. Grease trickled into the beards of the two scruffy villeins and down Quarle's stubbled chin.

"Ah," Quarle grunted, reaching for another slab of roasted pork and ripping the flesh from the bones. "We shall see if you are any less cowardly than old Lachaume."

Cacchot flushed. "You are too hard on our neighbor." And turning to Laire, he said, "Lachaume was not entirely to blame. He was ambushed, not a month after he took command. Half his troops were killed. Afterwards he scarcely poked his nose from the chateau's gates. The brigands had a free hand until Quarle and I joined forces."

"Pafh! Brigands! Why do you insist on calling them brigands? They are stinking peasants."

It was obvious from Adela's stony expression that she did not care for Quarle. She rose from the bench, passed the little girl to the nursemaid's arms and led her pouting son away toward the kitchens. The nursemaid followed, bouncing the little girl in her arms and making cooing sounds.

If Quarle noticed her frown of disapproval, he gave no hint. He plucked a meat pastry from a platter, sogged it in the remains of the sauce and stuffed it into his mouth. He quickly emptied the goblet of apple wine, and proceeded to raise a damning indictment of the local peasantry. "They will murder us all in our beds, if we do not put an end to them now!" he predicted, between choking down food and drinking.

He had a curious habit of hanging his nose over

the cup and sucking the wine through the gap in his teeth. It was a crude habit, disgusting and noisy, but very effective. He emptied his third goblet of wine in a wink.

Cacchot's manservant, who hovered round the table like a ghost, promptly refilled the goblet.

"Drink up," Cacchot encouraged, downing his wine as well.

Laire noticed that Georges, the cleric, needed no prompting. He drank as if there were no bottom to his goblet, and he was competing for his share against Quarle and his villeins.

Laire was forced to admit that the apple "wine" had a certain fiery spirit to it. And after the second goblet, he felt compelled to compliment its extraordinary properties.

Cacchot beamed with pride.

Quarle hammered on against the peasants, and with a greasy smirk warned Laire, "You will soon tire of your insolent peasants, and of Gaillard. The wind howls through its donjon and the curtain walls are crumbling."

"It is true," Cacchot agreed, wagging his head. "I have seen it. Lachaume had no luck at keeping workmen. Many were killed on the roads, the others were too fearful to venture from the security of the village. The chateau is falling to ruin."

The cleric, pausing to have his goblet refilled, remarked, "The chapel is knee-deep in rubble. Messire Lachaume would not trouble himself to clear it away. There is the reason for all his misfortune. I said to him more than once, 'This is an affront to our savior.' But he did not listen. Do you know what he told me? 'I give alms to the beggars.' Of course such acts are commendable. But glory to God! A chapel is more important, only there can souls be nourished.

"But, alas, I see in it God's infinite wisdom. For if not for the few obols tossed to the unfortunates of the world, how else would many a noble escape the flames of hell?"

Quarle gulped down a final fritter soaked in honey and chased it with a slug of apple wine. "Beggars, cripples, and peasants, they are all a scourge."

The cleric was something of a wit, though to look at him you would not have guessed it. And the more wine he downed, the more talkative he became. "Ah yes, the peasants," he began. "It is difficult to believe that God made them in his own image, for they are a filthy lot. Nothing but rain has ever touched their bodies. They are forever discontented and so doltish they must be prodded and beat. But in observing them and listening to their tales, I have discovered a wealth of humor.

"In Andelys the barber likes to tell the tale of a peasant driving some pigs past a perfumer's shop. The peasant did not progress ten paces when he was overcome by the unaccustomed smell and fainted. The perfumer rushed from his shop, thinking the man dead. But one of the peasant's fellows brought him round by waving a shovel full of pig dung under his nose."

Quarle gave a snort of laughter, then said, "I see

them differently, good cleric. More often they are clever, insolent thieves who would gleefully slit their seigneur's throat as quickly as a stolen pig's, had they the opportunity. Oh, they are doltish and dirty enough that even Satan wants no more in hell because they smell so vilely, but do not misread them, or they will bury you."

Cacchot swigged at his wine. "If there is murder in their hearts, then it has been put there by the English and the Flemish. They do not deceive me with their sheep's eyes and their talk of peace. All of Normandy is what they want, no matter how many treaties they sign."

Laire listened, sipping his wine. The brew had a pleasant enough taste, but it was as strong as the wrong end of an ox. The heat of the room seemed to have increased tenfold and his eyelids began to smart.

Across the table, he noticed Quarle's eyes appeared somehow comically smaller. Laire took another drink, looking first to Cacchot, whose eyes were bright as embers, then to Quarle, who opened his mouth to speak. Laire saw only the gaps in his teeth.

"I must admit," Cacchot quickly conceded, "the bandit hanged by the provost in Andelys was the son of my plowman. He swore his innocence. I am still haunted by his words."

"Then you do not know the filthy swine well enough, Cacchot. For them it is 'les gros, les grands,' the little people against the big. It will never be any different."

The cleric, unmistakably drunk, gave a hoot of laughter, and agreed, in principle. Lifting a single finger, he said, "In that there is some truth. Even in the bible, servants rise up and kill their masters. You have only to recall King Belshazzar and the writing on the wall. It is a theme old as time, as old as good and evil. And it is in the stories that the peasants tell by their cook fires. For often in their tales, the seigneur is cast in the role of the devil."

Laire felt distinctly lightheaded, and mildly amused by the fact that everyone else at the table looked drunk. The cleric, who had hardly paused to take a deep breath, was telling the tale of a peasant who had more children than holes in a sieve. Laire found it more and more difficult to concentrate. From the corner of his eye, he glimpsed the manservant moving beside the table, and had the uneasy feeling that his goblet had just been refilled.

"And so," the cleric said, "he sold his son to the devil for a year's time in return for a gold piece. But being a peasant, the man had never had so much wealth, and he squandered it. Soon he and his family were starving again. When the year was up, the son returned to his father. By then the son had learned a few tricks of his own. The father and son put their heads together and devised a plot to cheat the devil. The next day the son turned himself into a hunting dog and the father sold him to the devil. Once the father had the gold, the dog ran away home and changed back into the boy.

"The trick worked so well, the father and son

decided to try it again. But the devil was ready for them this time, and when the peasant sold a handsome horse to the devil, the devil knew it was the man's son and put a magic halter on the beast so it could not escape.

"However, the devil made the mistake of leading the horse to water, and at the stream the horse turned into a frog and swam away. So the devil, not to be outdone, turned himself into a fish and was about to swallow the frog. But ah," the cleric exclaimed, lurching forward and wagging a finger at them, "the frog turned into a bird and flew away.

"The devil, who was left to stomp his feet and swear oaths, transformed himself into a hawk and pursued the bird. Just as he prepared to pounce, it winged into the bedchamber of a dying man and became a ewer of wine. The devil, seeing this, wasted no time in changing himself into a doctor and demanded the wine for his services. But before he could lay hands on the ewer of wine, it spilled onto the floor and became grains of barley. "Eureka!" the devil shouted, "I have won!" And he quickly took the form of a greedy hen and began to gobble up the barley."

Suddenly, the cleric leapt up from his seat and made a flamboyant gesture, shouting at the top of his lungs. "But, ah ha! The wily peasant boy changed into a fox and devoured the hen, spitting out only the tail feathers. And that," Georges said with a chuckle, "is how the peasant told it to me. So you see, messires, the servant eats his master."

Quarle slapped his legs and laughed so hard the

scar on his face turned white. "There!" he guffawed, "that is what your peasants think of you, Cacchot." Quarle's villeins laughed as well.

Laire chuckled and took a drink of wine. His host, Cacchot, smiled good naturedly. "What has a peasant, but his tales? Authority, power, it would be no different than the gold. A peasant would not know how to use it."

Quarle grinned in silence and quaffed at his wine. No sooner than he emptied it, the servant quickly refilled his goblet.

"Tell us another story, Georges, a love story," Cacchot said to his cleric. "One that will give us something to take to our beds."

The drunken cleric gave a mirthful laugh and, wetting his lips with wine, regaled them with the tale of Flamenca, a promiscuous wife who finds the perfect way to deceive her jealous husband.

Apparently the cleric knew a hundred such ribald tales, and he went on indefatigably, sucking on wine and spinning stories like a spider spins a web. All continued to drink, for the nimble servant was omnipresent, leaving no goblet unfilled.

Mercifully, before any of the guests had the opportunity to slide beneath the table, the youthful Cacchot complained of a numbness in his legs, bid his guests good night, and was carried off to bed by his servants, while a little varlet, holding a torch almost as large as himself, led the guests to their quarters. It was unlikely they would have found them on their own.

Nine

Earlier that evening, Nicolette gratefully ate the meal the servant women brought. She was almost glad for Albert's company. At court she would have been insulted had someone seated a lowly squire at her side. When she thought of it, she was amazed that only a week had passed. It seemed another lifetime. As for Albert, he was polite, very bashful and for the most part silent. He treated her respectfully, which was more than she could say for the leering sergeant and his troop.

After they had eaten their fill and the platters were removed, Albert escorted her to the garderobe. On their return he remained outside the chamber. However, Nicolette did not believe for a moment that he had strayed far from the door.

Hours passed. Nicolette lay awake, listening to the sounds of the house, to the night noises that filtered down the passageway and drifted in through the shuttered window which opened onto the courtyard. Six beds lined the chamber. In appearance it was little different from the monk's dormitory. She chose the center bed. Illogical as it was, it seemed safer to her, being an equidistance from the window and the door.

The beds were all identical, save for the soft natural colors of the coarse homespun blankets, little more than boxlike shells filled with straw and topped with thick feather mattresses. The warm pastel colors of the blankets brought back memories of her childhood, of a time when she had been happy and full of dreams.

More than once she lurched up, startled by the muffled shuffling of feet beyond the door. It was no doubt Albert, but knowing this did little to calm her nerves.

She must have drifted off to sleep, for a loud, clear-cut thud woke her. The door jarred open. A long yellow triangle fell across her bed and she glimpsed the moving tail of torchlight from the corridor. In the instant before the darkness came flooding back, she saw two black forms, only heads, the line of the shoulders. Nicolette bolted up, her eyes wide with terror. "Who is there?" she gasped.

"De Fontenne," a voice replied too cheerfully. "Chevalier to our most gracious and beloved Philip, by the grace of God king of France." His tongue slurred over the words, and as he repeated them, he added little absurdities here and there, phrasing it backwards and forwards, and laughing a droll little laugh as he stumbled unsteadily across the darkened room. He was drunk, and Nicolette was alone with him. She did not see the squire, though a moment later she heard someone moving about on the bed nearest the door. Even so she was at de Fontenne's mercy. A squire would not raise a hand against his master.

She heard him fumbling nearby in the blackness. She did not realize how close until he sat down heavily on the bed beside hers. Not an arm's length separated the beds and the sound of his laughter tickled her ear. He smelled as if he had been steeped in wine.

He was so drunk he could hardly pull off his boots and as he struggled out of them he fell into an aimless, rambling reminiscence, concerning feet, footwear, and the occasion when he had first come to court as his uncle's squire.

"I was eight years old," he began, pausing to allow his head to stop spinning. "Fresh from the country and scarcely knee high to a horse," he added, grunting as he succeeded in removing one boot. "Like all squires, it was my duty to serve my uncle at the banquet table. That night there was a great feast, thirty courses or more, interminably long," he assured her as he tugged at the second boot.

"All this time we were forced to stand attendance. For hours there was nothing to do. I cannot tell you how bored I was . . . almost to insensibility. It was then I happened to notice a Spanish knight. From where I stood below the dais I could see beneath the table and I watched as he removed one boot with the other, so that his foot was bare, and he wriggled his toes."

Nicolette heard his loudly exhaled breath as the

boot broke free with a sucking noise and he dropped it to the floor.

"He had remarkably long toes, even for a Spaniard," he continued as he fell back onto the mattress. "I was intrigued, even more so when I noticed the lady directly opposite him raise her skirts and spread her legs most commonly. I can tell you that gave me something to look at, particularly when the Spanish knight slid his foot between her legs and proceeded to satisfy her right there before God, the king of France, and three hundred assembled nobles. All the while, above the table, the Spanish knight and the lady smiled and talked as if they were politeness itself. I could not believe my eyes. I must have turned a shade or two of scarlet, for just at the moment of ecstasy, my uncle called me to him to ask if I was ill."

Nicolette could not decide whether to laugh or be frightened. She had never seen anyone quite so abysmally drunk. Drink had always made Louis's vicious tongue even crueler. Invariably Nicolette had been the object of his scorn. More than once he had struck her.

But the man chuckling in the darkness gave no hint of aggression. Suddenly he stood up between the beds and she heard him fumbling in the darkness. He had forgotten to remove his belt and sword. In his pickled state the intricacies of such a maneuver were quite beyond him, and presently he began to laugh. "The end of my belt seems to have eluded me," he chuckled, rocking on his heels, his voice slurred with wine and amusement.

Nicolette watched as he swayed first one way, then the other. "Might I help you?" she offered, fearing he would topple onto her bed if she did not do something quickly.

He made a gallant bow and, pulling his face into a comic grimace, intoned, "You are too kind, madame."

She quickly climbed from bed, avoiding him as much as possible, and in the darkness began to fumble with the heavy buckle. But she had no success. "You must stand still," she whispered in a scolding tone.

He pulled himself up to his full height, promising, "Very still, yes." His soft laughter was at once infectious and disconcerting. Each time she caught hold of the elusive buckle, he tottered to and fro. All at once he lost his balance and, laughing, threw his arms round her and pulled her to him to steady himself.

A flush of warmth spread through her limbs, an odd trembly feeling. She was not frightened, nor even offended by his embrace. It was as if the gentle pressure of his hands and the feel of his strong, young body answered some inward desire, some secret hope that she held in her heart without really knowing it. As they balanced together, she could feel him looking at her intently in the blackness. She could make out little of his face, no more than the sensuous curve of his lips, and she became suddenly embarrassed.

Perhaps he sensed her bewilderment, for he managed to hold himself erect long enough for her to finally loose the heavy buckle. He thanked her in the most eloquent language and, with the sword in his hand, collapsed onto the bed. A moment later she heard a clunk of the belt buckle as he laid the weapon on the floor beside him.

From her bed, Nicolette listened, thinking he would go to sleep. But he simply went on talking in a charmingly foolish way about everything that came into his mind. Even after he had wrapped himself in the blanket, he continued to talk in a muffled voice about the most remarkable things. He told how while he was stationed in Pontoise, a merchant's wife took revenge on a lecherous curé who had pursued her relentlessly.

"One day," he related, "in desperation, the poor woman agreed to give in to his desires. Then after setting a time and place, the wife paid a local prostitute to await the curé in a darkened room." He paused, then remarked sleepily, "She had, of course, invited the town's most prominent citizens to be present, and the randy curé's shame was complete."

He had no sooner finished that tale when, laughing softly, he told how a clever friar from Naples had sold the king's brother, Monseigneur Charles, a feather from the Angel Gabriel's wings, somehow convincing him that the angel had lost it in the Virgin's chamber during the Annunciation. He went on and on, and much later, in the midst of a word he dropped off to sleep.

Nicolette was wide awake. How could she sleep with all his talking? She lay there for what seemed hours, brooding over her situation. She no longer feared Laire de Fontenne. Neither could she believe that he was in league with her husband. She felt, perhaps instinctively, that he would not harm her. He seemed incapable of cruelty. He would, however, lock her away. He would have no choice. And even if he treated her with a measure of kindness, she would nonetheless be imprisoned forever. The thought was too horrible to bear, incomprehensible really, to be denied every moment of her life.

No, she thought. She must make her way back to Burgundy. For even though her family would not, or could not, aid her, her father's loyal steward, Valdot, would surely give her refuge. Her mind was made up, she must escape and it must be done now.

She moved slowly, cringing at each crunching sound made by her shifting weight upon the straw. At last she sat up. In the silence of the room, she could hear quite distinctly their every breath. They were both of them asleep. With more stealth than she imagined she possessed, she crept from the bed and to the window.

The wooden shutter balked at her first attempt to pry it open. Determined, she tugged once more. Moonlight flooded into the room. She held her breath, expecting him to awaken and come after her. Her heart pounded in her breast like a tambour drum, so loudly that she thought he would surely hear. But when she hazarded a backward glance, he had not moved.

Beyond the long low window the court was bathed in moonlight. She had only to climb over the embrasure and put her feet down on the hard-packed earth. Lifting her skirts, she slid silently into the chill night air. A light transparent mist, silvered and gleaming, hung suspended above the ground, outlining every object in shadows. Nothing stirred in the shimmering silence as she stole toward the stables. Earlier, on their arrival, she had noticed a postern gate not twenty paces from the stable. She needed only a horse to complete her plans.

Moments later, Albert Drouhet awakened to a call of nature. He grappled from his blanket and looked stupidly about. The fullness of his bladder demanded that he leave his bed. Since he had no clue as to where he might find the chamber pot, he stumbled to his feet and made use of the window. That he found the shutter standing open had no immediate significance.

Only when he turned back and saw the lady prisoner's empty bed did he jolt to awareness. "She is gone!" he croaked, lunging away across the room to shake his master's shoulder. "Sire! Sire, she is gone!"

Laire jolted up into an agony of pain. He could not remember when he had awakened with such a headache. He reeled unsteadily to his feet and staggered across the room, half in a daze. Only her imprint remained in the mattress, and if that was not sobering enough, the cold air from the open window cleared his senses like a dousing.

Albert appeared, wild-eyed in the moonlight. "Shall I call out the sergeant and his troop?" he blurted in a rapid whisper.

"No!" Laire said, too loudly. "No," he whispered, shuffling back to his bed where he sat down heavily. His skull threatened to burst and his mouth tasted as if it had been stuffed with wool. He felt around in the darkness for his boots and rammed his feet into them. It occurred to him that the charming Adela might have somehow arranged the lady prisoner's escape. "What a deceitful little puss," he muttered as he lurched toward the window.

Albert, still fumbling with his boots, dashed to the door. "Where are you going?" Laire called. He did not wait for the boy, but threw a leg over the window embrasure and stepped out into the courtyard, as if he were walking on eggs. Only then did it occur to Albert, in his distracted, half-wakeful state, that it was the quickest way, and he darted back across the room and clambered from the window after him. Searching as they went, casting their gaze about the gauzy moonlit court, they walked swiftly toward the stable.

Meanwhile at the rear of the stable, Nicolette pushed against the heavy door, barely shifting it, as she glided in like a waft of breeze. Inside the humid air was heavy with the mingled scents of hay, horses, and manure. Nicolette's eyes, now somewhat accustomed to the dark, settled upon the stall nearest the door and the horse inside.

She waited, motionless in the dark silence, which

was broken only by the sounds of horses pulling hay from mangers and slowly chewing it. Plucking up her courage, she tiptoed toward the stall. The horse shifted, its ears twitched, and it turned its head to give her an inquisitive snort.

In the courtyard, Laire and Albert strode past the barracks. They heard voices, most notably the sergeant's, and they quickened their steps. In only a short time the sergeant and his troop would also be en route to the stable, witnesses to Laire's incompetence.

He shuddered to think what would happen were the prisoner to escape. His uncle had risked everything to spare him from the gibbet; now he, too, would feel the king's displeasure.

Laire found the rear door of the stable slightly ajar. A space too narrow for a man or horse, but sufficient for the lithe form of the lady prisoner. Speaking in hushed tones, Laire sent Albert round to the front of the stable. He paused, giving the boy time to reach the doors, then entered. As he did, he saw Albert slide noiselessly past the front doors.

In the stall, Nicolette's fingers blundered over the bridle's buckle. Unexpectedly, the horse moved backwards a step, shook, and tossed up its head. "Shush," she pleaded, reaching up to fumble frantically with the obstinate buckle. The horse's eyes were much sharper than Nicolette's. She did not see the shadow about to eclipse her.

The scent of wine tingled the inside of Nicolette's nose. Not wine rich and full, as it is poured from a ewer, but the pungent, fermenty odor she had smelled in the room. Her heart heaved into her throat. But before she could whirl about, a large hand clamped over her mouth and she was dragged from the stall. The startled horse lunged forward with a squeal, banging its sides against the boards. And Nicolette, kicking and thrashing, was plummeted backwards into the hayrick opposite the stall. With alarming swiftness, she found herself flat on her back, and Laire de Fontenne straddle-legged atop her.

At that same moment, Simon Quarle stomped unsteadily toward the stables, flanked by his two villeins. One carried a lantern. Quarle halted before the horse trough, dipped his helmet in the icy water and took a long noisy drink. His innards felt afire and his throat was dry as a desert. He belched, leaned over, and poured the remainder of the water over his thumping head, then shook like a dog.

"Why are you standing here?" he growled at the two men hanging dumbly by the trough. "Saddle the horses!"

Quarle's two drinking companions turned carefully, as if they feared any sudden movement might separate their heads from their bodies, and pushed inside the stable.

Albert, poised by the door, was about to spring to his master's aid when he heard voices outside and ducked back to hide in the shadows. Suddenly the door opened and the two villeins entered, a lantern swinging from one's hand. Albert molded himself to the rough hewn wall.

Laire, too, heard their voices and redoubled his attempts to subdue the girl, who kicked, twisted like a dervish, and pounded her fists against his arms.

Nicolette felt as if she was being crushed, driven deeper and deeper into the dusty hay. In desperation, she bit down savagely on his thumb. Spots danced before Laire's eyes. He dare not cry out. Neither did he pull his hand away, instead, he leaned forward, putting his full weight on her and hoarsely whispered in her ear, "Stop biting me! I have not a penny's worth of malice in me, but I swear I will throttle you, if you do not!"

Albert watched open mouthed as the two men halted just beyond the door to get their bearings, then ambled like sleepwalkers toward the rear of the stable. He was too stunned by what he had seen to make his escape. In the pool of yellow light from the lantern, Albert saw clearly the ornate silverwork on the hilt of the man's sword. It was identical to that on the knife left behind by the assassin at the abbey. He craned his neck, trying to get a look at the man's face. All at once the door jarred open and Simon Quarle blundered inside, swearing in a foul voice and following the footsteps of his two villeins.

Deep in the hayrick Nicolette sputtered, releasing Laire's thumb from between her teeth. She wrenched her face away, and hissed, "You stink like wine!" His response was to clamp his hand over her mouth once more, and threaten, "You will think even worse of me if you do not be still!"

Footsteps approached. Laire shoved a knee between her soft white thighs and spread her legs. Nicolette went mad, bucking against him and screeching into the moist warmth of his hand.

Simon Quarle mistook the muffled yipping sounds for cries of pleasure. His head swiveled toward the sound, his eyelids lifted, and with a loud guffaw, he exclaimed, "What's this?"

Laughter thundered above Laire's head. "Aha! ha! ha!" Quarle bent double, convulsed with amusement. The sight of the noble dandy frolicking in the hay atop a serving girl delighted Quarle. Particularly when Laire, wearing a rakish smile, turned and saluted him.

Crushed in the hay, Nicolette ceased her struggling. She could not see the rough voice's owner, but she understood at once the danger of their predicament. For despite her fury, she much preferred to keep Laire de Fontenne as her jailer. The thought that he might be replaced by the brutish sergeant, or someone of his ilk, numbed her with fear.

"My apologies," Quarle said, choking with laughter as he turned away. "You are more a countryman than I thought. A man like myself. Ha! aha! ha! ha! Quite a man after all!" he roared, his laughter trailing after him.

Laire watched his retreating back. When Quarle had put a sufficient distance, and the concealing uprights of the stalls, between them, Laire jerked

Nicolette to her feet and pushed her through the door into the darkness. He hustled her toward the outer door of the guest chambers, avoiding the court, where the sergeant and his troop had just entered.

Albert waited. When Simon Quarle and his two villeins turned to busy themselves with their saddle girths, he bolted out the door. He had no sooner breathed a sigh of relief when he ran head-long into the sergeant and his straggling troop of men. Albert ducked his head and dodged away across the darkened courtyard.

Inside the stable, Quarle and his villeins were still laughing when the sergeant and his troop arrived. From a word overheard, the story spread. It was, Quarle thought, too rich a sauce not to be shared and before long the entire stable rocked with laughter.

"I saw the sword," Albert said to Laire in an undertone. "I would swear to it, sire." But when Laire strode back to the stables, he found Quarle and his villeins had ridden out.

Aside from recognizing the hilt of the sword, Albert had noticed little about the man. In the darkness and terror of the moment, he had not seen his face, at least he could not remember it.

Laire's memory was no clearer. For if what Albert said was true, he had sat across the table from the man all evening, drinking, without realizing it. What's more, he could not honestly recall the face of either of Quarle's villeins, other than to say both were young men. The apple wine had fuddled all but his most basic memories of the night. And though he seemed to recall that one had a large nose, he could not say which one.

Later as they prepared to leave, Albert escorted Nicolette, sullen and shrouded in her penitent's robe, to her mare. Nicolette had hoped to see her benefactress, Adela, and thank her once more for her kindness. But, alas, it was not to be.

Good manners required that Laire bid his host farewell. He found him lying on his couch in the hall, red-eyed but remarkably cheerful.

"What a time we had," Cacchot said, a twinkle in his blood-shot eyes. Laire could not but agree, thinking that if enjoyment could be measured in pain, he had never known a night to equal it.

"My friend," Cacchot began, "if you have need of me do not hesitate to send a messenger. Between us, we can put an end to this lawlessness. Know that I will be a ready ally."

Laire clasped his proffered hand. "I am indebted to you, monseigneur, and for your gracious hospitality as well. I would consider it an honor to welcome you at Gaillard."

Adela, standing behind her husband's couch, smiled and wished Laire, "Safe journey," and in her sweet voice, added, "My heart is much at ease, knowing that you will be the lady's jailer. You seem a good and honorable man."

Laire accepted her compliment graciously. And, after exchanging further pleasantries, expertly touched his lips to her plump fingers. Cacchot, who was becoming more jealous by the moment, cautioned Laire to send riders ahead of him to scour the roadsides. "In every incident, these brigands have struck from ambush. I would send Gouin with you, but I have need of him and his men here."

Laire assured Cacchot he would be cautious. He was not overly concerned, certain that even freebooters would have more sense than to attack a troop of heavily armed soldiers.

The towers of the Chateau Cacchot gradually disappeared behind the russet and golden hills. The sun rose higher, the morning frost evaporated, and the spicy smell of autumn leaves and woodsmoke filled the chill morning air.

To the north, the road widened and narrowed accordingly, closed in by woods and opening to fields of wildflowers, of yellow, blue, and lavender. From a hillock wild with pine and low spreading shrubs, the road led steeply downward into an expansive valley of flat grass and broad sky. There they passed farms and villages where the harvest was being gathered. Roughly clothed peasants, whose faces and sturdy arms were as tanned as polished walnut, labored in the fields of rustling, golden grain.

By late in the day, rain clouds gathered, and a mutter of thunder sounded from beyond the distant hills. Presently the rain came in a great wall of mist, like a curtain being dragged across the meadows. It swept toward them, shaking the last leaves from the trees and laying down the weed stalks, until it overtook them and poured down on their shoulders and darkened their horse's hides.

The drenching rain transformed the road into a slippery wallow, so that they were thankful when the course led again into the woods where the ground was thick with leaves and pine needles. Wave after wave of rain passed over them and afterwards the wind picked up, blowing cold and sharp, stinging their faces.

From time to time Nicolette would cast a sidelong glance at her jailer. He had ridden beside her all day with the lead rein of her mare looped over the pommel of his saddle. In all he had not uttered a dozen words. At mid-day when they stopped, he took a drink of water.

It was his undoing. He brought it up again, almost at once, and twice that afternoon he was forced to stop and retch. It was no more than he deserved, she thought. She did, however, feel a twinge of guilt over his thumb. It was on the same hand which had suffered the knife wound at the abbey, and she noticed he had taken to holding his reins in his left hand and rode with the other tucked inside his tunic. In both instances he had been defending her, in his own way, though at the time his motives hadn't seemed so noble.

As they rode, darkness settled over them and the path led steeply upwards. Though the rain had ended, a dozen swiftly sluicing streams of water cut across the rocky path, cascading downwards to the valley and the river below. Nicolette leaned toward the hill, shifting her weight forward as the mare splashed through the foaming water. It was quite dark and the horses picked their way slowly up the path. Eventually they came to the top of a long broad ridge. In the distance they saw the towering, eyeless walls of Gaillard, black against a low and threatening sky. No light shone from its battlements. To Nicolette it looked like a grave, a place dead and deserted, a monstrous crypt of stone.

Ten

As they rode from under the trees, a damp gust of wind swept the ridge, driving the tall grasses before it like a wave. Nicolette, who had been warm beneath the woolen robe and clothing, shivered to the bone.

The billowing grass was belly high on their horses and the wind ranging swiftly through it made an eerie rustling sound.

At the drawbridge with its attendant towers, Laire pulled the chain to sound the entry gong. There was a rusty protest. Then a moment later it clanged hollowly somewhere deep inside, echoing back as mournful as a passing bell. No porter came.

Again Laire tugged at the chain. Still no one came. "Wait here," Laire called to the sergeant and, turning his horse, cantered round the walls seeking a postern gate. Eventually he found one, overgrown by vines, halfway along the south wall where the moat ended in an earthen dam.

He dismounted in the damp darkness and, fighting his way through the vines, put his shoulder to the iron-hinged gate. It was not barred; jammed perhaps, swollen by the rain. With another heave it opened, quite unexpectedly, launching him inside. He stumbled forward several steps, halted, walked back and, catching the reins of his browsing horse led him inside. He found himself in a long stone tunnel. Raising his eyes, he noted the blackness of the murder holes above his head, where in times past stones and burning pitch were showered down on attacking enemies.

The tunnel joined another. He followed it, and coming from beneath a stone arch, stepped directly before a stoop-shouldered old man.

"Merde," the old man cried. Laire, equally startled, leapt back. He dropped the reins, and his hand closed over the hilt of his sword. The bay lurched sideways, throwing up its head with a loud snort. In the gloom, the bent figure in the cowled cloak seemed faceless, almost ghoulish.

"Why is there no porter at the gate?" Laire demanded in a remarkably steady voice, considering the state of his nerves. The old man mouthed a few words that Laire could not make out, and swiftly turned away. "Wait," Laire called after him. "Where is your master, where is Lachaume?"

The old man hesitated, but made no reply. Slowly, as if he were speaking to a child, Laire explained that he was no ordinary visitor. "I am sent by King Philip. I am the new lord of Gaillard." The old man stared at him stupidly, and Laire wondered if he was not a half-wit. He was getting nowhere.

In disgust he left the old man standing there

and led the bay toward the drawbridge. Ronce went unwillingly, nostrils flared, and ears pricked forward.

After poking around in the darkened tower, Laire set the bridge into motion. The troop entered. The sergeant, shortening his reins, brought his horse round, and said to Laire, "I see you found a servant."

Laire turned to see the old man standing not ten paces behind him. Apparently he had followed. He seemed to have found his voice as well, for raising an arm he pointed to a distant tower surrounded by a jumble of buildings. "Lachaume is there." He said only that, and took off at a brisk stride across the outer court.

Away from the tunnellike structure that circuited the walls, the outer court was a derelict, a shambles of wooden and stone buildings. One had been a stable, judging from its size, housing as many as fifty horses. All that remained was a few skeletal timbers, sections of roofing thatch, and numerous muck piles. Nearby was the decaying framework of a barracks and, crouching in the darkness, assorted workshops, barns, and lean-tos. The cooking sheds were also in ruins, save for the huge stone ovens.

Amid the secular rubble rose an elegant gothic chapel with soaring pinnacles. Its roof had received a death blow, a gaping hole visible even in the dark of night. Having crossed the clutter of the bailey, they came upon yet another wall and before it another moat. It was not so wide as the first, but the drawbridge was braced with iron and its accompanying towers appeared stouter, more solid.

At the moat the old man called out in a shrill voice. Moments passed. There was the rattle of rusted chains and a loud groaning sound, as if a huge wooden bar was being dragged back. The bridge creaked ominously, then lowered into place with a resounding crash.

Beyond the drawbridge, an iron portcullis was cranked upwards in its grooves by an unseen hand. The last obstacle to the inner ward was a series of towers and a high iron-faced gate, wide enough for only a single horse.

A porter with a lantern stood to one side and hailed them as they entered. "Baron Lachaume awaits you," he called, and strode off into the darkness, the yellow arc of his lantern bouncing along the paving stones of the court.

Looking about her, Nicolette felt only despair. How could she ever escape from such a prison? On either side stone walls and pointed towers frowned down at her. Lurking before her in the dark was an ugly square stone building with tall slotted windows and a high sloping roof that blotted out the sky. And beyond it, looming upwards like a titan, was an enormous round citadel that dwarfed the other towers.

Another servant stood before the doors of the square building. He held a lantern in his hand and hailed to them. They dismounted. When Laire reached to lift Nicolette from her horse, she pulled away. "No," she sobbed, throwing off his hands. "I would rather die here, beneath the sky."

In the hard look he gave her, she saw it was useless to resist. She grasped his hand as he sat her feet on the cobbled stones, clinging to him, begging him, "No!" But he tugged his fingers from her grasp and, turning her by the shoulders, sharply whispered, "Be still."

Black figures milled around them, men and horses. The sergeant approached, blocked momentarily by Nicolette's mare as it was led away. A second man with a lantern appeared from a smaller court, and prepared to lead the troop to the stables and barracks of the inner ward. Albert followed the troop, leading the three horses.

A manservant waiting at the door walked several steps ahead, casting shadows before him. They passed from a small entry hall into the main chamber where two huge blackened fireplaces faced each other, and the windows, what few remained, were of glass.

Long in the past, the stuccoed walls had been painted with frescos of hunt scenes and religious subjects. One was of St. Martin, the warrior saint of France, another depicted the Last Judgment. All were faded, blackened with smoke, and in the momentary flashes of sickly light the ghostly images appeared to suddenly jerk to life.

At the hall's far end, a corridor opened to more chambers, dilapidated and dirty with an air of something long deserted, lived in only by mice and spiders, and the opportunistic wasps whose paper nests dotted the massive beams. The window shutters were rotted through, the lintels cracked, and upon the floors the dirt and leaves of seasons past crunched beneath their feet.

From the labyrinth of corridors and passages they came to a door and walked again into the night. It was but a patch of sky above their heads, for they were surrounded by the sheer walls of a long narrow court. Traversing the court's length they came to a stout iron-barred door. A servant peered out from a small portal.

At their approach, the door swung open. From the entrance and by a steep turn they entered the hall of the citadel. The interior was cleaner than the abandoned living quarters and had a more occupied appearance.

There was a kitchen at one end of the hall. An old serving woman and two young girls ventured from a storeroom door to stare at them. A faint odor of food clung to the stale air.

It was oppressively dark, and would ever be, for the only windows were mere loopholes at the end of deep cone-shaped passages built into the walls. Long trestled tables lined one wall, an immense fireplace graced another section, and above their heads, a wooden gallery made a complete circuit of the walls.

The servant led them to a stone stairway, whose steep cut risers were integrated into the wall and ascended through the gallery to the floors above. The second story was taken over by the chambers of Lachaume's knights.

Four middle-aged men came out into the corridor to gaze at the arrivals and fell in behind them as they ascended to the third level.

When at last they came face to face with Baron Lachaume, it was almost comical. His expression was like that of a rabbit pulled from a burrow. He cast his eyes about with furtive glances, as if he feared something might leap from the shadows, and hustled the visitors into his chamber. The knights followed.

Lachaume greeted Laire de Fontenne with something near to joy. In his distracted state of mind, Lachaume mistook the lady Nicolette for a monk. Speaking rapidly, he told Laire that a messenger had arrived the day before with word of the prisoner and of his recall to Paris. "I have never known such happiness," he said and hastened to introduce Laire to a plump woman seated by the hearth. "My lady wife, Jeanette," he announced, hardly pausing.

The chamber through which they moved was reasonably warm and bright. A low fire flickered in the hearth and a bronze oil lamp hung from a chain, providing a constant light. Apparently, Lachaume had feared an attack on the fortress and retreated to the safety of the keep. Sequestered as it was, the chamber did not lack for comfort. Saracen rugs adorned the floors and tapestries covered the window openings. To one side of the room a bed stood beneath a great canopy, hung with curtains of sendal silk. The bed and its heavy draperies obscured one corner of the room, but the other was cluttered with chests, benches, stacks of clothing, and even books.

Lachaume quickly plucked a candle from atop a chest and, lighting it from the hanging lamp, led them into a solar of sorts where there was a table and benches. Here there was no hearth, and the room was cold. Laire seated the lady prisoner on a bench beside a large prie-dieu and returned to the others.

Lachaume remarked, "Thanks be to God and the saints, I am delivered from this purgatory." Both Lachaume and his wife, watching silently from the door arch, had about their eyes the anxious look of those who live each day in fear for their lives.

Only after Lachaume had described in great detail his ordeal as lord of Gaillard, did he realize that "the monk" was in fact the scandalous Nicolette of Burgundy, daughter-in-law of the king.

Lachaume craned his neck to get a better look at her. "She must be secured," he said in an agitated voice. "I would be held responsible if she were to escape. She is in my charge until I am gone from this . . . this . . ." His voice dropped off suddenly and he called to his wife. She came at once, a ring of keys jangling at her belt. Her nimble fingers quickly produced the requested key and she placed it in her husband's trembling hand. He toyed with the key, turning it in his thin fingers.

"Henri, Jean," he called to the knights at the far end of the table. "Take her and lock her in the dungeon."

Nicolette's heart heaved painfully. No, her mind

screamed against it. No, she thought, watching in horrified silence as the two men climbed across the bench and came toward her. She shrank back like a child. Her dark eyes jolted to Laire de Fontenne. But the level blue gaze that met hers was cold as rain, impassive as his arrogant young face.

Nicolette looked away, sick with loathing. How she hated him. She felt betrayed, having been so certain that she sensed in him some sympathy for her. It pierced her heart to know that he was after all no different than the others. No less self-serving, no less a beast than Louis, nor any other man.

It took all the courage she could muster to gain her feet. She raised her head and, setting her eyes straight before her, walked from the chamber, oblivious to the stony-faced men who followed at her elbows.

From the hall a stairway led down to a vaulted chamber. In the lantern light a jumble of objects lined the walls, chests, heavy furnishings, the shields and weapons of departed generations. Somewhere amid the clutter of the storeroom was a hole chiseled into solid rock. From its gaping mouth a black staircase descended still deeper. Dampness seeped from the rocks and the fetid stench of mold and stagnant water assailed her nostrils. Where the stairs ended the floor tilted crazily and at one point they splashed through puddled water.

In the stinking darkness Nicolette could envision slimy creatures wriggling in the mire, and rats. For she was certain she had seen something dart before them from the shadows. The journey ended at a barred iron door. Nicolette sagged against the stones, sick with fear, as the lock was opened. She had heard stories of such cells. The vade-en-pace, depart in peace, where her father-in-law sent prisoners to languish in pitch blackness, to slowly starve and be eaten by rats.

Aside from a few monosyllabic grunts, the men had not spoken. They thrust her inside and slammed the door. "They should keep all of them locked up," one said. The other laughed.

She heard the key grind in the lock and the sound of their retreating footfalls, then only silence and the drip, drip, drip of water.

For a long while she stood rooted to the stones, afraid to move. When her eyes became better accustomed to the dark she began to make out shapes. The cramped room contained a wooden plank that served as a bed, what seemed to be a stool and wooden bucket. After a time she cautiously climbed onto the plank and, drawing her knees to her chest, pressed her face to them and sobbed.

Laire and the sergeant found beds in a chamber opposite Lachaume's. It was occupied by several serving women who peered suspiciously at the intruders and whispered among themselves. The stuffy air smelled of wool, and some other indefinably odd, oily odor. A large loom occupied one end of the chamber.

PRISONER OF MY HEART

The sergeant, bumbling in the dark, cracked his shin into a second, smaller wooden framework and blustered out an oath. Shaggy piles of wool lay stacked against the walls, amid spindles, rounds of yarn, and a jumble of other objects only half seen in the feeble candlelight.

Long before daybreak, Laire and the sergeant were awakened by clunking sounds and the trample of feet. Laire roused himself and looked into the corridor.

Lachaume's servants hustled past like ants abandoning a nest. One after another they trudged by, grunting under the weight of chests, carpets, and the many and varied belongings of their master. The exodus continued throughout the day, while Lachaume dashed about, harrying his weary servants, cursing and shouting orders.

On the second day, before the sun had crossed the inner ward, Lachaume, his heavily laden goods wagons, his knights, and servants, and the sergeant with his troop, trundled across the drawbridge and were gone.

In all of Gaillard there remained scarcely a dozen servants. Albert reported finding a former soldier at the stables, one who had defected from Lachaume's entourage, and three young boys who ranged in age from nine to fourteen.

At the guard tower of the inner ward, he came upon a club-footed man whose task it had been to operate the drawbridge. But in the rubble of the outer bailey, only rats survived. It was a wasteland.

Like the rest of the once grand chateau, the keep

echoed with emptiness. Laire discovered only a bald cook, three maid servants, one of whom looked to be as ancient as the chateau, and the stoop-shouldered old man he had met unexpectedly in the dark that first night.

The old man, who called himself Aymer, said that in his youth the population of Gaillard had numbered over two hundred souls. "But that was in the days of the old king, St. Louis, long before Philip la bel. You see Andelys? I was born there," the old man said, pointing to the rooftops of the town nestled by the sparkling river far below. "When I was but a child, my family gave me to the church. Those were famine years. Children starved, infants were left in the forest to die because their families could not afford to feed them. I was fortunate. The monks were not unkind, though it was not the life for me." His face cramped in a lean smile as he told the tall young man beside him, "I came here as a cleric when I was yet without a beard. I have no other home."

"Then it is a fortunate day for us both," Laire replied, also with a smile. "I have need of a cleric, and a good deal more it seems." At the moment he seemed to be the lord of nothing. He had no villeins and the village was in the hands of a neighboring lord's provost.

"Do not lose hope. Your villeins are there," the old man said with an all encompassing wave of his arm.

The old man had an odd halting manner of speech, disconcerting at times. Even so he was knowledgeable on many subjects. His mind was sharp, as was his tongue, particularly when he related how Lachaume had barricaded himself in the keep, while his provost was murdered and lawlessness spread across the countryside. "Without a lord to lead them, or sanction their actions, the villeins and the merchants were helpless to defend themselves. Now that Lachaume is gone, they will take heart. They will support a new seigneur."

Eleven

Nicolette awoke to the perpetual darkness. Someone was at the door. A snippet of light streamed through the barred opening and a key scraped in the lock. She saw only a black form silhouetted against the light, but she knew it was de Fontenne. Anger and spite boiled up in her throat. "Why have you come?" she asked hatefully.

"To take you out of this hole." He looked about, then stepped into the cell. "Lachaume is gone."

"Where are you taking me?" She stared into the blackness, wishing she could see his face. She moved stiffly to touch her slippers to the stones. Slowly she pulled herself erect, clenching her fists at her side, hating him, and yet terrified he would leave her there.

His eyes roved the darkened cell. "To the apartments in the tower."

"So that you can question me? You will only send me back!" Her voice broke off tearfully.

"No," he said decidedly. "I would not put an Englishman in this stinking place. Come," he urged. "The air is bad down here, the lantern flame is dying." It was not, but his insinuation that

PRISONER OF MY HEART 161

it might, the fear of being plunged again into total blackness, produced the desired effect. She followed him out into the passage without another word.

Together they climbed the damp and treacherous curl of stone stairs. Laire leaned his shoulder against the door leading to the storage chamber, and it creaked open. Nicolette, close on his heels, stumbled over the threshold. He grabbed her by the arm to steady her. They paused, hemmed in by the disarray of objects that cluttered the vast chamber.

Nicolette's eye caught a flurry of movement in the blackness just beyond the halo of lantern light. She tilted her chin so she might see from beneath the hood and saw a pair of luminous eyes blazing in the darkness. She gave a cry of alarm.

"It is a dog," Laire said, at the sound of her sharply indrawn breath. Suddenly it lunged into the circle of light. It was huge and white, so grotesquely thin that its every bone seemed visible. It slid between them, nuzzling their hands and bumping against their legs and wagging its tail.

Nicolette stroked the dog's broad head. Unexpectedly a large pink tongue curled about her hand. She smiled, riffling her fingers through the fine white fur. "Who does it belong to?"

Laire shrugged, "Lachaume, perhaps? I found it and half a dozen others wandering in the courtyard. This one has taken to following me everywhere." He had never seen her smile before that moment. There was something very sweet in her expression, an unfeigned goodness that was impossible to ignore. "Careful, there is a wound on its side."

"Poor fellow," she softly crooned. "He looks hungry."

"Dogs are always hungry," Laire replied, giving the dog a preoccupied pat on the head as he studied her face with a critical eye. "Bring your hood forward a bit."

Nicolette glanced up, puzzled by his command.

"It will be best if the servants do not have too clear a view of your face."

His reply made even less sense. She did, and afterwards asked, querulous, "Why? What can it matter?"

"I have my reasons," he said, and led off with the lantern. The dog trotted before them, white as a ghost.

In the hall, Nicolette took her first deep breath in days. All around her were the smells, sights, and sounds of the living. She felt as if she had just emerged from a grave. A boy shoveling ashes from the hearth looked up as they passed. And on the far side of the hall, two others spreading fresh rushes turned their heads to stare.

They took to the stairs once more, climbing past the gallery, the empty chambers of the second floor and on to Lachaume's suite of rooms. The dog bounded before them.

Nicolette took two steps into the room. At first she did not recognize the chamber. It was bare. Nothing remained of its splendid contents, save for

PRISONER OF MY HEART

the chain where the bronze lamp had hung and the smoke etched rectangles left by the tapestries. Inside one of the rectangles was a window. Autumn sunlight poured through its rotting shutters. But inside the smaller of the rectangles was a curiously low door set into the wall. It was of a height that a child might pass through easily, but an adult could enter only by stooping.

The dog sniffed about the room. Behind her, Laire opened the lantern, snuffed the flame and set it on the floor. Nicolette turned her head at the sound. The thought flashed through her mind that this was to be her prison. But an instant later she saw something which changed her mind. Before the low fire in the hearth she saw his leather satchel and a blanket.

"In here," he said, crossing the room to the solar where she had sat several nights before. The dog trailed after him. "It seems the table and benches were not to Lachaume's liking. Or perhaps they were too heavy?" Laire commented. "Take off the robe," he called back to her.

But she only pushed back her hood, exposing her wimple and coif, and followed him. There was a ewer on the table, a cup, and a platter containing chunks of cheese and several slabs of dark bread.

"Sit down," he invited, sprawling on the bench opposite her. "You must be thirsty, hungry as well."

She was famished, and forgetting all her courtly manners fell upon the food with the gusto of a peasant.

"Lachaume forbade anyone to bring you food."

He tipped the ewer to fill the cup, explaining, "He interpreted the written judgment, 'without comfort,' quite literally. There was nothing I could do."

Liar, she thought. Though she was too hungry to contradict him, or even care. "And now," she asked, stuffing her mouth with bread, "now that he is gone?"

He leaned back against the wall, placing his arms behind his head and lacing his fingers together. "It seems your fate is in my hands," he replied, watching the movement of her lips and imagining more than bread and cheese between them. He knew what he was about to do was foolish—deadly, if it was ever revealed to the king. And yet he also knew that he was incapable of locking her away.

She had become like some strange treasure to him, one which he had a confused and sensual need to see and touch. He had never felt so possessed by anything, certainly not a woman. He had deceived enough of them with little or no conscience, telling each he loved her best. But this woman was alarmingly different.

The three days she had been locked away had been a torture for him. Even in his sleep he had been visited by visions of her. She had come to him like a witch's charm with her pale little breasts and that feathery part of her dark as a stain. He had held her, possessed her, every soft curve. The lewdness of the dreams had both disturbed and relieved him. But in only a few hours the exasperating desires returned as strong as before. How could he feel anything for her, he wondered? She was, at the very least, in some way responsible for the death of his friends, the ruination of his life. Yet he was obsessed by this irritating and unreasonable longing to have her. "I have no desire to lock you in the tower," he confided. "To watch you slowly die of cold and boredom. On the other hand, if I were to offer you a life of freedom, within limits of course, would you be willing to abandon any thought of escape?"

She paused long enough to glance up suspiciously, then took a chunk of cheese and bit into it. "What sort of freedom?"

In the same calm, rational tone of voice, he suggested, "If I were to introduce you as the lady prisoner's serving woman."

The proposition, took her completely by surprise. For a moment she was speechless. "A servant?" she repeated, at once bewildered, amused, and uncertain. Could she, she wondered? She did not know how to be a servant.

"It is better than being mewed up in the tower. Perhaps you should see it first. Before you decide."

She took a gulp of wine to keep from choking. The bread felt as if it had lodged mid-way in her throat. After a moment she said, "No one would believe it. The servants would know only one woman came with you."

"How could they know? It was dark when we arrived. They saw riders wearing cloaks. They saw no one clearly. As for Lachaume and his wife, the men who escorted you to the dungeon, the sergeant and his troop, they have all gone."

"But the servants will see there is no one in the tower room," she countered.

"I have the key," he said, producing it from his tunic. It was long and with a cloven bow and he placed it on the table before her. "Only you will attend to the lady prisoner's needs."

"What if the king should send someone? And what of the man at the abbey? I am certain he was sent by Louis."

She looked very young and afraid, and there was something almost seductive about the way her lips moved when she spoke. He found himself studying everything about her, the tilt of her nose, the sudden flush high on her cheeks, and that her dark brows, which had been rigorously plucked in the arched fashion of the court, were beginning to grow, straighter, thicker.

He smiled abruptly at the thought of her, and said, "In the unlikely event that the king should send a courtier, I would delay him until you had time to take your place in the tower. As for the assassin, if that is truly what he was—He will not find you here."

"If he is from court, he would know my face!"

"Not dressed as a servant. I doubt he would spare you a glance."

She shifted uneasily on the bench. Sitting as he was, opposite her, his long legs stretched out before him, she did not know where to put her eyes. She did not wish to stare and yet each time she demurred, her gaze seemed to fall invariably to the apex of his legs and the bulge beneath the tautly drawn leather hosen. She raised her eyes, looking him full in the face. "Why do you care what becomes of me?"

He shrugged off her question with a smile. "Since we are condemned to spend eternity together, we should not be enemies. What do you say?"

From what she saw in his eyes, she had expected him to say something much different. She turned her head away, experiencing a flood of warmth, a strange restlessness that was both exciting and frightening. "Yes," she conceded, realizing to her shame that she would have agreed to anything he asked. She pressed the cup to her lips. Wine swirled over her tongue. She was very conscious of his eyes on her, the quickening of her pulse.

Only after, following him cautiously, she had climbed up the dizzy twisting staircase and entered the tower room, did she fully appreciate his offer. The dog, wise in his own way, did not follow, but sat waiting at the foot of the steps.

The room, itself, was a dismal place. Several filthy, threadbare tapestries hung from the walls, there was a sentry's bed of straw and a black iron brazier. But the soaring view from the window took her breath away. Far below a wild green island basked in the sparkling waters of the Seine.

"I must have a name. What shall I call myself?" Nicolette asked as she gazed out over the distant blue misted hills.

"Odette," he said, without a hint of hesitation. "It suits you somehow." From over her shoulder, Nicolette sent him a curious look. He came and stood beside her, leaning his shoulder casually against the stones. "You are very like her," he confessed, "the smile, the dark eyes."

She gazed down at the river, blue and blazing with sun needles. Her curiosity now piqued, she asked, "Who was she? Were you lovers?"

"For a time," he replied.

"Have you a wife, as well?"

"No, I have no wife."

"But you had a mistress?"

"Yes." His smile deepened.

There was something terribly annoying, almost superior, about his smile. It was the same sort of smile her father had always given her to let her know that she had said something foolish, and it irritated her beyond reason. "Was she your only mistress?"

"Odette. No."

"Have you had many?"

His blue eyes twinkled. "No, not many."

She felt suddenly angry, as if she had been in some way deceived by him. "How many?"

He laughed. "I have never counted them. And you?" he asked, "How many lovers have you had?"

Love, she hardly knew what it meant. There had been no love between Louis and herself, only hatred and disgust. She was still tormented by that one awful night they had spent together. The memory of his sweaty, grappling hands and that part of him like a hairy worm that tried to crawl inside her. He had blamed her for his failure, because her appearance was not to his liking. He could not abide brunettes. He had cursed at her and struck her full across the face. No, she had never had a lover. "None," she said. The sunlight pained her eyes and she gazed up at him from beneath her hand. "You do not believe me, do you?"

"Perhaps. I cannot decide."

"But you admit to it," she reminded him, "to having mistresses?"

"Yes, why not. It is different for men."

How arrogant they all were, she thought, conceited, too. "And Gautier and Pierre, did they have mistresses?"

"Yes, of course."

"You told me once that Gautier had a mistress at court. You believed it was me, didn't you?"

"Yes, at first." There was a look of absolute honesty in the clear blue eyes, and something more, expectancy, perhaps.

"Why? Why did you?" she persisted.

"Because you are the one I would have chosen." He smiled again and, pushing away from the wall, walked toward the door. "Come, it is time you were introduced to the servants."

With the dog close at their legs, they returned to the hall. Laire called the servants together. Nicolette hung back shyly. None of her pranks and play acting in the gardens of the Hotel de Nesle had prepared her for the stark reality of the moment, the dreadful sinking feeling in her stomach as he drew her forward by the arm and introduced her.

"This is Odette, the lady prisoner's serving

woman," he announced in his teasing, jesting manner. "She is from the king's court and therefore ignorant of any practical knowledge. You will have to teach her."

Nicolette sent him a blistering look. Her cheeks flamed amid their laughter. An old woman, squat and ugly as a monkey and two young girls crowded around her talking all at once.

The bald-headed cook whose face was red from the heat of the oven gave a hoot of laughter as Nicolette was towed along by the chattering women into the kitchen. She was so infuriated that she heard not a word of what they said. Her ears stung as if they had been stuffed with cotton wool and her face burned with outrage.

Just as Laire de Fontenne predicted, the servants accepted her without question. There was not so much as a flicker of doubt in their voices, nor the raising of a brow. However when she was alone with them, the girls, and even the old dame, Mahaut, plied her with questions about the Paris court. At first Nicolette was reluctant to speak of it, fearing she would give herself away. But their looks of eagerness soon drew her out, for she loved to talk, to be amusing. They were captivated by her tales and did not seem to mind showing her the proper way to stir a pot, pluck a bird, or boil salt into meat.

In the days that followed she learned a wealth of things, that yeast made bread rise and butter must be churned. Things that were unknown to her, at least things she had never before considered. Just as she had never considered sweeping a floor, scrubbing pots, and beating out bed clothes to rid them of fleas. At first her enthusiasm was boundless, but day in day out, the novelty soon wore thin. The servants, for all their kindness, had faults. The cook was often ill-tempered, the two girls, Josine and Dore, were lazy as geese, and the old dame Mahaut tipped wine whenever the opportunity presented itself.

Every morning without fail, Nicolette would lug a bucket of wood chips up the curl of stairs, enough to fill the brazier. In the evening, she would carry the lady prisoner's food to her. Food that she surreptitiously fed to the dogs, who were devoted to her. She would then climb the stairs, start a fire in the brazier with a bit of tallow and the flint striker, and fall onto her mattress, exhausted.

Each day she expected her jailer to press his attentions on her. At first she found the thought disgusting, but when he did not come to plague her, she began to wonder why. It was true there was much to do; the chateau was bare, as if it had been sacked. De Fontenne directed forays into the storage chamber in search of furnishings. He organized and even lent a shoulder to the arduous task of carrying weighty chests and beds and benches to chambers above. The majority were of another age, large and cumbersome, and the stairs were steep and narrow, so that the task became a trial of endurance.

While curses, grunts, and clunking sounds echoed from the stairs, Nicolette, Josine, and Dore labored in the garth amid a tempest of dust, coughing and sputtering as they beat a lifetime of filth from the ancient rugs. The tapestries required much the same treatment, for they, too, were dim with age and dust-laden.

Nicolette saw Laire de Fontenne only when the meals were served. He sat at the long table with his squire Albert, the cleric Aymer, and a former sergeant at arms, Etienne Judot. Lachaume, it was said, had broken him in rank for his insolence. Nicolette could easily reason why. He was short and swarthy, with a jaunty bravado about him. Dore, who was obviously without shame where Judot was concerned, had intimated to Nicolette that his punishment had stemmed from a disagreement concerning Madame Lachaume.

In the day to day existence of the hall, Nicolette would often catch snatches of a conversation taken over by matters of rents and dues, the peasants abandonment of the fife, and the much needed repairs to Gaillard's walls.

Occasionally de Fontenne would glance up at her, his expression as inscrutable as the look in his eyes, then turn again back to the discussion.

Alone in her tower room at night, Nicolette would think on her ruined life and pray. She felt no guilt in praying to God. He knew of her innocence, she thought, and even though His Church had deserted her, He in His mercy would not. But despite all her contemplation and prayers, she could find neither comfort nor an end to her anguish.

Her desire to escape her prison was tempered

with the realization that even if she could escape the walls of Gaillard, she would never be able to escape her fate. Before God she was the wife of the king's eldest son and only in death would she be free of him. She deluded herself to think otherwise, to believe her father's steward or anyone could defy the king of France. And she wondered how long her freedom, such as it was, would continue. How long before the king discovered Laire de Fontenne's duplicity. He would die for it, as cruelly as his friends had died, and the thought of it troubled her more and more.

Day by day Nicolette struggled to establish some sort of normalcy to her life. In spite of everything she had made a place for herself at Gaillard. She felt a sense of belonging, a feeling she had never known before. At times working with the others, she could almost put the past from her mind. Perhaps it was, after all, the past she wished to escape.

There was only the wimple to remind her. She had come to hate it, for the wimple and the stubbled crop of hair concealed beneath it were symbols of her imprisonment. The wimple chafed the tender flesh beneath her chin and at times felt like a band of steel about her face. In the privacy of the room she pulled the linen cloth from her head and ran her fingers through her crop of hair. She could only feel its unkempt texture, for she had no mirror, no bit of polished metal, in which to see herself. One day in the kitchen she had seen her reflection in a metal pot, a pale face, dark brows growing thick and straight, and staring eyes. For a moment she remained transfixed by her own image, for it was as if she had looked into the face of a stranger.

Just as they had done for days, Laire, Albert, and the soldier, Judot, set out from Gaillard at a brisk pace. The brittle leaves crunched beneath their horse's hooves. There had been frost during the night and with the rising sun the meadows and fields became a patchwork of brown and white.

At farmsteads Laire talked to the peasants and viewed first hand the destruction wrought by the brigands. He listened patiently to the complaints, and vowed to put an end to the lawlessness. He talked and laughed with them, entered their huts, riffled the hair of their children and smiled at their wives. To all he promised a reduction in rents and dues. And to those vassals with a horse and a strong arm, he offered two deniers a week to serve as soldiers. With a poor harvest and winter coming, the peasants listened, though warily, to this new seigneur. He had come to them with promises, not threats. He was young and handsome, and there was about him the irresistible look of a champion.

"You have won them over," Judot declared with a sly smile, as they cantered from a farmstead. "Though only Christ knows how you will pay them."

"That part is simple enough," Laire said, settling back comfortably in his saddle. "All we need do is relieve the village provost of his ill-gotten revenues."

Judot, coming up beside him, gave a grunt of laughter. "That will be tedious work. He will defend them like a badger."

As they returned to Gaillard, under a sky dark and threatening, the pine woods appeared black, and the slopes of the distant hills seemed somehow closer, drawn nearer in the gloom. In the welcome warmth of the hall, Laire found a delegation of merchants awaiting him.

The eldest of the four men, a chandler by profession, wasted no time in explaining the townspeople's dilemma. "We are all loyal subjects of King Philip. We have faithfully paid our rents and dues. It is through no fault of our own that they have not reached the king's treasury."

Laire listened with interest.

"The fault lies with our provost, Pons Vernet," a wool merchant dressed in brown velvet accused.

"What he says is true," a third man, a cobbler with calloused hands, attested, adding, "He collects our rents and dues, but keeps the payments for himself and his lord."

Laire heard them out and agreed to meet with the mayor in Andelys the following day. After the merchants had gone, Judot walked to the sideboard and poured Laire and himself a cup of wine.

He returned, a cup in each hand, and sank down on the bench. "If you rid them of Vernet, they will support you. Lachaume would not lift a hand against him. Not even the murder of his provost would draw him out of Gaillard. All knew the provost had been murdered by Pons Vernet. Many townspeople witnessed it, though none would come forward. They still fear Vernet. They will be of no use when it comes to the deed. We will be alone in it."

"We might muster six or seven men," Laire mused, naming several from the farmsteads who possessed horses. "And ourselves."

Judot sipped thoughtfully at his cup, "It would not do to meet him openly."

"No," Laire agreed, "I do not intend to."

In the pre-dawn darkness, Albert brought water for his master to shave. By candlelight Laire rinsed the straight blade of his razor and continued to cautiously scrape away the three day growth of beard. His fingers were numbed by the icy water in the bowl, and his jaw seemed to be of a different shape than the one reflected in the disc of polished steel.

"Two deniers is indeed a fair wage," Aymer agreed. He was seated across the room, and lapped his cloak about his bony legs to ward off the morning chill, before adding in a measured tone, "Unfortunately the strong box of Gaillard contains not one obol, let alone a denier."

"Are you trying to tell me that I am a pauper, Aymer?"

"Essentially, yes, milord."

Laire paused, razor in hand, and grinned into

the mirror. "All that is about to change." He assured him. "We shall have our rents and dues. What figure did you give me, 5500 livres?"

Albert looked in from the door, saw his master was still shaving and ducked out again.

The cleric nodded. "Yes, milord. And though I know such an action is right and just, I also know the provost of Andelys to be a violent man. He will not surrender the gold easily and if you attempt to remove him, it can only lead to mayhem. Oh, it is well and good for the merchants to wish to be rid of Pons Vernet, it will not be their blood which is spilt."

"Nor ours if we are wise," Laire remarked.

"Then you intend to go to Andelys this day to meet with the merchants?"

"Do not look so grim, Aymer. We are about to become wealthy."

The cleric folded his hands and took on an expression of forbearance. "As you say, milord."

In the hall, Laire ate a chunk of bread and drank a cup of wine. The stouter of the two girls, Dore, brought the wine.

"Where is Odette?" he asked her.

Her face was round as a cherub's and she had little pursed lips. "She's collecting the eggs, sire."

"Does she always do that?" Albert who was sopping a slice of bread in his wine looked up sleepily.

"Oh yes, sire," Dore nodded. "She's given the hens funny names and all." She gave a little laugh, then stiffened, as if she had said something she shouldn't have, and hurried away.

Judot, already in his cloak, came from the direction of the kitchen. As he passed the girl, Laire could have sworn he saw him swat her on the rump.

"Shall I have the horses saddled?" Judot asked.

Albert sucked the last of the bread into his mouth and, climbing over the bench, went to fetch the cloaks and his master's sword.

"We will need four," Laire said. The lack of horses at the chateau was becoming a problem. He took a bite of bread. It left a strange taste in his mouth, like straw. He rinsed it away with a slug of wine.

Across the table, Judot lifted a brow. "Aymer is going?" he asked, recalling the old fool had been deadset against it.

"No," Laire replied, taking his cloak and sword from Albert. "See that the mare is saddled," he instructed him. He took the sword from Albert and, sensing a presence behind him, turned to find the bald-headed cook.

"Milord," the cook began, "our store of flour is depleted. What's left I had to mix with chaff."

The thought disturbed Laire. He wondered what else was in the bread. "Then see to it," he told him, buckling on his sword.

The cook's smooth pink brow furrowed. "The miller will not give me the flour without payment, milord. And even when Lachaume paid him in full, he short weighted the sacks."

Judot turned at the door arch as he and Albert were leaving. "Aye, he's as much a thief as Vernet," he called back as he went out.

"Take the boys in the stables with you, and some stout staves," Laire instructed. "Tell the miller he will get his payment later."

The cook gave a fat, greasy smile. Today, he thought with satisfaction, he would have his revenge on that weasel of a miller.

The dawn sky was streaked with red as Laire walked toward the shed where the fowl were kept. No grass grew there and the heels of his boots made a sucking sound in the mud. All at once he heard an uproar from inside the shed, a startled yelp followed by a frenzy of squawking. An instant later a swarm of fluttering black hens dodged frantically, feathers flying, from the shed's door.

Laire sidestepped the frantic hens, looked inside and laughed. The air was thick with dust. "Don't move," he said, laughing and coughing at the same time. "You have no idea what you look like." It was not what he had meant to say, just as he had not meant to laugh. It occurred to him that she might be hurt, but, no, she just looked angry.

Nicolette was furious, her cheeks scarlet. She knew what she must look like beneath the mountain of straw. An armful was all she had meant to pry from the loft, only enough to line the nest boxes. Instead it had all come down atop her, an avalanche of sweet-smelling, dusty, golden straw. How foolish she felt, splay-legged and flat on her behind beneath a mountain of straw.

"Are you hurt?" he asked, attempting to stifle his laughter.

Her nose itched and she sneezed. "No," she

sneezed again, and asked, indignant, "How did you know where to find me?" She was certain that Dore had told him.

He did not answer her at once, knowing he would laugh. He crouched down, balanced on his heels, and began to clear the cone of straw from her head. "I came looking for you," he said finally, his lips curling at the corners. "I heard the chickens. I thought a fox was loose in the shed. Then I heard you cry out." Handful by handful she emerged from the straw. "What a mess you are," he laughed, dusting away the bits that clung to her coif. "What did you do, try to pull an armful from underneath? Couldn't you guess what would happen?"

"No," she said, gritting her teeth and watching his hands. After a moment she made a futile effort to help. He told her to hold still, and went on slowly clearing away the straw heaped upon her breast. He took his time, a handful here, a handful there. His fingers lingered over her modest decolletage, plucking away the last twigs. She held her breath, wondering what he would do. But all he did was go on clearing away the accumulation of straw. "There," he said, pulling her to her feet.

She shook out her skirts. "Turn around," he instructed. His voice made her start with surprise, and without her permission he began beating the last of the chaff from the rear of her skirts. "That's the worst of it," he said, straightening up.

Nicolette made several swipes at her skirt, then

looked up. He was still there. "Why are you staring like that?"

The smile spread slowly over his face. "Can't I look at you?"

"Why would you want to?"

"Because you are pretty."

"No," she said at once, quickly stooping to rummage through the straw for her basket of eggs. The dusty air, everything, smelled of chickens.

"No," he repeated with a laugh. "No you are not, or no you do not wish me to say so?" He saw the wicker handle protruding from a pile of straw, but let her go on searching.

"No! Yes!" she stammered, disconcerted by his attention, by the look in his eyes. She glanced away, searching the straw.

"Are you looking for the basket?"

Just then she saw it and made a grab for the arched handle. He caught her hand. It was cold as ice, and she tried to take it back. He held fast. "Do you want to ride with me to Andelys?" For a moment she did not know what to say. "No!" she snapped. "What will the others think?" Still, she wanted to go with him and was sorry she had been abrupt.

His smile deepened. "Do you care what they think?"

Her nose itched, she was going to sneeze again. "Someone may recognize me." She sneezed.

"In Andelys?" It made him laugh.

He was right, she thought, it did sound foolish. "Do you want to go with me?" he asked again.

Releasing her hand, he picked up the basket and held it out to her.

"Yes," she replied in scarcely a whisper and, snatching the basket from him, darted out the door.

Mud squished beneath her slippers as she hurried across the lot. In the kitchen everyone was busy and talking too loudly. She knew they had been watching from the doorway.

Nicolette saw Mahaut was seated at the table shelling beans. "I'm going to the village," she said to her.

"Alone?" Dore asked, nudging Josine with her elbow as she spoke.

"With de Fontenne. The seigneur," she corrected. She sat the basket on the floor near the flour bin. Not one of the eggs was broken. It was a miracle, she thought.

"Oh?" Mahaut said, dropping a handful of shelled beans into a bowl. "Why is there straw on your back?" she asked, her hooded eyelids crinkling into a thousand wrinkles.

"The straw fell on top of me."

Dore and Josine giggled. Nicolette ignored them. "May I wear your shawl?" She already had it in her hand. Mahaut assented with a nod of her grey head.

Nicolette wrapped the shawl deftly about her shoulders, before she advised, "One of the stable boys will have to set the straw aright, my arms are not long enough."

"How did it come to fall?" Dore asked.

Nicolette glared at her. "I don't know!" She shrugged. She noticed the cook was watching her, too. All at once the pot the two giggling girls were supposed to be watching boiled over and the cook cursed at them. Mahaut shouted at them as well. And when the old woman looked back, she saw only the swirl of Nicolette's skirts as she bounded out the door. "Well," Mahaut tittered, grabbing another handful of dried beans, "Did I not tell you she'd be in his bed in a fortnight?"

"I'd give him a sweeter cup to sup," Dore swooned with a wag of her ample hips. Beside her, Josine giggled, emitting a groan of feigned ecstasy. The bald-headed cook grumbled at their foolishness. He took up a knife and swiftly disjointed a chicken, and aiming his remark at Dore, said, "Your cup's been passed around so often, I doubt there's any left!" He raised his head, smirking through the woolly clots of steam. Dore rolled her eyes and looked away. But a moment later when the cook turned his back to tend a pot, she made a pickled face at him.

Nicolette did not care what they thought, at least not at the moment. She was far too excited as she dashed down through the garth, her heart beating with a childlike expectancy at the prospect of riding into the village at the foot of the hill. She did not know what she expected to see. It was only a Norman village with mud streets, but she was filled with delight. She ran past the row of scraggly hedges, her slippers skimming over the ground.

The sky had lightened to a creamy color, and

the chilly air made a frosty comma of her breath.
She filled her lungs with the cold, crisp air. It was
going to be a beautiful day, she thought, and she
wondered if it was because Laire de Fontenne had
chosen to spend it with her.

Twelve

In the stable yard the horses were saddled. Judot was tightening the girth of his saddle. He turned when he heard Nicolette's slippers crunch on the gravel, and gave her a cross look, as if he did not approve. But he said nothing. Albert's back was to her. He dropped the hoof that he had been inspecting, giving her only a cursory glance before mounting. He looked older somehow.

Laire brought the mare around for her and boosted her into the saddle. He was smiling, as if he were enjoying some private joke. Nicolette found her other stirrup, noticing the horse was the mare she had ridden from Paris, and she leaned forward and patted the animal's sleek neck before tightening the reins and giving her a nudge.

Beyond the gates, out in the tall grass, the world seemed boundless. The hills rolled gently away, lost in mist, and the sky arching above her appeared immense beyond imagining. She had not known such a sense of happiness since childhood.

A road, in reality a wide dirt path, led down the north hill and through the fertile Norman countryside. With the hill behind them, Laire dropped back to ride with Nicolette. The morning sun slanting through the lattice work of branches framed the perfect oval of her face with an ever changing dance of light and shadow. He smiled at her and asked, "Are you pleased?"

"Yes," she replied. She wished there was some way she might say, "you have been kind to me and I thank you," but there was no way that would not wound her pride.

"You will find Andelys grim and provincial," he predicted.

She glanced up from plucking a bit of straw from her skirt and squinted into the glare. "No more than the merchants will think of me," she said with a merry smile.

Judot turned in his saddle. Laire noticed, and cautioned her, "Say nothing to your mistress about today."

"No," she agreed in a modest voice, thinking his words were for Judot's benefit. That morning was not the first time Judot had looked at her strangely and she wondered if he did not suspect. His loyalty to de Fontenne seemed complete, but one could never tell about loyalties.

The valley spread before them in shades of brown and russet and through the barren trees the river sparkled in the distance. On the outskirts of the village a bridge of stone and timbers crossed a sluggish stream. Beyond lay Andelys, grey in the autumn sunlight: the proud steeple of its church, rows of shops, homes of wealthy merchants, the hovels of the peasants. The streets were unpaved, narrow and airless, and its market grounds a clutter of open stalls. Compared to Paris, Andelys was indeed grim. But to Nicolette, so long denied any contact with the world, it was a place of wonderment.

Traffic moved up and down the streets seemingly without purpose. Peasants herding pigs and geese, merchants, monks, and soberly dressed housewives. The sounds of commerce filled the clear, cold air, a fish monger, shouting his wares, a cooper setting an iron band on a barrel, the shouts of tradesmen. Without warning, a gang of filthy, half-dressed children with ruddy cheeks and snotty noses darted before their horses. Screeching and chasing they raced down an alleyway between two shops and disappeared among a row of ramshackle buildings.

Tall stone and timber buildings lined the maze of streets. Beside the church there was a burial plot enclosed by a low stone wall and before it an intricate black iron lyche gate. Here the houses were larger, grander, constructed of stone, with gardens and walled courtyards. It was to one of these houses they were admitted.

A serving woman led them up a flight of steep stairs to a solar where they were greeted by the florid-faced mayor and his wife. Nicolette hesitated at the door, suddenly intimidated by the room filled with men, but Laire pressed her forward by the arm. The mayor's wife clearly regarded her as a servant. She did not even trouble herself to smile.

Half a dozen men, merchants by their attire, rose from the table where they had been locked in a hushed discussion. At the far end of the comfortable room, Nicolette saw several children playing quietly on a rug. A nursemaid sat nearby bouncing an infant in her arms.

The men paid no attention to the servant girl who entered with the seigneur and his villeins. They greeted Laire de Fontenne with smiles and exaggerated enthusiasm. They jostled and crowded around the young seigneur, their voices and jovial laughter filling the room. Nicolette went to a bench that was scattered with pillows and sat down, gazing about the room.

Across the chamber, a hearth fire blazed under the hood of a huge chimney, and a servant boy seated on a stool beside it fed logs continuously into the leaping flames. Coming in from the cold, Nicolette had at first welcomed the warmth, but as the men's discussion dragged on, the unnatural heat made her drowsy.

Servants hovered over the men, pouring wine. One after another the merchants stated their case.

"After our provost was murdered, Lachaume refused to name another. We," the merchant said, glancing about as if to include the others in his words, "felt that if the king and his liege lord were not prepared to stand by us, we should seek another master."

A thin-faced merchant flapped his hand impatiently. "No, no, there is more to it than that. After the provost's death, Simon Quarle came to us and hinted that if we wished to live in peace, we should swear allegiance to his lord, the Baron of Artois, and accept his man, Pons Vernet, as provost. What were we to do, but agree? You have seen the state of the countryside. Only Andelys has been spared."

"The Baron of Artois?" Laire questioned. He knew of only one. "Raoul de Conches!"

"Yes," another of the men quickly confirmed. "We had no way of knowing Quarle and his provost would withhold the taxes."

Nicolette, sweltering in the oppressive heat of the hearth, stiffened at the sound of Isabella's lover's name.

A fat man in a blue silk tunic complained, "Now the king sends demands. But what are we to do? We have not the troops to oppose Quarle and his overlord."

Hearing their words, Nicolette felt a chill of apprehension. Was that why Isabella had proposed locking her away at Gaillard, with Raoul de Conches poised to do her bidding? She listened closely as one merchant said, "I know for a fact that our tax monies are still locked in a strong box in the provost's house."

"It must be done quickly," the thin-faced man urged.

"Where might I find this provost?" Laire inquired.

"He has taken over the money lender's house at the top of the square," another offered.

"There was murder done in that affair," a short, stocky man insisted. "The man and his family vanished. We are all guilty. No one less than the other." A grumble of discontent passed through the group, but the stocky little man went on determinedly. "We knew of the provost's plans, yet we did nothing. It was greed, simply that and nothing more, monseigneur. For with the money lender's death, our debts were canceled out. There, I have said it!"

"What could we have done to prevent it?" the others cried, defending their actions. "We have families and businesses to consider." The stocky little man, because he was in fact one of them, merely shrugged his shoulders, agreeing that the provost had threatened to kill anyone who defied him.

The conversation turned to other matters, and another hour passed before Laire finally rose from the bench, thus bringing the meeting to an end. Even so, it seemed to Nicolette that they would never reach the door, as first one merchant then another detained Laire with their problems.

Away from the drone of voices and the oppressive heat of the mayor's solar, the courtyard was cold and eerily silent. A servant brought their horses and they rode off toward the market grounds. The route Laire chose led by the provost's house. It was a large, three-storied structure of stone and timber, and little different from the other houses that lined the road. A low wall separated its forecourt from the rutted mud of the lane, and before its brightly painted blue door, a sturdy-limbed serving woman swept a whirlwind of leaves from a stone walkway.

As they walked their horses past the house, they caught a glimpse of a stable directly behind the house where a small group of men stood watching a horse being shod.

Nicolette, riding beside Albert, could not quite hear Laire and Judot's conversation, no more than their low serious tones, though from their solemn expressions she guessed they were discussing a plan of attack. At the top of the square she shifted in her saddle, glancing back the way they had come. She saw four men exit the front door of the house. They were dressed in the manner of soldiers, wearing mail vests and with swords swinging from their hips. From that perspective the house took on a new and more sinister appearance, that of an armed camp. A gust of wind greeted her as she turned the mare onto a narrower street that bounded the market grounds, and a sudden chill raised a rash of gooseflesh on her arms.

Where the road divided, Judot turned his horse and cantered down the slope toward the bridge that led away from the village. Nicolette urged her mare forward. "Where is he going?" she asked Laire.

"To speak to my steward, Rigord," he answered amicably enough, but seemed unwilling to say more and led off toward the noise and the ragtag collection of booths. It was a country market, spread haphazardly across a meadow, where a milling flock of people moved amid an array of goods, and the meltingly delicious aroma of bread and roasting meat drifted on the cold air.

They tethered their horses beneath a stand of limber, young hornbeams and joined the throng of shoppers. At a booth where buns were being baked in an iron kettle nestled in the coals, Laire bought one for each of them. They were marvelously fragrant with yeast, drizzled with honey, and almost too hot to hold, a solace that warmed their cold fingers and was devoured with relish as they slowly explored the gaudy colors and curious sights of the market.

Where the cloth merchants gathered, Nicolette's eyes were dazzled by a fluttering array of silken scarves. Laire, because he seldom saw anything but her, noticed her delight. "Would a scarf please you?" he asked.

"Oh, no, I have no need of a scarf," she insisted. "But they are lovely all the same, don't you think?" And she turned away, preparing to walk on, even though it was apparent to anyone with eyes that she longed to have one.

"Choose one," he urged.

"No," she said, reluctantly.

"Yes. Choose one," he insisted, and looking quickly among the scarves, selected one that was bursting with orange and yellows and greens, brighter than a jongleur's britches. He held it up to her, threatening, "If you do not choose, I shall buy this one and make you wear it. What do you think, Albert?"

"It would not be easily misplaced," Albert responded with a bashful grin. He was fully fourteen and old enough to understand what lay behind the profound looks that passed between his master and the doe-eyed lady, and it was that which made him blush.

After much bantering back and forth, Nicolette chose a scarf that was predominately scarlet with a small delicate design, one that matched the trim of her serviceable woolen kirtle.

Five obols was the price quoted by the wiry little woman with the sharp black eyes. Laire paid her three. It was too much, he thought, but well worth Nicolette's delighted smile.

He alone knew he had but four remaining obols to his name. The thought amused him. It seemed the singular constant in his life. He consoled himself with the thought that his sister was not there to lecture him.

Walking back to the horses in the glittering sunlight, Nicolette was already deciding how she would fashion the scarf into a coif. But even the thought of the beautiful scarlet scarf could not dispel her apprehensions concerning the provost's house and the words she had overheard in the mayor's solar. Above all she prayed none of the merchants would betray the plot to the provost. She shuddered to think what her fate would be if Laire de Fontenne was killed.

The sun was near to setting when they approached Gaillard, and a fiery glow outlined the towers and battlements. In the inner ward, Nicolette, preoccupied by her thoughts, dismounted and, passing her reins to a groom, hurried toward the keep.

Laire called to her. "Wait. Walk with me."

In the twilight of the walls it was cold. Nicolette wrapped the thin shawl tightly about her shoulders, and waited shivering. She watched as he dismounted and spoke briefly to Albert. Whatever he said sent the boy running toward the keep. Voices sounded from beyond the courtyard, male voices. She turned her head toward the sounds, and noticed half a dozen horses tethered in the inner ward. When she turned back, Laire was standing beside her.

As they walked toward the keep, she said, "We should not enter the hall together. The others do not like it."

"What do they not like?"

"The attention you give to me, they whisper about it behind my back."

"What is it they say?"

She looked up swiftly, frowning with displeasure. "I do not know!" she said in a loud whisper before glancing away.

"Then how can you be sure it is about you?"

"Because I know it is!"

"Do they say you are sharing my bed?"

She blushed, shocked that he had said so, and quickened her pace. She did not know how to oppose him with his handsome smile and smooth, blandishing manner. In another stride it was too late; they were before the hall doors.

Judot met them, flushed with success or wine. "The villeins are here," he exclaimed. Laire, too, had noticed the horses in the inner ward, and now he saw their riders. He recognized the men from the farmsteads—Rigord, who had been the steward to Lachaume and the seigneur before him, his two sons, and three others.

Nicolette fled to the kitchen. Later when she and the others served the meal the conversation of the men swirled around them. All the men were roughly dressed, their faces lined with determination. In their midst, Laire de Fontenne placed a chunk of cheese on the table to signify the provost's house. With bits of bread he surrounded the house and captured it. "When the moon is up," he told the men, "let us give them time to fall asleep."

Judot was flush with wine and joked that it would not be the sleep of the just. When Nicolette sat down beside Laire, she was conscious of Judot's critical eye. He did not like her, but she was more concerned with Laire's words. He was speaking of tonight, not the following day, as he had told the merchants. She glanced at him, her eyes wide with surprise.

But he went on talking, seemingly unaware of her. A moment later, and with the same easy unconcern, he covered her hand with his and, drawing it beneath the table, pressed it to his thigh.

Nicolette was so astonished that she neither protested nor made any attempt to take back her hand. The fact that he had done it before everyone, and not one of them had noticed, made her heart beat faster. There was something terribly exciting about the solid feel of his leg, the warmth of it. She felt weak and light-headed. It was the wine, she told herself, but even then she was thinking of his strong body and wondering how his embrace would feel.

He squeezed her fingers, then released them. "Go and see to the lady prisoner." His eyes said much more. Nicolette blinked and mumbled, "Yes," though when she stood up, her legs felt like water. Mahaut had prepared a platter for the prisoner and kept it near the oven. As she went to retrieve it, she said, "If you wish to remain in the hall, Dore or Josine can carry it up to her."

"No," Nicolette said quickly, "it is my duty. Just as I must sleep with her each night. The king has ordered it and so it must be." She took the platter from the old woman's hands, and as she turned to go, said, "I dare not disobey him."

Mahaut smiled to herself and went back to get a swig of wine.

The rutted lane before the provost's house was deserted. Leaves littered the ground and the cold air smelled of woodsmoke and frost. A low wall surrounded the yard and behind the house was a large stable and garden. A light winked through the shutters of a ground floor room. Laire waited for the men moving through the darkness to take their places. A dog began to bark, close by.

Judot, standing beside Laire, settled his sword belt on his hip. The dog's baying kept up, and a second dog began to howl. Laire moved from the shadows, signaled to Rigord, and began walking toward the house. Judot, cursing the dogs beneath his breath, strode after him.

A shutter opened on the ground floor of the house, and a man appeared outlined against the light. Laire broke into a run. Shouts sounded from behind the house. The man in the window disappeared. Laire and Judot lunged over the wall. Just as they reached the door, someone started to open it, then slammed it shut. From a window above, a woman screamed, "Murder! Murder!"

Scuffling sounds came from within. Laire and Judot butted their shoulders against the door. It moved, then slammed shut, as if it was being braced from the inside. The pair tried again with no more success. One of Rigord's men dashed from around the house. "We got two of them by the stables," he panted. "Where is the provost?"

"Inside!" Laire swore loudly. "Get some men and go in through the back!" The man dashed away.

Laire stepped back and drew his sword as Judot hurled himself against the door once more. Laire grasped his shoulder and motioned him away. Judot took several backward steps, drawing his sword.

"Vernet!" Laire bellowed. "It is ended! Open the door!" Shouts, a series of sharp cracking sounds and the metallic ring of swords sounded from within. The door groaned, sagging on its hinges. A woman began to scream in a high-pitched wail. Laire kicked at the door, and it jolted open.

Inside, the room was convulsed in combat. It was impossible to say how many men hacked and parried in the confines of the chamber. From the chaotic melee, three men sprang toward Laire and Judot. They met with a clash of steel.

Laire found himself fighting two men. They struggled across the floor, stumbling into others with the flash of steel in their eyes and the deafening clangor of battle ringing in their ears. Miraculously they escaped being brained or slashed as they blundered backwards and forwards amid the ongoing combat.

One opponent stumbled over a bench and Laire, gaining a momentary advantage, slammed him against the long trestle table and clubbed him with the hilt of his sword. He spun round to see his second opponent rampaging toward him, and lunged to one side as a blue haze of steel flashed past his face. The man came at him again, slashing from the side. This time Laire was quicker and with a mighty stroke split the man's head from scalp to jaw, and sent him down like a slaughtered beef. Judot's opponent, with his back to the wall and seeing the battle was ended, dropped his sword. Ribbons of blood streamed down his face and his arm was slashed to the bone.

The chamber was an appalling mess. Four of Vernet's men lay on the floor in wallows of blood, dead or dying. Laire took a hasty accounting of his men as Vernet's wife groped across the wreckage of the room to her husband, screaming hysterically. From the floor above there was the sound of children wailing and the piercing squall of an infant.

Under Laire's direction, some semblance of order was restored. Additional lamps were lit, and the children were reunited with their mother. Laire had intended to try the dishonest provost before the people of Andelys, but after he discovered Pons Vernet was a kinsman of Simon Quarle, he reconsidered.

Thirteen

Several times during the night Nicolette awakened, believing she heard horses in the inner court. She leapt up, wrapped herself in the blanket and anxiously pushed aside the moldering tapestry that blocked the window opening. But there was nothing to be seen, only the swirling blackness and the empty courtyard. Eventually she fell asleep, a fitful restless sleep.

She had no notion of how long she slept, thought it was yet dark when she awakened. Deciding it was futile to lie there staring at the walls, she rose from the mattress and hurriedly dressed. Without benefit of a mirror, she arranged her new scarf as a coif. It was a joy to be free of the wimple. The linen had been harsh, strict as a reprimand, whereas the silk was soft as a whispered word, a kiss. She smiled to herself, thinking she was silly to imagine such things. She wound the ends of the scarf beneath her chin, wrapped it about her throat and secured it at the back of her head, cleverly concealing the little knot. She was so weary of covering her head. It seemed her hair would never attain its former length. At first her dark brown,

PRISONER OF MY HEART

almost black, curls had grown quickly. But when the unruly crop had lengthened nearly enough to twine about a finger, it seemed to grow not a whit longer and she feared, despondently, that it would remain so forever.

She mourned the loss of her hair, perhaps even more than the loss of her freedom . . . for she had never truly been free. As a princess she had been watched over constantly, censored, and reminded of her duties. Only in her imprisonment had she truly known freedom, and now she feared the loss of it. Fumbling in the darkness she lit a candle from the embers in the brazier and, as she left the room, locked the door behind her.

At the foot of the spiraled stairs, she noticed the door to the solar standing open. She was certain the door had been closed when she passed it the evening before.

He has returned, she thought, much relieved. From the door arch she could see the hearth plainly. A low fire burned in the grate and the white dog was stretched out in the glow of the fire's warmth. The dog, dubbed Barbe for its whiskered muzzle, raised its head and gazed at her. Its tail thumped the floor several times, though it made no move to rise and presently laid its head down again. Beneath a tapestry, whose subject was the resurrection, Nicolette saw Laire de Fontenne's cloak, sword, and belt lying atop a chest. She recognized his belongings and was much comforted by the sight of them.

She stood there a moment, immobilized, then

nudged forward, seized by a sort of absurd anxiety, knowing that she would not be satisfied until she saw him, living, breathing, unharmed. Step by silent step she entered the chamber, for only then could she see the huge ancient bed and his half-nude form sprawled facedown amid the rumpled bedclothes.

The chamber was lit only by the flickering gleam of the fire and the mellow glow of the candle she clutched. She edged closer. Suddenly something banged against her legs, nearly unbalancing her. It was the dog, wagging its tail in greeting.

"Shush! Barbe!" she whispered, reaching out a calming hand. But the dog continued to prance and twist its large body, and its thick nails drummed against the wooden planks like hammer strokes.

On the bed Laire de Fontenne stirred, shifting his shoulders, and rolled onto his back, suspended in that uncertain state between sleep and wakefulness.

The dog's tail thumped against the bed's frame and though Nicolette tried to pull the animal away, it managed to nuzzle his hand. He stirred again, vaguely aware of the dog's presence, and gruffly mumbled, "Down Barbe, lie down." But despite Nicolette's best efforts Barbe lunged up and planted an icy nose against his bare chest.

Laire de Fontenne opened his eyes, regarding her through two blue slits. A smile lifted the corners of his lips and he said, "I am dreaming I see an angel."

Nicolette blushed at his foolishness and pulled

the dog from the bed. "No," she said, "no, you do not." She could not keep from smiling. "You are a worse flatterer than Monseigneur Charles, the king's fat brother. I think it must have been you who sold him the angel's feather."

He laughed. "Who told you that tale?"

"You did. You also told me what a charming woman Madame Cacchot was."

"Did I?" he chuckled, wondering what else he had unburdened himself of that night.

She smiled at him again, half innocent, half knowing. "All the same I am thankful you have returned. Was there blood shed in Andelys?"

"Some." He raised himself on one elbow and ran a hand through his tousled hair. "You have not heard?"

"No, I have only come down from the tower. It is not yet morning." Confounded by the sight of his naked chest, she bent to stroke the dog's back. "Was anyone killed?" she asked.

"Not of Gaillard. Rigord's eldest son was injured, but he will recover."

"What of the provost?"

"He is here," Laire said, lying back in the pillows and stretching. "Enjoying your dungeon."

Nicolette was glad. She walked to a small table and set down the candle. When she turned back the dog was sitting by the bed scratching a flea. "What will you do with him, hang him?"

"It is what he deserves. But then I could not ransom him."

"To Quarle?" she asked. "Why would he pay ransom for a provost? One who has failed him?"

"Pons Vernet is his brother-in-law."

"Truly?" Nicolette's eyes rounded. "Was his wife in Andelys, in the house?"

"His wife and three of his children."

"You did not harm them?"

"No. I sent them back to Quarle, with my ransom demand."

"And Vernet's men?"

"Dead, save for two. I sent them with the woman and her children."

"Then you have behaved very honorably."

"I doubt Simon Quarle will agree."

"Who will be provost, Judot?"

He smiled at her. "Do you find fault with that?"

Nicolette gave a little laugh. "He did not approve of me."

"Only because you are a female. Go and put a log on the grate. It is cold in here."

Nicolette went and dropped a log onto the embers, then another. A shower of sparks danced up, winking and glittering. She took up the iron stoker and poked at the logs, asking, "Do you mind that I am a female?"

Across the room the white dog leapt upon the bed. "Actually, I prefer it," he called out, playfully wrestling with the dog for a moment before throwing back the covers and escaping the animal's affectionate assault. He grabbed his hosen from atop the chest beside the bed. "I have something to show you," he said enthusiastically.

Nicolette leaned the heavy fire stoker against the wall, and turned round, brushing the back of her skirt self-consciously. When she raised her eyes she saw only an expanse of pink skin, the broad shoulders, his narrow hips and muscular buttocks as he hiked into his hosen. She whirled about and stared into the fire. He was splendid looking, lean and muscular, but it was all so hilarious, she could not keep herself from giggling.

"What?" he asked and, guessing, laughed out loud as he turned to tie up the front of his hosen.

Nicolette gave a little toss of her head and faced him. Laughter bubbled up in her throat and burst from between her lips. She could not stop it. And he, too, unable to resist it, took up laughing again even harder than before. The dog, bewildered, went from one to the other, wagging its tail.

The more she tried not to laugh, the worse it became and her giggles slipped out in little jerking cries. "Have . . . you . . . anything . . . else . . . to show . . . me?" she stammered.

Finally when Laire could speak, he said, weakly, "Help me find my boots, damnit."

After he had struggled into his boots, pulled a woolen shirt across his shoulders, and they could once more look each other in the face without laughing, he took the candle she had brought and placed it in a lantern. "Set Barbe out and lock the door."

She did as he instructed. He was fully dressed and it hardly seemed likely he meant her any harm. In fact the thought never crossed her mind as she barred the solar door. When she went back to him, she noticed he had thrown aside one of the larger tapestries, exposing the curious little door she had seen that first day. She glanced at him, her eyes bright and inquisitive. "Was this what you wanted to show me?"

He sent her a quick grin. "It was my intent, yes. Wait until I reach for your hand." Nicolette watched him duck beneath the low lintel, then followed, cautious as a cat.

Beyond the little door was utter blackness, darker than anything Nicolette could have imagined. Gripping his hand, she stepped out into nothingness, or so it seemed for one terrible instant. In reality the stout wooden plank beneath her feet abutted a flight of stone steps. She clung to his arm, gazing into the empty space between the square-framed interior and cylindrical keep walls. In the weak light she saw stairs curl away upwards into the black. "To the tower room," he advised. "You did not find the door?"

Nicolette looked at him with large, dramatic eyes. She did not believe him.

"It is behind the tapestry of St. John."

She would have questioned him, but he drew her into the void. Steep narrow steps descended into nothingness beyond the lantern's feeble light. Nicolette looked at him owlishly, the pale oval of her face made round by the saffron glow of the lantern. "Where do they lead?"

"To a vaulted chamber beneath the keep," he answered, "but that is only the beginning."

Nicolette felt her way, her body tingling with uncertainty. To her one side was the great timber frame of the keep's chambers, to the other the interior of the stone tower. The steps, like the inside of the wall, were rough and treacherously uneven. At each point where the massive frame came square, the stairs narrowed, so that it was necessary to squeeze past the ancient timbers, then widened again.

As they descended in the yellow arc of light, Laire revealed that the old cleric Aymer had told him of the passageway's existence. "Lachaume believed it went no further than the vaulted crypt. You will see why." He led on, glancing back every few steps to reassure her.

At the foot of the keep, the stairs plunged into a dismal hole, not unlike an animal's burrow. Almost at once they were met by a fetid breath of dankness and decay. The stairs ended abruptly in a small vaulted chamber, not unlike the dungeon in which Nicolette had been imprisoned. Heaps of rubble, rocks and mounds of clay ground littered the chamber.

Laire led toward one mountain of debris, and motioning for her to follow pointed to a hole large enough for a thin person to squeeze through. "This is what Albert and I cleared away," Laire disclosed. It appeared unimpressive, even to him, yet it had taken him and Albert several hours hard work each day for nearly a week to clear an entrance. "There is another tunnel over there," he said, pointing to the opposite wall of the chamber. "Aymer believes it may lead to the inner courtyard. When the walls were sapped during a siege, a section of it collapsed, just as the entrance of this one did."

Nicolette eyed her surroundings with a growing sense of uneasiness. There was something almost evil about the place with its pitted walls and rank-smelling mounds of earth. He seemed unaware of it, she noticed. He was far too engrossed in telling her how the fortress had been built by Richard Couer de Lion and fashioned after the castles of the east. "Why did you bring me here?" she asked, interrupting him.

He looked at her as if she were stupid, a little annoyed that she did not trust him or even appreciate the scale of such a work, the ingenuity of the ancient builders. "So that you would know a way to reach the river. You may have need of such knowledge one day."

He crouched down, angling his shoulders, then disappeared into the hole, pulling his long legs in after him. After a moment, he reached back for the lantern and called to her. Against her every instinct, Nicolette scrambled over the rock strewn mound of black earth and snaked through the ragged opening.

Here the tunnel was closed in with a forest of supports and beams, and in places dampness seeped through the walls, mirror bright where it puddled on the slanting floor of the earthen gallery. They walked for what seemed a very long distance, until finally Laire halted. "We are coming to the steps. They are steep, so you will have to be sure-footed." Despite the warning, when she saw the steps, she had to be coaxed forward. They were of stone and earth, in places dangerously eroded, and plunged almost vertically downward, haphazardly, like the footsteps of a giant.

They proceeded down single file, until a strange gusty sound, like the wind rushing past, reached their ears. A sudden draft touched the candle flame inside the lantern, causing it to gutter and dim. The cold stream of air smelled of water, meadows, and sky. As they made their way toward it they could see the starlit night beyond. From a narrow opening cut into a fissure of the chalk cliff they exited onto a rocky outcropping above the river.

The scene was fathomlessly silent, the starry night, the ragged expanse of woods stretching out below, and the lusterless black waters of the river. Nicolette looked back in wonder, raising her eyes to the ghostly sweep of chalk cliff and the massive fortress perched at its crest. And she thought how differently things might have been for her if fate had not united them.

In the darkness, she said, "You have been a friend to me. Believe that I would tell you the truth about your comrades. If they were lovers to Joan or Blanche, I swear to you I did not know of it. Gautier and Pierre were often in the gardens, but so were many other young men. I have thought much about the game of catchers and seekers in the maze that day, and of Joan's and Blanche's rings, for it was the rings which damned them. I swear they were not gifts of affection as the inquisitor suggested. I remember well that it was a musician who declared the rings should be the prize. I had never seen him before in the gardens, nor in the palace. It is the truth, I swear to you."

At that moment he would have believed anything she told him. And it occurred to him that he would die if he could not have her—and that was the plain truth. He suspected she wanted him just as eagerly, for he seldom misread the look in a woman's eyes. And who would care? Had they not already been punished? "Soon," he said to her, "the nights will be too cold in the tower room. Come and sleep in the solar." It was not what he had intended to say, but the message behind the words was too powerful to shade with indifference. And now he waited.

For a shocked moment Nicolette did not respond. She had known all along the price he would ask. What stunned her most was the realization that she truly desired him. "Must I share your bed?"

Her sudden bluntness embarrassed him. He glanced away to where a storm of light was gathering on the horizon. "Only if you wish it. I will not force you."

She sent him a teasing, provocative look. "Had I been locked away, who would you have chosen? Dore? Josine?"

He smiled, defensively. Plump little Dore, he hadn't even considered it. Definitely not Josine, who was lank and colorless as a washed-out rag. "Do you suppose that is all I have on my mind?"

"You are no different than other men."

PRISONER OF MY HEART 211

"That is a heartless thing to say. Particularly after you've seen me without benefit of my clothing." He was playing with her now, for there was a smile on his lips and no hint of malice in his voice. And when he said, "Come here and watch the sun rise," she went to stand beside him. Below, the landscape, the hills, the river were taking on a distinctness, the solidness of day.

He dropped an arm round her and, drawing her against his body, set his gaze on the distant hills. "There, do you see the first glow? It is beginning." Moments passed in silence. Nicolette watched mutely as spears of light fell across the hilltops. The warmth of his body and the weight of his hand resting lightly on her hip seemed to inflame her senses. Incredible thoughts filled her mind. She felt burning hot.

Above the river, the hills seemed to catch fire. The sky was changing minute by minute. All night he had thought of her, thought of everything that might happen. His eyes fell to the black velvet of her lashes, the pretty face, her skin which was the color of cream and roses. "What are you thinking?" he asked.

"Nothing."

"Tell me."

How could she say what she felt? In what way could she tell him? She did not understand it herself, the breathless longing, the empty ache of need. And the fear that at the last moment, she would experience the same creeping disgust, the revulsion, she had felt with Louis. She could still hear Joan's laughing words when she had told her. Perhaps it was true, perhaps there was something wrong with her, just as Joan had said. Sunlight spilled over the distant hilltops like an unpent dam. "Only that I am afraid."

"Not of me? I would never harm you."

She shook her head, allowing him to take her in his arms so that she was facing him.

"Then what?" he asked gently, smiling down at her in the half-light.

Her eyes filled with tears. "You do not know me . . ."

His answer was to bring his mouth down on hers. He had intended only to reassure her. But she slid her arms about his neck and clung to him, pressing her hips against his building erection. A surge of passion jolted through his body and the memory of what he had intended to say was lost, carried away by the same irresistible force that sent his hands to stroke her hips, cup her firm behind, and lock her against him. He could not hold her close enough.

The fierceness of his grasp startled her, though she did not attempt to break away. She had never known such pleasurable sensations, such excitement. On their wedding night Louis had come, unwilling, to do his duty, and climbed upon the bed in a drunken stupor to fumble over her. There had been no embraces, no tenderness. So that now she was bewitched by the wild pulsing thrills that tingled her breasts and set up a strange throbbing in her groin. Only when his tongue stole between her parted lips to invade her mouth did a soft cry gather in her throat and the odd constrained excitement she felt turn to fear. The thought tumbled in her mind that she must stop, stop now or it would be too late. There would be no turning back and nothing would ever be the same again. Suddenly panicked, she wrenched her mouth away and, unlocking her arms from around his neck, shoved against him.

He released her, slowly, his hands caressing her. He was trembling and his breath came whistling between his teeth in warm gusts. The shimmering light touched their faces. For a long moment they remained silent, staring at one another with dazed eyes and parted lips. A wave of sunlight broke over them, glittering and touching the air with enchantment. When he finally spoke his voice was scarcely audible. "You are too tempting." He touched her face. "We should start back, it is a long climb."

Nicolette nodded in mute agreement. The nudge of fear she had felt in his arms had now given way to a vague restlessness that both confused and tormented her. As they returned through the blackness of the passages she knew in some corner of her mind that it was already too late. She would go to him. It had been inevitable, from the first. Even before they reached the solar, they heard someone knocking persistently at the chamber door. The noise sounded far down the unseen passageway. It was Albert, his reddish hair standing on end, and breathless from running.

"He is here!" the boy gasped, "Simon Quarle

and thirty villeins! He is before the outer gate hurling curses and demanding the release of his kinsman! He is threatening to lay siege to us!"

Laire secured the small door and dropped the tapestry into place. The three set off at a brisk pace, down through the hall and out into the forecourt. By the time they reached the outer ward, the walls were lined with spectators.

Laire de Fontenne took the watch steps at a run, by twos and threes, Albert right behind him. Nicolette, holding up her heavy skirts to keep from tripping, lagged last. A crowd had gathered atop the wall. For the most part they were the peasants and men at arms from the outer ward. Nicolette spied the silent white faces of Dore, Josine, and the cook and squeezed in among them.

The sight of so many mail-clad horsemen sent a shudder of fear through Nicolette, particularly when she recognized the voice of their leader as the one she had heard in the stable. Astride his stomping horse, Simon Quarle was enough to strike terror in the heart of the bravest man. Beneath the helmet his face glowed with rage and his flat nose with its flaring nostrils lent his features a singularly hideous expression, like the snarling muzzle of some wild animal.

Atop the wall a breeze buffeted the faces of the onlookers and the air was cold despite the bright sunshine. Peasants leaned over the wall, men at arms craned their necks.

"What will happen?" Nicolette overheard one woman ask another. She, herself, understood all too well, and the shouted exchange only further terrified her.

She murmured a silent prayer, convinced that Laire de Fontenne was no match for the powerful adversary on the blood red horse. But when she looked at him, she was shocked by his appearance. His lively blue eyes had taken on the hard sheen of a steel buckler, his jaw jutted out at an obstinate angle, and his generous smile had twisted into something quite ugly. She hardly knew him.

Startled by the revelation, she looked back to the menacing form of Simon Quarle. With each volley of words, her eyes leapt from one to the other. Not a blow had been struck but the threat of violence was as unpleasantly real as the rattle of the horsemen's weapons.

Simon Quarle cursed and raised his mail-clad fist. "The time for talking is past! Release Pons Vernet!"

"Gladly," Laire responded, "for fifteen hundred livres!"

Quarle reined in his large stallion. "You are a thief and the son of a sow!"

"Surely Vernet is worth fifteen hundred livres, if only to your sister!"

"You have no right to hold my kinsman prisoner!" Quarle bellowed, swearing another obscene oath.

"You had no right to appoint him provost and even less to make merry with the king's taxes!"

"Vernet was chosen by the citizens of Andelys!"

"Because they feared your reprisals!"

"Bah!" Quarle spat. "They are a pack of pigs! Always squealing that they have been wronged! A year from now they will denounce you, too! I want nothing more to do with them. Release my kinsman and I will leave Andelys in peace!"

Laire stubbornly restated his demand. "Fifteen hundred livres!"

"Do you think I will pay fifteen hundred livres for a dolt, a niente!" Quarle railed. "He is not worth a single obol!"

"Then the world is better served if I hang him for his crimes!"

Quarle grimaced with rage. His horse stretched out its head and shook. "Five hundred livres!" he offered.

"I could skin him and sell his hide for a better price!" Laire replied with a note of mockery in his voice.

"Seven hundred then, and only because he is my sister's husband!"

"One thousand livres and your word before God that you will leave Andelys in peace!"

Beneath the helmet Quarle's face darkened to crimson. "You are a piss ant!" he squalled. "Do you see what is before you? I can muster five times this many villeins! Your walls will not save you, popinjay!"

"Then why do you trouble yourself to bargain?"

Quarle sputtered and cursed. "Eight hundred! You are more a pig than Lachaume. One day I will hang you from your own watchtower!"

"Nine hundred and your word," Laire called out in a loud, seemingly unruffled, voice.

There was a terrible silence. The brutal mouth beneath the helmet slammed shut, the jaws clenched. For a moment it seemed he might explode. "Agreed!" he conceded. "The bridge at Andelys, tomorrow at nones!"

"So you might ambush me," Laire muttered and, raising his voice to carry down the wall, said, "No! Here, and do not keep me waiting or I will hang him!"

A cheer went up all along the wall. Simon Quarle wheeled his huge horse around and with a string of oaths led his horsemen away at a fast trot.

Nicolette loitered nearby as the onlookers deserted the wall. She hoped to have a word with Laire, but a group of peasant men from the outer ward crowded around him, hoping to be taken on as men at arms, or be chosen as guards.

Josine tugged at Nicolette's arm, and Dore called, "Are you coming with us?" Nicolette balked, motioning for them to go on without her. But when she saw Laire, with Albert at his side, stride off with the group toward the barracks, she decided it was useless to wait and hurried after the others.

Neither did she have an opportunity to speak to him later in the hall. One by one they came, peasants, peddlers, and merchants from Andelys, all seeking something from the new seigneur. They brought with them their complaints of a neighbor infringing on a wood lot or garden, the theft of a cow, a sheep, or a pig. Peddlers came to complain of being robbed and merchants brought their feuds before the seigneur, shouting at one another and pointing accusing fingers.

Nicolette noticed one of the petitioners sported a blackened eye and a lump on his jaw. Dore whispered to her that it was the miller, and with a giggle, confided, "He has loudly threatened to kill our cook." Nicolette sneaked a second look at the infamous miller. He was a wiry little man with a pointed face, and she did not think their cook, who was twice his size and round as a tun of wine, had anything to fear.

Late in the day an errant pig from the outer ward was sighted in the kitchen garden, greedily rooting for turnips. Nicolette, Dore, and two household boys chased the squealing beast until they were breathless. As they herded it into the outer ward, they noticed a group of riders cantering toward the drawbridge, and dogs running before them.

"Look!" Dore cried, "It is Judot. Where do you suppose they are going?" Nicolette stared after the horsemen. She had no idea, but Laire was with him, as was Albert, Rigord, and the half dozen young men from the farmsteads who had come to be trained as soldiers.

Hours passed, the meal was prepared, but they did not return. Several times Nicolette went out into the kitchen garth to sight along the hill, but there was nothing to see, only the greying expanse, the empty road, and a heavy sky hung black with clouds. It would soon be dark, Nicolette thought uneasily, and it was growing colder. She returned to the kitchen where Mahaut was sitting in her usual corner, silently sewing, as if everything was just as it should be.

Dore and Josine were scrubbing pots and chattering nonsense and the cook was slouched with his hip resting on the table, gnawing on a roasted chicken leg.

It troubled Nicolette that Laire had left without a word. Angered her, perhaps, that he had left her to deal with the uncertainty, and the thought of the former provost locked in the dungeon.

The sight of Simon Quarle was still fresh in her mind and her worst fear was that he would attempt to free his kinsman. Nicolette mentioned her fears to Aymer as he sat opposite Mahaut at the kitchen table devouring his platter of food. For one his age, he had an immense appetite.

"No, no, no," Aymer assured her in his odd halting way. "Now that there are guards on the walls, Gaillard could resist an army. Indeed, demoiselle," he said, stuffing his mouth, "it has in the past resisted the armies of kings. Simon Quarle is nothing," the old cleric chuckled scornfully, "Simon Quarle is like a flea to an ox, he is no match for Gaillard's walls. No match at all." Nicolette prayed it was so, though it did little to ease her mind.

A short time later, the sound of voices in the garth sent Nicolette to her feet, but it was only Marcel the stableman and two of his boys with pails to collect their suppers. Nicolette questioned them closely as the cook filled their pails. But they only shrugged and shook their heads stupidly. On his way out the door, the stableman said, "They may have gone to Andelys."

The time dragged past and twice more Nicolette went out in the rain to search the distance. In the darkness there was nothing to see but the silhouette of the hill, black against the sky. To ease her mind she spent the evening helping the women to repair clothing in the kitchen.

"Lachaume and his wife were like this," Mahaut winked and rubbed her thumb and two fingers together to indicate their stinginess. "They would not give an obol for new cloth. What did they care if their servants went about in rags. We, none of us, have had new clothing in four years."

"Five years," Josine amended. "It was before old de Gantry died. He was the lord before Lachaume," she explained with a wan smile.

Mahaut nodded, adding, "He was a big man, fatter than our cook, and taller, too. A devil with the girls, but he was generous that one."

Dore laughed unexpectedly. "There was an old woman in the village who sold love philtres, perhaps she still does. At any rate she convinced the old seigneur that her fine powder could make him thick again."

Nicolette looked up from her needlework, bewildered by the word. "Thick?" she questioned.

Everyone laughed roundly, and Dore, making a lewd stroking gesture with her hand, giggled, "Can't you guess?"

When its meaning dawned on her, Nicolette

laughed too. She was curious now, because Louis had been afflicted in much the same way, and pressed Dore to continue.

"Well, the old woman told de Gantry he must mix the magic powders with honey. But she cautioned him that for the powders to be magical, he must have a young girl rub it on his terse." Dore's narrative elicited a chorus of giggles.

But Nicolette only smiled politely. She felt she had missed something. "Well, did the powders truly work?"

"Oh yes," Dore said, and burst out laughing.

Listening to the tales of the serving women harkened Nicolette back to the days of her childhood. She had delighted in eavesdropping on the tales told by the serving girls and her nursemaid, Ozanne. Though Nicolette and her siblings had been coddled and carefully tended, they had been exposed to the same superstitions as the peasants' offspring, for the serving women who saw to their every need were no more than peasants themselves.

Ozanne had among her repertoire a virtual litany of practical charms. She knew, for instance, a way to rid oneself of warts, by touching each wart with as many little stones as one had warts, then carefully wrapping the tiny stones in an ivy leaf and tossing it into a stream.

She knew also a sure method to capture the heart of a young man. It was simply to steal a feather from a black hen and wear it near your breast for seven days. Then dip it in a cup of wine, being certain you are not seen of course, and give the wine to the young man to drink.

Or if you wished to punish someone for a hurt they had caused you, you had only to cut a hazel branch, name your enemy, and lash the air with the branch. No matter where the person was, he would feel the sting. As a child it had been Nicolette's favorite way of avenging herself. She would shout and thrash and lash the air until she was exhausted and laughing, and no longer feeling spiteful.

The women continued to chatter until the light from the cresset grew dim, and old Mahaut reminded them that oil was too precious to waste over gossip. Nicolette agreed. In any case she had postponed taking the lady prisoner's food to her as long as she dared. After collecting a platter of food, Nicolette climbed the stairs with the others, then, taking the lantern, went on alone to the third level.

She paused a moment at the door to the solar, plagued by a welter of fears. An everchanging and frightening kaleidoscope of scenarios flashed through her mind. The worst was that Simon Quarle had killed Laire de Fontenne just as he had threatened. Equally terrifying was the thought that Laire would return, unharmed, to make love to her, and at the last moment she would panic and reject him. She was certain he would not come to her again and there would be nothing but bitterness between them. The thought haunted her, for she was truly fond of him.

Inside the solar, she set the platter on a long

bench at the foot of the bed. One of the household boys had set a fire in the hearth earlier in the evening, and little more than glowing embers remained. She added several logs and stood before the hearth watching little orange flames spring from the coals to lick the logs.

The bed appealed to her as much as the warmth of the fire, and she plopped down on the feather mattress. It was gloriously soft, not at all like the spiky straw mattress on the floor of the tower room. She looked up at the bed's trappings and an image of Louis, swaggering and naked, intruded on her thoughts.

Distressed by the memories, she pulled herself from the soft caress of the down mattress and walked about the sparsely furnished chamber, taking inventory of all she saw. Laire de Fontenne had few belongings, several articles of clothing and a knife with an intricate silver haft that she recognized at once as the knife the assassin had dropped when he fled the abbey.

Carrying the lantern with her, she wandered into the small chamber off the solar. On the table she found writing materials, quills, ink, and greek paper, so called because it was made of cotton and flax and was feather light, not at all durable. She ran her fingers over the paper. The feel of it pleased her, the texture and the rustling sound. The soft fluttery crinkle ushered back a memory of a night of torchlit celebration in the palace and of a confused little squire who slipped a note into her hand.

Surely a mistake, though there were no identifying names, neither the one for whom the missive was intended, nor a signature. In flowing script it read, "My adored one; For each moment of our separation I have suffered the torments of hell. My soul burns for your kisses and I am mad with desire for you. I cannot live another moment without your caress."

There was more, but she pushed it from her thoughts, recalling how she had read it twice over before gazing about the hall in confusion. Suddenly Joan appeared, in a flush of temper, two red dots high on her cheeks, and pried the note from her hand. "What foolishness," she laughed and, glancing at the note, made a joke of it. She even pretended to toss it away, but later Nicolette saw her tuck the note into the tiny pearl sewn purse she wore suspended from her jeweled girdle.

The recollection, total and sudden as a lightning strike, stunned Nicolette. Was it so plain as that? Had it happened before her very eyes? she wondered. And had she, out of innocence, or the misery of her own unhappiness, ignored it?

She wandered back into the solar, unable to stem the tide of memories, of the fetes in the gardens and Joan's endless games of courtly love. Even so she could not bring herself to condemn Joan and Blanche. If they had deceived their husbands she knew nothing of it. She had no knowledge of their lovers, and it was possible that the missive was naught but another of Joan's elaborate games.

Both Joan and Blanche had spoken to her of

courtly love. They had praised it in glowing terms as a love of the spirit, of denial, one untouched by carnal reality. But Nicolette, as childish and naive as she had been, had suspected otherwise. She was thankful now that she had chosen not to become involved. She had only to consider her own desires toward Laire de Fontenne to realize how easily intimate imaginings might lead to stark reality.

She felt shamed by her own admission, and twice she decided that she should go to her room in the tower, but she went only as far as the solar's door. Defeated, she returned to the bench by the hearth. Her dignity demanded that he not find her in his bed, and so she remained on the hard oaken bench, where, finally, drugged by the warmth of the fire, she lay down amid the pillows and fell asleep.

Fourteen

Voices, garbled and distant, woke Nicolette. She did not realize how wickedly uncomfortable the low wooden bench was until she rose stiffly to her feet. For a moment all was silent, and she thought she had dreamt the sounds. But, no, she heard them again and much closer. She dashed to the door and flung it open. Huge and white, Barbe brushed past her skirts, wagging his tail in greeting, scenting the air with the unmistakable odor of wet fur.

A haze of light glowed above the curl of stone steps, rising like a fog, growing larger and brighter until it revealed Laire de Fontenne with a lantern in his hand, followed by two household boys carrying pails. The sight of the bizarre procession swept the remainder of the cobwebs from her groggy brain, though it did nothing to clear away her confusion. She simply stared dumbly as he directed the two boys to set the pails before the hearth.

Water sloshed and slopped, splashing onto the scarred wooden planking, and the boys, whose round faces appeared red in the fire light, smiled at one another, exchanging glances. When they had gone, Nicolette turned on Laire and whispered, hotly, "They will tell everyone."

He smiled, and his gaze made her blush. "It is what they all believe anyway." Unconcerned, he took up the fire iron and swiveled the blackened cauldron outward on its armature. He emptied a pail of cold water into the hot iron pot, raising a cloud of noisy steam, and added several logs to the fire before swinging the cauldron back over the flames.

He took several steps and slumped down on the bench to remove his boots. "I am wet to my skin," he muttered. A wedge of damp hair fell onto his forehead, and with an impatient gesture he raked it back into place.

His boots were worn out; they no longer kept his feet dry. He thought fleetingly of the pair of boots he had ordered that day in Paris and wondered if they were still waiting for him. He dropped one soggy boot and then the other. When he glanced up, she was staring at him with a peculiar searching look. He smiled at her. "What is it?" he asked.

"I am pleased that you are safe. I should go now."

With an agile swiftness he placed himself between her and the door. "Stay," he coaxed, circling her lightly with his arms. "It is too cold for you in the tower. It is raining, it will be damp. Stay," he repeated, "I will share my hot water with you."

A dozen words of protest were poised on her tongue, but before she could speak, he flashed a smile and said, "Here, I have brought you a present." After a fumbling one-handed search of his tunic, he presented her with his closed fist.

As always his manner was charming, but she smiled and turned her head away. "It is only your empty hand," she accused.

He exhaled softly, and dropped his head to hers. "You are a suspicious little puss. Give me your hand."

She could feel that he placed something on her palm, but now he folded her fingers over, so that she could not see what it was.

"Would you give me a kiss for such a fine gift?"

She laughed. "Perhaps, after I have seen it."

"No, you must kiss me first, to show your gratitude."

"What if I do not like your gift?"

"You will be enchanted, I promise you."

She looked at him slyly, ready to smile again. "Is it a feather from an angel's wing?"

He gave a soft laugh and released her hand. "I should never have told you that."

At the sight of the perfumer's vial, her eyes widened with delight. "It is perfume," she exclaimed, holding the little vial of amber-colored liquid to the fire light. Already she could smell the faint tantalizing scent. The little cork was difficult to dislodge, but when it was opened the air bloomed with fragrance—roses, hyacinths, and something more, a dusky sweetness that brought to mind sultry summer nights and moonbeams. "It is lovely," she gushed. "How did you come by it?"

"The merchants of Andelys wish to have my protection on their journey to the Michaelmass Fair in Gisors. Judot and I met with them tonight. A perfumer gave the vial to me as a trinket for my lady."

His words made her heart quicken, but the reality of their situation soon sobered her. "You must not call me your lady. Someone may guess."

"What will they guess? That I have lost my senses over a serving girl?" His fingers toyed with the silken knot of her coif. "I do not think anyone will trouble their thoughts over it."

Carefully she replaced the little cork and tucked the vial into the pocket of her skirts. "If we are discovered, you would be killed for your deceit. I could not bear for you to die that way . . . or at all . . . not for my sake." The scarf was slipped before she realized what he was about. She did not know whether to snatch after the floating blur of color or cover her shorn hair with her hands. She hadn't time to do either, for he caught her wrists and drew her close so that he might lower his head and bring their lips together.

She was too startled to resist and when his tongue slid between her parted lips she responded by locking her arms around his neck and pressing herself to the solidness of his muscular body. His hands moved over her breasts and down to cup the curve of her buttocks to press her to him.

She had no defense against the mindless surge of passion that flared in her abdomen and set up a pulsing heat between her legs. She felt his shaft hard against her belly and, shameless as the serving girl she pretended to be, she lifted her hips, and rubbed against him.

He had to free his mouth to gasp for air. "Take off your clothes," he whispered, embracing her once more and pressing a series of quick kisses down her throat.

The heat of the room made her dizzy. And when he broke away from her, she reached after him, crying, "Where are you going?"

"Our wash water is boiling away," he replied, taking up the fire iron and swiveling the pot outward. He quickly shed his tunic, then his shirt, and with his foot pushed a three-legged stool before the hearth. Wrapping the shirt about his hand, he grasped the pot's handle and hefted it onto the stool. The wadded shirt he shook out and tossed toward the bench.

Nicolette stood beside the bed, paralyzed with indecision. Her passions had cooled sufficiently to permit her some semblance of rational thought. What am I doing? she wondered, falling prey to her old fears. Her hands moved hesitantly over the laces of her kirtle. It was inevitable, she concluded. If she did not give in to him this night, then it would be another. What was the sense in waiting any longer?

Hurriedly, before she had time to change her mind, she unlaced her kirtle, lifted it off over her head and laid it on the long bench at the foot of the bed. As she did, she noticed the platter was empty. She thought of Barbe, and when she looked she saw the dog stretched out asleep on the floor.

His voice called to her from before the hearth. "Look in the chest . . . the one beside the door," he directed. "There should be soap and linen in it." He watched her cross the room. The light loose chemise clung to her, betraying the supple curves, suggesting so much more. After a moment he took up a pail of water and tipped it into the pot. A fog of steam filled the air.

A waft of odd fragrance rose from the interior of the chest. Nicolette found several lengths of linen and a disc of soap. The soap was scented and satiny, the sort she had been accustomed to at court, not at all like the greasy bit of lard soap she had secured from the well house where the laundry was done and with which she washed herself in the tower. There she had only a small bowl of icy water. Nicolette had all but forgotten the luxury of warm water. She came and placed the items on the bench beside his shirt.

Laire added yet another log to the fire. As he rose up something brushed his bare shoulder. He did not realize it was her chemise until he looked up and saw her naked body glimmering in the orange glow of the fire. The sight of her, the thought of her beneath him, set his heart to pounding with a wild motion. He stood up, unfastening the ties of his hosen. He was at once delighted and tortured, so intoxicated by the notion of this perfectly beautiful person being his entirely, that he could hardly struggle from his britches.

Nicolette seemed stunned by the sight of his body. Modesty told her she should avert her eyes, but she simply stared at this hitherto only imagined frontal view of his well-developed physique. Her eager gaze played across his broad shoulders, his muscular arms, and wide chest with its heart-shaped patch of golden brown hair. Almost against her will, her eyes were drawn downward by a faint tracing of fair hair to his hard, flat abdomen and to where his erection bloomed from the crisply curling hair of his groin. The firelight gleamed upon his sinewy muscles, tinting him gold. "You are so pretty," she said to him suddenly, reaching out a pale, cool hand. Her remark, her childlike spontaneity, amused him. And even though he laughed, she could see the words had pleased him.

He took her face gently in his hands and kissed her, almost overcome with joy. He had no harsh words for her, only kisses, caressing hands, and praise. She was infatuated by his manner, the hard muscles of his body and that part of him that jerked up and down to tickle her thigh. She was both bemused and fascinated by the impudent thing. And the knowledge that her hands could excite him as much as he excited her made her bold.

Amid their soft laughter and murmured words they passed the soap between them. With slippery hands they formed a rapid intimacy, discovering all the curves and hollows, all the little secret, concealed places of their bodies.

They soaped themselves from end to end, water splashing upon the floor to puddle beneath their bare feet. She let him lather her curly crop of hair, and rinse it with generous, sloppy handfuls of water. She did the same for him, his hair so coarse and thick she delighted in the feel of it between her fingers.

Laire could not have enough of her. She had made a conquest of him that first day in the forest, exciting and bewitching him. For she was tantalizing, beautiful, and funny. She had become somehow indispensable to him. He could not imagine losing her, he could not live without her. Just as he could not resist planting kisses on her neck as he buffed her dry with the rough linen towel. His little nibbling kisses shivered her, made her hot and cold, and restless with desire. She wriggled, wanting to go and to stay, unable to decide. And when she pleaded with jerking giggles and begged at last for mercy, he rolled her in the towel, swooped her up, and carried her to bed.

The mattress yielded beneath their weight and he pulled her to him. He told her all the things he had said to other women, thinking that, perhaps, after all the words had always been meant for her.

She was warm and rosy from the fire, she smelled of soap and he could not wait to have her. Nicolette went eagerly into his arms, unafraid even when he laid her down and moved atop her.

He began kissing her again, caressing her little round breasts, sucking at her nipples and planting a pattern of light butterfly kisses down her body. Only when his head went between her thighs and his tongue touched her, did she arch with shock, and in a startled voice, plead, "No! No, you must not!"

But he merely closed his hands over the hollows of her hips, and held her fast. "Yes, let me . . . let me kiss you. You are beautiful." His voice was deep and vapory, and his warm breath pushed against the dark, feathery curls.

"No!" she pleaded, moaning softly when he did as he pleased with her. It was like an exquisite torture, an aching, pulsing need that only he could remedy. She reached for him, clutching distractedly at his arms, his shoulders, attempting to draw him to her, driven by some nameless fear that he would leave her thus, longing and discontented. But there was no danger of him abandoning the hunger that had been building inside him for so long.

Mindlessly, without really seeing, she was aware of him poised above her, of his hands stroking the tender insides of her thighs, spreading her legs. She felt his swelling muscles bunch and heard his sharply indrawn breath as he entered her.

A searing, stretching sensation coursed through her. She wanted to cry out. Hush, she told herself. She felt as if she were about to die. And in that same instant, like a stab, he plunged hard into her, sending her body heaving upwards in agony. A sob of pain tore from her lips and, reeling with panic, she tried to pull away, escape the hurt. It was too late, she was pinioned helplessly.

Her silent voice cried out. Stop, she thought. But he would not obey, and with another swift, hard thrust embedded himself in her. She cried out, she could not help herself. Her mewling cries mingled with his quick, ragged breaths.

He held her there, his eyes glazed, struggling to control the escalating spiral of his passion. Then she felt him begin to move inside her, slowly, rhythmically, until the pain was replaced by a tingling excitement, an urgent driving need that carried her along with him.

Instinctively she clasped her legs about him. His thrusts came faster, harder. Suddenly everything was changed. She was not about to die, but was alive with exhilaration, throbbing with pleasure, open to him and ready to be filled with what was coming.

Afterwards, still joined, he leaned forward and touched a kiss to her parted lips, her cheek. "You cannot have been a maiden," he whispered softly to the little curls over her ear.

For a moment she was still as death. Then she slid her slender arms around him. "I am no longer," she confessed without a trace of guilt. Indeed she felt good. She knew now that the fault was not with her. Tonight she had been mated, and the experience was such that she would desire it again. It was as if a door had been opened, and there could be no turning back.

Laire shifted his weight from her, freeing himself. His head was a void and his heart pounded against his ribs. He did not understand. He drew her into his arms. "Tell me," he said.

Her lips brushed his shoulder and the hand that

held her. "There is naught to tell," she shrugged. "It was as I said. Louis found me ugly."

"No man with eyes could find you ugly."

"Yes. It was my darkness, I think. His mistresses are all very fair. One, I am told, his favorite, has hair the color of a Rhine maiden's . . . even in certain private places."

Laire said nothing.

She looked at him full in the face. "He could not abide me!" she said impetuously. "He blamed me for his failure. He could not perform the act with me. He said that I was cold, that I disgusted him." Slowly, painfully, Nicolette told Laire of her wedding night, of her shame and of the fear she had lived with for so long a time. A fear that she was somehow different from other women in her affections.

Laire could scarcely believe what he was hearing. "Your marriage was never consummated? You were never a wife? Why did you keep silent? There was your proof of innocence."

"How long do you think I would have remained thus in Nogaret's charge? From the first, Louis threatened to have me killed if I told. I believe he would have done so, had it not been for the incident of the rings."

She was silent for a moment, deciding. She had shared her innermost fears with no one, until now. Her gaze darted away, then back. She said, "Louis spread rumors at court, that I was cold, strange inside my head, that I did not have the desires of a normal woman. When Joan and Blanche heard the gossip and learned that Louis never came to me, Joan advised me to flirt with courtiers and the king's chevaliers. She said I should have courtly love affairs, so that my senses would be aroused, and in longing for a lover, I would come to desire my husband."

He pressed his lips to her hair. It was still damp, curling about her face. "Did you?" he asked.

Nicolette shook her head, "No," she said in a hushed voice.

"And Joan and Blanche? Did they play at games?"

"Only games, I think. Not what we have done. At least I have no knowledge of it. I know that their husbands came to them. Joan, and even Blanche spoke openly of it. They mocked their husbands." She felt a wetness beneath her and, lifting a pale leg, noticed the linen cloth was spotted. "I am bleeding," she announced with a mingling of emotions. In the days before her wedding a matronly court lady had advised her of what to expect. She recalled how embarrassed she had been to hear such things.

He glanced over, determining it was not serious and gave her waist a squeeze as if to reassure her. "I am told it is not fatal," he teased, taking her into his arms, and shifting her away from the stain. "It is a first for me as well," he said and dropped his head to nuzzle her neck, confiding that he had never had a virgin before, never had a woman who had been his exclusively.

"We are guilty now, aren't we? Guilty of all they—"

He touched his fingers to her lips, silencing her. "Since we have suffered the punishment, it is only just that we should take some pleasure in the sin."

She lowered her eyes, kissing the fingers of his hand. "You may grow tired of me, just as you did of Odette."

"Odette was faithless." He smiled at her, thinking he would take her again. "She was a 'bonne amiee,' a tournament girl."

"You said I reminded you of her?"

"Only that your face resembles hers. I saw in you what she might have been . . . what I once deceived myself that she was. You are real, and what I feel for you, I will never feel for another. Perhaps it is love—it is unreasonable enough."

Tears filled Nicolette's eyes. Had he not confessed to loving her? She took his hand, threading her fingers through his. In the back of her mind was the vague realization that in some strange way, she had always known, from the moment she had first seen him, beaten but defiant before the council, that fate would unite them. She found herself wondering about the other women he must have had, and if he had made love so tenderly to Odette.

His jaw brushed her cheek, stubbled and prickly. He kissed her, his lips moving lightly downward, skimming her throat, her shoulder. She felt his mouth on her breasts, his lips and tongue teasing out her nipples. His fingers stole between her legs to fondle her and she was seized by the same wild and mindless emotions that had swept through her before.

He leaned over her and her body moved to accept the hot, pulsing prod of his entry. Cradled in his arms, Nicolette did not want to think of anything but the fact that he wanted her. She was little aware of his whispered words of love and her own soft cries, only of his rhythmic, probing thrusts. Her body arched, straining against his. Her hands slid over his back, feeling his muscles bunch and flex. As her pleasure built she heaved her hips against him, harder, faster each time he drew back, building her excitement higher and higher until at last she sobbed and shook with fulfillment.

Her response, the spasm of silken contractions, destroyed any hope Laire had of forestalling the oncoming waves of his climax. With a sob of release he felt his seed spurt from him, and groaning with pleasure, he emptied himself in her.

When it was ended they lay together talking quietly. In only a short time, Nicolette's hushed voice stilled and she snuggled against him, her breathing deep and gentle. He shifted full length beneath the blankets, drawing her into the curve of his body. She stirred, but did not wake. She was sleeping soundly as a babe, a picture of innocence. As Laire drifted off to sleep, a single last thought imprinted itself on his mind, and it was that he had never been so contented in all his life.

Morning light winked through the single shuttered window, though perhaps it was the dog's long, low growl that woke Laire. For he was already awake when he heard Albert's voice and the tapping on the door. "A moment," he called, his voice coarse, still thick with sleep. At a glance he saw the fire had died to ash. The room was cold as death. He lay there a moment longer, loath to pull himself from the warm bed and the soft body beside him.

His movement woke Nicolette. She bolted up, wide-eyed with alarm, thinking it was surely late and that it would not take much imagining for the others to guess why both she and the seigneur were still abed.

Bumbling in the half light, Laire found his hosen, though not where he had expected. Groggy and unsteady, he hiked into them. The dog circled his legs, darting back and forth to prance before the door and whine. The room was in complete disorder. The pail he had overturned in his search clattered against another, clothing was strewn everywhere, the pot atop the stool was edged with soap scum and the floor beneath it was puddled with water.

Laire no sooner opened the door than the dog bounded out, past Albert, loping toward the stairs. Albert stepped inside, pretending not to notice the room, nor the fact that someone was in the bed. She had ducked beneath the blankets, but Albert knew perfectly well who it was.

When he spoke his voice betrayed his embarrassment, for it sounded to him high-pitched and stilted, which only further embarrassed him. He struggled to modulate it as he reported, "The foresters have been waiting since before first light, and Rigord is here concerning the peasants, those who fled Lachaume's service and have now returned." In a side-long glance he saw the lump had altered, buried deeper in the covers.

Laire banged open the shutter of the solar's single window and relieved himself. "They expect to be fed, I suppose?"

"Rigord thinks you should take them back, he says they will be needed to work the fields in the spring."

"Does he?" Laire remarked. He found his shirt lying on the floor. He had no idea how it got there. The sleeve was lying in a puddle of water. He jammed his feet into his boots—they were also damp—and went in search of another shirt. "The foresters, have they brought wood?" From a tall chest lined with camphor wood, he took a fresh linen shirt.

"They have come to complain," Albert said, his eyes following him.

Laire whipped the shirt over his shoulders. God deliver him from Norman peasants, he thought, and strode into the antechamber in search of his leather jacque. "I suppose Lachaume owed them as well?" Oddly enough, it was where he had left it, draped over the ancient prei-deiu. He felt warmer at once.

"Four livres, or so they claim. Aymer was arguing the sum when I left. What of Simon Quarle?"

Laire returned to the solar, raking a hand through his hair. "What of him?" He paused angling his face before the polished steel mirror above the washstand, confirming his three-day growth of beard. He took up his brush and made several swipes through his tousled hair.

"It is nearing mid-day," Albert reminded his master. "If he should arrive—"

Laire's jesting remark cut across his words. "If he does not, we shall be forced to go and search for him, so we might pay our creditors." He straightened his shoulders and looked at Albert. But Albert's eyes were on the bed. "Go and serve Rigord some wine. Tell him I will be down in a moment," Laire said to the boy. Albert blinked to attention. He was across the room in three strides and out the door.

Laire went and leaned over the mounded form on the bed, and in a teasing voice, murmured, "Don't you know you cannot escape from me, ma mie?"

"Is he gone?" Nicolette's muffled voice came from the warmth of the bed covers.

"Yes."

Slowly Nicolette emerged from beneath the blankets. She was mortified and now his soft laughter annoyed her, particularly when he nuzzled her throat and kissed her. She turned her face away and pushed against him. "No, do not look at me, I am a sight."

"You are delicious. You smell of bed and love . . . and I would like nothing better than to stay." He ruffled her hair as he stood up. At the door, he paused and said, "Do not forget that you are mine."

Nicolette threw on her shift and, shivering, made use of the chamber pot. She felt tender, bruised, and suddenly bedeviled by thoughts of guilt and sin. She quickly dressed and dashed about straightening the room.

It was with the same determination that she washed the stains from the linen towel he had thrown across the bed prior to their lovemaking, plumped the feather mattress, hung the blankets up to air, gathered up his shirt and the tunic he had worn, sopped the water from the floor, returned the monstrously heavy pot to its rightful place, and emptied the chamber pot in the garderobe. Finally she sat the empty pails before the door, paused a moment to compose herself, sighed deeply, and descended the stairs.

The hall was deserted. It was the same in the kitchen, where pots bubbled unattended and bread was set out to rise. She reasoned everyone had gone to watch the exchange of the captive provost and sprinted into the forecourt. The gates of the inner ward stood open.

In distant glimpses of the outer ward she saw a crowd mingling before the walls. She set out, walking swiftly. The morning was cold and overcast, and the tarry odor of woodsmoke stung her nostrils. A shiver passed over her shoulders, and as she walked she wrapped her arms tightly about herself to ward off the chill.

Nicolette arrived just as the drawbridge was being raised. She caught only a fleeting glimpse of riders on the long flat meadow beyond Gaillard's walls. The ward echoed with the shouts of the onlookers, insults for the most part hurled at Pons

Vernet and his lord, Simon Quarle. Some shouted, "Death to them," "Swine," and other less eloquent phrases. Many of the new arrivals to Gaillard's outer ward were well acquainted with Simon Quarle and his former provost's brutal brand of justice.

Above the clamor of the crowd, dogs barked and children dodged in play. Nicolette threaded her way through the throng, attempting to reach the drawbridge.

As Nicolette pressed her way forward, the crowd opened before her and she saw Laire surrounded by his young men-at-arms, Albert, the cleric, and Rigord. Four of the young men-at-arms carried a small chest bound with ropes between them. She imagined it to be the ransom payment.

Dore, Josine, Mahaut, leaning heavily on Josine's arm, the cook, and others from the household hailed Nicolette. "You are too late," Dore shouted. "Yes," Josine concurred, "You have missed it all." Mahaut wagged her grey head. "No good will come of it. Wolves do not stop eating sheep. The seigneur will rue the day he did not hang that pig Vernet." Turning her sharp little brown eyes on Nicolette, she asked, "Where is your cloak, child?"

"I did not feel the cold at first," she lied. "Was there violence?"

"No, no," they chorused.

"Only words," the cook chimed, strutting along with the group of women like a huge, fat rooster.

"No good will come of it," Mahaut muttered.

"Nonsense, it is all to our advantage," the cook

chided and, with a hearty laugh, remarked, "Now I shall be able to pay that weasel of a miller. I feel so generous, I may pay him half of what he asks."

The group could move no faster than old Mahaut, and they lagged far behind the victorious procession striding toward the keep.

In the hall, the chest was placed on the long table where a smiling Laire de Fontenne counted its contents in the presence of a jubilant crowd. Wages were paid. Aymer, seated beside the young seigneur, duly noted each amount in his account books. The foresters had remained in hopes of just such a development. After a huddled discussion, they settled on a payment of three livres, which included wood for the coming winter.

Eventually, late in the afternoon, the chest was carried up the keep's winding stairs to the seigneur's chamber. Nicolette saw its gleaming contents that night. For all that she was the daughter of a comte, and had been wife to the king's eldest son, she had never seen so large a quantity of gold coin. There was no doubt she had been extravagant, but her debts had always been paid by others, by her parents, and later the king's ministers.

Now she laughed as Laire spilled a handful of gold coins onto the bed where she lay. There would be money for cloth. The household servants would no longer look like beggars, and there would be draperies and trappings, pewter cups, all the luxuries that had been absent from Gaillard. Later as she lay in his arms, she became very serious and said, "We should repair the chapel."

He laughed softly. "If it is to compensate our sin, we would have to build a cathedral."

"Do not jest about such things," she frowned. "No, to thank God for the good fortune he has given us."

He did not say yes or no, merely that they would talk of it later. For his soul did not occupy him half so much as the taste of her lips and the feel of her warm body against his.

Fifteen

For several days the merchants of Andelys shuttled back and forth between the village and the chateau, finalizing their plans for the journey to Gisors.

The kitchen buzzed with talk of Gisors and the fair. Both Dore and Josine had once attended, in the days before Lachaume became lord. They had accompanied old lord de Gantry and his wife, and spoke of the fair in glowing terms. So much so, that Nicolette took it into her head that they must go to Gisors.

Laire in his present state was unlikely to deny her anything. However, there was the matter of the lady prisoner, and Nicolette was expected to carry her food every day. It was a chore which could hardly be left to a household boy. True, Gisors was not a far distance, scarcely twenty leagues, but the merchants' carts and chars would move at a snail's pace. Even if they were to set out before dawn, they would not reach the fair until late in the afternoon. Nicolette, though clearly disheartened, was forced to agree.

On the day before he was to depart for Gisors,

Laire drew Nicolette into Aymer's counting room, for the old cleric was nowhere about. After devouring her with kisses and telling her how desperately he would miss her embraces, he asked, "Does it mean so much to you, this fair at Gisors?"

"No, of course not," she said, though everything about her, her eyes, her voice, her expression, said differently.

"The truth, ma mie?" When he told her that Albert could be trusted to carry food to the lady prisoner, she was ecstatic. She threw her arms around Laire's neck and kissed him, then dashed off to the kitchen to tell Dore and Josine.

In the chill before dawn, the merchants of Andelys gathered in the square before the church. Shouts rang up and down the line of carts, charettes, and pack animals. Men fumbled and cursed the darkness, horses nickered, restlessly shaking their harnesses, and donkeys brayed. At a signal from the new provost, Judot, the procession rumbled past the church.

For the merchants, the Michaelmas fair at Gisors presented an opportunity to offer their goods to a much larger clientele, as well as to purchase raw materials and items they might later sell in Andelys, at a slightly higher price of course.

By pre-arrangement, Laire and his heavily armed troop awaited the jolting black mass of vehicles and riders at the stone bridge. The squeak of wooden wheels, the trundle of hooves, and the babble of voices echoed down the slope at their approach. Snug in their hooded cloaks, Nicolette, Dore, and Josine spoke in excited, penetrating whispers, chattering and giggling as they urged their horses forward to join the parade of carts and chars.

The starlit night gave way to a fair day and the few leaves that still clung to the trees glinted russet and amber in the sunlight. The meadows they passed were strewn with splashes of red and yellow and the world appeared like a glittering page from a breviary. At the farmsteads they passed, peasants came out to stare at them and wave. And where the pastures gave way to woods, several times they spotted deer, shy, graceful creatures who flicked their tails and bounded away. At every turn huge oak trees rose tall and straight, their trunks mottled with grey and green moss.

It was past mid-day when they first glimpsed the spire of Gisors' cathedral and the pointed rooftops of the village rising above the russet hills. Near the village's walls, the meadows were ablaze with gaudy colored pavilions and booths.

Banners fluttered in the sunlight and the sound of music, of drum and flute, danced on the breeze. But as they drew nearer, their noses discerned something less pleasant, the aroma of pigs. Not a pig here and there, but large herds of swine, as well as other less pungent beasts. For there was no cattle market so large as Gisors, and from many parts of Normandy, pigs, sheep, horses, cows, and oxen were brought to Gisors for the best prices.

"That stench is the smell of gold," a merchant

with baggy eyelids informed the young women as they rode beside his char, pinching their noses. "Pigs and apples," he said with a jolly laugh, "That is Normandy's wealth."

Perhaps, Nicolette thought, he was right, for she would not have believed there were so many pigs, not in all of France. She saw, also, a scarlet abundance of apples. They overflowed carts and wicker baskets and their spicy scent came in waves, interspersed with the odor of pig.

While the merchants set about bartering for space and unloading their wares, Laire oversaw the making of the camp. The young men-at-arms were eager to be off to take in the sights. "The taverns and the demoiselles," Judot remarked as he saw the last of them disappear into the crowds.

Nicolette, Dore, and Josine had wasted not a moment, there was too much to see. A vast array of goods spread from the meadow into the village beyond. There was armor and spices, all manner and color of cloth, and leather goods. There were dealers who sold kohl and rouge and cures for all diseases, old women who would read your fortune in the lines of your hand for an obol, jewelry from the east, pewter, crockery, jugs of honey, and barrels of cider. Musicians strolled amid the throngs of people and jongleurs vied for coins with feats of juggling and tumbling.

At booths misted with a blue haze of woodsmoke, it was possible to buy chunks of pork roasted on skewers and sweet fritters filled with apple bits and fried in a great bubbling pot of lard. Exotic sights and scents awaited them at every turn, but above all was the pervasive odor of pigs.

Nothing, however, not even all the swine in Normandy, could dim Nicolette's cheerful mood. She and the two maid servants mingled with the crowds, warming their fingers and their stomachs with apple fritters as they blithely strolled through the market in search of cloth for new garments.

Inside Gisors' walls the winding narrow streets were mobbed with peasants, brethren, townsfolk, and local nobles dressed in brocades and furs and sparkling with jewels, and pigs, pigs, and more pigs. Cries of vendors rose in the brisk air, for despite the sunshine, the breeze was cold and everyone they met had rosy cheeks and a running nose.

A large chateau rose from the midst of the village and frowned down upon the clutter of close set buildings. Everywhere the pointed rooftops of the houses duplicated those of the chateau, lending it the appearance of a mother whose many children clung to her skirts. Nicolette squinted her eyes in the late afternoon sun. Her glance swept upward, admiring the fairylike towers as she walked along.

Josine saw the obstacle first. Her hand shot out and grabbed Nicolette's arm just as Dore gasped a warning, a single startled "O." Several men stepped from an alleyway directly before them carrying a coffin. The three young women stared at the long, black box with startled expressions.

"It is worse than seeing a black cat," Dore exclaimed as Josine simply watched the men maneuver the coffin through the crowded street.

"We should not cross its path," Nicolette said, and hastily made the sign of the cross upon her breast. "If we do not cross its path, it cannot bring us ill fortune."

The detour led them down the alleyway past the house where the coffin had exited. Surely it was the very house, for the door stood open and the sound of weeping carried into the grimy alleyway.

They followed the twisting alleyway to another street. There a merchant who wished them to buy his woolen cloth assured Nicolette that the lady mistress of the chateau bought his cloth with regularity, and that he had heard from certain individuals he dare not name that the lady had several gowns fashioned for herself from his handsome cloth.

Nicolette thought him an oily fraud, and was quick to point out that his price was twice what his neighbors asked. He adamantly argued his cloth was of a finer quality. Nicolette did not agree. Dore and Josine concurred, pointing out that the colors of his woolen cloth were not as vivid as some.

The merchant's replies were well rehearsed, as were his moves, for when it seemed they would desert him for another, he all but dragged them back to his stall. His efforts, though, were wasted and, much to his chagrin, the women purchased their cloth from his smiling competitor.

The trio moved on, their arms loaded down with folded cloth. They browsed along the street of shops, untroubled, unconscious of everything but the seemingly endless variety of tempting goods.

At an open shopfront given over to headdresses, Nicolette gazed longingly at cauls and crispines of gold and silver net, chaplets of silver filigree and ribbons to twine into long luxuriant hair. The sort of hair, she thought sadly, that she had once possessed. Her hair had been her secret pride, dark and shining curls that had never known the touch of shears. They had rudely taken it from her, and with it all the years of her youth, her innocence. All trampled underfoot in the dungeon of the Cite and swept away with her beautiful hair.

She raised her eyes from a chaplet set with tiny coral beads, preparing to step away from the open shopfront, then halted abruptly, her eyes expanding in fright. Threading his way through the mobs of shoppers was Raoul de Conches. Simon Quarle strolled at his side, their heads together as if they were locked in a discussion. Several burly men-at-arms trailed after them.

Nicolette was hollow with dread. Her legs trembled so that she could hardly force them to obey. Without a word, she left Dore and Josine gaping at the headdresses and fluttering ribbons and pressed her way into the midst of the shoppers at the next booth, where jeweled broaches and highly polished buckles were displayed on velvet cloth.

From the shelter of the shopfront, she looked back over her shoulder. Raoul de Conches was still talking, his head down. But Simon Quarle gazed about as he walked, glanced her way, then turned back and said something close to de Conches' blue-tinted jaw.

What a fool she was to look back. She turned away, desperately trying to recall if Simon Quarle would have cause to remember her. She was almost certain he could not have seen her in the stable that day, and it was unlikely he would have noticed her on the wall when he came to bargain the price of his brother-in-law's ransom. Raoul de Conches, on the other hand, would recognize her the moment he saw her face.

She turned back, holding her breath, her eyes frozen on the gleaming buckles displayed on squares of green velvet cloth. A fat matron crowded in at her elbow, pushing her aside. Nicolette stepped quickly backwards to avoid being squashed against the side of the shop front. As she did, she collided with a noble lady, dressed in brocade and wearing a fur-lined cape.

Nicolette murmured an apology and, raising her eyes, nearly swallowed her tongue. It was Adela Cacchot, plump and fair, looking just as she had the night Nicolette had first seen her. "Madame," Nicolette finally managed in an unsteady voice, one that grew surer and rang with politeness. "How wonderful it is to see you again," she said with a slight curtsey, acting out her role, and being careful to keep her face, beneath the hood of her cloak, concealed from the passersby.

Adela Cacchot looked at her in amazement. She was dumbfounded. The sight of the exiled princess left her momentarily speechless. Even so, she did not miss the look of warning in Nicolette's eyes.

With every stride, Raoul de Conches and Simon

Quarle drew nearer. Nicolette focused her eyes on Adela's fair face and with a smile, said, "You appear well, madame. And your children, how are your little ones?"

Adela swiveled her head. She recognized Raoul de Conches. She was certain he would know the princess royal by sight. Although he was lord of Clermont, he spent far more time at the king's court in Paris. Adela set her eyes on Nicolette. "I am very well, thank you," she said, "and yes, my children are doing splendidly."

"My heart is glad, madame," Nicolette replied, sensing Raoul de Conches and his minion, Quarle, closing ground. Quickly Adela stepped before Nicolette. De Conches, Quarle, and the men at arms passed before them and walked on; Nicolette relaxed. Adela took her arm and guided her toward another booth where pewter cups and bowls were displayed. In a swift glance Nicolette saw Dore and Josine still chattering over the headdresses.

Nicolette pressed the cloth one-handed to her breast, and with her other grasped Adela's hand. "I am truly pleased to see you," she said, "that I might thank you once again for your kindness."

Adela gave her an encouraging smile. "You look so frightened. There is no need. I will not betray you, not even to Cacchot," and with a little laugh, she added, "Like all men he can not be trusted to keep a secret." They spoke in undertones as they slowly walked. "You have often been in my thoughts and prayers," Adela said softly. In hushed whispers, Nicolette told her of being locked in Gaillard's dungeon, of the events in Andelys, and of her and Laire's deception. Nicolette, who kept a wary, watchful eye on the passersby, noticed Dore and Josine walking past the booth where the buckles were displayed. To Adela, she said, "I am glad we met today, but I must leave you now. If we are seen together, it would be dangerous for you."

Adela nodded that she understood. "There are many nobles from the king's court here in Gisors, be cautious." Adela noticed her serving women gawking from where they stood in the street, waiting. The crowd flowed past. She must go, she thought, and she murmured to Nicolette, "If I can ever be of help to you, you must not hesitate to ask me."

"I promise," Nicolette responded, watching as Adela joined her serving women. Just then, Dore and Josine came up beside her. "Was she a lady from Paris?" Dore asked. Both she and Josine looked after the young woman in the fur-lined cape. "Yes," Nicolette said, turning her attention to the next booth. "She was very kind to me once."

A blare of trumpets split the bright, cold air and a babble of voices rose up afterwards. "Come!" a bystander urged. "It is the blessing of the swine!" "Yes," another said, "the king's bishop, himself, has come!"

Nicolette raised her eyes toward the square. "Hurry!" Dore and Josine urged. There was little choice but to go, for the crowd propelled them along. Above the milling sea of people and pigs, the clergy gathered on the cathedral steps. Nicolette shielded her eyes from the late afternoon sun. It was just as the peasant had said, for there was the king's bishop, Renoul D'Enbeau.

Nicolette felt suddenly cold. Why should the king's bishop come to Gisors? Certainly he had not come for the sole purpose of blessing pigs and apple trees. Was his final destination Gaillard? she wondered. And had the king sent him to fetch the prisoner back to Paris?

Unnerved, but not yet panicked, Nicolette reasoned she was safe enough amid the crush of people. Until she drew her gaze back across the men assembled beneath the columns of the holy building and her eyes fell upon a squat man garbed in brown velvets and fur, a man with a protruding paunch and spider's legs. It was Gullimae de Nogaret, the crown's inquisitor, the keeper of the seals.

She paled. Pigs squealed above the Latin benediction and incense pots smoked. She shook Dore's arm. "I do not feel well," she said in a choked whisper. "I am returning to our tent."

Josine, watching the ceremony with rapt attention, did not hear. "Wait, we will go with you," Dore said.

"No," Nicolette told her. "Stay and watch, I will be fine." A lie, for her knees were trembling as she made her way from the square.

Earlier that afternoon, Laire and Judot had ridden out to the cattle market which sprawled across the far meadow beyond the walls of Gisors. Laire intended to purchase horses and cattle to replenish Gaillard's stock, but today he was content merely to scout out what was available. If he bought them on the first day of the fair, he would have to feed the animals all week. Better to buy them on the final day. There was also the possibility that the prices might be somewhat lower as the fair drew to a close.

He and Judot walked along, leading their horses. A handsome grey mare caught Laire's eye and he and Judot halted to have a closer look at her. From behind them, a voice boomed, "My God, it is you, de Fontenne!" Laire recognized the voice even before he spun round to see Francois Cacchot bearing down on him, his steward, Gouin, at his side. Cacchot looked a bit taller standing in his boots, though he was still short. A solidly built fellow, a Norman to the roots of his hair, with a thick neck and pink cheeks.

After a jovial greeting, an exchange of pleasantries and introductions, the four men proceeded together in high spirits, talking as they perused the market of horses and other subjects. Cacchot was in search of a suitable mount for himself, and in his own words, "Something huge and rank, with good bone and wind and great courage."

Gouin grinned and shook his head. "He is searching for the devil, so he might put a bit in his mouth and ride him about."

They had not gone another twenty paces, when Cacchot spied the very creature his steward had so aptly described. It was in the form of a large roan stallion, an unruly beast, whom Cacchot admired at first sight.

Suddenly, a distant blast of horns signaled the approach of a large group of riders and charettes. They watched as the procession of nobles came into full view. Grandly attired gentlemen swathed in furs and laden with jewelry led the way. In their wake followed extravagantly gowned ladies who gazed out from upholstered charettes, and a company of soldiers, armed to the teeth, whose mail and weapons glinted in the chill sunlight.

"I had no notion Gisors's pigs drew such noble attendance," Laire remarked.

Gouin's eyes followed the charette and its female cargo. "It has never been the case before."

"There is a north wind blowing this year," Cacchot said with a wry smile. "I have heard rumors that the north Norman barons desire proclamations of freedom for their cities and an end to the maltote tax. It is said that if the king refuses to give in to their demands, they will join forces with the Flemish and oppose him." Cacchot was silent a moment, his eyes searching the group. "I see they have all come," he said. "There on the bald-faced chestnut, that is de Gers, beside him, with the red hat, is d'Urville. Directly behind him on the black horse is de Varentot, and the fat man at de Varentot's right is de Sevry. Though, wait, I do not see de Conches. He is their leader."

"Perhaps he is awaiting them in Gisors?" Judot

remarked, wondering, uneasily, if Simon Quarle was with him.

Gouin lent his voice in agreement. He and Cacchot had arrived only an hour before. As for rumors of the barons' revolt, Gouin added, "The treaty may well come to pass, there is talk of it even in the taverns of Vernon."

"I, too, heard something of the sort at our tavern in Andelys," Judot attested. "I thought it no more than idle talk. A person hears many tales in a tavern."

Laire shifted his gaze back to Cacchot. "If all you say is true, the king may be forced to agree, in the interest of unity."

"I believe it will be so," Cacchot replied, buffing his nose with his sleeve. "But de Conches will never be satisfied with a treaty. He is too ambitious. He has set his teeth for all of Normandy, and de Varentot and de Sevry are one with him in thought and deed. The others are honorable men, but in the end they will be forced to choose."

"And you?" Laire asked. "Have you made your choice?"

Cacchot did not look away. "I would like to see an end to the maltote, certainly. It is a crippling tax, but I will not join de Conches."

Laire believed him. "Quarle will oppose you."

"I have ever suspected that he was at the root of our 'peasant' uprisings," he imparted. "Though I had no proof of it until last week." And he related the incident in installments as he again examined the roan stallion. "Two of my shepherds were found murdered, their flocks stolen." He halted as he pried open the horse's jaw and looked into its mouth. Satisfied, he continued. "My shepherds notch the ears of their best ewes." He lifted the horse's hoofs, each by turn, and ran his hands over its legs. "Not a week passed," he went on to say as he lifted up the horse's tail, "when I saw the ewes at the market in Vernon. After questioning the new owner, I learned he had bought them from Simon Quarle." Cacchot had more to say on the subject as he circled the stallion. Between phrases, he deliberated over the beast from every conceivable angle. Finally he stood back, buffed his nose once more, and offered the horse trader a silver coin to hold the beast until the following day. "I must consider it," Cacchot said. "If I decide against the animal, the denier is yours to keep. That is fair enough, is it not?"

The horseman readily agreed and stowed the coin in his tunic, assuring the young noble, "You will not find a stud with more spirit, sire, not in all of Normandy."

The four men made their way through the tethered horses, pausing to look and comment, then moving on to another. The sheep market lay just beyond, and a throng of buyers and sellers mobbed the wattled enclosures. Bleating sheep were flipped onto their backs, examined from nose to tail. The length of the wool and the strength of the fiber was loudly praised by the sellers, and met, appropriately enough, with skepticism by wary prospective buyers.

Gouin was quite knowledgeable where sheep were concerned. Cacchot, too, knew what traits to look for in the best animals. "I know a healthy sheep when I see it," he told Laire. "And Gouin, here, is as clever as anyone where they are concerned, but it's my wife who will make the final choice. She knows the wool, they cannot fool her."

Laire, having spent the entirety of his young life as a chevalier, knew absolutely nothing about sheep, save for a wealth of randy jokes, which he shared, amid much laughter, as they walked along, leading their horses.

Laire did not at first notice the lone rider skirting the sheep pens. The moment he did, he halted, his features stiffening involuntarily. The others, curious to learn what had distracted him, turned to look. "It is my squire," Laire said, by way of explanation, his eyes following the rider's progress. Laire passed his horse's reins to Judot. His mind raced quickly from one imagined disaster to another, wondering desperately what had sent Albert from Gaillard in search of him. Laire walked swiftly to meet the boy, catching the horse's reins. He had obviously covered the distance with all speed, for the horse's hide was wet with exertion, steaming in the cold air.

Albert kicked his feet from the stirrups and slid from the saddle. His face was flushed from the cold, near as red as his hair. Almost before his boots hit the ground, his hand flew to his leather jacque and he drew out a missive. "A servant of madame your sister arrived at the gates not an hour after you left. He insisted you must have it in your hand without delay. Have I done wrong to bring it?"

Laire's eyes moved quickly over the careful script. "No," he mumbled, and turning back to the expectant faces of Judot, the young lord Cacchot, and his steward, said, "It seems the king's bishop is arriving to question my prisoner. I regret I will not be able to join you in the tavern tonight."

"You will be returning to Gaillard?" Cacchot asked.

"Yes, unfortunately I have little choice."

"If this business with the bishop is completed before the week is out, ride back. Perhaps we shall have the opportunity to sample some of Gisors' fine ale after all."

"I would like nothing better," Laire laughed, accepting the invitation. After parting company with Cacchot and his steward, Laire, Judot, and Albert walked their horses toward the merchant's campsite.

"I will ride back with you," Judot pledged.

"No, you are needed here. If I am unable to return before the fair ends, the merchants will be expecting an escort. They have paid for it, after all."

The sunlight turned Albert's hair to flame. "What of the lady prisoner's serving woman?" he asked.

"She will only slow your pace," Judot remarked.

As Laire hoped, Judot did not suspect. "I can not return without her, there would be questions."

He said no more, for he had learned long ago that the most successful lies were but half a lie.

At the campsite, no one had seen Nicolette. Even so Laire was not too concerned. If indeed de Conches was in Gisors the likelihood of him sighting Nicolette amid the crush of people was slight. But as the time passed, the thought nagged at him and he knew he could not be content to wait. Moreover the missive from his sister had taken three days to reach him. He had no clue as to when the bishop would arrive at Gaillard's gates. The shadows were growing long when the three set out to search through the crowds for a glimpse of the blue cloak with the tasseled hood.

Their search led them through Gisors. The sun had begun its fiery descent and the town's narrow, winding streets were deep with shadows. In the square the ceremony was ended. People and pigs streamed through the streets returning to their lodgings and campsites for the evening.

Laire led off through an alleyway near the square. The trio emerged from the shadows and came face to face with Simon Quarle and three of his villeins. For an instant the group stared at one another in total astonishment.

Laire's lips quirked into a smile. It seemed the only solution, short of drawing his sword. "We meet again," he said in a voice touched with amusement.

Quarle's sudden grimace might just as easily have been a snarl. "Well, well, my fine Paris friend, are you enjoying the fair?"

The moment of silence only served to deepen Laire's amusement. "I was," he remarked. "What brings you to Gisors . . . selling cattle, perhaps? Or have you come to be blessed?" He knew it was not a wise thing to say, but he could not stop himself.

Quarle's eyes narrowed and a menacing chuckle rose in his throat. "One day, my proud popinjay, I will wring your fancy neck."

Laire grinned. "A bird so fine as me? You would have to catch me first. Surely you must know . . . pigs can't fly?"

For an indescribable instant it seemed the confrontation would explode into violence. All at once Quarle's scarred face creased in an ugly laugh. Squaring his thick shoulders, he shoved past into the crowd, his men glancing back as they followed his lead.

Not twenty paces down the street, Quarle ducked into a shopfront, where the merchant was in the process of closing his shutters for the night.

"We are closed, messires, return tomorrow," the shop owner said, attempting to shoo them from his premises. Quarle gave him such a vicious look, that he shut his mouth and went and stood inside his door.

"Pincot, Gargan," Quarle motioned, "Follow them, I want to know where they are lodged."

Laire halted. All around them merchants were gathering in their merchandise and closing shopfronts. "We should split up," he said, sending

Judot to search the square once more and Albert toward the cloth merchant's stalls.

"I will be at the town gates," Laire advised. "Meet me there before dark." Judging from the deepening shadows, it would be scarcely an hour. Laire hoped it would not take that long to find Nicolette.

He made his way slowly through the crowds, searching for one face among the hundreds, thousands, that streamed past. For it seemed all of Normandy had come to Gisors. Looking out through the town gates Laire realized the immensity of the makeshift markets and campsites. A multitude of tents and lean-tos, crudely constructed stalls, carts, chars, and tumbrils sprawled across the rolling meadows. Their winking cookfires twinkled in the smoky dusk and the frost-scented air reverberated with the babble of voices and lowing cattle.

Where the crowd slowed and thinned to flow through the gates, Laire found a niche by the wall and waited, his eyes roving over the passing throng. Presently he saw a blue tasselled hood amid the mix of bobbing heads and shoulders.

He moved off into the stream of people, certain it was Nicolette even before he glimpsed a pale slice of face. He fell into step beside her. Nicolette did not realize he was there until he dropped a hand on her waist. At first startled, she sagged against him.

"He is here," she said in a whisper.

"Quarle, yes, I know, I have met him."

Nicolette gave her head a frantic toss.

"De Conches, as well?" he guessed, judging from her alarmed expression. It seemed likely, in light of what Cacchot had told him.

The cold air stung her throat. "Nogaret!" she breathed. "He and Bishop d'Enbeau!"

"Here?"

"They have come to take me back to Paris," she cried, biting her lip to keep from sobbing.

"No, the king would never agree to that," he said in a quieting voice. Though the thought had occurred to him as well. He guided her back to the niche by the wall. "It is about the annulment."

"You cannot be certain?"

"Yes, my sister sent a message to Gaillard. Albert brought it, not an hour ago."

"Albert?"

"Yes, we have been searching for you."

Just then she caught sight of Albert. Judot was with him. "You have not told Judot?" she asked in a horrified whisper.

"No, he believes you are the lady's serving woman. Why?"

"He may suspect. Now that we . . ."

Laire pressed his fingers to her lips.

She would not be still. "What will we do? If we are not at Gaillard when they arrive?"

"Surely they will not leave until morning." He gave her a smile of assurance and squeezed her waist. "We will be safe within the walls by then."

Quarle's villein, watching from the shadows, leaned his shoulder against a shuttered shopfront and waited, observing the young man and the girl in the blue cloak. They appeared to be talking. There was a certain intimacy in the way they touched, stood so close together. All at once the young man pressed a kiss to her forehead, then another.

The villein was so intrigued by the drama that he did not notice the approach of Judot and the red-headed boy until they were beside the pair. Farther back in the crowd two young women hailed the group, and together they all set off again.

A sudden movement behind the villein spun him round. When he saw it was his comrade, he swore an oath. Together they moved to mingle with the knots of people trudging toward the town gates. Shoving and pushing, the two villeins struggled to keep the group in sight.

Meanwhile at the chateau in Gisors, torchlight, music, and laughter filtered into the corridor beyond the glittering banquet hall.

"Go and fetch him!" Simon Quarle growled. "Tell him the words I have said to you. Go on! Go, you little wart! Before I lay my fist to the side of your head!"

The wisp of a page shrunk back, eyelids fluttering, then darted into the hall, dodging musicians and servants. His zigzagging course led him past the long festive tables and splendidly attired guests. The boy's legs, one green, one white, looking frail as sticks in the parti-colored hosen, carried him unerringly toward the dais where Raoul de Conches sat in splendor amid the northern barons.

De Sevry, seated mid-way down the table, had risen to his feet and in scathing terms began to damn the king's policies. His gravelly basso echoed through the hall.

All eyes were on de Sevry as the little page approached Raoul de Conches on silent feet and whispered in his ear. De Conches's lips tightened and his gaze slid toward the door arch. In a sweeping glance he captured de Sevry's eye, making known his intent to rise from the table.

Frowning in the torchlight of the corridor, de Conches turned on Quarle, impatiently. "What?"

Quarle hesitated, glaring at the page who fidgeted nervously within earshot. Under his scrutiny the frail-looking boy turned a shade paler and stepped back inside the hall. "De Fontenne is here in Gisors," Quarle said, his eyes on the doorarch.

De Conches looked at him with disbelief. "You are certain?"

"I have seen him."

"What jowl the bastard has!" de Conches remarked with a snort of indignation. The man's audacity knew no bounds. He behaved as if he had received a mandate from the king, rather than a sentence of exile. De Conches smiled suddenly. "Well, he has outfaced himself this time. If he is not at Gaillard to greet the bishop and de Nogaret, the king will see the error of his leniency. I could insist the Burgundian woman be placed in my charge until a decision is reached in Avignon."

"De Fontenne is certain to hear of the bishop's visit." Quarle reminded his lord. "On a fast horse, he could be at Gaillard in a matter of hours."

"Then you must see that he does not leave Gisors."

Quarle made a puzzled face.

"I will make it simple for you," de Conches sighed. "Hold him captive, chase him over the countryside, if you like. Just see that you keep him away from Gaillard. Do you understand?"

Quarle's heavy brow furrowed. "Yes, milord," he responded. Even so he did not understand. He left the chateau grumbling to himself and trying to make some sense of it all. In Normandy, Quarle thought, a man kills his enemy, he does not play games with him. No, it made no sense to him at all. What strange fowl these dandies from the Paris court were, and no surprise the kingdom was in such a state.

The merchants' encampment was a sprawling area of tents, booths, lean-tos, and carts. Crude aisleways led through the mobile market place. The trade for the day was ending, yet there was a din of voices and activity, a constant coming and going of people through the chill, smoky twilight. All along the aisleways, meals were being prepared over cookfires.

The walk had not seemed so far to Nicolette earlier in the afternoon. Now she thought despondently how her happiness had been suddenly changed to despair. Since the moment she had first glimpsed

Gullimae de Nogaret standing before the cathedral, she had been plunged into depression. She could think of nothing else. The fear was like a dark cloud over her mind and she was overcome by sensations of helplessness and dread.

She had withdrawn from the conversations around her, even avoiding, as much as possible, Dore's and Josine's endless prattle. Only vaguely did she hear Laire say to Albert, "You have ridden far enough today. Your horse has earned a rest, even if you have not." His jocular tone mystified her. He behaved as if nothing was amiss and went on discussing the most trivial of matters. Even when Albert handed over the key for the lady prisoner's tower room, Laire shrugged the matter off as if it were nothing.

It was no different with Judot, who laughed and made broad jokes about introducing Albert to Gisors' infamous street of taverns.

Albert, keeping in step, blushed at the suggestion. He had caught but a glimpse of the buildings, of women hanging from doorways. He was no stranger to such sights, for life was much the same in Paris and everywhere, yet it made him feel embarrassed.

"Will you be returning later in the week?" Judot asked Laire.

"If all goes well," he replied. "If not, the merchants' return journey will fall to you and Albert."

Judot nodded. His thoughts swept back to the present, to the immediate need to reach Gaillard.

"Take my stallion for the lady's maid," he offered. "He is faster than the mare."

"No," Nicolette spoke up. "It is kind of you to offer, but I am accustomed to my mare."

Behind her back, Judot sent Laire a meaningful glance, as if to say, you are letting this little puss have too much her own way.

Laire responded with the slightest of shrugs. There was a touch of wit in his smile.

Judot grinned. He understood.

Nicolette sensed the by-play behind her back. She did not care what they thought, she would ride her mare. In her fear, she fancied the mare her charm. A magic horse that would carry her away from danger to a future filled with happiness.

Sixteen

Atop her mare, Nicolette glanced back. She could no longer see the lights of Gisors, the myriad of cookfires spread across the meadows. Riding in the dark, it was safer to keep to the center of the road where there was less chance of losing your head to an over-hanging branch.

After a time, Laire set Ronce at an easy pace. Nicolette's mare, whose stride was not so long, lagged slightly behind, content to follow. There was no great rush; Laire determined they would reach Gaillard long before morning, in all likelihood before the bishop and de Nogaret even ventured out from Gisors.

The blackness of the night was sharply contrasted by the brightness of the star-filled winter sky. Where the road forded a rocky creek bed, the dark water slid quickly away, lapping over the rocks. They dismounted and let their horses drink. A little crescent moon peeked through the bare branches and the frosty air tingled the insides of their noses.

In the darkness, Laire could not clearly see her face. Still, it seemed to him that she was crying.

He smiled at her and reached out to gently brush her cheek with the back of his fingers. "Do not forget that you are mine," he said.

She threw herself into his arms, sobbing, "They will take me to Dourdon and lock me away forever." She could not stop the flood of hot tears.

He dropped his head to hers. "Do not weep. No, ma mie, ssh. I will not let them take you from me. I swear to you, we will live out our lives together, even if we must be fugitives."

Tears wet her cheeks and trickled into her mouth. "How can that be?"

"Oh easily enough," he said, tilting her chin and touching his lips, cool and moist, to her cheek. "Italy is a land in love with tournaments, and if you are willing to follow me. Well, we would at least be together."

The thought that he would willingly face the dangers of the tournament, support himself by fighting as he had in his youth, and all for her sake, brought more tears to sting her eyes. "You would do that for me?" she asked, looking into the handsome face and wishing desperately to believe that there was yet hope for them.

He pledged that it was so, and lightly kissed her once again. There was an absolute confidence about his broad shoulders, something irresistible and almost dangerous that Nicolette desired to touch, to hold. She twined her arms about his neck, pressed her lips to his, and for a moment would not release him.

He laughed softly, sounding a little helpless, and

lifted her arms. "Do not tempt me," he murmured. "We have too far to ride." Behind them a horse moved in the darkness, sloshing from the black water that lapped over the rocky creek bed.

Mounted once again, they continued south. The scent of woodsmoke in the frosty air betrayed the presence of unseen farmsteads nestled in the darkened woods. Where the road's track dipped into a long ravine, their horses shied and balked. The bay pranced sideways, its ears swiveling, grasping for sounds, and the normally placid mare stomped and shook her bridle.

Laire's senses became suddenly alert. The atmosphere of lonely wilderness, all that had been calm and serene, seemed oddly changed. Though sighting down the ravine, he saw nothing, only empty blackness. Still he was unable to explain away the queer feeling of premonition that bristled the hair on the back of his neck.

Nicolette felt it, too. As if the cold air was charged with the same nervous apprehension that shuddered through the skittish mare.

Silence. Starlight.

Suddenly a chorus of piercing shrieks split the cold air, followed by a thunderous crash of brush. Horsemen plunged from the blackness of the ravine. Others charged down the hillock above the road, blocking any hope of retreat.

Instinctively Laire's hand went to his sword hilt. But the riders held back, circling, tightening their reins, and keeping out of range. He did not draw the sword, he waited.

From the dark, a voice rasped, "Hoy, popinjay!" Simon Quarle nudged his red horse forward. "Now it is my turn to set a ransom. What do you suppose you are worth with all your fine feathers? Aha, ha, ha, ha!"

"Tie him to his horse's tail and drag him back to St. Eloi," said a familiar voice. Laire wheeled the bay to put himself between Nicolette and the menacing riders. As he did he saw Pons Vernet's taunting face. "I've a taste for serving girls tonight—what say you, men?"

Hemmed in by the shouting, jostling riders, Nicolette's heart heaved with panic.

"She had no part in this! Let her pass!" Laire demanded. "It is between you and me, Quarle. Or is honor something you only speak of when you are full of wine?"

Quarle's lips twisted in rage. "I spit on your honor, tournament knight. In Normandy, we do not play such fancy games. And do not draw your sword, unless you wish to see your little slut cut in half!"

Nicolette heard a sword rattle from a scabbard, then another. "I have always thought you a swine!" Laire goaded. "I was wrong. A pig has more scruples!"

A string of stinging oaths issued from Quarle's gap-toothed mouth and, kicking his horse forward, he slammed the big-boned red into Laire's bay stallion.

Laire felt the stallion gather under him, and saw Ronce's ears flatten to his head. He knew what was coming and braced himself. The outraged bay, pressed beyond his dignity, lashed out with the swiftness of a snake, lunging and savagely sinking its teeth into the red horse's neck. The terrified beast squealed and reared to its hocks, dumping Simon Quarle onto the ground.

The red horse's panic seemed to infect the others and they blundered into one another as their riders fought vainly to control them. Quarle, dodging hooves, rolled in the dirt screaming curses.

In the mayhem, the road before Laire and Nicolette lay open and clear. Laire wheeled the mettlesome bay and, with a mighty swat, he brought the flat of his hand down on the mare's rump and sent her galloping off into the ravine.

One rider, Vernet perhaps, wrestled his horse around, sword in hand and charged Laire's flank. Laire heard the blade sing past his ear, as he and the stallion shot forward in pursuit of the mare. A litany of curses and shouts echoed after them, and soon the trample of hooves.

Laire and Nicolette kept to the road. The heavy undergrowth would only slow them. Where the woods thinned and the giant oaks were older and more widely spaced, they plunged among the trees. They clattered through creek beds, loped across hillside meadows and down rock-strewn slopes thick with gorse and young pine. After an hour or two, only silence followed them.

All night long they had a sense of continually traveling downward. The first grey light of morning revealed a boggy area, studded with clumps of frost-burnt sedge and matted reeds. Dark, stagnant pools of water, lusterless and looking deep as wells, dotted the marshy ground.

Nicolette looked at the desolate scene around her. The feeling of confidence that had come over her with the lightening of the sky quickly evaporated. "We are lost," she announced from atop the mare.

"We are somewhere between Gisors and Andelys," Laire informed her. He was not yet prepared to agree.

"We are lost," she repeated.

He would have been forced to concede had the sun not come wandering from the clouds in the eastern sky. Nicolette was glad to leave the eerie solitude of the marsh behind. They set off toward a line of misty hills. Pines, dull and monotonous, populated the hillsides. In a high meadow warm with sunlight, they came upon a shepherd's lean-to. It was constructed of pine boughs, and in the not too distant past, for the resinous scent of pine still clung to its interior.

They dismounted and, with trailing reins, let their horses move off to crop the meager grass.

Laire strolled over to where Nicolette was inspecting the crude lean-to of pine boughs. She looked up at his approach. "Do you think the shepherd will return?" Nearby was a circle of rocks filled with the ashes of many cookfires.

Laire looked both ways and made a foolish face. "I don't see him anywhere."

Nicolette pressed her dark brows into a scowl.

He looked at her and laughed. "No," he said, "he has moved on. The grass is gone."

She hadn't noticed until then. It was true, she saw the horses were finding precious little. After she had gone behind some nearby shrubs to relieve herself, she rested a shoulder against the lean-to. She felt it give dangerously before she quickly took her weight away. She was so very tired. Her muscles ached with a burning weariness, and she looked longingly at the soft mat of moss and grasses inside the hut.

Sunshine poured into the open-fronted structure. It was too tempting, and she plopped down to rest in the pool of yellow sunlight. Laire had walked a short distance away to sight into the valley. The countryside had a familiar look. He expected to find farmsteads at the foot of the hill. Gaillard, he reasoned, was but several leagues away.

Presently he returned to the lean-to. He took off his belt and sword and sat down beside her, informing her of what he had seen. He was confident.

"Are you certain?" she asked, drowsy and wishing she could fall asleep in the sunshine.

Laire nodded, but his thoughts had wandered off to the coming confrontation with de Nogaret. Only when she spoke again did he look at her.

"Do you think Quarle and his men have followed us?" she asked. Her thoughts were also in the future, and she tried not to think of the moment she would again be forced to face the inquisitor.

Laire lay back on one elbow and crossed his legs.

"We would have seen some sign of them," he said, watching her with tempting eyes.

She was busy with her coif. Her arms were lifted to her head and her bosom rose with every movement she made. A chill breath of breeze riffled her hair as she removed the silken scarf. The once lovely coif was snagged and tattered.

He watched her, thinking, memorizing the curve of her cheek, her chin, her lips. He felt a vague, voiceless desire to kiss her, hold her, and he raised his hand to gently run a finger down her spine. "What are your thoughts?" he asked.

When she raised her face, there were tears shining on her cheeks and her dark eyes flashed beneath the black silk of her lashes. "Is it true what you said to me last night?"

He sat up and took her on his lap. "It is true."

She laid her hands on his shoulders and looked into his blue, almost violet eyes. "Perfectly true?"

He smiled. "Before God, it is true." He touched his lips to hers and then, speaking in a low tone almost into her mouth, he said, "Do you suppose I could live without you, ma mie?" He held her on his lap, his open hands on her back, beneath the cloak.

For a moment they contemplated one another, acutely aware of the confines of their clothing and the warm flesh entrapped beneath. With only that single thought in their minds, their weariness vanished. They were aware of nothing beyond the aching need to gorge themselves on one another.

Mute with desire they fumbled with their clothing, enough that they might join. There was barely room for the both of them inside the lean-to, and so she sat upon his lap with her hands on his shoulders and her pale legs straddling him.

His open hands slid to her waist to anchor her, and he felt her tightness close around him. He began to move inside her, thrusting, probing, until they rocked together, their hearts pounding, the blood rushing in their ears.

An indescribable feeling began to build inside them, a feeling that could not be spoken, nor held back. A moment of sudden, convulsive contractions that rushed through them like some glorious holy shock, and left them clinging to one another, wonderstruck and breathless. "There is the reason I would rather die than lose you. Do you feel how I am trembling?" His voice, like his breath, came in short rapid gasps.

The kiss he planted on her neck still had the power to send a thrill tingling to her fingertips. "I will always love you," she murmured, leaning against him, resting her cheek on his shoulder. For a moment they remained there, embracing, too weak to rise.

Outside the lean-to the air felt cold once more. Laire buckled on his sword, and Nicolette shook out her skirts. A short distance away, the mare raised her head and made a nickering sound. As quick as that the bay's head went up and its ears swiveled toward the hill they had crossed no more than an hour before.

Laire ran and grabbed the horses' reins and hustled them back across the high meadow. Nicolette hurried toward him. "Riders!" he told her in an urgent whisper. He had glimpsed them a moment only, but enough to recognize Quarle's red horse. He boosted Nicolette upon the mare, drew the reins over the bay's head and swung into the saddle.

The high meadow was empty when Quarle and his men halted their horses by the shepherd's lean-to. One of the men dismounted and, looking about, asserted, "These hoofprints are no older than an hour."

Quite naturally he stooped and poked his head inside the crude shelter of pine boughs. A human scent mingled with the earthy breath of resin, moss and couch grass. A distinctive amorous scent, one that excited and teased his nostrils.

He rose up laughing, and loudly proclaimed his discovery. "I wager they were rolling on the ground when we rode up the hill!" The crude remarks and laughter had hardly died away when a sharp-eyed villein caught sight of the pair galloping into the valley below.

The desperate game of catchers and seekers continued throughout the day. Several times Quarle nearly overtook them. Each time Laire and Nicolette were forced to abandon their course. Finally, in desperation they made a race for Gaillard.

From the edge of the thicket, they saw they were too late. De Conches and his advance guards were approaching the walls. The bishop's entourage with its heavy, slow-moving charettes rumbled behind.

A backward glance only confirmed Quarle and his villeins were still pursuing them. Laire looked at Nicolette, trying to hide the feeling of utter hopelessness in his heart. With de Conches and Nogaret before them and Simon Quarle and his villeins at their back, they were neatly trapped.

There was no way they might enter the walls without being halted, save for the passageway that opened onto the chalk cliff far down the rock-strewn hillside. Laire wavered, knowing it would be dangerous to descend the cliff, perhaps impossible. At last he called to Nicolette and swung the bay back into the thicket that extended toward the precipice.

Nicolette turned the mare and cantered after him, thinking it could not be so difficult, for they would be going down, not climbing. Deep in the brushy thicket of windswept scrub and bramble, they dismounted and led the horses a short distance over the rocky ground before abandoning them.

Laire took her hand, guiding her through the rough stretch of tangled vines, thick-set cedars, and thorny bramble.

Nicolette glanced back at the horses, alarmed. "They will wander away," she cried, balking at the last moment.

Laire caught her by the shoulders and hurried her forward, promising, "They will not go far."

The ground beneath their feet was steep and uneven, and Nicolette was forced to concentrate on keeping her footing. She ran now without thinking, without looking beyond her next stride. Suddenly the thicket into which they had plunged opened, and the expanse of the great valley with the river twisting through it lay before them.

When she looked down, the dizzy height took her breath away. The cliff had not looked so treacherous on the morning she had stood at the entrance of the passageway and gazed upward.

There was no path for them to follow, and little time for them to choose one. Laire led off, following a depression in the rock that led obliquely down the hill. It was no more than a gully wearied out by erosion, worn by the wind and rain, not an arm's length in width and slippery with loose stones. Nicolette held her breath, afraid to look down, knowing that one slip, one misstep, would send her tumbling irretrievably down the jagged cliff.

Like dogs who had lost a scent, Simon Quarle and his villeins milled about. Quarle drew his red horse to a halt and stood in his stirrups. He could see no hint of de Fontenne and the serving girl. They and their horses had vanished into the dense wild thicket below the chateau's north wall and the crest of the precipitous cliff.

"I wager there's a postern gate in that section of wall!" one villein called out. Quarle said nothing, though it was what he thought. There could be no other explanation. What little he could see of the cliff's craggy face appeared impassable. Quarle cursed out loud and towed at his reins.

In backward glances, Laire could no longer see the riders, the stark white spine of the craggy cliff hid them from view. He prayed they could not see him and Nicolette.

Loose rock scattered from beneath their feet, raining down on the boulders below. Where a huge section of rock had slid away, the gully deepened and became a maze of deeply eroded trenches. One track led only a short distance before ending in yet another slurry of chalky white stone. Several other rutted tracks vanished around an outcropping of rock.

It was one of those Laire chose, and unwisely. They made their way slowly. But when they reached the point where the track swung around the massive outcropping, there was nothing before them but empty space and a sheer precipice over which the spring rains cascaded to the river below.

The track had so narrowed that now they were unable to turn, and they were forced to retrace their steps, slowly backing to the point where the slide had divided the gully.

In choosing another twisting ravine Laire was luckier, for it widened to a wash, broad as a dry stream bed and choked with heaps of loose stone, as it twisted down the cliff. On its sides, low frost-burnt shrubs began to appear. They could move faster now, stones clattering underfoot. Only the huge mounds of boulders checked their speed. In places it was possible to squeeze past them, at others they were forced to halt, panting with exertion, and scramble over them. Their hands and clothing were white with chalk dust.

Where the stream bed plunged steeply downward, it was less cluttered and they began to run. Soon the slope surrounding them was covered with scrubby bushes, and farther down, a clump of stunted trees. Laire had marked the spot in his memory. The entrance to the passage lay just opposite the stand of gnarled trees. He reached for Nicolette's hand and slipping and sliding pulled her along with him. In a matter of moments they reached the guardian stones and dropped safely into the entrance.

They paused to catch their breath, for now they had to climb the passage. The darkness swallowed them. There was neither torch nor candle. The close, silent blackness of the tunnel was broken only by the scuff of their feet and the heaviness of their breathing as they struggled upward.

From the vaulted chamber beneath the keep they made their way up the irregular stones of the inner stairs. In the darkness Laire stooped, prying open the little door that led into the solar. Once he had pushed from beneath the tapestry, he lifted up the corner of the fabric so Nicolette might enter.

Their clothes were ripped, caked with chalk dust, and laden with burrs. They began to shed the telltale clothing as quickly as possible. Laire flung open a chest, stowing their clothing as they removed it and dressing himself in whatever he found.

Nicolette stripped to her linen chemise and underskirt. Her legs beneath the tattered linen petticoat were scratched and bruised. In desperation she used the skirt of her blue woolen gown to brush the chalk dust from her slippers.

By the time she and Laire had climbed the stairs to the tower room and unlocked the door, Nicolette was shivering uncontrollably. Once inside she grabbed the coarse-woven penitent's robe and wrapped it about herself.

Laire sighted down from the window of the tower. Far below, the bishop's entourage of elaborate charettes, and the remainder of de Conches' troop, were crossing the broad ridge toward Gaillard's walls. He reported the news with a note of satisfaction. At the door, he turned, brandishing the key, and gave her a winning smile. She heard the key click in the lock as she took up the flint striker to light a fire in the brazier.

Laire descended the steps at a trot. In the hall, a young guard from the outer ward stood restlessly, shifting from one foot to the other. He turned at the sound of footsteps.

Aymer, peering from one of the circular windows, did not hear. A maelstrom of thoughts ran through the old cleric's mind. He would have no choice but to admit the king's representatives. And yet, to do so would reveal the fact that his young lord was absent from his post.

The sound of a familiar voice brought him from his thoughts, his face blank as a sheet of paper. He quickly stepped from the recess in the wall, and seeing Laire de Fontenne, exclaimed, "Milord, how have you . . . ?" All at once his face crinkled into a smile. So, he thought, the passage had served some purpose after all.

Laire sent the guard away with orders to open Gaillard's walls. He then went into the kitchen in search of food. Aymer followed, bombarding him with questions as he took a loaf of bread and tore it apart. The cook hastened to bring out a wedge of cheese and Mahaut fetched a cup of wine.

"Has Odette come with you?" the old woman asked, concerned, recalling that the serving girl was sworn to remain with the lady prisoner at all times.

"She is with her mistress," Laire replied, between mouthfuls of cheese and bread. He could not ever remember being so hungry. As he ate, he sent one of the young boys to gather up the household servants.

"Men from the king's court are coming to question the lady prisoner," Laire told those gathered in the kitchen. "Be cautious with your words. Tell them nothing. If I am sent away, Simon Quarle may well be your new master." Laire was correct in assuming that it would require only the mention of the hated Simon Quarle to seal their lips.

He emptied the cup of wine, belched loudly and entered the hall to greet the bishop. Even as Laire made his reverence, he was alert to Raoul de Conches and Nogaret.

The inquisitor looked at him, looked *through* him, or so it seemed to Laire. People, humanity, had no place in Nogaret's grand scheme. Enemies and allies were all the same to him, existing only to be used or destroyed.

De Conches's reaction was much more gratifying. He smiled his disbelief. Clearly, he was surprised to see Laire.

The bishop wasted no time in installing himself and his clergy at the great table. Seated comfortably near the warmth of the fire, he called for the lady prisoner to be brought before him. "A dreary place," Bishop d'Enbeau said of Gaillard, and made known his intention to conclude his business there as quickly as possible. It was his desire to reach the abbey of St. Severin by nightfall.

Nogaret and several of his men accompanied Laire to fetch the lady prisoner. There was no doubt of the men's unquestioned loyalty to the inquisitor. They were young, perhaps still in their teens, yet there was already a look of evil about them.

Several times they halted, waiting while the inquisitor opened chamber doors, peered inside and gawked about. It was no different in the tower room. There Nogaret strolled across the chamber, studying it with an appraising eye, weighing the harsh, miserable conditions against the severity of the lady prisoner's sentence, or vice-versa.

As Nicolette was led across the dusty planks, Nogaret gave her a scornful look. "Well, madam," he said, "You have filled your bed with thorns, and now you must lie on them."

Nicolette's features remained rigid, but her large, dark eyes flared with hatred. She was exhausted, cold and hungry, in that there was no pretense, and she wondered if Nogaret was as convinced of her misery as he appeared.

The servants were sent from the hall and, Nicolette was made to swear to answer truthfully all the questions put to her by his grace, the bishop.

Nogaret sat nearby, listening. Occasionally a tic of nerves would cause his head to bob or jerk suddenly sideways. Raoul de Conches lounged on a bench by the hearth. If he was listening to the course of the proceedings, he gave little sign of it.

At one point, Laire noticed de Conches staring fixedly at Nicolette. And later, while the bishop's voice droned on hollowly, Laire had the uncomfortable sensation of someone staring at him. He raised his eyes. He and de Conches looked at one another. Laire recalled the night of his arrest; perhaps de Conches recalled it too. There was no need to translate their thoughts into words, they were reflected clearly in their eyes.

The bishop's scriveners worked in feverish silence. The ample sleeves of their scapularies dragged across the table with each swooping stroke of their quills, each carefully arched letter set down upon the parchment.

The petition dealt with matters of consanguinity, an attempt to prove both Louis and Nicolette shared a common, though distant, blood relative. It was ludicrous, for most noble marriage partners did. The petition also cited the fact that their union had been childless. It was a feeble case, but Pope

Clement would hardly rule against the wishes of the king who had sat him on the Papal throne.

The questions Nicolette feared most were not asked. No mention was made of Louis's lack of sexual vigor. Neither were there any accusations of Nicolette's aversion to the conjugal act. Even the crimes for which she had been condemned were strangely omitted.

After the last reply had been set down on the parchment, the bishop leaned toward Nicolette, and said, "Hopefully, my child, our Holy Father will agree that this marriage was no right match. Do not fear for your soul. Remember, salvation is not closed to sinners, only to those who do not believe in Christ. Sin is inherent in us all, but can be cancelled out by penance and absolution. Pray his Holiness gives his approval to this petition and grants you your freedom."

Nicolette raised her voice hopefully. "My freedom, your Grace?"

"Yes, my child, the freedom to enter the convent of St. Catherine de Vincennes where you might pledge your life to penance and to prayer."

Nicolette's face remained impassive, but she could not have felt his words more sharply had they been a knife. No, she thought, she would never sign. There was no stain of guilt upon her soul, no cause to commit her life to penance. And if what she felt in her heart for Laire de Fontenne was a sin, then she preferred to remain a prisoner forever.

Laire heard the words as well, and the thought

of losing her appalled him more than he dared to acknowledge. He did not look at her, or at anyone, fearing the truth was all too plainly written on his features.

In another hour the unwelcome guests, with their clergy, servants, and soldiers, were gone from Gaillard. The bishop, his hands glittering with jewels and his silken robes flowing after him, climbed into his gilt and blue-upholstered charette. The inquisitor, who often made a show of shirking luxury, seated himself in one of equal splendor. Raoul de Conches mounted his fine destrier, gathered his knights and men-at-arms and led the long procession through the gates.

High in the tower, Nicolette threw back the hood of the coarse brown robe and leaned against Laire. Snugged to his side, she looked down from the slotted window and watched the magnificent entourage traverse the broad ridge like a moving band of color. "It is a strange view," she mused. "From here they do not appear so mighty, only small and insignificant as . . ."

"Lice," he supplied. His observation brought a bitter little smile to her lips.

The entourage had hardly faded from view when a guard atop the wall called to his comrades in the gate tower.

"Hoy!" he shouted, waving his arms above his head. His comrades trotted toward him, "What, what is it?"

"Look! A pair of fine horses, saddles and all. Where do you suppose they have come from?"

"Our patron saint." The taller of the group grinned. He was already counting the money in his purse. Even divided among them the profit from the sale of the horses in the village would be handsome.

"It might be a trap," the more cautious of the trio warned, and he peered down suspiciously at the horses browsing in the tall brush close to the wall.

"Nah," the bolder of the group said, mockingly. "Where is the trap? I see nothing."

"He is right, we are fools if we do not claim them."

The guards were still arguing when the seigneur and several stable boys rode up to the gate tower, preparing to leave the chateau to search for the abandoned horses. In only a moment the mystery was solved. The horses were retrieved. The guards received a coin for their alertness, and the incident provided them with an entire evening's worth of speculation.

Nicolette would not be satisfied until she had gone to the stable and looked upon the mare with her own eyes. She carried a clutch of spicy-scented little apples from the kitchen in her apron, which she fed one by one to the gentle-eyed mare.

Juice dripped from the animal's soft brown muzzle. "She is my charm," Nicolette murmured, cooing softly to the mare, and stroking her satiny neck. "She has carried me from danger, saved my life. Only a little brown mare, but she is very brave."

The mare gratefully accepted her praise and another apple.

"It is true," she said to Laire, who had taken an apple to the stallion. "Have you ever thought of it?" she called, "Thanked your horse for saving your feet and your life?"

"He is well fed," Laire replied, laughing, as he teasingly passed the apple from hand to hand. The determined stallion, wanting the apple and tiring of the game, bumped its muzzle against his chest.

"He will nip you," Nicolette warned, "and it will be no more than you deserve."

Laire looked at her and laughed softly before turning back to his game. "He enjoys it, don't you, Ronce?"

"You are cruel," she accused, petting her mare. After a few more tosses of the apple, Laire opened his hand and offered the shiny red fruit to the stallion. Then Nicolette heard his boots crunch in the straw as he crept toward her. She giggled. But he caught her before she could dodge away, and tickled her until she was weak.

That night Rigord came to the hall at Laire's summons. When Nicolette heard they were planning to ride to Gisors in the morning, she was angry. She said nothing until they were alone in the solar and she lay on the bed.

"Why?" she asked Laire, as he sat down beside her to remove his boots.

"To buy cattle. I have explained all—"

"No," she said, sitting up and narrowing her eyes, "That is not why you are going. It is to prove you do not fear Simon Quarle. Because you are a great, huge fool, and afraid people will say you are a coward, like Lachaume."

He turned and regarded her with a chuckle before he took her by the shoulders and playfully pressed her to the pillows. "You are like a little buzzing, biting fly tonight," he told her, burying his face in her neck and giving her kisses. "A nip here, a nip there. A tempting little Spanish fly."

It was no use to try and argue with him, and soon she had no wish to.

Seventeen

The arrival of Bishop d'Enbeau threw the abbey of St. Severin into chaos. An attack some weeks before had dealt the order a severe blow from which it had not yet recovered. A number of brethren and servants had been killed or maimed, their chapel looted and their cattle driven away. The blame had been set on marauding peasants, those who had lost the fear of God. Bishop d'Enbeau was horrified by the abbot's retelling of the bloody night of terror, so much so that he found it difficult to sleep despite the copious amounts of wine he'd drunk. Even the comfort of his silken bed, which traveled with him wherever he went, could not give him solace.

A fear of marauding "peasants" was the last thing on Simon Quarle's mind as he hastened into the red torchlight of the abbey's crowded forecourt. He was, however, keenly concerned that his lord Raoul de Conches would not take lightly this latest failure. And as he strode past the line of splendid charettes, Quarle grumbled to himself, thinking nothing would better please him than to chop that crowing popinjay, de Fontenne, into small pieces.

The frost-starred earth crunched beneath his boots. At a door well to the rear of the huge complex, a lay brother with a lamp led Simon Quarle through the darkened inner precincts of the monastery and to a room bright with lamp light.

Raoul de Conches sat on one of a pair of velvet upholstered chaises, turning a cup of wine in his hand. When he looked up, his blue tinged jaw was clenched and his eyes were bright with rage.

Before Quarle could say a word in his own defense, de Conches snapped, "Do not bore me with your feeble excuses. You are worthless, a clownish peasant. I should dismiss you, I should have you flogged and dragged behind your horse, dragged all the way to Clermont!"

"Milord," Quarle pleaded, slowly pulling the fur cap with a rolled brim from his head, "De Fontenne was far and away before I had the report of his leave taking." And forgetting he had not his lord's permission to be seated, he plunked himself down upon the chaise opposite, mouth open, prepared to give a full account. Not a particularly truthful account, but one he felt might spare him further retribution.

"You dare to sit without permission!" De Conches's sharp reprimand sent Quarle lurching to his feet. The damage was done. Wherever his cloak and hosen had brushed the pale lemon-colored velvet they had left behind a litter of notched triangular pods, little heart-shaped burrs. De Conches let go a string of obscenities. "You oafish pricklouse! See what you have done!"

"My pardon, sire," Quarle murmured, stumbling to one side, at once clumsy as a bull and timid as a serving wench. "It is no great damage, sire. It is naught but burrs. See milord, I will pick them away."

A sudden strangeness came over Raoul de Conches's features. "Burrs," he mumbled, as if he had never heard of them before. "Burrs, of course," he repeated, and with a flash of comprehension recalled Nicolette of Burgundy arranging the folds of her coarse robe as she sat before the bishop. He recalled the momentary glimpse of ankle and the ragged linen underskirt flocked with black speckles. Had what he mistook for flecks of menstrual blood, for that was what had occurred to him at the time, actually been burrs? And where would a woman confined in a tower room catch burrs on her petticoat? The more he thought of it, the more he was convinced. She had not appeared to be a woman deprived, ill-kept, ill-fed. No, her color was too high and her limbs firm and supple. He looked to Quarle, stooping, picking burrs, and said, "You rode through weed fields, did you not?"

"Yes, milord." He pinched away the last of the little opportunists and shook the handful into the fire crackling in the hearth.

"As you pursued de Fontenne and the serving girl," de Conches, continued.

Quarle raised his eyes from the glowing hearth and nodded stupidly.

"This serving girl, you have seen her clearly?"

Quarle answered in the affirmative, and with some prompting described the pretty face and slight physique of Nicolette of Burgundy. De Conches's mood lightened by the moment. Quarle, giddy with relief, went a step further and, chuckling like a man who has just recalled a joke, related how he very nearly caught the pair coupling in a shepherd's hovel.

It was too droll, de Conches nearly laughed. "My God, what a game they are playing." It was madness. Unbelievable, save for what he knew of de Fontenne, the tournament knight whose recklessness had won him fame, and the unhappy princess who squandered a fortune on fetes and plays in the gardens of the Hotel de Nesle. "In a shepherd's lean-to," he repeated.

Quarle responded with a nod and yet another mirthful snort.

"Do you not see?" de Conches remarked, somewhat exasperated. The man was dense as a stone.

Quarle, still chuckling, noted his lord's amused expression had suddenly waxed serious. Puzzled by this new turn of events, he pulled a straight face. Quite by habit, his hand went to the back of his head and his fingers crabbed at the oily scalp beneath the stringy hair. "See, milord? See what, sire?"

"Why, that she is Nicolette of Burgundy, you fool! Yes, I am certain of it. Find a way to abduct her, hold her at your chateau until I return from court. With her in my hands," he began, but he did not complete the thought in words. He was already considering the possibilities.

"But, milord. How am I to—"

De Conches's voice cut savagely across his. "Do not fail me again, Quarle."

"No, milord," he stammered. "It will be done—just as you say. I have hunted foxes before."

Morning came with a steely grey light, a bleak wind and low dragging clouds. At Gaillard, Nicolette followed Laire out into the courtyard. Into the winter cold where dogs barked, and horses stamped and snorted. Rigord and two of his younger sons waited while a stable boy led Laire's bay stallion forward. Laire and Nicolette's brief words of parting were no more than the proper words of a seigneur to a servant, his instructions for the household in his absence, but the flicker of expression in Laire's eyes, the look of mute reproach in hers, did not go unnoticed. For earlier Rigord had shared such a parting with his own wife.

With the seigneur and his men-at-arms away, and now the steward as well, a pall of fear swept over the chateau. There was wild talk among the guards of an attack by Simon Quarle and his villeins. Everyone jumped at shadows and more than once a false alarm was raised when the guards sighted enemies that existed only in their overwrought imaginations.

"Well," Nicolette asked expectantly. She stood in

the middle of the yeast-scented kitchen, dressed in one of Dore's cast-off homespun kirtles, displaying the blue gown on her arm. She had painstakingly plucked away the multitude of tenacious little burrs from the wool frock, beaten out the chalk dust and scraped away the mud. Now she waited. All work in the steamy kitchen came to a halt.

Mahaut drew back a step, the sharp little black eyes amid the wrinkles quickly appraising the gown. At last she shook her grey head and, making a clucking sound with her tongue, declared, "It is ruined."

Nicolette's hopeful expression fell. "If we were to mend it?" she suggested. She hated the thought of discarding the blue gown; like the brown mare she considered it a charm. The thought of the gown being ripped into smaller, usable pieces of cloth distressed her as much as the thought of a black cat crossing her path.

Mahaut took the skirt in her gnarled hands, inspecting it closely. "It is beyond mending," she concluded once again. "See here, the briars have shredded the hem. Here it is ripped, and here and, oh, see here. No, no, there is no hope for it. Though we might use it for a pattern," she mumbled, more to herself than Nicolette, for she was deciding how to go about it. The old woman looked up suddenly, quick as a little bird. "Tell me of the cloth once more, the colors you chose and all."

The old woman was happy as a child to hear it all again. Work resumed around them. Nicolette and the old woman sat at one end of the slab-topped table and, as the dough was being twisted for the oven, they spread the gown and carefully loosed each seam. To everyone's delight, for all in the kitchen lent an ear as they worked, Nicolette described the cloth, the vibrant colors, and then, prompted by her listeners, told of the fair, of its scoundrels and jugglers, and all the strange sights.

On a cold, wet afternoon as the week came to a close, the church bells of Andelys heralded the merchants' return. At mid-day the bells rang out sext, and shortly thereafter began to toll again. Not the slow, dull iron stroke of the conical hours but a steady rolling peal.

The procession appeared like phantoms in the misty fog. People ran shouting through the puddled rain toward the walls. Children and barking dogs chased merrily along. With a rattle of chains and groaning wood the drawbridge was lowered. Cows and pigs clattered into the outer ward, followed by the riders and a string of pack horses neck-roped together.

From atop the wall, Nicolette, shivering in the icy drizzle, waved to Laire. He drew his horse aside and waited by the guard tower steps. What would people think? she wondered, as she hurried down to him. Dressed in the cast-off homespun and wrapped in Mahaut's ragged shawl, she looked more a peasant than a proper lady's serving woman. Laire seemed not to notice, for he pulled her up to ride before him. His stubbled jaw scratched her cheek. "Have you been lonely for me?" he whispered close by her ear. She did not

PRISONER OF MY HEART 303

answer him with words, but her cheeks were flush with color and the smile she gave him was filled with promise.

The cattle were secured, the goods unloaded, and in the mad excitement, Nicolette saw little more of Laire. He went with the men, his white dog at his heels. Nicolette became a captive of Dore and Josine, who were determined to tell her in rapid, gushing terms of their experiences.

Mahaut was presented with a new shawl, the cook with the spices he had requested. For everyone of the household there was some trinket, and the hall rang with laughter and merriment as if it were a feast day.

During the meal, there was endless talk of the fair. Indeed Nicolette believed there would still be talk of it at Easter! The young men-at-arms spoke of it with glowing faces and even Albert, who lately tried very hard to be blasé about everything, joined in their banter.

Laire made his excuses and went to his bed early. He was waiting for Nicolette when she climbed the stairs with the lady prisoner's platter.

Once she was inside the solar and the platter set aside, he caught her up in his arms and kissed her until they both lost their breath. Afterwards he held her to him and moistened her throat with his lips. In a husky voice he said to her, "My soul burns for your kisses. I am mad with desire for you. I cannot live another moment without your caress."

The words, recalled, sent a chill through Nicolette and turned her blood to ice. They were the very words that had been written on the note!

She stiffened and pushed against him.

Laire looked at her, bewildered. "What?" he asked, "What have I said?"

"Are those the words you say to every woman?" she accused, her voice changed suddenly to a hiss. She was angry now, filled with rage, prepared to believe he had been a part of Louis and Isabella's plot from the first, prepared to believe her wildest doubts. It was irrational, absurd, but she was so furious she could think of nothing but the words.

However, he only laughed softly, "I have done so in the past," he admitted, "though the words were not entirely my own invention. It was some foolishness Gautier, Pierre, and I made up as a wager one night when we were drinking." He studied her face, deliberating, trying to decide if a further confession would put an end to his evening's pleasure. "At the tournaments," he began to explain, "we would say the words to every handsome lady we met. Sometimes we would receive a slap, but more often an invitation."

Nicolette was incredulous as he went on to tell how each of them would put up a gold ecu, and when the tourney ended, the man with the most conquests, won the coins.

Nicolette felt as if her heart were breaking. It was suddenly so clear, Gautier and Joan, Blanche and Pierre, why had she never seen it before? The two brothers who had been so often in the gardens and in the corridors of the palace, so often that

PRISONER OF MY HEART 305

their presence was hardly noticed. Had Joan's talk of courtly love been meant to lure her into their games? Did Joan and Blanche feel they could not trust her unless she was as guilty as they? And was she not, after all?

"Have I offended you?" he asked, thinking he should not have told her. She looked so strange.

"No." Her voice was no more than a whisper. She drew his hand from her waist and walked away.

He followed her, and sat down beside her on the bed. He could think of nothing else to say.

The crippling silence continued. Finally, in a quiet voice, she told him of the letter Joan had secreted away, and of the words, Gautier's surely. She told him also of the summer's day she had come upon Blanche and Pierre in the rose arbor, of their disconcerted expressions, and Blanche fumbling to arrange her skirts.

As she spoke, she recalled a dozen other little happenings that had no meaning until then. At last, she said, "You knew, didn't you?"

"No, not a name, only that the lady was royal. I tried to warn Gautier, to tell him it was a different game at court, not like the tournaments. For myself, I preferred not to have a jealous husband catch me with my hand under his wife's skirt and break my arm. And if the jealous husband wore a crown, well, so much the worse. But Gautier made a joke of it. He said I was becoming moral, that it did not suit me. The day of the arrests, I stopped by his quarters. He was writing a letter. I only glimpsed the first line. It read, 'My adored one, my queen of hearts.' At the time, I assumed it was meant for you, since you were the wife of the eldest son. I was mistaken."

Even then, Nicolette was unwilling to believe Joan and Blanche were guilty. "The rings were not Joan's doing, nor Blanche's. It was Isabella who gave us the rings. It was she who planned to trap us. She and her hateful brothers!"

"Isabella had the most to gain," Laire thought aloud. He had never really considered it before. But with her brothers' wives disgraced, there was no chance of legitimate heirs. And after her brothers, who stood nearest the throne? Only Isabella and her son.

Nicolette looked at him with tears in her eyes. "It will make little difference to you and me," she cried. "I will be locked away in a convent, dead to the world, and you will be left here to grow old. We will have no opportunity to run away. There will be nothing you can do!"

"Dead to the world," he repeated the phrase, taking her in his arms. "Yes, perhaps that is the answer. For if the lady prisoner were to die, there would be no need of an annulment, and Odette her faithful serving woman would be free. What would you say to such a role?"

"No one would believe us."

"Why not? They believe you are Odette."

"If someone was sent from court, they would see."

"What would there be to see—only a grave!"

* * *

A chill mizzeling of rain and snow fell on Paris. Cargo ships arriving at the Place de la Greve were met by customs officers, weighers, porters, and merchants. The streets were no less crowded nor any less squalid for the winter cold. At an apothecary shop on the Petit Pont an apprentice was macerating the herb scelerata and kneading it with pig dung to be offered as a cure for boils.

While at the Palace of the Cite, Isabella was again enjoying the luxuries of her father's court. Its splendor differed vastly from the rather crude, almost provincial English court at Westminster and at Isabella's apartments in the Tower of London.

The unsettling news of the annulment arrangements had brought Isabella quickly from England. She had easily convinced her philandering husband to allow her to journey back to France on the excuse of paying fealty for her dowered lands of Ponthieu. On this occasion she had succeeded in bringing her young son, Edward, heir to the English throne. Isabella had long ago determined that her son would also be the king of France. She had made a vow even before the child quickened in her womb, she had been that certain she would give birth to a son. Now she would stop at nothing to wrest the crown from her weakling brothers.

The magnificent chamber where Isabella lay upon a richly upholstered couch was hung with silken trappings and tapestries that gleamed with golden thread. She had inherited her father's love of grandeur, as well as his rapacious greed. No luxury was too grand and no pocket to poor to pay the cost.

A serving woman brought a tray of candied fruit. Isabella gave instructions to her mistress of the wardrobe, before sending her away. She then turned her pale eyes sharply on the serving girl massaging her limbs with scented oil. "Softly!" Isabella snarled, "You are clumsy as a cow!"

The stormy channel crossing aboard a wind tossed ship had left Isabella's fair skin red with chill-blain. She still felt the cold sting of the salt air, even in the warmth of the chamber.

"Ouch!" Isabella shouted, and made known her displeasure with the serving girl's ministrations by giving her a swift kick. "It is my foot, you fool of a peasant, not a lump of dough!"

Just then Madame Beaurain, who was employed as a nursemaid, appeared at the chamber's door arch leading Isabella's toddling son by the hand. He was a plump child, very fair, and his clothing was stiff with jewels. Isabella smiled at her son and offered him a candied fruit. She spoke to him briefly, and let him roll a silver pomander about the chamber while she questioned Madame Beaurain. "Does he eat well?" she asked. "Is he warm enough?" Satisfied that she had fulfilled her maternal duties, Isabella told the nursemaid to lift up her son, so she might kiss him. "There," she said, "I have kissed him. You may take him away now."

The little pot of scented oil slipped from the

serving girl's grasp and struck Isabella on the toe. She squalled and kicked out viciously. "Enough!" she screamed. "I shall have a bruise. Get out! Get out, you ugly sow!" The pale-faced serving girl scrambled from the room.

"Seraphine!" Isabella called. Across the chamber, a thin, sharp-faced woman seated by the hearth leapt up and came quickly forward.

"Madame," she said, careful to curtsey low.

"Arrange my robes," she commanded. "Now, you may send in the gentleman who is waiting."

A moment later, Stanis Rapet was ushered into the chamber. Rapet, an alchemist and an astrologer, bowed majestically before Isabella. She was as coldly regal as the old man recalled. A statuesque blonde, a beauty, yet in her fair loveliness there was something perverse. It was her mouth, Rapet decided. She had a cruel mouth, one that was at once sensual and ugly with the lower lip too thick for the thin dry upper lip.

Isabella regarded him with a strange smile. "Have you brought what we discussed?"

"Yes, madame," Rapet replied, producing a slender silver phial from the dagged sleeve of his particolored jupon. The phial contained a potent grey powder, fine as dust, a deadly poison with mercury as its base. Rapet referred to the poison as "serpent de pharah," serpent of the pharaoh, and often told his wealthy clients that it was this most potent of all poisons, not the bite of an asp, that had killed the tragic queen Cleopatra.

Isabella cared only that the fine grey powder

brought a violent, almost instantaneous death to its victims. She questioned Rapet closely about its qualities; then smiled once more, a strange, rather evil smile. "Seraphine!" She motioned to the thin woman. "Go and fetch the serving girl who was just here."

Several days later, a cold gust, a foretaste of a long winter, drove a whirlwind of brittle leaves across the square opposite the church of St. Jullian. A thin woman wrapped in a grey cloak hurried through the iron gates toward the house of Jerome de Marginay, the tax collector. The woman had no sooner taken a seat among the throng of people waiting in the antechamber when a young serving girl came and led her through the rear of the house to a staircase. The narrow steps led to a room above, where Agnes de Marginay sat with her needlework in her lap. The serving girl, having shown the woman into the room, turned and closed the door behind her.

"I understand you have information for me?" Agnes said, securing her needle in the material she was working.

Seated in the wintry shadows of the room, the woman's thin nose, which fell a little sideways, appeared fantastically long. "Yes, madame," the woman said, inclining her body forward and speaking softly as though she feared being overheard. "I must have payment in gold, as was agreed," she whispered. "For what I have to say could easily be my death."

Agnes dipped her fingers into her sewing basket and withdrew a tightly cinched satin pouch, heavy with gold, and passed it to the woman's waiting hand.

As the woman related her story, her fingers moved nervously over the coins beneath the satin cloth. In a soft, rapid whisper she told of Stanis Rapet's visit to her mistress, of the poison, its hideous properties, and of the poor serving girl dead upon the chamber floor.

Agnes shuddered at the thought of Isabella's cruelty, though it was no more, or less, than she expected of the wicked slut. "For whom is the poison meant?" Agnes pressed expectantly.

The thin woman's shoulders raised in a shrug, her eyelids fluttering. "Who can say, madame? Though I can tell you there is much turmoil in the palace. Madame Isabella argues with her father, the king. She and her lover quarrel incessantly, and only yesterday she had a violent dispute with the inquisitor, de Nogaret. I heard their angry voices, but I could not make out their words. However, later, I heard from another servant that madame Isabella struck the inquisitor across the face with her hand and accused him of treachery."

After the woman had gone, Agnes sat sewing, thinking on what she had heard. For all her thrift, Agnes considered the gold well spent. She was not at all surprised when a week later she heard of Gullimae de Nogaret's death. "Taken by a seizure of the heart," at least that was the opinion of the king's physicians. The words of de Nogaret's servants were more graphic, for they said he had been seized by a terrible fit, fell upon the floor and voided from every orifice like a strangled duck.

Every day more news came to the house of Jerome de Marginay. From her uncle, de Orfevres, Agnes learned that the king would soon be journeying north to parley with the Flemings and with the Norman barons. And from another source, she heard Isabella had attempted to persuade her father to set aside her brothers and name her son as his heir. King Philip had refused.

Alone in her solar, Agnes put her thoughts in order. She felt she must warn her youngest brother. In her letter, she entreated him, "You must influence your lady prisoner to sign the annulment. If she refuses, I fear her days are numbered and, more to my caring, yours as well. For the king desires that Louis should have a moral wife and heirs as soon as possible."

Not long afterwards, on a sullen December afternoon, Simon Quarle's chateau appeared a derelict in the drifting mists. The structure near St. Eloi was not truly a chateau, but rather a rambling manor house with enclosing palisades and a network of ditches. There was a shabby, ill-kempt look about the place, like an animal's lair. That day neither man nor beast was to be seen moving about the courtyards in the chill, heavy air, and there was no sign of life save for the columns of bitter blue woodsmoke that rose from the chimneys.

Inside the hall, Simon Quarle brooded before his hearth, swilling hot spiced wine. Since he had been forced to take in his sister, her children, and his brother-in-law, Pons Vernet, he had known no peace. His hall rang with constant consternation, children whooped and squabbled, and short-tempered women hissed at one another like angry cats.

Quarle was not a happy man. Added to all the petty annoyances that surrounded him was the thorny problem of finding a means by which to abduct the "serving girl." Any attempt to lay hands on her during one of her infrequent visits to Andelys was bound to failure. She was always in the company of two other serving girls and more often than not within earshot of de Fontenne and his men-at-arms. Worse still, Quarle's prospects of forcing his way into Gaillard were not worth considering.

Jehan, Quarle's villein, who had lost his fine silver hafted knife at the abbey, lay stretched on the dusty stone flags before the fire, cracking hazelnuts and popping the sweet kernels into his mouth. Two other villeins lounged nearby. One was sharpening a knife blade against a stone, the other yawned. Pons Vernet sat in a chair to one side of the hearth, sleeping. His chin had dropped upon his chest and his mouth hung open.

From somewhere in the rear of the house, Simon Quarle heard his sister's strident voice berating one of the servants. An infant began to squall. Quarle took a deep draught from his cup. As he did, two of his sister's children burst into the hall chased by several of his own bastards. He had no wife; he preferred to take his pleasures with this or that serving woman, and therefore had no legitimate children. The children dodged back and forth, galloping around the table, shouting and tossing a little sack filled with grain.

He felt the air move as the sack zinged past his head, and he leapt up in a rage, loudly cursing and sending the lot of them, much subdued, back toward the kitchen to annoy the women.

"Go and saddle our horses," Quarle grouched, directing his words at the villein sharpening the knife and the fellow beside him. Jehan, looking up from the dusty stone flags, popped a final nutmeat into his mouth, dumped a fistful of hulls into the fire and got to his feet. Awakened by the ruckus, Pons Vernet blinked like a badger roused from a long winter's sleep. "Where are we going?" he asked.

The thawing, muddy trail led through the forest, south toward Andelys and the smaller neighboring village of St. Eloi. The section of forest they passed through was populated with towering old poplars, and there, a creek, swollen and swift with rain water, flowed through the ravine. They had not ridden far when they sighted an open char, containing a coffin, lashed down with ropes, and drawn by three mules. They saw only two conversi—lay brothers, for their heads were not shriven. One was seated on the char, the other astride the lead mule.

"What a sight to come upon," Pons Vernet said

with distaste, hastily crossing himself as if to ward off the thought of death. Out of habit, the others did likewise, all but Simon Quarle. Slowly but surely, as he watched the char jolting over the rutted trail, a notion was forming in his brain. Who could refuse a night's lodging to churchmen escorting a good and holy monk to his final resting place, he thought. And what better means to carry off the "serving girl" than inside a coffin?

Eighteen

Days passed. At Gaillard Laire and Nicolette awoke to the steady drumming of rain. Laire went and opened the shutter, as was his habit. Outside it was a miserable day. The rain fell in a steady drenching deluge, obscuring everything in a watery grey mist. The cold, heavy air gave him an instant chill, and the pinpricks of rain felt like ice upon his bare flesh. He completed his task quickly and closed the shutter.

On the bed Nicolette stretched voluptuously. The thought of her new dress being drenched by the rain, its hem dragged through the mud, discouraged her. She asked sleepily, "Do you think it will stop soon?"

"Surely by Assumption Day," was his reply, for such went the joke. Summers were often dry.

Before the fire, Barbe stretched out his front paws and lifted his haunches, his muscles rippling beneath the fine white hide. The dog stood up, shook himself and waited, wagging his tail. Laire crossed the room, wearing not a stitch, save for his gooseflesh.

He opened the door and let the dog out. Nicolette rolled onto her stomach and watched him crouch down to tend the fire. "Will there be gossip if you dance with me today?"

He cast her a side-long glance from over his shoulder. He was grinning. "Only if I go dressed as I am."

The sound of her soft laughter floated across the chamber. "I wish everyone would come dressed in such a suit of clothing! What a sight that would be."

His erection, which had retreated from the chill and drooped fat and lazy between his legs, began to build, bobbing up to brush against his thigh. "You are indecent," he told her, pushing into bed and taking her in his arms.

"I?" she piped, giggling, parrying his hands. "I don't walk about looking nasty," she said with a mischievous lilt to her voice, and rolled her eyes, even though she loved the sight of his strong, young body. There was, she thought, a sort of insolent beauty about him, his hard muscles, the easy grace of his movements.

"Now you have offended me," he teased, laughing and mauling her over. "You will have to beg for what you want."

The household servants no longer took note of their coming late to the hall of a morning. It had become so commonplace that it was no longer worthy of gossip. At Gaillard it was more or less accepted that Odette held the seigneur's favor.

In the village, too, the merchants were well aware of it, for at the candlemaker's, the oil merchant's, and the cobbler's it was she who decided what would and would not be purchased, and she who paid with the seigneur's coins. There was talk, of course. It seldom happened that a noble, even a petty one, showered a serving girl, no matter how pretty she might be, with the respect and considerations due a wife. The women of the village, the mayor's wife and those of the wealthy merchants, particularly those with young daughters, thought it a disgrace, the girl impertinent, the young seigneur, bewitched by her.

The celebration in Andelys that day was to be hosted by the mayor. But all the merchants had contributed to the feast, which was being held in honor of the new seigneur, and the prosperity his leadership had brought to the village.

Dore and Josine could hardly wait to wear their new gowns. Albert, handsomely decked out in his new attire, was ready hours before anyone else, and sat in the hall looking bored. Six of the young men-at-arms, who were to serve as the escort, polished themselves and their weapons to a fine sheen. Aymer thought them all young fools and went about the chateau shaking his head. "I am fortunate to be old," he muttered to himself.

By afternoon the rain had ceased and the last dark scudding clouds raced away toward the horizon. When Laire and Nicolette and their entourage arrived at the mayor's house in Andelys, the cobbled stones of the courtyard appeared polished by the wind, bright and gleaming as a hound's tooth.

Inside the house, servants dashed about and the scent of roasting meat hung in the warm, heavy air. Guests dressed in finery spilled into the corridor, and the hall which encompassed the full length of the grand house was jammed with people. A large table draped with silken cloth had been arranged upon a dais. Those below were little more than lengthy boards, though covered with linen cloth they conveyed an impression of opulence.

The mayor's plump wife, bursting from a gown of azure silk trimmed in marten fur, stood gabbing and smiling amid a knot of women, broad matrons and young daughters, all clothed in equal, if somewhat provincial, grandeur.

As seigneur, Laire was the guest of honor. Judot sat at his right, the mayor at his left. There was a place at the table for the serving woman, Odette, but only because to refuse her one would have been an insult to the seigneur.

Toward "Odette," the women's manner was sugary and mawkishly polite. The mayor's wife, her cheeks heavy with powder and golden necklaces gleaming beneath her double chins, looked down her nose, seemingly offended by her presence. The wool merchant's wife regarded her with a stiff and stony countenance, as did her two daughters.

It occurred to Nicolette that Andelys with its petty jealousies and social order was no different than the king's court; smaller, less significant, but just the same. And she wondered if it was so for every little village, everywhere. Each of them in order, like little worlds, eclipsed by larger ones and all of them alike. She had never thought of such a thing before, and it made her smile, though she could not say why.

The others, perhaps from curiosity or because they were lower on the social ladder, spoke pleasantly. Gossip had come to them concerning the imprisoned princess royal of Gaillard, and of the scandalous liaisons with the king's guards.

Nicolette had hoped for such an opportunity. She held them spellbound with her recounting of "her mistress's" story. She told how Nicolette of Burgundy had been falsely accused. "It is a sin that they have branded her with such malicious lies," she said, and as she had intended all along, added, "My poor mistress is not well. At times she burns with fever. Their lies have broken her heart and I fear God may call her to him."

By the time Nicolette had finished with her tale, the women were sighing sympathetically. Even the socially conscious wives of the mayor and the wool merchant were genuinely touched. Once in the gardens of the Hotel de Nesle Nicolette would have taken a bow after such a grand performance. But she felt no such thrill of accomplishment. The women for all their haughtiness were, after all, compassionate to another of their sex. Nicolette consoled herself with the thought that the "lie" was necessary, for if she was to live, the lady prisoner must die.

In all, the celebration was a great success. The tables groaned with roasted game birds, larded mutton with herb sauce and pastry tarts. With much ceremony a venison roast stuffed with onion and saffron was presented to the guests, along with patties filled with egg yolk, cheese, and spices.

Afterwards the tables were disassembled, musicians played and the guests took to dancing heartily, for every Norman, low born or high, loved a good hard dance.

Laire's attentions were monopolized by the merchants and Judot. Only when the dancing began was Laire able to speak to Nicolette. In glimpses, during the meal, he had seen her talking to the women. And now in her eyes, he saw the answer to his question. She had planted the seed in their minds. It would seem perfectly reasonable when in the future the sickly lady prisoner died of a fever and was laid in her grave.

Before them the hall throbbed with the lively melody of a "tourdion," and gaily laughing dancers whirled furiously past in their gaudy finery. Later, the mayor requested that the musicians play a courtly "dance of the chaplet," and insisted the seigneur lead the dancing.

Laire gave Nicolette an encouraging smile. She was blushing when he took her by the hand and led her before the crowd. It was obvious to all who watched the young couple glide across the hall that there was much between them.

At a cue from the musicians, the other dancers followed. With the last sweet, slow notes, the gentlemen delivered a kiss to their lady's cheek. Applause echoed through the hall.

One after another the musicians struck up faster and more enthusiastic tourdions. Nicolette saw

Dore gallop past on Judot's arm, her laughing face a blur. She did not see Josine among the dancers, but when she glanced toward the brace of tall arched windows, she saw her talking quietly with the candlemaker's son.

The musicians, fueled by endless cups of wine, played on indefatigably and, as the hall grew dim, the mayor's servants came to light the oil lamps. Albert and the young men-at-arms from the chateau stood together talking, laughing and shyly watching the young girls. Beyond the brace of tall arched windows, the sun had set, leaving behind a fiery band of purple twilight that tinted the rooftops of Andelys with a rosy, yellow glow.

Guests began to take their leave. Nicolette, Dore, and Josine were already wrapped in their cloaks, waiting by the door, when a porter pressed past them. He hurried, pushing his way through the crowd, making toward the mayor who was engaged in a conversation with Laire and the proprietor of the local tannery. Judot, nearby, was talking to a grain merchant.

Nicolette could not hear what the porter said. His words were lost to the gabble of voices and intermittent shrills of laughter. A tragedy of some sort, she guessed, judging from the porter's agitated expression.

The crowd of men dispersed. Laire, Judot, and a group of young men came toward the door arch where Nicolette and the others were waiting. The porter was with them. Dore leaned forward to catch Judot's arm. "What has happened?" she asked.

"Some men have drowned," he told her as he brushed past, striding down the corridor with the young men following after him.

"Drowned in the river?" Nicolette asked Laire as he and Albert shepherded the women into the corridor. Two of the young men-at-arms were waiting for them in the courtyard with their horses. The others had gone with Judot and his recruits.

"No, the creek," Laire corrected. "Some peasant children found three dead men by the bridge."

"Just now?" Nicolette inquired.

"Earlier, I suppose." Laire took Nicolette by the arm and guided her toward the horses. Dore and Josine followed after them. "Could they have been there when we crossed?" Dore wondered aloud. "Eugh," Josine grimaced. In the winter darkness of the courtyard the guests departed. There was the red tossing of torches and the clatter of hooves upon the cobblestones.

At the bridge, a ghastly scene awaited them. In the flaring torchlight, the stone arch of the bridge appeared grotesquely misshapen. Judot tramped up the sloping bank to speak to Laire. They exchanged a few words. Laire dismounted and followed him along the bank to where a group of dark figures gathered in the leaping torchlight. Albert swung down from his horse and forged after them, trailing through the brushy weeds.

Nicolette shortened her reins to alert the mare and squeezed with her legs. The mare moved forward. Nicolette raised herself in the stirrups to see.

"They are naked!" She said in a hushed but startled voice. She wished she had not looked.

The torchlight revealed three hugely bloated creatures, glistening and white as the bellies of fishes. Nothing about them appeared human. Nicolette turned her head away. She heard Josine's sharply indrawn breath, and saw Dore stretch her neck to see.

The black water swirled past a few paces from where the bodies had been dragged onto the shore. "They did not drown," Judot announced. "Look at this." He took a torch from one of the men and held it close to the first body. There was a gaping wound in the corpse's left side, just below the armpit. The wound was deep.

The second corpse had suffered several knife wounds, as well as a severe blow to the head. But the third corpse, that of an older man, nearly bald, with only a fringe of grey hair, looking almost as if it had been tonsured, had not a single mark of violence. His body bore only the inconsequential damage of being bounced along by the swift running water.

Horses shifted restlessly, and the cold breeze pulled sparks from the smoking torches.

The fact that the men were nude was not altogether strange. Obviously whoever had murdered them considered their clothing of value. Perhaps they were rich merchants with fine leather boots, silken jupons, and fur-lined capes. That in itself would be a boon to robbers. There was even the possibility that the children who found the men had stripped them of their clothing.

Judot gave the last body another nudge with his boot. "Not a mark. It is strange, is it not?"

"Perhaps he was thrown into the stream by the thieves?" Laire suggested.

"These are the first in weeks." Judot passed the torch back to the young man. "Merchants, do you think?"

Laire shrugged. "We may never know. They might have been killed far to the north. The stream has carried them. Keep them at the church for a few days, someone may come searching."

As they rode toward the chateau, there was a sort of nervous excitement in the cold night air. In the kitchen, Dore and Josine told the story to everyone.

The grotesqueness of the scene and the sight of the corpses troubled Nicolette long after they had returned to Gaillard. She was plagued by disquieting thoughts of death and decay.

In a dream that night she wandered through a wood. At last she came upon a pond nestled among the trees, a water-filled depression, shallow and dark with decaying leaves. When she drew near, ripples shook the surface and a hideously bloated corpse leapt at her with clutching arms and Louis's face.

She bolted up in bed with a startled cry. Her sudden movement woke Laire. He reached for her and pulled her near. Secure in his arms and lulled by the warmth of his body, Nicolette fell asleep once more.

***

Three days passed and the routine of the chateau went on undisturbed. Toward the end of the week, Rigord came early to discuss the sheep tithes and the feed allotment for cattle.

At mid-day Judot arrived to report that no one had come to inquire about the three dead men, and the curé wished to bury them. Judot could have easily sent a messenger for permission to bury the bodies.

He had come to pass the time, drink a cup of wine, and to make use of the well house for a bath, which he did every week or two. Judging from his and Dore's secretive smiles, Nicolette guessed they had planned a tryst in the well house. All morning Dore had been merry as a little bird, humming to herself.

Sometime later, Judot, looking cleaner and much satisfied with himself, shared a cup of wine with Laire, the old cleric, Albert, and several of the young men-at-arms.

The jolly conversation was punctuated by laughter even before Judot began to tell of a dispute that had recently flared between two merchants whose shops adjoined one another. The disagreement had turned ugly when one merchant's wife dumped the contents of a chamber pot onto the head of her husband's enemy as he stood shouting threats before their shop door.

The entirety of the afternoon was devoted to such foolishness. Hearty laughter filled the hall as the men sat around the table eating and drinking, exchanging reminiscences and rough jokes.

A new morning found Laire once again engaged in the monumental, and oft times tedious, task of removing rubble from Gaillard's outer bailey. He did not lack for laborers. The influx of peasants after Lachaume's departure had created a ready workforce.

Laire had quickly decided to allow the peasants to set up households in the outer ward, in exchange for their labor. The arrangement benefited everyone. The ward was slowly being reclaimed from the rubble. The area now bustled with activity, and had about it an almost prosperous air.

As was his habit of late, Laire spent a good deal of time in the outer ward. When he was not directing the workmen, he was conferring with the carpenters and stone masons. It was a learning process for Laire and he found himself enjoying it. He had come to understand, at least in part, the measure of Cacchot's pride in his chateau and lands.

As the winter day darkened, wood was unloaded from a trio of ox-drawn carts, fuel to warm the inhabitants for the long winter. Laire stood, watching, passing the time of day with the elder forester.

Agnes's messenger, no more than a boy and stiff-legged from long hours in the saddle, found him there before the chapel. Laire sent the boy off toward the hall to be fed.

Hours later, after Laire had thought upon the letter's contents, he touched the corner of the parchment to the flames in the hearth. He held it a moment, watching the edges curl and blacken.

He did not mention the letter to Nicolette until late that night when they lay together quite exhausted. For a little while she was silent, and then she said, fiercely, "I did not believe there could be such wickedness in the world. It is not true, is it? It is only rumors?" All at once her eyes filled with tears and she pressed her face to Laire's chest, sobbing, "What will we do?"

"It changes nothing. We must not lose our nerve."

She looked up at him despairingly. "They will not believe the lady prisoner is dead."

"Yes, they will believe, we will see to it. I will not lose you, ma mie. Before God, I will not."

The following day, the first snow fall of the winter began. An uninterrupted curtain of white drifted from the low-hanging clouds. Soon the guards on the wall were white with snow.

Toward evening, an open char drawn by three mules approached the gates. The two men upon the char were blanketed with snow, as was their cargo. They announced themselves as lay brothers from the abbey of St. Maur. "We are escorting the remains of a holy monk to Vernon where he was born. Can you give us shelter?"

The guards felt sorry for the lay brothers beneath their snow-laden cloaks, and one ran to ask permission for their entry. He returned quickly and the draw bridge was lowered.

"You have been invited to the keep," a guard

informed the lay brothers, directing them toward yet another drawbridge and the citadel beyond.

The lay brothers saw to their mules, settling them in the stable of the inner court. They pushed the char with its gruesome cargo beneath a lean-to beside the iron smith's shed.

When they had eaten, Laire graciously offered the lay brothers a bed in the servants' dormitory.

Aymer was curious about their abbey. "St. Maur, you say, at Dorental?" Aymer had not heard of such an abbey, but he had not been farther than a stone's throw from Gaillard in twenty-five years, and he reasoned that was the explanation.

As the meal was served, Laire questioned them about the roads and asked if they had met with many travelers. There was something oddly familiar about the taller of the two conversi, though he could not say exactly what it was. Perhaps his nose, for it was large and humped, one not easily forgotten. Laire could not rid himself of the notion that he had seen him on another occasion.

During the conversation, Nicolette mentioned Gaillard's ruined chapel. She told them something of its history, their plans to restore it to its former glory, and lamentably that they had been forced to store firewood in the chapel's nave because the chateau's woodshed had collapsed. "The good brother who last served the chapel has long since died," she told them. "He is buried in a crypt beneath the altar."

"It is a just tribute to a man of God," the conversi

with the prominent humped nose said. "Such a noble grave awaits our brother Bertin."

The evening passed uneventfully. Darkness came early that time of year and oil for lamps was costly. By the time the moon had risen the chateau's inhabitants were abed.

Not all were asleep. In the solar, high in the keep, Laire and Nicolette were lying on the bed clasped together without the knowledge of anything beyond their building passions.

Thus far their matings had resulted in only a deep sense of shared pleasure, though each month they had anxiously awaited the arrival of her flux. Soon, Laire promised, it would not matter. He would marry "Odette" before the village priest and if there was a child, there would be no danger of punishments or accusations. Laire felt in every sense a husband to her. Since he had first held her, he had not even thought of another woman. She was his, she would always be, and her fate rested on his conscience.

That morning before dawn, a man's voice, talking very low, sometimes swearing, came from the end of the stable. The air was cold, the damp cold of a snowy night, and Marcel the stableman, wrapped tightly in his blankets, was not inclined to rouse himself. He did raise his head enough to see the faint, far off light of a lantern. Presently he heard the rattle and tinkle of harnesses, the stomping of hooves and the brusque shake of a freshly roused animal. He reasoned it was the two lay brothers come to harness their mules for an early start on their journey. The stableman tucked his head back in his blankets and closed his eyes.

Not long afterwards in the outer ward of the chateau, a teenaged boy and girl were embracing in the loft of a cow shed. The girl was surprised to see a red glow through a gap in the boards. "It is the sun!" she gasped.

"No, it can not be!" the boy said fearfully, and leapt to his feet. He had been warned to keep away by the girl's father. The boy was afraid of him. If they were caught together it would be the end. The boy pressed his face to the gap in the boards and saw a sight that was at once breath-taking and terrible. "Fire!" he exclaimed. "The chapel is on fire!"

"Do not leave me," the girl cried.

"Go back to your family, hurry! I must warn everyone!"

Together they shimmied from the loft. No sooner than the girl had slipped into the shack where her family lived, the boy began to shout at the top of his lungs. In only a few moments the entire population of the outer ward had stumbled from their beds and were standing in the cold night, shivering and staring at the flames.

Several men ran toward the smaller drawbridge that separated the outer and inner wards of the chateau. Now that guards patrolled the walls, the smaller inner drawbridge was seldom raised. The men stampeded across the wooden planks. Behind them a pillar of flame burst from the hole in the chapel's roof.

It spewed like a fountain, scattering showers of bright sparks.

A pair of household boys, who slept by the hearth in the hall and whose job it was to stoke the fire at night, were awakened by a frantic hammering at the doors.

"Fire!" the men yelled as they stumbled into the darkened hall. "Fire! The chapel is burning!" The words streaked like lightning through the keep.

Albert raced up the stairs to wake his master. Laire and Nicolette came down together, but no one noticed. All the inhabitants of the keep, the seigneur, his squire, his men-at-arms, the household boys, the cook, and the serving women, poured from the hall. The lot of them, half-awake and dressed in whatever they could lay hands on in the dark, went sprinting across the drawbridge. Snow mashed and crunched beneath their feet as they pushed their way into the throng of onlookers. People stared. No one spoke.

All at once the whole roof caught fire with a loud whooshing sound. A cry went up from the jostling crowd. Roof beams crackled and snapped as the flames devoured them. The smell of burning hung in the air and everything was bathed in a trembling red glare.

Clouds of sparks drifted in the cold black night. Glowing embers rained down on the roof of the barn close by. Laire pushed and shoved, rallying the peasants, shouting orders. "Turn out the cows and pigs!" he commanded. "Bring buckets to the well! Wet down the barn roof!" he roared. "Everyone to the well!" The crowd obeyed. Laire caught several men from the running mob. "You! You! Fetch an axe, break the ice in the moat! Here!" He grabbed several more men from the crowd. "Some of you with buckets, to the moat!"

Dogs barked, men cursed and children cried. Dore and Josine, panting, ran to carry water from the well for the barn roof.

With chattering teeth and a sinking heart, Nicolette watched the chapel burn. "There's nothing can be done for it," Mahaut said. She had only just arrived. Nicolette and the old woman hugged arms to ward off the cold. Soon they began to feel the fire's heat on their faces and, in the glare, saw red people, pigs, and cows.

Dore and Josine passed buckets from the well until the chapel roof crashed in with a rumbling sound more terrible than thunder. It frightened them so badly, they drew back in awe. People running past grabbed the buckets from their hands. Defeated by their fear, they went and stood beside Nicolette and Mahaut, staring, dazzled by the light. "It might be an omen," Josine said in a queer little voice.

"Go back to the keep!" Laire told Nicolette when he found her. "All of you," he told the women, "Go back to the hall!" Nicolette shook her head stubbornly. "No, I want to stay." Laire was going to send her back, despite her objections, when some men came running up to him. They shouted, "The manure pile is afire!"

Laire ran off with them, to where the mountain

of manure beside the barn smoldered and hissed. Buckets of water sloshed onto it, and men attacked it with rakes and pitchforks, pulling it apart.

Nicolette trailed after him, shivering and gazing about at the confusion. Ash floated down like snowflakes, and underfoot the snow was transformed by turns to slush and ice. After a time she lost sight of Laire.

Flames continued to leap from inside the chapel, but with each incendiary flash and subsequent burst of flame, the voice of the fire grew weaker, wheezing, gasping. Nicolette paused for one last look. She was very cold and had decided to go back to the keep.

"At times it is difficult to understand God's wisdom," a voice from behind Nicolette said. She whirled about to see the hump-nosed lay brother's smiling face. "It is a pity," he observed, removing his cloak and dropping it over her shoulders. "Come." He gently turned her. "You are shuddering with cold. I will return to the keep with you."

She was at once warmer. "The chapel was to be repaired as soon as the weather warmed. Well, after the fields were plowed, when the men were free to work." She had told him all that earlier in the evening, but she wanted to say it again, to tell someone. She was so disappointed.

He let her go on talking as they walked. Below the drawbridge that separated the outer from the inner bailey, the moat was black as doom and locked in winter ice. Everything was silent, no one was about. All were either at the scene of the fire or gone in from the cold. The snow made a crunching sound beneath their feet.

A shadow fluttered, separating from the pool of blackness beneath the high snow-capped hedges, and a slim figure materialized before Nicolette. She saw only the flash of eyes beneath the slanted hood. A hand gripped her shoulder, another clamped over her mouth, and before she could utter a sound, another grasped her about the waist with a steely grip.

She grappled wildly, flinging her body back and forth, convulsed by her efforts to free herself. Something hard struck her jaw a stunning blow. Swirling lights danced before her eyes and she felt herself being dragged into the shadows.

Nineteen

At dawn a sputter of snow drifted from the low clouds. In the outer ward of the chateau, a man shouted, "Here! Someone help me!" A frightened cow charged past him. He gave chase, cornering the cow between two wooden huts. Another man and a half-grown boy came running with a rope. Wedged in the narrow space, the cow began to bawl. At the approach of the men it lowered its head and pawed at the snow, refusing to budge.

All that remained of the chapel was a fiercely smoking hulk. Steam rose from the scattered piles of manure and the water doused upon the barn roof had frozen to a sheet of shimmering ice. Fantastic icicles scalloped the eaves and glittered in the bleak morning light.

A group of men stood about with Laire as he watched smoke roll from the gutted interior of the chapel. "The barn was saved, at least," he said to the exhausted faces of the men around him. The fact that their supply of firewood had been reduced to ash was too depressing to consider at that hour of the morning.

Why? Laire wondered. What had caused the

PRISONER OF MY HEART 337

blaze? He was considering all the possibilities as he, Albert, and a small group of men and boys poked through the smouldering remains with wooden staves.

One of the men poking through the hot ash speared a distorted chunk of metal, all that remained of an oil lamp.

Near the well, a group of people were congratulating themselves on having saved the barn, the cows, and the pigs. Laughter rang out from the lively conversations as one, then another rehashed the night's events, while the lay brothers' char drew up before the drawbridge.

The guard who had been carrying buckets of water all night quit the discussion of the fire and went toward the drawbridge. "Did you see the fire?" he asked the lay brother seated on the open char. The hump-nosed conversi shook his head. "Brother Gui and I were not aware of it until this morning," he said, gazing at the smoking ruin.

"The barn was spared, and all our cows and pigs," the guard told him, remarking how the people had worked to save it and the beasts from the flames. The guard was still talking when the char rumbled off across the drawbridge.

Inside the coffin, Nicolette was gripped by an inexpressible dread which seemed beyond her strength to bear. Bound and gagged and unable to move, she thought she would surely lose her senses. The strict confines of the wooden box closed upon her like a grave and the suffocating air reeked of decay.

Numb with cold and shock, at first she could not think beyond the horror of the moment. But as the char jolted over the frozen ruts of the road, tossing her against the sides of the coffin, the full horror took hold of her mind. Did her captors intend to bury her alive? Surely they had learned of her identity; what other reason could there be to abduct her? Were they paid by Louis? Or was this at last what Isabella had intended for her?

Laire would come after her. She clung desperately to the thought, refusing to believe they had killed him in the confusion of the fire. For it was clear to her now why the chapel had burned, and who had set the blaze.

Her torture, both mental and physical, continued until the char lurched to a halt, driving her head into the fore of the coffin. She heard voices, dimly, and the rattle of ropes being dragged from atop the coffin.

A blaze of daylight blinded Nicolette as she was dragged from the coffin. She was shaking with cold, bruised and terrified. Her two abductors had been joined by two other men leading riderless horses. Nicolette had no time to consider what this new and startling development meant. She was roughly seized by the hump-nosed brother and her feet unbound. After he had mounted his horse, he pulled her up to ride before him. "My name is

Jehan," he whispered close to her ear. And in a voice ugly with insinuation, he promised, "You will have cause to remember it."

Simon Quarle strode out through the snow-blanketed yard of his manor house. He had been advised of Jehan's return. Pons Vernet exited the door after his brother-in-law, raised a hand to shield his eyes, and blinked in the unaccustomed glare.

Both men watched as the riders picked their way through the maze of defensive ditches and approached stone and earthen palisades. Simon Quarle raised a fist in the air and gave a hoot of victory. A shrill response echoed back across the snow.

Quarle pounded his sides with pleasure. "Well, well, if it is not the popinjay's pretty little mattress!" He gave a broad, gap-toothed smile, poked his brother-in-law in the arm so hard that he nearly knocked him off his feet, and made several other lewd, mocking comments.

Nicolette's face which was already numb with cold, stung from the vileness of his words. With an increasing sense of alarm she saw an army of scroungy-looking servants and soldiers. They seemed to crawl like vermin from every doorway and crevice of the ramshackle buildings. Just then, the horse on which she was seated halted and swung about. She saw Quarle's moving hand, the obscene gesture, and heard the whooping laughter of the men in the yard.

She was dragged from the horse and hustled inside the manor house. As in the yard, people appeared from everywhere, women, some with infants in their arms, half-dressed men, and a gang of filthy children. The hall was dingy, small compared to Gaillard's vastness, and smelled rankly, a mingling of unwashed people, urine, and stale food.

"Where are you taking her?" a broad, coarse-featured woman challenged. She gave Nicolette a look of unbridled resentment, and loudly complained that she was a slut and she belonged in a sty with the rest of the swine. Quarle cursed at her and knocked her aside. Only later did Nicolette understand that the woman was Quarle's mistress and that she had been routed from her sleeping quarters so the prisoner might be secured there. It was, apparently, one of the few chambers with a lock upon the door.

It was a miserable room, small and without a single window. Nicolette saw at once that there was no avenue of escape, save for the heavy, iron-hinged door. The room contained only a bed, covered with a fox fur rug, a chest containing a few articles of clothing, a chamber pot, and a small bench. Only after a close examination of the walls and door did Nicolette feel safe enough to use the chamber pot. Afterwards she felt warmer, but no less fearful of what fate awaited her.

A small group of riders broke from the encircling woods and galloped toward Quarle's manor house.

PRISONER OF MY HEART

At the first line of defensive ditches, they slackened their pace.

The drowsing guard atop the wooden watch tower roused like a man doused with water. He leaned from the tower, shouting and flailing his arms. Below, a dozen or more men armed with crossbows scrambled to their positions atop the stone and earthen palisades.

As the riders reined in their horses to weave a path through the ditches, the men atop the palisades recognized the shields of their master's suzerain lord, Raoul de Conches.

De Conches and his two noble traveling companions were accompanied by a small troop of archers carrying their long bows slung over their backs. From that distance and silhouetted against the stark whiteness of the snow, they seemed to be winged creatures.

Again, Quarle hastened from his hall. He was bursting with good cheer, thinking of what a coup he had pulled off in capturing the lady. De Conches's arrival had taken him completely by surprise. He had not been expecting his lord to return from the Paris court so quickly. What good fortune, Quarle chuckled to himself as he took a deep breath of cold air, to have the lady brought in only hours before.

Servants and archers milled about, and the exhausted horses were led away. The nobles made their way through the trampled snow and entered the hall. At the door, de Conches placed a gloved hand on Quarle's arm and halted. "Do you have her?" he asked, his voice hushed but emphatic.

"Yes, milord," Quarle responded proudly. "The lady of Burg—"

"Keep your voice down, fool! I trust you have followed my instructions?"

"I have told no one of her identity," Quarle assured him.

"Good, see that you do not."

"Are you taking her north with you, milord?"

"No," de Conches said quickly, "not today. I have no time. I leave her in your care. I will send for her later. Guard her with your life. She is my best bargaining point." That said, he stepped past Quarle into the smoke-scented warmth of the hall.

Quarle ordered the servants about. Food and hot-spiced wine was offered to the guests. After they had eaten, the two nobles drowsed and napped by the hearth. Quarle, after making some excuse about the fief's account books, led de Conches up the stairs to the room above the hall.

The sound of footsteps alerted Nicolette. She leapt up from the bed, where she had been lying wrapped in the mangy fox fur, and faced the door.

The hinges squealed a rusty protest as the door jarred open. A shaft of milky white daylight flooded in from the shuttered window across the corridor and Raoul de Conches entered the room. An instant before the door closed, Nicolette caught a glimpse of Quarle standing in the corridor.

De Conches moved slowly toward her, his slick black hair gleaming with oil. He smiled with recognition. "I had to be certain it was you," he said, savoring each word. "It is a comfort to my soul to know that you are as immoral as your sluttish cousins, Joan and Blanche. Indeed," he said with raised brows, "it would have pained me beyond measure to think that you were truly innocent."

"Pray, do not concern your soul for my sake, messire de Conches. I am certain you will burn in hell for a thousand other sins."

A flicker of emotion flashed in his eyes, mockery perhaps. "Alas, none so grand as yours, madame—nor so unwise." His hand snaked out to brush her cheek. "There will be no more charades for you, my deceitful little actress."

Nicolette struck his hand, flinging it aside. "Has she sent you to murder me? Your queen of whores, the regal Isabella!"

A murmur of laughter rose in his throat. "Murder," he said with a note of surprise. "No, not at all—at least not yet. She has planned something far more entertaining for you and your lover de Fontenne."

"Where is he?" The note of pleading in Nicolette's voice betrayed her. "What have you done with him?"

De Conches only chuckled. From the door, he sent her a look of mock reproach and chided, "A common chevalier. Women, who can understand them?"

Nicolette turned her head away, fighting back the useless tears. She heard the door close, the lock click. She threw herself down upon the ratty fur in despair. The fear that Laire was dead, murdered by the men who had abducted her, suddenly was too much to bear. She began to weep, hysterically, exhaustingly.

At first she heard only the pounding of her heart, her sobbing breaths. But as she lay there, she fancied she heard voices, very close, as if the sound came from inside her head. The wind, she thought. But, no, she heard laughter, a man's voice. It seemed to be coming from beneath the bed.

Intent, she moved to the edge of the bed, where its frame stood near the wall, and glancing down saw a splinter of light winking up at her through the dusty floor planks. Again she heard a man's voice. He seemed to be standing directly beneath her. It was Raoul de Conches. The realization stunned her as much as the words.

"It is only fitting," de Conches said in his lazy amused fashion, "that a pig should be the end of our beloved King Philip." Another voice, one Nicolette did not recognize, deep and gravelly, asked, "Are you certain you can separate the king from the other hunters?"

A third voice remarked, "Boars are notoriously unpredictable. How can you be certain the beast will lead the king within range of the archers?"

"My men are well versed." It was de Conches's voice again. "You seem to forget, gentlemen, I have had some experience in hunting accidents." His comment was followed by a round of laughter and some mention of an incident in Blois.

"This damnable storm will slow our pace," the graveled voice cursed and swore an oath.

"Have no fear, gentlemen." De Conches spoke once more. "We will be in Clermont long before the king's entourage arrives. Time enough to spin our web. Drink up. Ah, here is Quarle. Are the horses saddled?"

Quarle grunted affirmatively, and afterwards the voices faded. She heard a door open, the sound of the wind gusting past, as if a storm was blowing. And then the door closed and she heard only the sounds of the house.

Nicolette could not at first comprehend the magnitude of what she had overheard. It was too fantastic to believe. De Conches and the unknown men in the room below had just plotted to murder the king! Surely with Isabella's blessing, perhaps with her direction, for de Conches had been her sucklouse even before he climbed into her bed.

Nicolette felt no pity for the old king. He was cruel and ruthless. And if Isabella was a she wolf, well, perhaps it was justice after all. Nicolette might have even found some wicked sense of comfort in the thought, had it not been for a sudden terrible realization, that, from the very first, Isabella's singular objective had been to seize the crown of France for her son.

The thought sickened Nicolette. That it had been no more than Isabella's overweening lust for power. Not envy, jealousy, or even hatred, but greed alone that had caused her to denounce her brothers' wives. Poor, unhappy Joan and Blanche, who had so foolishly played into her hands.

How Isabella must have rejoiced to rid herself of her brothers' wives and her father's personal guards with one fell stroke. How easily Gautier and Pierre had fallen into her trap. And what of Isabella's brothers? Nicolette wondered. Would she murder her own brothers? Could even she do such a thing? Would she exile them? Or perhaps they would simply bow to her, for they had always been weak and foolish.

With Isabella's hand on the crown, Nicolette knew there would be no future for her and Laire, no new beginning, only a violent and brutal end.

Her thoughts were plunged into havoc. She lay there with her cheek pressed to the fox fur trying to think of a way she might escape.

At Gaillard, hours passed before "Odette" was missed. Only when Laire and the others had returned to the hall cold, exhausted, and hungry, did Dore look up from slicing bread and ask, "Where is Odette?"

Laire slumped down at the table. "What do you mean? She is here, isn't she?"

"No," Josine said, coming up to the table and wiping her hands on her apron. "She told us she was going to watch the fire." Dore inclined her head, adding, "But she has never returned."

The chateau was searched from top to end. Laire even looked in the tower room. It was necessary to climb through the passage for the only key was in Nicolette's possession. She was not there. She was not anywhere. In desperation Laire had men pull apart the charred timbers of the chapel to search for her.

It was the same story at the stable. She had simply vanished. "No one was here today," the stableman attested. "Only the two conversi who came in the middle of the night to harness their mules. They were a foul-mouthed lot, not at all reverent, I can tell you."

"They brought us bad luck with that coffin," one of the young stable boys said with a sage wag of his head.

Laire cursed his own stupidity for not seeing the truth sooner. There was but one way she might have left Gaillard. The sudden significance of the coffin, and of the three nude bodies, found by the river, staggered him. The conversi, of course, had been Quarle's men. Laire was left to wonder if Quarle had abducted "Odette" simply as revenge, to recoup his brother-in-law's ransom, or because de Conches had somehow guessed her true identity.

Laire could hardly confide the last possibility to Judot and the others. As it turned out they were satisfied with the explanation that Quarle had carried off Odette for revenge.

It all made perfect sense to Judot, save for the notion that a serving girl, no matter how pretty or otherwise talented, could be worth ransoming. The idea was somehow obscene, certainly nothing a sound-thinking Norman would do.

In less than an hour, Laire, Albert, Judot, and a dozen men set out to search the countryside. The day had grown darker with each passing hour. Masses of black clouds stacked upon the horizon and the wind came in icy gusts. Less than two leagues from Gaillard they found the abandoned char, three sad-looking mules and an empty coffin. The snow was trampled, marked with hoof prints where riders had been waiting.

Laire sent Albert and several of the men back to Gaillard with the mules and the char. He, Judot, and the others followed the tracks through the silent snowy woods. Toward evening they came within sight of Quarle's manor house.

Concealed in the encircling woods, they settled down to watch the grey stone buildings sink steadily into the winter darkness. Slivers of light escaped from the tightly shuttered window openings, and everything was still, buried beneath a mantle of snow. Only the sound of the wind rattling the branches above their heads broke the eerie silence.

Laire sat on his heels in the snow, continuing to stare at the untidy clutter of buildings. He was sick with worry. He could not even be certain that Nicolette was still being held by Quarle. In the trampled snow they had seen evidence of many riders approaching Quarle's shabby chateau, a score of which had continued on north. He tried not to think of what her fate might be as de Conches's prisoner.

Fate seemed very cruel to Laire at that moment, and he considered how close he and Nicolette had come to succeeding. In only a few short weeks they would have buried the lady prisoner and the past once and for all, and been free to live out their lives in peace. Of all the tortured thoughts sifting through his consciousness there was above all else, the recollection of the tenderness that had existed between them. It was as if he could recall the touch of her lips, the scent of her skin, the clear, sweet sound of her voice, her laughter. The thoughts consumed him.

Judot crouched down beside Laire, laying a hand on his shoulder.

Laire jumped.

"What do we do?" Judot asked.

Laire shrugged. "Wait," he said, casting his glance back across the snowy landscape. "Later, I am going in to find Odette."

Judot arched a brow. He did not say what he was thinking. One does not tell his seigneur that he is unwise. Instead he said, "I am with you." A murmur of agreement sounded from the young men who had gathered round. "We do not fear Quarle," one said. "Our swords are sharp," another boasted, and from yet another, "It is justice."

Laire looked over the young faces, red with cold and burning with enthusiasm. They were the sort of faces that restored a man's faith in rightness and decency. He felt a certain sense of pride in that. "You are good men and brave," he told them. "But we are outnumbered by twenty or more. In open battle they would cut us down. Alone, I may be able to reach the hall. If I can locate Odette, perhaps, through stealth, I will be able to free her. However, if things should go amiss, then I will need your support."

Judot and the young men voiced their determination. "We will be ready to ride." Judot spoke for all. "If an alarm is raised, we will charge the palisades, that should give them something to think about. With any luck we can draw them out and lead them on a merry chase."

Unaware of the men plotting in the snowy woods, Simon Quarle sat basking in the warmth of his hall, counting out gold coins, one hundred gold ecus to be precise. The exact amount given him by Raoul de Conches for his success in abducting "the serving girl." Quarle's brother-in-law, Pons Vernet, sat beside him, placing the coins in neat stacks. "We should celebrate," Vernet suggested. The villeins seated round the table, awaiting their share of the wealth, were in hearty agreement. Quarle laughed. He was in a rare mood that night, and sent a servant for wine.

The hump-nosed Jehan was inspecting his windfall of five coins and thinking of the pleasures he could buy with such a fortune. His accomplice, Gui, sat at his elbow, fingering his payment, holding the coins up to the light of the oil lamp and inspecting each piece. The servant returned with cups and wine.

Simon Quarle rose and called a toast. "To popinjays! And other featherbrained birds!" he roared, shaking with laughter. The villeins rose to their feet, shouting in agreement. The wine was soon gone and they sent for more.

Again and again Quarle called on Jehan and his confederate, Gui, to recite the tale of the abduction. Quarle had heard the story at least six times, but laughed harder with each telling of how Jehan and Gui had duped de Fontenne. Not only had he admitted them into the chateau, but the fool had even invited them to sup at his table.

The story grew with each telling. More wine was required. Before long Quarle and his villeins were all quite drunk. Jehan's much embellished description of the blazing chapel renewed their thirst. Quarle wished to hear it several times. They drank and drank. Crude jokes were told. They laughed like lunatics and drank some more.

Outside an icy wind came gusting over the rooftops and soughing past the eaves. The wind swept the snowy courtyard in gusts, blowing the drifted snow into the air in swirling, sparkling clouds. Locked in the darkened room above the hall, Nicolette lay there hearing every word.

She did not know what to do. A thousand dark and dire possibilities leapt into her mind. She thought of Laire again. Her heart ached.

There was, perhaps, a single ray of hope. The men below, for all their bragging, had not once mentioned killing Laire. She was certain they would have bragged of the deed had they done so.

Their laughter rang through the floor planks, louder than the wind moaning past. The men were getting drunker by the moment, and Nicolette more fearful of what they might do. Her only hope was that they would drink away their wits.

Time passed, light still winked up from below and Nicolette lay there listening. For some unknown reason she thought of the geese she had seen at the market in Gisors. Pretty blue- and green-feathered geese with shiny yellow bills, locked in a wicker cage and waiting to have their heads sliced off by the butcher's knife. She knew now how the poor geese must have felt.

A sound of staggering footfalls jerked her head toward the door. She heard two men quarreling. A glow of yellow light crept beneath her door. She heard scuffling sounds, grunts, and the thud of blows being landed. There was a loud thump, a crash, then she perceived panting noises and gasping, and suddenly hoarse, almost silent, laughter. Perhaps the men discovered one was no stronger than the other?

"Look here," a voice slurred. "We can both have some sport."

Nicolette's heart skipped a beat, realizing it was surely her they were referring to.

Twenty

One of the men staggered against the door as they rose to their feet. "We will need to be careful. We will have to watch for one another, give a warning if someone comes up the stairs. I'll go first. You stand watch."

"Nah, yah, yah . . ." The second man protested. At least, from his tone, it seemed a protest. His voice was so blurred by drink it was impossible to discern his words. "Go on," the soberest of the two insisted. "When I've had my fun, I'll watch for you." There was a mutter of disagreement. They were both drunk. At last the one who was so fuddled in his brain that he could only babble agreed. She heard him stumble away.

Nicolette jumped at the sound of the bar being raised, and the door creaked open. In a fit of panic she flung herself beneath the bed and lay in the dust and filth. The dingy room bloomed yellow. Boots flashed before her eyes, as he paced past her, weaving across the room. He was drunk. She could smell his sour, fermenty stench.

He was not, however, drunk enough to believe she was gone. He began to hum to himself, a mindless sort of hummn, hummn, hummn. He sat the lantern down on the chest and continued to hum. Suddenly, he fell down on all fours and pounced forward. He leered beneath the bed, a look of triumphant malice on his laughing face.

Nicolette screamed. It was Jehan. With a mighty shove she sent the chamber pot careening toward him. It sloshed and toppled over, spilling over his hands and across the floor.

He spat out a single furious obscenity, leapt to his feet in a rage and seized the bed's wooden frame. With the strength of a madman, he lifted the bed and flung it to one side. Nicolette scrambled across the filthy planks, keeping beneath it.

Ranting with fury, he lunged for her, his hands grappling, plunging after her. She kicked at him, knocking his bag cap from his head, battering at his hands. No matter how he came at her, she whirled to aim her feet at him and kicked.

Back and forth they went. At last he was too quick for her. His sweaty fingers clamped down on her ankle like a steel trap. She kicked out viciously with her other foot. Her shin struck wood and jarred with pain. He was dragging her forward. She grasped at the rope fretwork suspending the mattress, but he gave her ankle a brutal twist. She gasped with pain, and the ropes slipped from her grasp. He caught her other leg and towed her screaming and struggling from beneath the bed.

She lunged sideways, her mouth open to scream again. But before she could, he clamped a hand over her mouth. She felt his fingernails dig into her cheeks. She struggled wildly, thrashing out with her legs, pushing against him with her arms. When he tried to climb on top her, she thrust her knee upwards and felt it sink into his groin.

He yelped with pain and fell back. Nicolette scrambled sideways. She felt her coif ripped from her head. He cursed and grabbed for her again. She lunged away. He caught her by the hair, flinging her head backwards. It cracked against the floor with a sickening thud.

A dizzy blackness filled with swirling lights swam before her eyes. She lay there stunned, her resistance momentarily shattered. He flung himself atop her. Still dazed, Nicolette tried to scream, but no sound came out. Blind with terror, she began to buck and toss in a frenzied effort to free herself.

His hand grasped her throat. She went insane, flailing her arms against him, thrashing out. The knuckles of her outflung hand cracked against the chamber pot. She grasped the pot's lip and, swinging it with all her strength, clouted him alongside the head. It made a dull, hollow sound. He fell heavily forward, pinning her beneath his weight. The unwieldy pot tumbled away, rolling against the bed. She shoved him aside with a grunt of disgust, and fought her way to her feet.

All at once he groaned and tried to raise himself on his arms. A chill of panic raced through Nicolette. She grabbed the pot, this time with both hands, and clubbed him. Afterwards he did not move.

For a moment she crouched there, trembling, trying to decide what she must do. Perhaps it was fright that sharpened her wits, for in a flash of inspiration a thought came to her. If she could be mistaken for Jehan, mayhap she could climb from the window in the corridor and walk right past the guards at the watch tower?

She tugged and pulled, working quickly, stripping the unconscious Jehan of his clothing. Though she was loath to do so, she shed her once beautiful emerald green dress and rapidly donned the filthy hosen, sherte, and jupe. They were too big for her, especially the boots, but she hardly noticed. She stuffed the damp bag cap on her head, and peeked from the door.

The corridor was black as the inside of a cow. She saw nothing. She slipped outside and set the bar on the door. She did not see the man who was supposed to be watching for Jehan, and wondered nervously where he had gone. Fumbling in the dark, she found the window. The shutter would not open. She jerked, she tugged, she could not budge it. At last she gave up.

Now she was truly desperate. From below the sounds of their drunken conversations and hooting laughter rang up the stairs and down the corridor. Nicolette knew the men in the hall were drunk as rats, half-blind on wine, but would they be duped by Jehan's clothing? And where was Jehan's accomplice?

She crept down the corridor, hardly daring to breathe. At the top of the stairs, she saw Gui. He was perched precariously on the top step, snoring away in a drunken stupor. A wash of light from the hearth played on the stairs, enough to light her way. Across the hall the men sat before the fire, drinking and carousing. Their backs were to her. Several wailed an unmelodic song while another kept time by slamming a mace against the tabletop. She saw no servants, save for two young boys who were asleep, leaning against the wall. The others had apparently all crawled away to their beds.

The hall doors were not twenty paces from the foot of the stairs, but she could not bring herself to be so bold. Surely they would see her. She would have to walk right past them. To the right of the steps was a door arch which led into a passageway. Surely the passageway led to the kitchen, but which way, to the right or to the left? She chose the left, and moving furtively with her back close to the wall, inched through the darkness.

She felt her way blindly, trying to hurry. Her heart was beating so wildly it seemed that it would suffocate her. Then before her eyes she saw the dark outline of a stone oven. She had found the kitchen. She took a deep breath. All was silent. She saw a door on the far side of the room and moved toward it.

Her clumsy boots seemed to have a will of their own and collided into something soft. She sprawled forward over a large formless mound. It stank of wine and vomit and uttered a muffled grunt. A huge fat hand groped from the darkness. Nicolette dodged away. It was a drunken man. She sprang to her feet, choking back the startled cry that rose in her throat.

Lurching away she cracked her hip on the corner of a table. She gasped and blundered on toward the shadowy door. She grasped the wooden handle with both hands and pulled as hard as she could. Blackness and the odor of rancid, half-rotten meat wafted over her. It was a storeroom. Behind her she could hear the scuffling sounds of the drunken man on the floor, moving about and grumbling.

Near to hysteria, she closed the door and sagged against it. Her eyes roved wildly over the clutter of the darkened room, searching. At last she saw the outline of another door and started toward it.

A man's voice boomed out. She jerked around, her eyes wide with fear. She bit her lip to keep from screaming. The drunken man took several swaying steps toward her and, reaching out his arms, pitched forward and fell on his face. He did not move. She stood there paralyzed. But there was only the distant sound of the drunken men carousing in the hall.

She began to move quickly, groping toward the door. The blackened room seemed endless. At last her fingers grasped the latch. She pushed against the door and, stumbling in the oversized boots, nearly fell into the snow. She pushed the door to and hung there a moment, giddy.

It seemed she had neglected to breathe and now she drank in long draughts of air. Faint with fear she raced across the snowy ground toward the shadows cast by the odd collection of buildings. A gust of icy wind stung her face, and for a moment took away her breath.

She was free of the hall, but there remained before her the hopeless task of reaching the woods. Gazing about, she saw no sign of life. There was but a single watchtower. Apparently the guards had retreated there from the bitter wind. She could see wisps of smoke curling from the slotted window openings and a faint light, no more than a glow, and cast, no doubt, by a brazier.

Nicolette molded herself to the wall of a shed and waited, gathering her courage. An open expanse of snowy ground lay between her and the low, earthen palisades. From nearby a crunching sound reached her ears. She stiffened. The sound, baffled by the buildings, seemed to come from all directions. The wind gusting past stung her ears and filled them with a rushing sound. She paused. Convinced it was only the wind, and her imagination, she slowly edged toward the corner of the shed. Her next objective was a long, low building whose shadow and tall, snow-covered hedges would conceal her route of escape from those in the watchtower.

With a leap, she flung herself forward. All at once a pair of arms fell over her, plucking her from the snow. The ground vanished from beneath her feet as if she had stepped off into the air. Her legs cartwheeled madly, the oversize boots threatening to fall from her feet. She filled her lungs to scream, but before she could, something cold and tasting of leather clamped over her mouth—a gloved hand.

A voice breathed her name into her ear, louder than the wind whipping past. "Shh, it is I, ma mie. At first I was not certain it was you. I did not mean to frighten you. I was afraid you would scream."

"Laire!" she softly sobbed. She turned in his arms, clinging to him. She began to whisper a thousand questions in a rapid, excited voice. He pressed a gloved finger to her lips, promising, "Later. First we must reach the woods without being sighted." He took her by the arm and, keeping low, they ran together. In the stillness, the sound of the snow crunching beneath their boots was alarmingly loud. They progressed by short bursts, then crouched in the snow, listening, then ran again.

Voices carried from the watchtower, followed by a hollow thumping sound. Laire halted, pushing Nicolette down in the snow beside him. A form, black against the snowy landscape, descended the watchtower steps. A moment later the man mounted the steps with an armload of wood. They waited, and presently puffs of smoke belched from the slotted opening.

"Now," Laire whispered, pulling her up with him, and sprinting toward the palisade. In an instant they were over the crest and down the other side, slipping and sliding, running toward the ditches. At the last ditch, they paused, glancing over their shoulders. All was still, nothing stirred. They moved off once more, dashing across the open snow toward the concealing blackness of the woods.

In the darkness, men moved to surround them.

A hand reached out to steady Nicolette. "It is Odette!" a voice whispered. "What in the name of Christ!" another declared. Nicolette looked up to see Judot's broad face and furrowed brow beneath the felt hat. He and Laire exchanged words, and other voices joined in until the cold air buzzed with their whispered words. Someone threw a cape about her shoulders. A shiver shook her from head to foot. Horses were led forward in the darkness.

Once Nicolette found her voice, her breathless words tumbled out in spasms. Her story halted and leapt forward as she told how the lay brothers bound and gagged her and forced her into the coffin. She told them of de Conches's visit, the words she had overheard, of Quarle and his men, of how they had become drunk, and of her escape. "The one called Jehan came to the room . . . he was drunk . . . I hit him with the chamber pot." She paused abruptly to catch her breath and, looking up in the darkness at Laire, the faces surrounding her, she said, "They are bound for Clermont to kill the king! A hunting accident, they said."

No one spoke, though their thoughts were clear enough, even in the dark. Nicolette, herself, felt no sympathy for the old king, but her whispered plea was filled with passion. "We must stop them! Isabella is worse than Satan!"

Rigord's youngest son shook Laire's shoulder. "Lights!" he reported, gesturing toward the chateau. Before their eyes, lanterns appeared at doorways and windows, a barrage of sounds came cannoning across the snow, and black figures burst from the buildings. The scene was one of utter confusion. Shouts and curses were hurled into the wind, doors jarred open and slammed shut, and reluctant horses balked and sidled.

Laire hauled Nicolette up to ride before him, and the group set out through the woods, ducking low-hanging branches, avoiding windfalls. Many of the huge old trees lay rotting where they had fallen, and the young woods springing up around them was thick with undergrowth. Where the wood thinned to pasture land, Laire halted.

Judot turned his horse. "Do we ride for Clermont, milord?"

"No." Laire had already decided what must be done. "Quarle is a more immediate danger. You must warn Gaillard and the villagers."

"And you?" Judot asked, perplexed.

"I have no choice. I have sworn an oath to defend the king."

Nicolette, twisting her body in the saddle, said, "I am going with you."

"You are going back to Gaillard, where you will be safe."

"As I was safe before?" she contradicted. He was not about to give in, and she, noting well the stubborn set of his jaw, threatened, "If you send me back, I will follow you—even if I have to walk to Clermont." Nicolette's eyes flashed defiantly. She felt she had proven herself to be more than a foolish, helpless female. "It is all because of Isabella, think what evil she has done."

It seemed she was about to reveal everything, and

PRISONER OF MY HEART

in an effort to silence her, Laire said, "There is no horse for you."

Several voices rose from the group of horsemen. "Take my horse," each offered. "The demoiselle may have mine," Rigord's youngest son insisted, quickly dismounting his stocky sorrel gelding.

Nicolette scrambled from the saddle. Laire barely had a chance to give her an arm down. He could see it would be useless to argue further, and there was no time.

The youth boosted her atop the sorrel. "His name is Sable," he said. "He's quick, and he can jump like he has wings." The youth passed her the reins and climbed up to ride pillion with another of the men-at-arms.

Astride the milling horses, Laire gave Judot and the others their instructions. Judot and several men were to make for Andelys, Rigord's son and the others for Gaillard. Quarle would be forced to divide his forces. Hopefully he would overlook the pair of tracks heading north. Laire and Nicolette turned their horses into the cold north wind, and crossed the meadow at a lope.

They rode without speaking, for they would have been forced to shout into the blustery wind to make themselves heard. Near dawn the wind died down, and the countryside was wrapped in a strange, almost religious silence. Above them a fiery winter sunrise streaked the sky with scarlet, and filled the air with a mist of ice crystals.

They halted where a black ribbon of water meandered through a snow-covered field. Beyond the shoreline reeds with their heavy burden of snow, the dark waters, slowly freezing, flowed sluggishly past. The sound of a single Angelus bell carried on the silent air.

"Do you know what you are doing?" Laire asked as he stood her on the snowy ground.

"Yes, I am going with you," she sighed, hugging her arms about his neck in a vehement embrace.

He was so overcome by the desire to feel her against him that he took her in his arms and held her for a moment before he kissed her.

With her lips still against his, she mumbled, "Do not hate me for defying you. I could not let you go alone—"

"Shh, it is not important, only that I have found you again. We should ride south, make for Italy, let them murder one another. They deserve no better."

"If Isabella and de Conches succeed we will be killed. De Conches said as much to me. He said, 'She has planned something special for you and de Fontenne.' Those were his words. Oh, Laire, she would not rest until she found us. We would not be safe in Italy, there would be no place in all the world where we might hide. What can we do? How will we stop her?"

He glanced away, toward the horses and the frosty white vapors rising from their muzzles. His gaze swept back to her. "In my sister's letter, she wrote that our uncle de Orfevres was traveling with the king. That he was to be present when the treaty with the Flemish was signed. If he is at Clermont, and we can manage to get a message to him . . ." He did not complete the thought, but said, "Tell me again what you overheard. Try to remember each word."

Nicolette repeated the dialogue once more, concluding, "They spoke only of a hunting accident, not how the deed was to be done."

They talked for awhile, neither willing to admit that it seemed hopeless, then crouched by the stream and dipped their hands into the stinging cold water to drink. Before they set out, Laire made Nicolette take his gloves. As they rode north the sun peeked from a sky which was thick with clouds, tinted yellow and looking curdled as milk.

By afternoon the snow began to fall again. At first only a few snowflakes, huge and lacy, drifted lazily to earth. But within the hour the snowflakes grew smaller and more numerous until they filled the air and blotted out the distance. As the day progressed the wind grew stronger and they, riding into the howling teeth of the gale, lost all feeling in their hands and feet and their faces grew rigid with cold.

Laire reckoned their position to be somewhere near Clermont, but in the whirling, shifting snow it was difficult to judge which direction was north.

Quite by chance they came upon a merchant's char and two hapless horses embedded in a snow bank. The merchant, a large man wrapped in a fur blanket with a ball-shaped belly before him and a red face lost in whiskers sat in the snow, bemoaning his fate. On sighting two riders, he leapt to his feet, shouting, "Hoy! Travelers! My char is bogged completely! My servants have deserted me, left me to freeze! Help me! I will pay you—pay you well!" he yelled, fearing the man and boy would pass him by.

"How long have you been here, my friend?" Laire asked.

"Hours. God bless you, sire. My beauties and I," the merchant said, gesturing toward the two miserable-looking horses, "would not have lasted the night."

As Laire dismounted and studied the char from every angle, he asked the merchant if they were near Clermont.

"Oh yes, this is the road to Clermont, though one would hardly know it today. But yes, I have traveled it for twenty years." The merchant went on to curse his servants who had deserted him, and to tell how twice a year he sold alum to the tanners guild of Clermont. He was still rambling on when Nicolette climbed onto the char and took the reins, and he and Laire put their shoulders to the rear gate of the cart.

The char wobbled, the whole body groaned. The wheels turned slowly, slowly, creaking protest as the glistening horses slid and struggled. Steam rose from their hides and puffed from their nostrils. Finally with a violent effort from man and beast the char lurched forward and was free.

The merchant gave thanks to the saints, and to the travelers. When Laire refused payment, the merchant said, "If you will not accept my coin, then you must allow me to buy you and your young squire a meal. There is a tavern, this side of Clermont where I always make my bed. It is not but a league or so. Travel with me?"

The day darkened and the storm grew fiercer. The single league drew out into two or three or more, at least it seemed so with the howling wind and snow in their faces. They did not sight the tavern through the swirling clouds of snow until they were upon it. Carts and tumbrils littered the tavern yard.

Before the stable doors, Laire helped the merchant to unharness his weary horses. They led their animals inside away from the stinging cold of the wind. In the dim, humid warmth of the stable, a half-grown boy took their payment and directed them to a stall. The stableboy tagged along at Laire's elbow. "Psst," the stableboy said in an undertone. "If you want a place to sleep, its three obols for the loft, two for the boy, he's smaller. You won't find a place inside," he warned. At first Laire declined the offer.

"Is that true?" the merchant asked, understandably cautious, being something of a scoundrel himself and not above a little dishonest profit.

"See for yourself," the cheeky boy remarked, adding, "I may not have a space left by then."

While the merchant dickered with the stableboy over the price of a sleeping space, Nicolette went to fetch the horses a pail of water from the barrels at the rear of the stable. As she returned with the water, two burly-looking men with cross bows slung over their shoulders stepped from a large stall. The men's cloaks were white with snow. They appeared huge as mountains to Nicolette, who was forced to jump aside to keep from being trampled as they shoved past her. Icy water sloshed from the pails and onto her boots.

After they had disappeared from view, she glanced into the stall they had exited a moment before. There were three horses inside, two still with saddles, and the third, a pack horse, carried some sort of shapeless burden on its back. It was wrapped in heavy dowlas cloth. In the dim light of the stable there was something almost sinister about its appearance, and Nicolette wondered if it was not a dead body, though it could have been anything, from a merchant's goods to a tent.

Just then the pack horse shifted, swinging its hindquarters toward her, and she fancied that she saw a dark, hideous snout protruding from beneath the heavy cloth. It was nothing human. A fang like tusk lifted the lip in a stiff snarl and the eye that stared out was fixed and glassy, like the eye of a dead beast. She had about decided it was some sort of ferocious looking pig, when a hand touched hers.

Twenty-one

"What are you doing?" Laire asked, taking one of the pails from her hand.

Once she had recovered her composure, she whispered, "Look, it is some sort of pig."

Laire gave it only a cursory glance. "A boar, most likely," he said, and walked away. Nicolette hurried to keep step with him.

The merchant, who had exhausted his bargaining powers, was waiting for them. He was still grumbling as they stepped from the stable into the storm. "Every year it costs more. An honest man can no longer afford to make a living. I don't know where it will end. The world cannot go on this way for very long," he swore angrily.

They followed a trampled path through the snow to the tavern. Little light filtered from its hide-covered windows, and a cobwebbing of snow all but obliterated the sign above the door which creaked to and fro with each blast of wind.

Nicolette made it out to read, "The Merry Pilgrim," and beneath the frost and snow perceived a crudely painted figure in a penitent's robe. Immediately it brought to mind the feel and scent of the rough brown robe she had been forced to wear, the indignities she had been forced to bear, and she was seized by a sudden uneasiness.

The steamy heat of the tavern enveloped them like a fog. The two low-beamed rooms were jammed with muleteers, carters, merchants, pilgrims, and brethren, indeed all those upon the roads that winter's day.

Once the trio's stinging noses thawed, they were overwhelmed by the mingled odors of stale grease and ale, of wet wool and people too closely packed.

The merchant, good to his word, paid for their wooden bowl, for that was how the meal was sold. One rented a bowl into which a stout peasant woman dropped a chunk of bread and then dumped a ladleful of pork cruet atop it. The cruet, a stew more or less, contained more juice and turnips than pork. If a dusting of spices, salt among them, was desired, there was an extra charge. The merchant gasped upon hearing the price, and remarked it was above the cost of a seat in heaven. Laire and Nicolette declined the spices as well.

A group of brethren seated at the end of a long table near the door, made a place for the new arrivals. The brethren were a jolly group and told of their long pilgrimage to pray before the gold encased skull of St. John the Baptist in Clermont's cathedral.

Ale was sold at the tables by sturdy Norman peasant girls. Laire insisted on paying for his own ale. He bought a single cup and he and Nicolette shared it. According to the brethren, what the stableboy had told them was true. There was no hope of obtaining a pallet inside the tavern. All were sold, several times. In many cases the original buyers, with an eye for turning a coin, resold them for a profit, much to the tavern keeper's annoyance. A noisy argument broke out over just such a transaction as Laire and Nicolette were finishing their meal.

Before the loud disagreement, Nicolette had been watching the two men with cross bows slung over their shoulders. They were seated at a coveted table near the hearth, eating and drinking heartily. They were certainly not merchants, for their clothing was as rough as their manner. It occurred to Nicolette that they might be foresters, but her attention was drawn away by the shouts of the irate tavern keeper.

Later, the merchant became locked in a discussion with the brethren concerning religious relics. "I, myself," the merchant acidly remarked, "have seen two crowns of thorns, four feet all purported to belong to St. Margaret, and enough wood from the true cross to build an ark."

Laire and Nicolette exchanged smiles and left them to their arguments. It was yet afternoon, but with the gloom of the storm it was already dark. They made their way back to the stable through the wind and snow. The stable felt bitterly cold after the heat of the tavern. In the darkness they climbed the ladder to the loft, feeling the pressure of the rungs beneath their feet. The loft above was littered with people wrapped in blankets like moths in cocoons, humped forms, blacker than the black of the interior.

Laire found a space for them near the ladder. They had no blanket, and so they lay together wrapped in their cloaks. The wind groaned past the eaves, buffeted the thatch of the roof and found the gaps between the boards. Laire and Nicolette spoke in hushed whispers. "What if we are too late?" Nicolette sighed.

Laire drew her closer, and in an assuring tone, said, "Not even the king, who lives to hunt, would go out on such a day as this. According to our friend the merchant, Clermont is less than three leagues away. Tomorrow I will find a way to contact my uncle."

"I could carry a message to him," Nicolette suggested. Laire chuckled silently, and pressed a kiss to her cold cheek. "Non, ma mie, you would fool no one."

"The merchant was fooled," she reminded him sharply. It annoyed her to be made fun of, even at such a time and place.

He made a laughing sound. "Only because he is old and cannot see over his whiskers."

"Oh, then tell me how would I betray myself?" she demanded, seizing his marauding hands and holding them prisoner. He was not in the least hindered by the loss of his hands, and buried his face in her neck, covering it with little kisses. "It is your derriere," he murmured. "When you walk, it does the most remarkable—"

She jabbed her elbow into his ribs. "I can walk

differently." Her words, though whispered, flared with temper. He made an amused sound in her ear, perhaps it was a groan. "No, no," he croaked. "It is poetry. I think you have broken my ribs."

She turned in his arms, wearing an alarmed expression. As she did, she saw his grinning face. Before she could react he kissed her full on the lips, though it was more playful than passionate. "Now," he said, with his lips touching hers, "It is time to sleep, if only for a few hours."

She was disarmed, defeated by him as she always was. She turned and snuggled into the curve of his body. A moment later, she said, "Laire?"

He made a mumbling reply, like a man already asleep.

"What will we do? We must stop them from killing him."

"Yes," he agreed. "Tomorrow."

She lay there in the blackness listening to the rumbling snores of the surrounding sleepers, the flatulence, and the tossing and turning of bodies. It was no use, she could not sleep. Her body ached with exhaustion, but her mind would not rest. Too many fears tore at her heart, haunted her thoughts. She felt like a creature pursued by some terrible, inescapable doom, and each passing moment brought her that much nearer to perdition.

Below a door jolted open and slammed back against something solid, a wall, a stanchion. At first she heard only the stableboy's startled voice. Then another voice rang out, a man's voice, harsh and questioning.

Nicolette gave a breathless little gasp. Jehan! she thought. It felt as if all the air had gone out of her lungs. She had not killed him. Perhaps she was relieved, she was too frightened to give it much thought, though she was certain he must have a sore head and was now seeking revenge. She was terrified, even more so when she heard a second voice, that of Simon Quarle. "Laire." She shook his shoulder, whispering frantically and motioning below. The sleepers around them heard as well, some grumbled, and shifted, but none shouted a protest.

Laire raised his head and pulled himself up on one arm. He heard the voices and was instantly alert. Simon Quarle's voice boomed from below, interspersed with the stableboy's shrill denials. Laire recalled that the stableboy had not seen them return from the tavern, fortunately. More men entered the stable, several voices rang out, and there was the tramp of feet on the hard soil of the stable floor.

Laire edged to the ladder and peered down. He saw Quarle stride out of the stable and make toward the tavern, followed by four men. The stableboy banged the door to and, mumbling and cursing, returned to his bed.

Moments passed, the silence returned. Quickly Laire and Nicolette descended the ladder, saddled their horses, and led them from the stable's rear door. They mounted in the whirling snow and cantered toward the encircling woods.

With food in their stomachs and their horses

somewhat rested, they forged on through the gusty wind and snow. Toward evening the storm abated, though a flurry of snow still drifted in the air.

The city of Clermont and its grand chateau glistened in the winter twilight. Its towers, rooftops, and church spires appeared opalescent, polished by the wind and dazzled with ice.

A snow-filled moat crossed by a drawbridge marked the city's south gate. It was yet open that hour before sunset. There was little evidence of guards. Laire and Nicolette passed without challenge, though when they rode slowly past the double-leaf iron doors of the inner gate they noticed a curl of smoke rising from one of the watchtower's windows. And at another window, Laire glimpsed a man's face.

They encountered little traffic on the city's main thoroughfare, most likely townsfolk hurrying home to a warm hearth on a wintry evening. The shops had closed, and only the taverns were alive with activity.

As they rode past the guildhall Laire and Nicolette sighted a group of children playing in the snow. Seemingly immune to the cold, the children packed handfuls of snow into rounded missiles and hurled them at one another, amid taunting shouts and jeers.

Away from the main thoroughfare and the taverns, the snow choked alleyways were muffled in silence, save for the occasional crowing of a cock or the barking of dogs. It was nearly dark by the time they had found their way to the great square occupied by the cathedral of St. Sebastian. At the opposite end of the square, with its back to the city's walls, stood the Chateau de Conches. It appeared to be of ancient design and consisted of a trio of imposing towers, a square hall, and all surrounded by a forbidding walled courtyard. The remainder of the square held the homes of wealthy burghers and church officials.

Torchlight flared in the courtyard of the chateau and lights twinkled from window openings. Laire viewed the scene from the darkness of an alleyway leading onto the square.

Nicolette looked on despairingly. She twitched the reins and moved her horse beside Laire's. "How will we manage to speak to your uncle?" She was cold and exhausted, and at that moment the task seemed impossible.

"We will find a tavern, a place where we can escape the cold, then we will talk." In truth, Laire had already decided on a plan. It was simple and direct. He would arrive at the gates late in the night, declare that he carried a message for Marshal de Orfevres and bluff his way inside. The only problem was, Laire had no way of knowing if his uncle was truly in the chateau. It was entirely possible that he had gone on to Arras with the king's ministers to arrange for the signing of the treaty with the Flemish.

At best it was a risky plan, and Laire did not want Nicolette involved. He was prepared for her arguments. He understood perfectly what was at stake. It was their future, and it depended on thwarting Isabella's and de Conches's plot. His greatest fear was for Nicolette. He felt he could face any danger so long as he knew she was beyond Isabella's grasp.

Their search for a tavern led them down a pitch black street where the upper stories of the close-set houses all but met. They had traversed half its length, when at the far end of the narrow lane a torch appeared, carried by a man trotting before several horsemen. Laire assumed the riders to be nobles, at least one of them, and the others his servants. Laire reined in his horse and waited for them to pass. Nicolette drew the sorrel gelding in behind the bay, careful not to get too close to Ronce's hindquarters.

As the horsemen drew nearer, the flaring torchlight revealed the lead rider's features. Laire could hardly believe his eyes.

Twenty-two

Laire gave the bay a nudge of his leg and moved out smartly to intercept them. "Thierry!" he shouted. "Thierry de Fontenne!"

The procession halted. The man with the torch scurried out of the way as the horsemen came forward as a group. The rather bulky figure wrapped in a fur-lined cloak nudged his horse closer. He craned his neck and peered into the uncertain light. "Laire?" he said in a voice overcome with amazement. "You," he sputtered and, seeing it was truly his brother, immediately lowered his voice. "By the blood of the holy saints! Where have you—? What are you doing in Clermont?"

Seeing that he was not welcomed with any particular enthusiasm, Laire flashed a smooth smile, as he was apt to do, and remarked, "I knew you would be pleased to see me, brother. Are you staying at the chateau?"

"What?" Thierry muttered in distraction. "No. I am hardly among the chosen guests. I am here only as my father-in-law's representative." Thierry's uppermost thought was to get his brother off the street, out of sight, before he brought more embarrassment down on the family—or worse. "I am staying in the home of a banker. You have not answered me. Why are you here?" he asked, even though he was not sure he wanted to know.

"To visit you, brother, of course."

"That is a stinking lie. Is that your squire?" he questioned, glancing at the boy astride a horse deep in the shadows.

"Yes. Can you give us shelter for a few hours?"

"And then you are leaving."

"Yes," Laire agreed, "Eventually." He was never at a loss for words, and as they crossed the square to the walled villa of the banker, he drew his brother into a discussion on the previous night's storm and how an astrologer had once told him that such matters were controlled entirely by the stars.

Once inside the banker's hall, Thierry introduced Laire as his kinsman, which was not altogether a lie. "My cousin from Limousin, and his squire."

The banker, an affable, prosperous-looking man with a bald head, a thick neck, and short arms, directed his servants to prepare the chamber adjoining his guest's room for the late arrivals. "We have already taken our evening meal," the banker said, apologetically. "But I will have the servants bring food and wine to your chamber."

Laire was most gracious. His years at court had left him well polished and his manners were above reproach, most convincing to all, save his brother. For some unknown reason, lack of sleep perhaps,

Nicolette found it all enormously funny and smiled into the collar of her cloak. He and his brother were so vastly different, Laire full of farcical devilment, and Thierry, humorless and stiff as a stile.

The moment they were alone in the guest chambers, Thierry said to Laire, "You miserable scoundrel, what are you doing in Clermont, and do not lie to me!"

"You are beginning to sound like Agnes," Laire remarked in an amused voice. When he looked at Nicolette, he pulled a clownish face and propelled her by the shoulder toward the bench before the hearth. The orange flames crackling in the blackness gave off a blissful warmth. She had not felt so warm in days. The heat was potent as a drug, and immediately began to drain the weary tenseness from her muscles.

Laire remained beside her a moment. Before he took his hand away, he winked at her, and gave her shoulder an encouraging squeeze.

Thierry, whose back was to them, stripped off his sword and belt and slammed them down atop a chest. "Damn you, Laire. Do not provoke me. The king is not a league away, and you know full well wherever the king is, so is court. You are under sentence of exile. Do you wish me to believe that you are so stupid as—" he hesitated, too furious for a moment to put his thoughts together. At last, his voice jerked from his throat. "If you wish to flirt with death, I prefer it would not be at my expense!" His eyes fell nervously on the boy seated before the hearth. "Can he be trusted?"

"Yes, completely."

"Well? I am waiting for your explanation!" Thierry had no sooner spat out the words, when there was a tapping on the chamber door.

Laire admitted the servants, two of them, both women of some years. One carried a ewer of wine, the other a tray of food and several pewter cups. They set the food and wine on a side board and were quickly gone. Laire watched them until they were out of sight, then closed the door.

When he turned back, he asked, "Is our uncle de Orfevres in the chateau?"

"*Your* uncle de Orfevres," Thierry said pointedly. He crossed the chamber to the side board and poured himself a cup of wine. "No, he has gone on to Arras to organize the king's signing of the treaty with the Flemish." Thierry's eyes narrowed. "Why? What have you and he been plotting?"

Laire followed him to the side board and also poured a cup of wine from the ewer. "You have an evil mind, Thierry." He was beginning to understand why his brother had always annoyed him. "It has nothing to do with Lagrume Woods." He took a drink of wine from the cup and, crossing back to the hearth, handed it to Nicolette.

"I?" Thierry cawed. "You were always the liar. And if this is another of your elaborate jests, I swear—"

"Isabella and de Conches intend to murder the king. They are not alone. De Sevry is with them, de Varentot, and there are others."

Thierry all but strangled on the wine he had swallowed. "No! What are you saying?"

"Exactly that, a hunting accident. Once the king is dead, Isabella will denounce her brothers as incapable of producing legitimate heirs and, with the Norman barons to support her position, have her son crowned king, with her as regent, of course."

"How can you know these things?"

"De Conches was overheard," Laire said, returning to the side board to look over the food.

"By whom?"

"A serving girl." Laire selected a wedge of cheese and sampled it.

Thierry stared at him. "You are mad. You are becoming like madame our mother's cousin, Depuis. He was locked in a room and left there, and that is where you belong!"

Nicolette pulled off her cap and rose from the bench. "What he says is true."

"Who is this person?" Thierry demanded.

Laire was tempted to tell his brother the truth, but thought better of it at once. "Odette Druhot, the sister of my squire."

"My God, Laire, you are a lunatic!" he swore, turning his gaze again on the girl. "So he has drawn you into his—"

"No, messire, he has not influenced me in any way. I, myself, heard Raoul de Conches and several men whose voices I did not recognize plot to murder the king during a boar hunt."

Thierry said nothing for a moment. She was hardly more than a girl, and quite pretty now that her face was no longer hidden by the turned-up collar of the cloak. He was impressed by the way she had faced him, and there was something very compelling about the smoldering dark eyes.

Thierry said nothing. He slowly crossed the chamber, the cup of wine still in his hand, and sat down heavily on the bed. "There is to be a hunt tomorrow, and, in truth, the prey is the wild boar."

Again Laire was tempted to tell his brother the entire story. But, no, he decided. The fewer people who knew the truth concerning Nicolette of Burgundy, the safer for all concerned. "Thierry," he began.

"No," his brother said, raising his hand as if to ward off the words. "Do not tell me. I do not want to know."

"Think for a moment, Thierry. It involves you as well, you and Gardiner. What do you suppose will become of you and your father-in-law if Isabella's hand is on the crown?"

For a long moment, there was only the hiss and crackle of the fire. At last Thierry said, "Isabella is here, at the chateau. And it is true that de Conches, himself, has arranged the hunt on the morrow, for the king's entertainment." He looked directly at Laire. "The king would not believe you. He would not believe me. There is nothing we can do."

Sadly, Laire realized what he said was true. "You are riding in the hunt?" he asked his brother.

"Yes, at dawn. How do they plan to murder him?"

"I don't know," Laire confessed. "An ambush, perhaps? Though they could hardly strike him down before half his ministers. De Conches would have to find a way to separate him from the main body of the hunt. If we could prevent that—"

"We! Oh no, you are not going anywhere near the king. You will get us both killed, we will end like the d'Aulnays on the rack."

"There is no other way, Thierry. Together, the three of us may be able to save him."

"The three of us! No, I forbid it. You can not take her with us!"

"I cannot leave her here. Besides, dressed as she is and on horseback, no one will think her anything but a squire." Laire poured himself a cup of wine and, with the ewer filled their cups.

"If someone should recognize you." Thierry paused.

"In a melee of riders," Laire argued, returning the ewer to the sideboard. "I do not think so. I will keep far back." He raised his cup to them, and took a swallow of wine. "People see what they expect to see."

Thierry finished his wine with a gulp. "You have the nerve of a marble saint," he said, releasing his breath with a hiss. "And I am insane for listening to you."

After they had ravaged the platter of food and discussed their plans for a final time, Laire and Nicolette retired to the adjoining chamber and to bed.

***

Earlier that evening, Simon Quarle and four of his men at arms entered the city of Clermont. Quarle's frantic search for de Fontenne and "the serving girl" had now escalated into a matter of life and death—his. For if they managed to somehow warn the king, Quarle knew his life would be ended. The lord de Conches was not a man to be thwarted.

The group of riders proceeded down the snow-filled streets of Clermont. The men were bone weary and half frozen. Pons Vernet buffeted his dripping nose with a gloved hand and remarked, "There is yet time to alert the lord de Conches."

"Alert him!" Quarle mocked, glaring at his brother-in-law. "You idiot. And confess that I have failed?" He looked murderously over to Jehan. "Idiots!" he repeated. Quarle preferred not to think of the consequences. De Conches would kill him. He must find de Fontenne and the girl. It was fear alone that drove him on, for he was every bit as cold and weary as the others. There was yet time, Quarle told himself. He would find them. But the thought did little to allay the gnawing sense of desperation that tore at his gut.

At the top of the square, Quarle pulled up on his reins and brought his horse to an abrupt halt. "You know what you are to do?" he said to the men surrounding him. All indicated they did with a nod or an affirmative grunt. "Search the taverns, the churches. Find them," Quarle ground out.

* * *

That same frigid night in the Chateau de Clermont, Raoul de Conches had just returned from speaking with his foresters and huntsmen. All was in readiness for the morning's hunt. De Conches had arranged everything personally, so as to insure his final triumph. All of Normandy would soon be his for the taking, and after that, well, who could say?

A brief walk through the drafty, torchlit passageways brought Raoul de Conches to the door of Isabella's suite. He paused a moment to smooth his slick black hair. He was majestically garbed in a close-fitting jypon of scarlet velvet on which the fierce boar of Normandy had been lavishly embroidered in gold thread, and set with rubies and other precious stones. His hosen were of a deep, rich blue shade of Flander's weave and his tall, soft leather boots and silver spurs gleamed with polishing.

He greeted Isabella with a courtly bow and lightly touched his lips to her cool fingers. When their gazes met, his eyes shone with confidence. He withdrew to stand before the hearth, and spoke of trivial matters while Isabella's serving women labored to dismantle their mistress's elaborate hairdo.

Isabella was in the process of preparing for bed after a day of feasting. She was dressed in a silken robe, and her pale-golden hair, carefully unbraided and combed, fell over her shoulders in flaxen splendor. With her toilette completed, she promptly dismissed her serving women.

When the last of the women had hurried from the chamber, de Conches presented her with a conspiratorial smile, and said, "All is arranged."

Isabella pursed her lips in an expression of impatience. "Have you arranged for an end to this miserable weather, as well?"

"Alas, my love, there is little one can do about the elements. However, my astrologer has promised fair skies for the morrow."

Isabella's features softened, and she rose from the embrace of the ornate arm chair. She, herself, placed much faith in astrologers. Indeed it was an astrologer who had predicted that her firstborn son would wear the crowns of both England and France. *"Bon,"* she replied, coming to stand before him. "I am prepared to ride."

For all his cynicism, Raoul de Conches was inexorably drawn to Isabella. There was something almost frightening about the fair, audacious daughter of Philip la Bel. Perhaps it was simply the sense of danger which he found so irresistible. He said to her, "Then tomorrow belongs to the victor."

"Yes, dear Raoul, to me. I am always triumphant." Since her return from England, Isabella had resisted the baron's ardent entreaties to resume their affair of the heart. But that evening before the hearth she spoke tenderly to him, laying her jewel-laden hand on his arm and stroking the velvet sleeve of his jypon.

* * *

There was no light in the small chamber that adjoined Thierry's, nor any source of heat. In the cold dark, Nicolette removed her oversized boots and huddled beneath the blankets. It was too cold to undress, and there would be little time in the morning. Laire shed his sword and belt, pulled off his boots and climbed into bed beside her. The bed was icy except for the soft, cozy hollow they had warmed with their bodies, and they lay together being careful not to move. Finally Nicolette whispered, "Can you trust him?"

"Thierry?" Laire also whispered. "Not ordinarily." He chuckled, and after a moment assured her, "Yes, he is my brother. And you," he murmured, snugging her against him. "You are my love. You must promise to stay close tomorrow."

She did not answer him with words, but nodded her head.

"What is it?" he asked.

"I am afraid."

"Yes," he agreed, brushing her hair with his lips, "So am I."

Before Nicolette succumbed to the bone-weary exhaustion of the past days, she whispered a prayer, a fervent plea that God might grant her and Laire the future they had planned. They slept like the dead, without dreams or awakenings.

* * *

PRISONER OF MY HEART

Nicolette's eyes blinked open. A wavering light moved through the darkened chamber toward them. She felt Laire's sudden movement shake the rope sling bed.

"Sire," a voice came from the darkness. Suddenly a face appeared in the yellow halo of light. "It is time to rise."

Laire bolted up, his heart pounding against his ribs and his hand on the sword which lay beside the bed. Blinking to awareness, he recognized the man as Thierry's. "Tell him I am awake."

The face, made grotesque by the leaping shadows, nodded and withdrew.

Braving the icy chill of the room, they grappled in the dark for their boots and made use of the chamber pot. Laire buckled on his sword.

Thierry greeted them with a glum expression. He looked as if he were about to be crushed by the weight of his thoughts. Someone, a servant perhaps, had brought a ewer of hot cider and a platter of bread from the kitchen. Thierry took a sip of the cider. It was too hot and he sat it down, went to the shuttered window, and tinkered with the latch. "I have sent Gaspard and Randel for our horses." He pushed open the window a crack and sighted the distance. "The hunters are gathering in the square."

Laire and Nicolette hardly had time to devour a bit of bread and take a swallow of cider. The cider hadn't much taste, but it was hot enough that you knew your tongue was still there. In a rush, they donned their cloaks and hats and followed Thierry down through the house and out into the crunchy snow of the courtyard where Thierry's men waited with their horses. The sky had lightened, but in the courtyard it was still dark.

Gaspard, Thierry's squire, carried his master's crossbow and quiver of bolts as was the custom. The younger boy led Thierry's horse forward for him to mount. "Randel," Thierry said to the youth, "fetch the other crossbow for my kinsman." When the boy returned, Laire took the weapon from him, intending to sling it over his shoulder. "The squire must carry it," Thierry reminded his brother, "As you well know."

"I am capable, hand it here," Nicolette insisted, modulating her voice, and wondering uneasily if she could carry off her disguise. She wore the weapon slung over her shoulder. It was incredibly heavy and even more awkward than it appeared. As they rode out from the courtyard and into the square a flutter of fear touched Nicolette's heart, and her mouth felt dry as dust.

Moment to moment the sky grew lighter. The square before the chateau was already crowded with nobles astride fretting, stamping horses. Occasionally the air was split by the raucous blast of an ivory hunting horn. An assortment of dogs barked and strained at their long leather leashes, towing their handlers to and fro. The dogs lunged and tangled together. They mixed and mingled, some brindled, some fawn, others white and spotted. Among them were coursing hounds, sleek dogs with narrow heads and long legs, and scent hounds, heavier and more fierce in appearance, all baying in anticipation of the hunt.

At first the group had no luck in sighting the king amid the crush of riders. Fifty mounted hunters, perhaps more, handsomely outfitted gentlemen and ladies, milled in the trampled snow before the cathedral. A number of townspeople watched and cheered from the sidelines, adding to the noise and confusion.

There was a flurry of horn blasts, and through a gap in the crowd of riders, Thierry glimpsed the king. He brought his horse even with Laire's. "There he is," he indicated with a toss of his head. "Do you see him?"

Laire nodded, craning his neck to see while at the same time keeping a tight rein on Ronce. The bay fretted and stomped, slapping the air with his tail, not at all happy in the jostling crowd.

Viewed from across the wide square, the king seemed in high spirits, joking with those around him. To the king's left was a cadre of riders. Raoul de Conches sat in their midst astride a large black horse. He and the Baron de Varentot appeared to be laughing at something the Baron de Sevry had just said.

Nicolette pressed the sorrel gelding forward so she might see. She glimpsed the king and de Conches and, as her gaze swept over the clutch of riders, she noticed a fur-clad lady mounted on a pale grey horse. Her eyes seized on Isabella. The sight of her haughty chalklike face rimmed in fur brought a wave of bitterness to burn Nicolette's throat.

Shouts of "To the chase! To the chase!" preceded a harsh, strident chorusing of horns. A tremor of excitement shook the air as the hunters departed the square. Horses and riders bunched. The hunters, funneled through the narrow streets, strung out in a long colorful line, accompanied by barking dogs and the stares of curious onlookers. Townspeople gawked from shopfronts and leaned from windows to see the grand procession pass. The route led down through the city's winding streets to its ancient east gate. Out beyond the walls lay the mills, their wheels stilled, and ponds locked in winter ice. The stubbled snow-choked fields gave way to pasture land and then to the vastness of Clermont's primeval forest.

The dogs dragged their handlers forward through the underwood, eager to be loosed. The call was given and the yelping dogs lunged away, spurred on by the blasting horns. The riders pursued through the snow, at first at a brisk canter and then breaking into a lope. Laire, Nicolette, Thierry, and Gaspard rode far back. Thierry came up beside Laire and signaled his intention to move closer to the king. Spurring his horse to a gallop, he and his squire, Gaspard, wove their way through the pack.

The tonguing of the hounds grew frantic and shouts of "Hou, hou, hou!" carried on the icy air. The boar was a formidable beast, a wily creature that had to be driven from its lair. A boar could lead a hunt for leagues. Once brought to bay, it was

PRISONER OF MY HEART 393

a vicious fighter. Its razor-sharp tusks could disembowel a dog with a single thrust.

A fat noble bouncing along beside Laire and Nicolette called, "Cold trail!" But as they plunged along the narrow forest paths, a man before them yelled from over his shoulder, "They are running, they are running!"

Up hill and down, the hunters chased the dogs, until they came to a long ravine, deep and overgrown, an immense thicket whose undergrowth was so dense that in places it was impenetrable. Here the hunters were forced to disperse, to forge new paths. The king and his squire, far forward, found themselves in the company of his daughter, Isabella, de Conches, his closet companions, and their men. Off to their right they heard the horns and crashing progress of the remainder of the hunters.

Deep in the thicket Laire and Nicolette could see neither Thierry nor the king. Several times the accursed crossbow became snared by limbs and brambles, and Nicolette narrowly escaped being towed from the saddle. Her face was scratched and bleeding, and she was certain she must have a lump on her head where she'd been soundly thumped by a low hanging limb. Only her hands, because of Laire's heavy gloves, had been spared the abuse of the branches and thorns.

They progressed slowly and with difficulty. When at last they and the stampede of riders broke from the thicket, the king, Isabella, de Conches, and his minions were nowhere in sight. Hunters thundered past Laire and Nicolette in pursuit of the tonguing dogs. After a moment of mad confusion, Laire spotted his brother and, raising an arm to hail him, called out. "Where is the king?" Thierry's reply was a much exaggerated shrug. "He must be ahead," he shouted, spurring his horse until it reared and galloped off after the mob of riders, with his squire racing close at his horse's heels.

It was Nicolette who first heard the far-off cry of a second pack of dogs. "Do you hear?" she yelled. She snatched the sorrel to a halt and turned him shortly. "There," she pointed. Laire heard it now, behind them and far to their left, still deep in the thicket.

"They have done it!" Laire said the words aloud as the thought exploded in his brain. How stupid he had been. Clearly de Conches had chosen the thicket as a means to divert the king from the others, to lead him away to his death.

Twenty-three

Deciding it would be useless to reenter the thicket and attempt to track them, Laire chose to take the hilly ground, a succession of wooded ridges which skirted the entanglement. With any luck, he hoped to intercept the king. He motioned Nicolette on after the riders. "Find Thierry!" he shouted as he sent the bay lunging up the hillside thick with snow-shagged shrubs.

For an instant Nicolette hesitated, then turning the sorrel, she galloped after Laire. He did not realize she had followed until the sorrel drew up on his horse's flank. Where the trees thickened Nicolette reined down and fell back, taking the bay's path as black barked trees flashed past.

The ridge of oaks fell away sharply into a deep hollow cut by ravines and criss-crossed by fallen trees. They plunged on, the horses bracing their forelegs as they skidded downward. Where the ground leveled out the horses lengthened their strides. They clattered across an ice-bound stream, blue as steel where it had been polished by the wind. Branches and brambles reached out like claws. A limb clipped Laire's knee and sent a pain shooting to his hip.

Where the ground rose abruptly toward another ridge, the horses scrambled upwards, their hooves slipping on the stony surface beneath the snow. With every stride the sound of the dogs grew louder. And as they crested the ridge, the furious barking swiveled their heads to a stretch of meadow broken by stands of pine and hardwoods.

Below a horseman raced before the dogs. It appeared to Nicolette's stunned and staring eyes that the man astride the horse was one of the foresters she had seen at the tavern, for his cloak had been of a like color. What she saw next convinced her she was correct. As the rider streaked past, she saw a rope stretched taut and the bouncing carcass of a dead boar cutting through the snow.

The rider crouched low over the horse, racing the dogs, barely ahead of the king's fleet greyhounds. They flashed past, brindle, white and fallow, giving no tongue at all, saving their wind for their legs and speeding after the boar silently as death. Close behind them, baying furiously, the alaunts, boar hounds, twenty strong, bounded along, their cries shrieking across the cold air.

On the far edge of the meadow, a movement among the trees betrayed the ambush. An archer moved into position, then another. Six in all readied their bows. The meadow was empty, only the trampled track of the dogs remained. The man dragging the boar had disappeared, taking the dogs with him, for their baying receded into the distance.

All at once a brace of riders broke from the trees far to the left, at the head of the long meadow. The king and his squire rode at the fore of the horsemen. De Sevry and the others lagged back.

Laire did not see de Conches. In that there was a terrible clarity. Laire shuddered to think how cleverly de Conches had planned. For his men had scented an earlier track to lead the hunters into the thicket, where the king could be separated from the others. The forester with the dead boar then returned to the thicket to wait, and with the king's approach led off with a fresh scent. The baying of de Conches's judas hounds would have undoubtedly lured the king's dogs onto the trail, and they, on the track of a boar already dead, would lead the king into eternity.

There was no time to think, hardly time to act. A look of panic passed between them. "I am coming with you," Nicolette cried. "No," Laire shouted back, and when she moved to turn her horse, he caught her elbow and jerked her backwards in her saddle. "Do not follow me! Go back, it is too late!" For he truly believed it was and, like a soldier who fights on when the battle is lost, was reconciled to death.

She did not answer but watched him and the bay plunge down the hillside. Tears stung her eyes. She let out her breath in a sob, kicked her heels into the sorrel, and in a headlong rush followed after him.

At the bottom of the hillside, Laire flung the bay into a copse of young oaks, limber saplings that whipped back, stinging like nettles. The saplings gave way to larger trees, and here and there pines had taken a hold. He was in sight of the open meadow when he gave the bay its head. Between the flashing trees, he glimpsed the hunters, the king and his squire far ahead of the others.

Laire urged Ronce onward, praying he would not be too late. From the edge of his vision, the sudden image of a horseman fixed upon his retina. He saw the flash of a sword as the rider hurtled toward him through the undergrowth.

Close on his left a second rider burst from a clump of snow-heaped pines, his cloak a swirl of scarlet. Raoul de Conches rode full at him, a sword in his hand, a steel buckler on his arm.

Laire sawed at the reins, wheeling the bay hard to the right, nearly colliding with a tree. Dragging at the reins he turned the bay, and one handed, drew his sword from the scabbard.

Nicolette, galloped into the clash and clangor of steel. She reined down, horrified by the sight of Laire, de Conches, and another man hacking away at one another, their horses skidding and jarring together in a furious battering assault.

Blow by blow they were driving Laire back into the trees where they would trap him and slash him to death. Desperate, she thought of the crossbow, but she had no idea how to load and fire the weapon, much less the strength to cock it. There was but a single use she might put it to.

She looped her reins over the pommel of her saddle, pulled the awkward wooden crossbow from her shoulder, and wielding it as a club, galloped toward them. De Conches, pressing his attack, saw her. The distraction altered his vicious overhead stroke. The blade whistled past Laire's skull and bit into the tree beside him. She heard Laire's shout above de Conches's, but not his words.

The man whose back she had targeted wheeled his horse about. Startled, she slung the crossbow with all her might, and veered away. As she swept past she saw the man topple from his saddle. She had not killed him, she thought, but she had taken some of the fight out of him. Leaning forward, she groped for her reins. She had but one objective now, to reach the king.

"After her!" de Conches screeched at the man staggering up from the snow. The villein reeled drunkenly about, caught his horse's trailing reins, and pulled himself into the saddle.

Laire, seeing his chance, sprang from between the trees in a withering assault. The tip of his sword caught the turned edge of de Conches's buckler and sent it tumbling away into the snow. Without his shield de Conches was forced to give ground. He checked and turned his horse, and rising in his stirrups, charged, swinging his sword in a deadly arc. Laire saw the blue haze of the blade flash past. As de Conches roared by him, Laire slashed out, swinging his sword from the side. Laire expected him to check and turn for another pass, but he sagged forward in the saddle and his horse cantered on, coming to a halt a short distance away.

When Laire looked for the villein, he was gone. He turned the bay and galloped toward the meadow. Coming from beneath the trees he saw the scene all at once. The king and his squire, intent on the chase, thundered toward the ambush. Nicolette, on the spent sorrel, raced across the meadow to intercept them. They did not seem to see her, nor the villein who was closing fast, about to overtake her.

Nicolette heard the crash of hooves close at her horse's flank, and saw her pursuer's shadow racing across the snow. He must not catch me, she said to the wind, and set her eyes on the two horsemen galloping toward the archers. The one to the fore was unquestionably the king, for he sat the horse in the same rigid, uncompromising manner with which he had ruled his family and his kingdom.

Blinded by the stark whiteness of the meadow and the storm of her emotions, Nicolette did not see the brush-filled ravine with its camouflage of snow until she was almost atop it. Her lips parted with alarm, realizing it was too late to check and turn, to skirt the ravine. The gap yawned before her, dauntingly wide, wicked with brambles and tangled limbs, pointed and stout as lances. She held her breath and let the reins slip through her fingers, as the little sorrel bounded up and off.

As if he had wings, the gelding sailed over the obstacle. His forefoot touched neatly down, then the other, followed by his powerful hindquarters.

PRISONER OF MY HEART 401

In another loping bound, the spunky little horse gathered himself and, with a final spurt of endurance, sprinted up the slope toward the two swiftly galloping horsemen.

In his single-minded pursuit of the boar the king did not see the horse and rider hurtling toward him at breakneck speed. But his squire did, and the youth's eyes expanded with an expression of consternation, near panic.

Meanwhile, the archers, who lay in ambush, watched the scene with an ever mounting sense of apprehension. More and more riders appeared across the meadow. "What has gone wrong?" one blurted out. "What is happening?" another asked in alarm. Their leader, confused but determined to carry out his orders, sighted across his bow, and shouted, "Loose your arrows!"

The squire lunged forward, frantically grappling for the reins of the king's galloping horse. He seized them, wrenching the animal's head to one side, and turning it just as the smaller horse cut before it.

Nicolette saw only a jarring blur of color. Suddenly the air around her trembled with a thrumming sound. Arrows whined past like angry hornets, and she felt herself thrown savagely forward. Her hands clawed at the air as she tumbled. She did not see the horses collide, though she heard them squeal with fright.

As he galloped up the slope, Laire saw the animals skid, locked together, and go down in the drifted snow. By the time he had halted the bay, thrown his leg over the saddle, and dismounted, the floundering horses were again on their feet.

He ran toward Nicolette and pulled her from the snow, "Are you hurt?" he gasped in a voice near frantic with concern.

At first she could not answer him. All the wind had been knocked out of her and there was none left for words. Finally she said, "Oh God, you are safe! I was so afraid," and threw her arms around his neck and kissed him.

"You are not hurt?" he asked, holding her away from him so he might look and see for himself.

"The king?" she cried. "Where is the king?"

In truth, Laire had not noticed, his only thought had been to find Nicolette.

When they found him, he was struggling from the snow on his hands and knees. He, too, had been thrown from his saddle. Laire helped him to his feet. He was covered with snow, his hosen torn, and his hands cut and bloodied from the fall. An arrow protruded from the heavy material of his cloak. He shook off Laire's hands, and tore the arrow from his cloak. In a fit of rage, he broke the brightly feathered shaft and threw it into the snow.

The hunters, those who had lagged behind the king and others who had turned back from the false trail now, converged upon the meadow, adding to the confusion.

The king ranted for his men to run the archers to ground and arrest them. Only then did the king look for his squire. He was lying dead, an arrow in his breast. The king howled with anguish, "That arrow was meant for me! My God! They meant to murder me!"

In only moments, several of the archers were captured. They were inarguably de Conches's men, for they wore his livery. Dragged before the king, they confessed, and begged for mercy, knowing there would be none.

A startled hush fell over the crowd as a horse and rider slowly approached. Raoul de Conches swayed in the saddle, clasping his side. Blood poured through his fingers, soaking his clothing with an expanding dark stain.

"Traitor!" the king screamed. "You will die on the rack for your treachery!"

De Conches, his face ashen, slid slowly from his saddle.

Nearby, Isabella looked on. Unlike the others, she had not dismounted. Her face, framed by the fur-lined hood, was masklike. She stared at him in deathly silence, as if he were a ghost.

De Conches struggled to speak. "I did not act alone," he said. A tremor shook his voice, and a froth of blood bubbled from his lips.

Isabella's darting glance flicked to de Sevry and de Varentot. As if they read her thoughts, the men stepped forward, their hands on their daggers.

De Conches took several shambling steps toward the king, "Do you suppose I am the only serpent?" His staring eyes fixed on Isabella.

She seemed to recoil from the malice of his gaze. Her lips twisted into a snarl. "Kill him!" she screeched. De Sevry and de Varentot leapt forward, plunging their daggers deep into Raoul de Conches's chest. His body crumpled to the snow.

"Enough!" the king bellowed, motioning for his men to seize the pair. He was certain they were no less guilty than de Conches. For all their scheming he had survived, yet what he knew in his heart was far more painful than any death. He turned on his daughter and, in an accusing voice, demanded, "What do you know of this, Isabella?"

Isabella's pale, beautiful features contorted into something quite ugly. She said not a word, but swiftly turned her horse and cantered away.

By every right, Nicolette should have felt avenged, but she felt only sadness. Securely hugged to Laire's side, she could not help but feel sympathy toward the king. His sons were fools, and his own daughter, who was after all so very like him, had plotted his murder to satisfy her greed and lust for power.

The king, looking suddenly very old and shaken, turned and asked "Where is the boy who rode before me?" His gaze fell on Laire. "De Fontenne?" he said, astounded.

"Yes, my lord. It is true I have violated my exile. But if I must die for my loyalty, so be it. I could not allow them to murder you."

The king laid a trembling hand on his shoulder, "Do you believe I am so heartless as that? Your exile is ended!" He then turned his gaze upon the boy, whose short, dark hair curled about his face. At once, he realized the finely molded features were not those of a boy, but of a young woman.

PRISONER OF MY HEART   405

Looking into the large, dark, dramatic eyes he knew at once they were the eyes of his daughter-in-law, Nicolette of Burgundy.

Laire saw the king's hesitation, and quickly seized the opportunity. "Her name is Odette Druhot, my lord. She is Nicolette of Burgundy's serving woman, and your loyal subject." Pressing his luck still further, Laire said, "Her mistress lies at Gaillard, near to death." He waited breathlessly to see the king's reaction.

Fear constricted Nicolette's throat like a noose. She knew only too well Philip la Bel's treacherous nature. He might yet condemn them. Had they not disobeyed the sentence of his council?

In the confusion of the meadow, people and horses milled about, trampling the frozen snow. The distant sound of dogs snarling and fighting over the carcass of the boar carried from the hill beyond.

Finally, in an even voice, the king said, "You have saved my life, de Fontenne. How might I reward your loyalty?"

"I ask only for my freedom, and the right to wed Odette Druhot, my lord." Laire fancied that he perceived a spark of emotion in the king's pale eyes.

Perhaps he had, for the king was a wily man. He understood perfectly and, seeing it as a means to put an end to his own dilemma regarding Nicolette of Burgundy, remarked, "You say the prisoner is dying?"

"Yes, my lord."

Something very near to a smile stirred the king's

lips. "Return to Gaillard," he pronounced. "Make a grave for Nicolette of Burgundy and take this woman for your wife." His stern eyes fell on Nicolette, and he asked, "Does that suit you, demoiselle?"

"It does my lord, though there is one more favor I might beg of you. Do not judge too harshly Joan and Blanche."

The king did not answer her, but what she sought to hear in words, she saw in his eyes.

"Go now," the king bid them. "Before I have a turn of heart. Go with God, and the sure and certain knowledge of the resurrection."

Epilogue

The procession passed through the streets of Andelys and across the stone bridge. April mud was everywhere and the bright sunshine spanked off the water, paining the eyes of those who crowded the edges of the road to watch.

The newly married couple rode first, followed by the groom's brother, a neighboring noble and his wife, the mayor, the provost, and the merchants. Townsfolk who hovered about the route shouted cheers of, "Long life!" and "Many children!" All craned their necks, moving in and out of ranks to see the seigneur and his pretty bride pass by.

To the amazement and delight of all the village gossips, Laire de Fontenne had married the doe-eyed Odette, the lady prisoner's serving girl. Certainly she had no dowry, or so the wagging tongues insisted. The more romantic of the townswomen thought it only fitting that an occasion of great joy should follow on the heels of sadness. For the death of the disgraced royal princess was indeed sad. To be scarcely eighteen and already in her grave!

At Gaillard the gates stood open and guests flowed across the drawbridges and through the gates. They made their way through the outer ward and past the partially constructed chapel rising from the ashes. In the ward, more crowds of well-wishers awaited, cheering them along.

The courtyards buzzed with activity, and a sort of vapor, an overwhelming and delicious odor of food, drifted from the open doors and windows to mingle with the scents of the balmy spring afternoon. A long string of guests extended through the courtyards, all dressed in finery, riding on their palfreys, smiling and high spirited in anticipation of the wedding feast.

As Laire and Nicolette dismounted and walked toward the hall, the line of guests was still arriving, making their way across the drawbridge. Men, women, children, and dogs mixed in the crowded courtyard, all wishing to greet the seigneur and his beautiful wife. Nicolette's dark hair was fixed in a caul of woven gold thread, topped by a golden circlet. In her gown of pale yellow Tripoli silk with its matching, brocaded mantle, she was radiant as the spring sunshine. Laire was garbed in equal elegance, in a fitted jypon of rich brown brocade worked with golden thread. His dark brown hosen were of Flander's weave and his soft, tall boots with their silver spurs had been fashioned in Andelys.

Gaillard's large hall was lined with tables and quickly filled with guests. Laire and Nicolette moved among them, exchanging pleasantries and smiling. Later, on the dais, Laire and Nicolette began the celebration by sharing a bit of bread and a cup or blood red wine. The cup they passed between them was of fine silver, a gift from the mayor and his plump wife, who looked on proudly.

With the taste of the wine still on their tongues, Laire leaned forward to kiss Nicolette, and the feast began.

Thierry, Laire's brother, had only arrived the day before on his way from Arras after witnessing the signing of the treaty with the Flemish. The negotiations had lasted four long months. The Marshal de Orfevres, still concerned for the king's life, feared to leave his side. It was just as well, for Thierry and his uncle were constantly at odds.

After Thierry proposed a toast, Francois Cacchot took a turn, and more wine was drunk. The feast progressed and all around the hall people swallowed food and drink as if they had not eaten for a score of days. Tray after tray was brought from the kitchen, the gorging went on for hours while the guests sat sweating and red-faced, sweltering in the unseasonable warmth and the heat of the blazing hearth.

One by one people sat back from their plates, full enough to burst. Judot loosened his belt, and Dore, who was seated beside him, fanned her face with her hands. She had drunk too much wine and now she could not stop laughing. All along the tables men were opening their jypons and pushing up their sleeves. The women's faces shone as if they had been polished, and under the tables they hiked the skirts of their gowns to get a bit of coolness.

Before the musicians began to play, the men trooped outside to stretch their legs, or so they said.

Thierry, his face flush with wine, strolled along with Laire. As they took a turn down past the inner gates he asked, "When will you be coming back to Vezeley?" Since his arrival, they had found little time to discuss the future.

Laire shrugged. "Late this summer, perhaps. I can not leave until the king appoints another man to Gaillard."

Thierry was about to say that it would not be long if old de Orfevres had a hand in it, for the matter of Lagrume woods was to come before the judges soon. But he did not; it was, after all, his brother's wedding day. There would be time enough for all that later.

When the men began drifting back into the hall, the women walked by twos and threes through the mild evening to the latrines. Among them were Nicolette and Adela Cacchot. "You must tell me all," Adela said, taking her friend's arm. "It is too wonderful that you have been given back your life. You shall be happy with de Fontenne, I am certain of it."

"Oh, yes," Nicolette agreed, smiling and hugging her friend's arm as they walked. She was at that moment happier than she would have believed possible. "I have but one unfulfilled desire," she confessed, "I want more than anything to have a child."

Adela, whose abdomen was swollen with a third pregnancy, laughed a little and cautioned, "Do not be so eager. You will soon have more than enough of babes," she tittered. "My husband's favorite jest is that he has only to hang his hosen on the bed to get me with child. For him it is all sport, but for me it is a good bit different."

Nicolette laughed with her and sympathized. But in her heart, a child was what she wanted above all else. And it had been so since the day they had returned to Gaillard and buried an empty coffin in the grave plot. Only four months had gone by, but because she was young and impatient, each month when her flux arrived, Nicolette cried bitter tears of disappointment. Indeed, she had confided her desperate desire to have a child to everyone, except Laire. Mahaut had advised her to take a few sprigs of vervain, steep it in some wine and drink it every day for a week. But the brew, like all else she had tried, was without results.

When Nicolette and Adela returned to the hall the musicians were playing and a number of guests were kicking up their heels to the merry tune. At the long linen-draped tables food was still being served. Nicolette took her seat. As she did, she noticed Judot coming from the dance floor, out of breath and more red-faced than before. Dore clung to his arm, and when she squeezed past, she winked at Nicolette and slyly put something into her hand.

As the feast continued, music throbbed in the air, jests were tossed back and forth, and laughter rang off the hall's massive beams. The usual jokes concerning brides and grooms circulated through the hall, so that Nicolette's face appeared rouged with embarrassment.

"If I was a foolish scoundrel like yourself," Thierry told his brother, "I'd play a good jest on you tonight."

"Now I shall not sleep at all," Laire replied. The double meaning of his words drew a score of crude remarks and sent everyone nearby into fits of laughter.

Afterwards, Laire, still chuckling, held up his hands and said, "My friends, I have a tale to share with you. It concerns my brother, who wishes everyone to believe him innocent of all foolishness."

Thierry knowing well the tale he was about to tell, laughingly protested. "Confess to them, who was my confederate."

Laire freely admitted his part in the ruse, and went on to tell how he and Thierry had all but frightened to death the priest who had taught them Latin. "Our priestly tutor was a man who believed devoutly in the existence of demons and devils. And we, having discovered a means to crawl inside the chapel's stone and fretwork altar, decided to torment him. That night we squeezed into the crypt armed with an oil lantern and a bellows, and waited for him to come to say his prayers. Just as he knelt down and began to pray, we commenced to howl and groan and pump the bellows. He jumped up, white with fright, tripped over his robes, and galloped from the chapel on his hands and knees. It frightened him so badly that he went on a pilgrimage, and we escaped our Latin for several weeks."

Thierry laughed even louder than the others. "I

have no doubt that he is warming a corner of hell for us at this very moment."

More jokes and tales made their way round the table. While the musicians played, Cacchot shared a humorous reminiscence with the men. Halfway along the table, Adela and the merchants' wives sat close together speaking of children and female matters. Albert and the other young people danced on, perspiring mightily, their hair plastered to their damp foreheads.

Laire took Nicolette's arm and they rose to bid their guests goodnight. Since the evening's business was nothing new to them, they remained to enjoy their guests a while longer. But when they finally climbed the snail curl of stairs, Nicolette was trembling with expectation.

In the solar, Laire set the oil lamp on the chest by the bed and went to open the shutter. The warm night air was scented with the musk of spring, and a sliver of moon, like a tilted horn, hung suspended in the starry sky.

Nicolette sat the half-filled silver cup beside the lamp and, stepping before the polished metal disc that served as a looking glass, removed the caul and circlet from her hair.

As Laire undressed, he watched her from the corner of his eye. She had removed her gown, and was naked save for the thin chemise, which concealed almost nothing. She had something in her hand, a sort of packet, and was shaking it over the silver cup.

He crept across the room, making not a sound

for he had already removed his boots, and put his hands around her waist. She gave a startled little cry and whirled to face him, dropping the packet. Laire picked it up from the chest. "What is this?" he asked.

She did not reply at first, but as he remained looking at her intently, she felt impelled to say, "It is nothing."

He held the packet to his nose. The piquant scent of herbs tickled his nostrils. "Where did you get this?"

Nicolette's dark eyes darted back and forth, until finally she said in a small voice, "It is nothing harmful. It is only a tonic so that you will get me with child. Will you drink it?" She looked at him tremulous with hope.

Suddenly he grinned. "If it means so much to you, yes, I will drink it."

Nicolette threw her bare arms around his neck and kissed him, then quickly took up the cup and passed it into his hand.

He took a drink, and stood there looking very solemn. All at once he made a horrible face, rolled his eyes, clutched his throat, and pitched onto the bed.

Nicolette screamed and dashed to lean over him.

It was then he seized her, pulled her to his chest and, laughing, pulled her over.

Nicolette could not decide if she should laugh or cry or hit him. She cocked her head back and looked at him. Her eyes were bright with tears. "What if I cannot have a child?"

He brought his face to hers and kissed her lips, little teasing kisses. "It would not matter to me. It is you I love."

She kissed him back, loving him and thinking they would have the whole of their lives to enjoy the effort.

MAKE THE ROMANCE CONNECTION

Z-TALK *Online*

Come talk to your favorite authors and get the inside scoop on everything that's going on in the world of romance publishing, from the only online service that's designed exclusively for the publishing industry.

With Z-Talk Online Information Service, the most innovative and exciting computer bulletin board around, you can:

- ♥ CHAT "LIVE" WITH AUTHORS, FELLOW ROMANCE READERS, AND OTHER MEMBERS OF THE ROMANCE PUBLISHING COMMUNITY.
- ♥ FIND OUT ABOUT UPCOMING TITLES BEFORE THEY'RE RELEASED.
- ♥ COPY THOUSANDS OF FILES AND GAMES TO YOUR OWN COMPUTER.
- ♥ READ REVIEWS OF ROMANCE TITLES.
- ♥ HAVE UNLIMITED USE OF ELECTRONIC MAIL.
- ♥ POST MESSAGES ON OUR DOZENS OF TOPIC BOARDS.

All it takes is a computer and a modem to get online with Z-Talk. Set your modem to 8/N/1, and dial 212-935-0270. If you need help, call the System Operator, at 212-407-1533. There's a two week free trial period. After that, annual membership is only $ 60.00.

See you online!

brought to you by Zebra Books

KENSINGTON PUBLISHING CORP.